Also by Sister Souljah

LIFE AFTER DEATH

A Novel

SISTER SOULJAH

EMILY BESTLER BOOKS

—

ATRIA

New York   London   Toronto   Sydney   New Delhi

EMILY
BESTLER
BOOKS

―――

ATRIA

An Imprint of Simon & Schuster, Inc.
1230 Avenue of the Americas
New York, NY 10020

First Emily Bestler Books/Atria Paperback edition February 2022

EMILY BESTLER BOOKS / ATRIA PAPERBACK and colophon are trademarks of Simon & Schuster, Inc.

For information about special discounts for bulk purchases, please contact Simon & Schuster Special Sales at 1-866-506-1949 or business@simonandschuster.com.

Interior design by Yvonne Taylor

Manufactured in the United States of America

1   3   5   7   9   10   8   6   4   2

Library of Congress Cataloging-in-Publication Data has been applied for.

ISBN 978-1-9821-3913-1
ISBN 978-1-9821-3914-8 (pbk)
ISBN 978-1-9821-3915-5 (ebook)

WE SAY WE DIDN'T FEEL IT
BUT WE FELT IT.
WE SAY WE DIDN'T SEE IT
BUT WE SAW IT.
WE SAY WE DIDN'T HEAR IT
BUT WE HEARD IT.
WE PRETENDED WE NEVER KNEW IT
BUT WE KNOW IT.
Who?
ALL OF US

1.

Gunshots! Brooklyn born, I know the sound. No matter whose finger is on the trigger, a nigga vs. a nigga, niggas vs. the law, or the law vs. niggas, gunshots fired anywhere in the world means pay attention motherfuckers. But after these three shots, I don't hear no clap back, running feet, or screeching police sirens. I don't hear no cops calling out bullshit commands, like freeze! I don't hear the scream of the ambulance or the swift feet of the curious running to the scene of the incident. I don't hear the director calling out "Cut!" after first having called out "Action!" I don't hear the cheers, shout outs, or big ups from the VIP crowd, who I know had gathered, because I am the one who arranged their VIP passes to be the *only ones* invited to accompany the film crew on my prison release day. I can't even hear the howl of the wind, which normally is so loud upstate New York where I was locked up, that we could hear it from inside the prison walls, depending on where we were in the building. Fuck hearing, *I can't even see*. Everything is deep black. Oh shit! That's how I know. I, Winter Santiaga, am the one who got shot dead.

I don't have no big fear of death, never really even thought about it. Fifteen years on lock, I knew chicks who chased death, thought it was the better option over the rough lives they were living. I knew women who cut themselves, beat themselves, begged other inmates for their meds and swallowed a handful of game-changing pills in one gulp. I even knew six chicks who one by one successfully hung themselves within those fifteen years I served.

In the prison dayroom chilling, or on the yard, when the conversation got on that suicide bullshit, I stepped off. Everybody know Winter Santiaga is all about action and hustle, plotting and planning, making it and taking it, and a dead bitch can't do shit.

This is fucked up though. Seconds after my prison release, right when I was about to earn a big bag, lights out. I'm dead. When I was first approached to do a reality show that was gonna be so real that it would start with cameras rolling the moment I stepped foot through the prison release door, I was like *Ah, hell no!* Seated side by side with cellies, I had seen bunches of bitches on reality TV ridiculously playing themselves like crazy. They'd never catch Winter Santiaga on camera, finally easing outside with some Department of Corrections–issued clothing, which was all inmates had to wear other than the clothes they had on their back at the time of their arrest. After that vicious fight me and Simone had on our Brooklyn block fifteen years ago, right before the cops snatched up both of us, my clothes were shredded. Yeah that's how we do it. It's not a showbiz on-camera, off-camera thing in the hood. We fight with full fury.

Thinking over the reality-show offer while speaking on the prison phone with the show creator and executive producer, my brother-in-law Elisha Immanuel, I told myself, *Nah Winter, never let them see you sweat. Never let them see you down. Never reveal even one chink in your armor. Keep your game face on!*

"Good looking out, Elisha," I told him. "I thought about it like you asked me to do. But I gotta turn you down for the third time. Let it be the last."

"Well then, *negotiate*," my sister Porsche said, who I didn't even know was on the call that I made to Elisha, 'cause she remained silent up until the moment I turned him down. "You heard what my husband wants out of the show deal. What does Winter want out of it? There must be something you're ready to gain. Just let my husband know what that is. Winter, you are the star of this show. Only you can make it happen. Until you sign the contract, you're in the power position," Porsche added softly.

My mind started speeding. *That's right!* What *do* I want out of it? But I hated that I didn't think of it from that angle myself. Caught up in my hustles on the inside, I didn't consider that I was in the power position in a deal that would go down on the outside even before I get out. This show he's proposing is not just another prison show. That's right! This show is about me! And it's about me for a reason! After all is said and done, there are 'bout five hundred thousand bitches serving mandatory minimums for basically no fucking reason beside being the girlfriend of some low-level or mid-level drug dealer. Elisha chose me because I'm that bad bitch, the royalest of the royal precisely!

Six days after my sister had said over the phone, "Well then, negotiate," and after referring to my fashion-magazine library that spanned over fourteen years and was a small source of revenue to me on lockup, I finalized my list of star demands. The first thing was for Elisha to contact the warden and get clearance for me to receive a customized wardrobe and accessories to wear out of the prison on my release day, which coincidentally was in the winter season.

"I got you," Elisha said calmly. "I already planned to communicate with the warden, and of course the city officials for the license to film in the area."

"And Elisha, no brand substitutes, nothing generic, everything genuine, top quality no matter what anyone says," I told him. I knew what I was about to order. I didn't want to hear him tell me shit about some crazy fucking animal rights protesters.

"I know who you are," Elisha said, buttering me up.

"Starting with outerwear, since that will get captured on camera first, a hooded white three-quarter-length pure mink coat. Red Python 'sky-high' thigh-high boots, a red alligator Birkin bag with an activated iPhone inside in my name. Red Gucci driving gloves. Oh, and if you're going to continue the film with me being driven home, I want my own house."

"Porsche said you were going to move in with us. She already decorated a whole wing just for you. It has your own door and driveway; your own bathroom, bedroom, living room, and full kitchen; and even your own mailbox. Once you see it, and since we are all family, I'm sure you'll want to stay. Besides, it's located in Brooklyn."

"Truth is, I want my own house. I plan to have some of my girls move in with me. We plan to build a business together."

"Okay . . . how 'bout a compromise? Something that will make you and my wife and your girls straight and satisfied," Elisha swiftly shifted the convo like someone accustomed to these tough negotiations. I wondered if Porsche was listening in on this call again but I didn't ask, and if she was, she didn't say shit and I couldn't detect any extra breathing noises or movements.

"We will put your girls, up to five of them, in the reality-show cast and pay them a nice appearance fee. This way, they can afford their own apartments. You can live with us like Porsche planned." I was silent 'cause I was thinking about it. I thought it would play out better if I am the only star of the show. I make all the paper. I invest the paper into the business that I own, and allow my girls to run it so they could earn off of what I have provided. Elisha must've sensed something 'cause he interrupted my thoughts and said, "Winter, you're the star. Your deal is worth fifty thousand per show, sixteen episodes per season. After it hits—and you and I both know it will—you'll be in position to renegotiate and clear even more than the eight hundred thousand that is generated for you in season one. The five supporting cast members, your handpicked home girls, will only each earn three thousand on the episodes they actually appear on. They're backstory. You're on every episode. They're not. You are the main story. You are the show."

Elisha's pimp game is mean, I thought to myself. Eight hundred thousand dollars for me alone, that's right. Of course I would put my girls on the payroll. That's not coming from my stacks, but it is being paid out to them based on my say-so. Three thousand per episode was more than enough for them to pay their rent at the goddamn projects or for each of them to move on up into something new. My on-camera supporting cast, sounds good. I could not wait to give them a heads-up and dangle the deal. I did more time than each of them. I would roll out last, but on top and even save the day for each of them, who after their releases still had not managed to cake up. And let's be serious here. I'm not big on living under the same roof with none of their kids anyway. Now that I am in position to put them on, all of my bitches will bow down.

"I want VIP passes for everybody who I select to see me styling on my release day. I want a red carpet that runs from the prison release door to the black Bentley that I heard Midnight pushes, and of course, Midnight in person waiting on me to walk the red carpet straight to him."

"You know he's a married man, right?" Elisha asked smoothly.

"I know, but I knew him first. I saw him first. And this is my show we doing starring me, right?" I reminded him.

"A reality show . . ." Elisha said.

"You make him show up. I'll make it a reality," I told him with full confidence.

"Anything else?" Elisha asked patiently in his cool tone, not huffing or puffing or making it obvious that my demands might be over the top. So I told him, "Have the Bentley fully stocked, from the old shit to the new shit; Moët Rosé Impérial, Hennessy XO, Cîroc Blue Dot, and Ace of Spades, the thirty-liter Midas bottle. Oh, and me and my man must sip our champagne from authentic crystal flutes. So order me a set."

I gave him full details of the fashions I wanted to wear beneath the mink, even though they wouldn't show up on camera for my "kiss my ass" walk to freedom. Then I added, "And there's one serious really big thing I need to happen, although I won't say it over the phone. Elisha, plan to come up and visit me this week. I'll tell you face-to-face."

"No problem, I can do that. It's all good. We're in business now," he said as though my list of demands were all things within his budget, influence, connects, and grasp, and I liked that.

"But the thing is . . . Elisha, if you can't do the one big thing that I tell you in person, the whole entire deal is canceled," I said in a firm but nonthreatening tone even though it was a threat. It was more than a threat. It was a promise, a guarantee.

"We will work it out. See you soon," he said, unfazed, and hung up. Some next chick was waiting to use the prison phone. Although I had already hung up, I was still blocking it, wondering if I had undersold myself in the deal. Should I have demanded even more? Nah, I knew I would get even more than I demanded anyway. From my young teen years, I saw how entertainers, hustlers, and ballers got all kinds of perks, party passes, food and drinks, kicks and cars, trips and wardrobes and a bunch of other free shit that regular niggas had to grind for a whole year to get one of, or maybe to never get nothing at all. When I was done thinking and blocking I looked at the chicks on the phone line. They dropped their eyes like they suppose to. Not one of 'em dared to even look like they had a complaint. *They know who run dis.*

*   *   *

Lights-out on that same night of the deal convo, even though I was on track to get what I wanted out of Elisha, I was tight that now Porsche, my younger middle sister, would be able to say that she convinced me to do the show that I had said I would never do. Porsche would have me living in their place, eating off of her plate, and engulfed in her actively annoying overkill concern. I don't hate Porsche. We full blood. However, certain little shit that she does and how she is, I definitely don't like. For example, starting with the way she always says these two words, *my husband,* instead of just calling that sexy brown-skinned nigga by his well-known name, Elisha Immanuel, young, rich, black, and famous independent movie director. Also, Porsche is the quiet type. I didn't mind that. But I hated the way she always let her feelings show. On her one visit upstate New York to where I was serving time, she walked in with her eyes filled with watery tears, her voice and her fingers trembling. The only reason I overlooked it at the time was because other than that, she was picture-perfect. She had the meanest-ass manicure, that matched her haute-couture fashion and thigh-high Fendi boots that hood bitches would murder her for. Slide them right off her legs and feet and onto their own.

Once we were seated at the table in a prison room filled with inmates seated at separate tables, she sat trembling and silent like she was in some weird dreamy phase. When she finally did talk, her voice was all filled with emotion. Then suddenly her watery eyes spilled tears onto her immaculate diamond wedding rings. I was through. I took her off my visitation list, even though she was the only one on there. I blocked her. It was a smart move on my part. I know Porsche. She is annoyingly overconcerned about me. After I cut her off, she'll send her sexy husband to check up on me instead. He's a Brooklyn-born Brooklyn nigga, not the hardest moneymaking murderer, but he's definitely not soft. Me and Elisha could sit and talk at ease. I been locked up for so long with a bunch of bitches that I easily prefer men, and probably preferred men even before prison. I wasn't trying to lure my sister's man. No not at all. I don't get down like that. But I respect Elisha. He's my nigga 'cause over time he put money on my commissary, but never mentioned it. Most importantly however, Elisha visits Santiaga, my father, who is in prison serving life. That means way more than the world to me.

2.

Can a dead bitch think? My thoughts shifted as soon as my mind mentioned Santiaga to me. Santiaga is my first love. The number one father on the planet. The number one hustler in the streets. The number one ruler of my heart. Santiaga is the only man in the world who when I was eighteen years young and even fifteen years later while all alone in my cell, in the dark, deep into the night, beneath my one blanket, could cause me to shed silent tears.

Suddenly I was yanked out of my thoughts and on the move. I mean, I could not actually feel my feet taking steps, or my heels clicking on the ground beneath me, or mashing the snow, or sliding on ice. But somehow I knew for sure I was moving. I couldn't see or hear. Everything was pitch-black. But suddenly I was speeding like someone had hit the fast-forward button. Oh shit, it felt like I had puffed some of that Purple Haze and hit the Henny as well.

After a time, I felt myself jerk to a stop, like a car that was just about to run a red light but the driver jammed on the brakes. Still, my high remained. Next, ah shit, I felt a floating feeling. The blinding darkness eased up to a black gray, then an electric blue. Through a type of fog, I could see Santiaga standing right in front of me. Stuck staring, I didn't say a word 'cause I was struck at how chiseled and handsome and young he looked, even though he was seventeen years deep into serving a life bid. Obviously, he had worked out hard daily for six thousand, two hundred and five days. Yeah, I'm swift with numbers. In fact, my father, Santiaga, was the one who taught me to add, subtract, and multiply like a motherfucker. When I was six, I would be the first one in our Brooklyn projects apartment who would catch Poppa just as he walked through the front door. It was like I could feel him even before I heard his key turning in the locks. Then I would smell the scent of his cologne coming through the tiny space in the door. He would bring home gifts, lay them out on the table, and tell me the cost of each one, one time. Then he would say, "What's the total?" He'd snap his fingers three times and if I called out the right answer, I got first dibs on whichever gift I wanted to have. And since Santiaga knew me so well, everything he bought, I wanted to keep. Soon he would lay out the gifts, knowing I had mastered that adding-up shit, and then take one item away, and then be like, "Now, what's the new total?" After I caught on to that subtraction kind've lovely, he taught me how to multiply. It was like we would be chilling at the table, or I'd be in the bathroom brushing my teeth and he'd pop up at the washroom door.

"What's twelve times eight?"

"Ninety-six!" I would say rapidly like he required. No matter how fast I would come up with the answer, he'd be like, "Nah, it took you too long!"

I'd laugh and be like, "It didn't!! That was quick, Poppa!"

"Not quick enough!" He'd challenge me. "If you want to hang out with me, you gotta be so quick with your times tables that I can't see you thinking."

"See me thinking?" I'd ask, still laughing.

"Yep, swift with the right answer and with your game face on."

"Game face?" I followed up.

"That's what you call a face that doesn't reveal what you are thinking or feeling on the inside. Only you should know that. Everybody else shouldn't."

After that I mastered multiplication super-rapid response with the right answers. I would also stare in the mirror every morning and every night practicing my game face.

In his cell, Santiaga was getting dressed. He stepped into his boxers, every muscle defined. Even his hands were rough and gorgeous and just the right size. When he turned, I could see the bullet-wound scar on his sculptured abs. His haircut was sharp and he was dapper even in Department of Corrections digs. His eyes were brighter than his atmosphere. His stare was solid, masculine. His complexion was not showing that charismatic glow he flashed naturally before hitting the pen, where there's rarely any sunshine. But I'll fix that. I'll be the one to get him out of here even though he is serving life. Poppa's release is sure to happen. It was the condition I gave Elisha. The one thing that would cause the whole entire reality show, followed up by a major motion picture, followed up by a television series, followed up by a Winter Santiaga video game, to fall through and be nothing at all. Money makes shit happen. I read the many magazine articles on Elisha and how smart he is. How he had gotten accepted into six of America's top universities. So in my six days of thinking about my list of demands, the answer to what Winter really wants is, Santiaga. I want my father to be released. I want both of us to come up, back to where we belong. To be the royal high that we were before, *but even higher*. I bet my whole eight-hundred-thousand-dollar bag on that. Three gunshots later, and the most perfect plan exploded.

I rushed towards Santiaga. His facial expression showed me what I had already figured out the second I arrived in his cell. *Poppa cannot see me*. Long ago there was a smile that would come to his face and even to his eyes naturally whenever he saw me after not having seen me for a few days or hours even. Here I am standing right in front of him and that smile is not there.

"Poppa," I spoke, but even I could not hear my own spoken words even though I was speaking them. "Poppa, I . . ." I moved in close to him and ran my fingers through his hair. My fingertips traced his iconic face. My palms rested on his strong shoulders. Then I touched his fingers and then held his hands. He walked away from me. I followed him and saw that he had a short stack of magazines with a tall stack of letters on top. I dashed to the letters and went to pick one up or push the whole pile over even, in order to grab my father's attention. I wanted to give him a hint that I am here. But my fingers weren't working properly. I couldn't lift the letters up, even though I could see clearly that the letter on top was one of the many letters that I had written to him. My father, Santiaga, and I had remained close even while both being separately incarcerated. I tried to knock everything over but couldn't.

Now Santiaga was leaning against the cell door looking out the narrow slot. I'm familiar with that stance. How many days had I stood still staring through the cage bars, and then later through the metal door slot. Sometimes staring at the floor because at that moment in lockdown, there was nothing else to do. So I eased towards him. As soon as I did he turned his head. His eyes on the lookout but he didn't move. I could tell by his gaze he felt something. Like a man who had looked over his shoulder as hustlers gotta do all da time. Then he spun a one-eighty. His feet on pivot. His eyes on search. I ran into his arms, wrapped my arms around his neck, then closed in and hugged him extra tightly. I moved my lips to his ears and said, "Goodbye, Poppa. In all of the whole wide world, you were my favorite person, my best friend, my realest teacher, my deepest love." I pressed a closed-lip kiss on his lips.

"Santiaga, hands," the familiar authoritative voice of a corrections officer called through the slot.

"Don't interrupt!" I screamed. Santiaga walked back to the cell door he had been staring out of a minute ago and put his hands through the slot. C.O. cuffed him.

"Why are you cuffing my father? He's already locked in!" I yelled. Santiaga drew back his now-cuffed hands.

"This is just a precaution," the C.O. said, downshifting his tone like he should have in the first place. The heavy cell door slid open.

"Wait, don't come in here," I said forcefully. "I need a little more time with my father!" Then I stepped between them and turned to face Santiaga.

"Poppa," I called out. "Somebody got me! But don't you worry about who did it. Stay still for me. Don't kill whoever did it. I'm gonna get you the fuck out of here. I'm gonna put you back where you belong. Trust me, your Baby Girl. Poppa, you did everything in life for me. Now I'm gonna be the one to king you!"

"Bad news . . ." the C.O. said as though I was not even standing there blocking him from speaking directly to my father. So I started screaming to dead the sound of C.O.'s voice. It must have worked because just as the words "Your daughter . . ." came out of C.O.'s filthy mouth, I dissolved.

3.

Heat, I was nothing but heat now. Like heat coming through the radiator or incinerator or any hot place. Who killed me? That's all I wanted to know. Revenge, that's all I wanted to get. Yeah I was mad about losing out on the moneybag that I was about to earn, but I was more furious that I would not be there to see Santiaga get out and come home. Now I want to put down whoever shot me, before Poppa got home and gave the order to eliminate that person and whoever was on that person's team. No, erase that. Poppa would pull that trigger himself. That's the kind of man he is.

Of course I love, admire, and respect that deadly element of my father. However, it was hard and costly work to get to the point where he would possibly be released. I didn't want him finally freed only to return to the box for avenging my murder. So my mission is to murder first. They couldn't charge me with murder in the first, 'cause I'm already dead in the first place. I started laughing. Like real shoulder-shaking laughter that makes the whole body shake. Somehow the volume of my own laughter was increasing like someone slipped a mic on me or was in the DJ booth fucking with the fader, controlling the sound. Soon the volume doubled. So, I stopped laughing, but the laughter didn't stop. It tripled. It was the first time I ever got pissed and aggravated at the sound of my own voice. The more vexed I got, the more the laughter increased.

It grew so loud it mutated and started sounding like some old guy laughing.

"Shut the fuck up!" I screamed. When I couldn't out-scream the laughter I stopped caring. I'm good at that 'cause I didn't care in the first place. Once I thoroughly ignored the laughter, it thoroughly disappeared. I can't say how long it took to stop because I was realizing that I could no longer count time. That may sound like no big deal but to a locked-up bitch time is everything and the countdown from capture to release is as important and necessary as a pulse or a heartbeat. Without being able to count down time . . . well now that I think about it, that's like death. For example, is today the same day as the day I got shot dead? When I saw Santiaga, even though he didn't see me, was I seeing him right after I'd been murdered? Or was it days after or weeks after or months after?

Eventually my temperature decreased. Once it did I was more than just a glob of heat. I could feel my limbs again. It was like I got my body back and now the heat was just moving in my chest like my titties were on fire. After calming myself, I accomplished turning myself back to cold, my natural state. That's when I promised myself, *I'm moving whoever murdered me to the top of my "payback's a bitch" list*. It had taken me fifteen minutes after my arrest to put together my payback list. But it took me fifteen years to put together each scheme on exactly how I was gonna do it. Smarter, I knew I had to take revenge without getting found out. If I made one mistake I could end up back in prison and that wasn't even remotely a possibility no matter what I had to do to prevent it.

In my payback plot there was no murder. I'm not a murderer, I'm innocent. I served fifteen years for nothing. True, I wanted to hustle and blow up big in the streets. But who the fuck gets arrested for their thoughts? I never actually sold one rock, powder, or pill. But now that someone crossed the line and deaded me, I would turn into what I never was before. Even if that means monster. Who did it? I didn't even have no murder-type beef like that with anyone anymore. *Who did it? Who did it and why? Think, think,*

think, I told myself. Then it felt like something shot through my chest and grabbed me. I was on the move again after being stuck for who knows how long.

When the whirling feeling stopped, a sort of free high that I was starting to appreciate, my hearing came back, but not my vision. Ah shit! I could hear Biggie on the track "Who Shot Ya?" I was like, *Yeah is that supposed to be funny?* But I was excited to hear music, loud, clear, and crisp like it was coming through some even better than Bose, McIntosh super expensive speakers, not some bullshit Department of Corrections radio. I was even more excited to hear the livest music of the '90s, when I was a teenager at the absolute tip-top of my royalty. After I was locked down and the '90s slowly disappeared, and when we had the DOC radio turned up, I couldn't feel nothing from the music. It wasn't just because the radio was cheap. The new artists just didn't have "that thing." They were not the type of hip-hop heads or singers that got me rah-rah excited, hot, and kept me listening and loyal. The '90s had power-house artists who spit that rhyme and sang the songs that snatched a bitch's heart out her chest, made her go temporarily insane or caused her legs to open voluntarily. Nineties rappers and hip-hop music ruled the airwaves, reflected our culture, and moved our streets. It was dominant, not only in Brooklyn, but in all hoods in America and around the world. All my peeps knew that even without ever traveling far from the block. Nineties hip-hop shook the planet. And, in the real lives of real niggas, what was said, rhymed, or sung on a hip-hop track even dictated which niggas lived and which niggas died. Word.

Ever seen a dead bitch dance? Me neither, but I was doing it. Ol' Dirty Bastard was killing the track of his hit titled "Brooklyn Zoo." I stayed grooving all alone until I realized that I could hear muffled, murmuring voices. It sounded like a group of people talking, but the music prevented anyone from hearing what they were saying exactly.

I stopped dancing and waited for the track to end, but Ol' Dirty merged into Jay-Z's "Jigga What, Jigga Who" and I was like, *Oh hell yeah. It's a party!* Then I got pumped and was like, *"It's my party!"* My private after-party, after coming home from da joint. It was scheduled to start at 11 p.m. after all the reality-TV shit and promotions was finished for the day. It was exclusive for only my girls who been through the same shit as me, did time with me too and of course they was each allowed to bring their nigga. Wait! That after-party was supposed to take place the same night of the day I got released. Then I got tight. *Is this the same day I got murdered? Felt like forever. And, are they having my after-party on the same night even though I got killed?*

The music flowed on for a long time. I could only tell 'cause I was counting the tracks that the DJ spun. Eighteen cuts, sixty-six minutes later, a non-nineties joint came on. That nigga Young Jeezy a'ight. But to me it signaled that my throwback after-party was about to end. Then the music lowered and a girl's voice shouted, "Y'all ain't gotta go home but y'all gotta get the fuck outta my crib! I got two kids and they won't keep their asses in the bed till y'all leave." It was the voice of my girl Asia, which confirmed yes, this is my after-the-reality-show-party after-party. The crowd laughed and I could hear the door opening and closing and people's Timbs, heels, kicks, and flats walking out.

"Nigga gimme back my Bacardi before I embarrass your ass!" Asia shouted. Obviously one nigga tried to steal a bottle. Asia caught him.

"Come on girl, you got mad shit in here. Can't a nice nigga get more nice without you getting mad?" I heard a tussle. Then the door slammed. I'm thinking how it wasn't really Asia's Bacardi. I put up the paper to fix up her place and buy her a sound system, a new couch, and for her to get weed free-flowing and the bar fully stocked. I had a budget and could arrange for shit like that. I could've only had the one party at the club celebrating my debut on the first day of filming the reality show. Elisha covered costs for that. But that was like for the film crew and other professionals connected with the show. That's why I needed the after-the-after-party

party. Ain't nothing like a house party, at least in my memory. I wanted to capture that and just chill with my girls and their niggas, all men and women who been high and low and locked, but because of my show, was 'bout to be high again. A house party, where we could and would do whatever off camera.

"Fuck that bitch, she thought I forgot," I suddenly heard Simone's voice, an angry whisper. A little light started bleeding through the darkness that had just surrounded me. My vision now was dim, like there was a vision-control button. The type of buttons we had in our Long Island mansion after Santiaga had suddenly moved us out of Brooklyn right after my sixteenth birthday. In every room we were able to adjust the intensity of the lights. But here, where I was standing in Asia's apartment, I was stuck on very dim vision, but it was better than the blackout I had just had.

"I never forgot. Winter like to play dumb. So I went along with it and played dumb too. Fuck, we was locked up in the same joint. I had to look at her regardless. So I used her." Simone was close up in Natalie's face. Natalie is short, so Simone was looking down on her, like dominant.

"Yeah, well, if you gonna use a bitch, use her all the way! Winter got us the TV show! She put us on! You kilt her. Now all of us lost a bag," Natalie said.

Simone shot me! Simone shot me! Simone shot me! was running through my head.

"Word, we should beat your ass for fucking up everybody's paper," my girl Reese said, cutting her eyes while unbuttoning her coat that she had just been buttoning.

"Reese, if any of y'all could of beat my ass you would have tried it already. But y'all know what time it is," Simone threatened. Reese lunged forward fast and punched Simone in the face. Simone bitch-slapped Reese in return, which sparked Toshi to jump wild, and all three of them started thumping.

"Don't fuck up my house," Asia screamed. Then my girl Zakia started flicking the light switch on and off, off and on, as though that could influence or stop the fight. She was messing up my already-dim view. But I did see Natalie creeping up on Simone. She tried to crack Simone over the head with a bottle of Cîroc. Simone leaned, dodging the direct blow, and the bottle impacted on her shoulder but didn't break. Simone snatched it from Natalie's grip. Zakia stopped flicking the lights.

"Y'all some stupid bitches," Asia screamed.

"Why?" Simone asked, laughing in a greasy way. "'Cause Winter bought you a couch and fixed up this little dump?" Simone said as she put herself back together from the brawl and was dusting off her shoulders as though to say and show them that she wasn't even hurt, fazed, or impacted from their little rumble. She then opened up the Cîroc and started gulping it, a fourth of it spilling out on her face and her trying to catch it and lick it up with her tongue.

"Winter bought the couch and the bottle you drinking from and your ass is drunk! I fixed up the rest of my house myself with my paper," Asia said, but she was lying. She don't have no real paper yet. She was just about to come up when I got released and would put her on.

"Y'all was so busy kissing Winter's ass," Simone spit. "Y'all was so happy she put y'all on and was about to get you paid a little paper . . ." Simone burped then farted.

"So was you!" Natalie said.

"Y'all was so stupid y'all forgot to ask how much was Winter getting for the show?" Simone grimaced.

"I asked her," Natalie said swiftly.

"And?" Simone quick replied. As I looked around the room, I could see that Simone's question caught Reese and Toshi's attention and changed the expressions on their faces from fury to suspicion.

"Winter said she couldn't discuss how much she was getting because she had to sign a confidentiality agreement with the television production company and had to promise not to discuss the deal details," Natalie answered like a street lawyer.

"Slick bitch," Simone said.

"True dat is kind've slick," my girl Zakia said. She had been standing quietly in the same corner where the light switch was located, watching everything going down, smoking a blunt. Zakia was like that from being locked up with the rest of us. Hers was the shortest bid but her nerves got wrecked from just putting in a little time and a little work on the inside. She used to stand around silent same like she was now, when she was locked. She'd pay anybody selling, any amount, for even a fifth of a cigarette, smoked all of the time and said next to nothing. But we held her down anyway 'cause she was our home girl.

"It's Winter's sister's husband who got Winter the deal in the first place. So why she had to sign a no-talk agreement with her own brother-in-law?" Reese stated.

"Because that's how Winter gets down," Simone rushed and answered, cutting Natalie off. "She does the least and gets the most. Y'all gotta remember! Winter got me arrested the first time for stealing a dress *she wanted*. A dress she planned to put on her back and pretend that she paid full price for it herself. Then I got arrested for slicing *her face*. More than y'all, *I* did real time. She deserved to get cut but I should've really murdered her in the street, right then and there. She killed my daughter!"

"She did not!" Natalie scolded. "Your big pregnant ass chased Winter and fell down the steps and lost the baby. Back then I told you to stay home and let us handle Winter. You should've listened."

"That's what happened. I was there," Reese confirmed.

"That . . ." Asia screamed, "was fifteen! Years! Ago!" She said each word with space in between and mad emphasis. "Y'all old bitches better upgrade and update! What we gon' do now?"

"You the same age as us," Zakia's nervous one-liner bombed Asia. Then she just stared off, not even looking at the rest of the girls in the room.

"Y'all better wise up. Winter be lying all da time. 'Member how she used to gas us on lock-up about how that nigga Midnight was gonna pick her up on her release date pushing a half-million-dollar whip?" Simone said. My girls all started laughing. Somehow what Simone had mentioned wiped out the tension between them. But I was slowly heating, headed towards furious. I hate when anybody talks shit about something they don't really know and had no way of finding out what really happened in certain situations. I hate the way people talk shit either after somebody got locked up and ain't around to say it how it really was. I hate how people would go hard against someone who if they was standing right their in the face, they wouldn't dare to even look at too long or ever say shit to. Same way I hate how people talk shit about anybody after they was dead and gone and can't clap back. All that is sucker moves. Only suckers move and do that way.

"The show must go on," Simone said in her low, manly voice. "'Life After Death,'" like B.I.G. said. And dead entertainers sell more merchandise than living entertainers ever did, like B.I.G. did. Bet y'all didn't know that! Winter wanted to be the star. So she got murdered on camera, a dramatic debut." Simone waved her arms in the air, still holding the Cîroc. "You think any of these showbiz niggas, whether they Winter's brother-in-law or not, gonna delete that footage of that murder? Hell no, they gonna let it roll, air it, sweep the ratings, collect and count the cheddar and continue to show the show!" Simone bragged.

"And how long before they figure out it was you who pulled the trigger?" Natalie said, and she was pissy.

"They ain't gon' find out. And y'all ain't gonna tell 'em. That's why I don't give a fuck talking about it. Y'all need me. And y'all need the show. And everybody know in hip-hop the real making-moves murderers, the shooters, get the shine."

Back to black, I thought Zakia was messing with the lights again, but she wasn't. I had turned back into being nothing but a blob of heat, numb limbs and all. Couldn't see no more or feel my face and I was back to being blind, deaf, and dumb.

4.

I'm not no fucking firefighter. So I do not know how to put out the raging fire that is me. I don't know how long it would take, or how much water is needed to cool me off. I don't have no fire extinguisher. Besides even if I did, would I use it on myself? Plus I can't figure out this dead shit. I'm used to being able to figure out any situation no matter how complicated it is. Now I'm thinking, *Since I'm dead, shouldn't my mind shut off?* How come I could still know my own thoughts?

Afterwhile, I figured out that the angrier I get, the worse the impact is on me. The only reason I reached this conclusion is because I thought about how I never ever in my lifetime was that *angry bitch.* I never had a reason to be dat. I was always calm and cool and cold and steady. Even when shit was fucked up, I knew how to flip shit in my favor. Even on lock I flipped everything and everyone in my favor. If any chick was mad at me, even if it was for a good reason, the next step was for that bitch to get glad because I had a crew she couldn't resist. That crew started out with just me, and believe it or not, became me and Simone.

Yeah, the same Simone who cut my face with the jagged edge of a broken bottle, giving me the only scar I ever got in my young royal life, that could only be concealed by my silky hair if I wore it loose, which on lock I could not do. I hated Simone for impacting my flawless face. She hated me too. But in prison math, we were both better off using our mutual hatred together against others who probably hated us both more. So we did. We got on some beauty-and-the-beast-type shit breaking bitches down. My look, still stellar even with the scar, made them want to serve me or join me. Simone's beasting made them have no other option. So they gave in and got glad and ganged up beneath us. But I don't want to think about Simone. I just did and it caused my heat to flare up 'bout six notches. I was figuring out that when my heat peaks, I dissolve. When I dissolve, I disappear from whatever I was seeing, hearing, and feeling. *But* my thinking continues on. Who wants to be a glob of heat with thoughts, trapped in an infinite black space? Not me. So I figured I had to lower my temperature by thinking of anything that could make me feel good. Feeling good would be the opposite of feeling bad and then my anger might go away and the feeling in my face, arms, hands, legs, feet, and even my toes would return.

After Santiaga, there is only Midnight as far as real men in real life who I really know. Midnight still gives me that *ooh-ah* good feeling. It's stronger and deeper than the spark a hot rapper or huge movie star or amazing baller could ever shoot through my pussy like lightning. Midnight is a man who makes all of my body parts pulsate, even when he is not doing anything but standing still. His effect lasts over time, no matter how much time passes. To the point where even if I don't see him except in my mind, my whole body, including my heart, still feels the throbbing sensation. If you don't know what I mean, it means you never met him, never seen him. And you never ever even met any man like him. Which is extremely possible.

When men see women, they grade us. They be like she's a five, six, seven, or eight. Ten represents the top bitch, which is rare for them to say. When men see even a glimpse of me they automatically and naturally say ten, the highest. It's the reason they call me, Winter Santiaga, a dime. So why not grade them, the men, the same way? Now I'm entertaining myself and getting excited, in a good way. Well let's see. We will start at the bottom, which obviously is the lowest. The lowest type of man is a zero, a dude who actually fucks his children or anybody else's little children. A man who molests and rapes because he feels like a zero and knows he's a zero. So he stalks little kids and women who he's pretty sure even his weak backward ass can overpower. Zero-type slime balls like this also molests and abuses and rapes his girlfriend's children or his stepchildren who are not his biological kids. So sick is he, he even rapes his own or her own sons. I wouldn't say none of this greasy shit if I didn't know that it actually happens. Having been locked in with so many women coming from so many places across the country, I know it goes on.

Don't misunderstand. I ain't all kid-crazy. I think having babies is a burden that breaks a bitch down. Mostly it fucks up her figure and lessens her value. Same way a new whip is worth major paper, soon as you buy it and drive it off the car lot, it's worth a lot less. It's used. With babies, once you have one, all of a sudden you have two and then three. Then the only thing you have more than babies is problems. A bitch used to have the luxury of being all about herself. Even from the first baby everything becomes all about the kid. Instead of going for manicures and makeovers, she's left wiping up piss and cleaning up poo. Washing diapers and dishes and your whole pizzazz is stolen and gone. Unless you got paper piles forget having babies. Better to have the cheese to pay the servants to do all of the dirty work, while you style. That's the only way kids are all good with me. Still I don't respect no nigga who hurts, rapes, or molests the children. Even if he got money stacks and status, he's a zero nigga to me.

Men who are the next lowest type are the ones who are straight cowards. I don't know what happened to cause so many men to fit this description. I do know that a coward can never get a bitch like me hot, and probably not you either. A lot of chicks on lock, when we got into talking about their men, had cowards. These guys were the ones that blamed everybody else for their circumstance. Especially they blamed their woman or their women. Most of the females I met who had gotten beat up bad by men were the ones messing with some coward who they were supporting and providing for and whose dick they were sucking. He'd take her money, go get drunk with it, and come back and beat her ass 'cause he spent it all, didn't have no hustle, business, or a job, or any way to save face for his failures. So he used her as a punching bag.

Some niggas who got jobs or a business they own is also cowards, but instead of them being rated as a lowly one, they would be a two or a three 'cause at least they work! These types might beat up their woman or women, or might not. But, they are also still cowards in other ways. They the type that fuck a bunch of chicks, but not discreetly. They purposely leave clues that they fucking around randomly, just to set these bitches to battling one another, instead of all of the bitches linking up and catching him in his lying bullshit. Some of the females I was locked with been fighting some coward's other broad for a whole decade! These bitches be baby battling instead of thinking. They be competing to give this coward a baby first. Then the next bitch gives him one soon after. The first one thinks she's better 'cause she gave him one first. The second one thinks she's better because she's younger than the first one. On top of that she feels more relevant 'cause now she has his baby, too! Next thing you know, both of them got three or four kids from this fool who is still broke, still beats their ass, and spends their money from their nine-to-five or even their social service check. Meanwhile, he recruits a bitch three and a bitch four who are running around talking greasy 'bout his babies' mommas 'cause now they old news, and number three and four don't nag and sweat him 'cause they the new pussy he's poking. He's spending one and two's money on three and four, and besides, three and four both ain't pregnant yet.

A man in the four-to-six range definitely gotta have a business or a job, but he also, to earn those numbers four through six, gotta have a decent look. Some niggas stay stuck at number four because their style, ways, and look is limp and lame. If you need your teeth fixed, drag your ass to the dentist. Bad breath, funky armpits, puss-filled pimples, dirty rotten cheesy dick, shit-stained boxers or drawers, and toe jam are all disqualifiers. Don't have long nails ever, especially not with last night's dinner trapped underneath them. Never ever wear cheap soiled kicks, cheap or mismatched socks, or run-over shoes . . . even if you gotta eat out less. The kicks and shoes are way more important than a bucket of chicken or shrimp fried rice or even lobsters. Sacrifice, you idiot! When I started laughing, it felt like my temperature lowered 'bout twelve notches.

For a man to be a seven or eight, he has to have a hustle, a business or a job, and not beat his woman up ever. I'm not counting play fighting. I like sex to be a lil' rough sometimes and always very physical. I like to look at a man's body first 'cause I get wet by the design of something stunning. I don't mind a few scratches during the love-making, long as there is no passion marks on my face. I like make-up sex, after we had a lil' argument. I might even cause a lil' argument to get that passionate thrust going on. But brutalizing is bullshit. I met several females on lock who agree. They murdered a man or two for laying into them repeatedly like they were professional fighters. These women would arrive at the joint black and blue in the face and permanent scars were all over their bodies when their uniforms dropped.

For the seven- and eight-rated men who do what a man is supposed to do but keep a bitch on a bullshit budget, even though he's caked up, that's why he's stuck in the seven–eight range. Or the type of guy who over-monitors his woman, doesn't buy her a car or hire her a driver and don't give her taxi money and space to be a woman so she can get herself right. Get her look perfect so she can enslave him in the bedroom which whether he knows it or not is what he really wants! I'm cracking up now. I'm feeling my toes tingle and my calves and my knees are no longer numb.

Nine is next to perfect, but not quite. A man who is a nine definitely owns his own business or is CEO of someone else's business. The key is, his endeavor, whatever it may be, has got to be profitable. A seven or eight can have a business, but it's one thing to have a business by name only, but no dividends. That's why there are sevens and eights that have mastered frontin' and even done a great job at it. They have a business, but the small profit they earn is spent on what they are wearing on their backs, what whips they are leasing, and the apartments, condos, or houses they're renting but can't keep 'cause they don't own. They make it all look good, but after the look there's no equity, assets, or cheddar left over.

Nine distinguishes the man who's big banking, legit and illegit, with corporate credit and corporate cash, personal cash and personal savings, and a slush fund as well as a stacked-up hood stash, from all of the lower-numbered men beneath him. Meaning a nine, in addition to his legit capital, has got to also have a dirty-money pile in his backyard, or in a super secret can't-be-discovered place, stitched into his furniture, built into his wall, buried beneath his pool, floating in his yacht, or stuffed in his momma's attic in the house he bought her. To be a nine he gotta be all that, as well as neat and clean and fashionable and manly. He can have any size dick because his status makes chicks overlook it and come with creative ways to get the sex and keep the sex exciting.

Ten is Santiaga and Midnight, the only men who are perfect to me. Stupid-ass Simone was talking 'bout how Midnight didn't show up for me on my release day like I said he would. But, she didn't know what really happened. I'm action. Simone's after the action. She always been an after-the-action bitch. She waits for somebody else to build up their business and she robs their shit that they built. That's why she's after the action to me. When we was locked, our little crew was organizing in the dayroom what business we were gonna run once we got released. I of course was plotting a fashion empire. I would design the clothes 'cause I'm nice with it. Then I'd employ a bunch of chicks who was nice with the needle to sew. A lot of locked-up women were working in a sewing factory on the inside. They was nice with regular needle-and-thread sewing. Plus they knew how to work the sewing machinery.

I was not only going to be a clothing designer, merchandiser, wholesaler, and retailer. I planned to get into interior decoration. I figured no matter what anybody wore or possessed or imagined, I could make it look even better. I would set up the most meanest-looking images and make the whole hood and whole world chase it. Of course that means, *more money more money for me.*

Seated in a crooked circle, Simone was cheering my ideas on. Then she was like, "Winter, that's the perfect setup. You look pretty and lure the clients with that interior decorating shit. I'll lay low for a month or so after your work is done. Then, surprise motherfuckers! It's a stickup! Get butt naked. Keep your hands where I can see them. Don't make me check your orifices. If you're hiding diamonds in your asshole, shit 'em out while I'm asking you nicely." Simone dramatized, and we cracked up. "I'll rob they whole crib, whoever's home, even the bitch from next door who just stopped by to drop off a blueberry pie! I'm swiping everything that Winter convinced them to buy: their appliances, merchandise, cars, jewels, cash, credit cards, and even their dogs. Rich motherfuckers will pay high ransom just to get back one kidnapped dog. They'll pay even more than they would for one of their kids! If not, I heard the black market for pets be bubbling." Simone laughed. So did the rest of us. But in my mind, I knew she could never come up with a good business idea other than stealing. That shit must've been in her bloodline. That's why she's an after-the-action bitch. Oh no, my thighs are numbing. I wasn't supposed to think about Simone. I didn't want to get heated all over again.

Anyway, back to Midnight. When Elisha came up a week after we discussed on the phone that there was one thing I needed him to take care of that I needed to say face-to-face, he gave me a full report on the status of my reality-star demands. He said wardrobe was a 100 percent go and even threw in a diamond necklace, like a real motherfucking G. The VIP passes, liquor, parties, and perks was all a go. He got the warden and the city working on the permits and licensing to do the film shoot, and they were excited, 'cause nothing good really happens up there where I was, in locked-up territory. Plus I think they was just on Elisha's balls and would give him anything he wanted for a close-up or selfie to brag about after he and his film crew packed up and left and their little prison city flipped back to dreary gray.

"Porsche had asked Midnight to promise that he would show up on your prison release date. She asked him way back, right after she came up here to check you. Midnight agreed. He's a 'word is bond' type of brother," Elisha said, speaking discreetly to me as every prisoner is always monitored even in visitation.

"But . . . when I followed up with him this week and told him about the reality show, he said, 'No cameras.' I started to try to convince him but he's not the type who can be convinced once he has made a decision. So I stopped myself from asking again," Elisha explained. "But Porsche could not be stopped. She called Midnight and said, 'You promised, and a promise is a promise.' Midnight told your sister, 'I never promised to be a character in a show. That was never part of our agreement.'"

I was disappointed. For some seconds I didn't say anything back to Elisha. I was thinking of ways to flip it in my favor, like how lil' smart-ass kids used to try and maneuver that Rubik's cube when it was hot.

"If you succeed with getting my special request done, I will still do the reality show," I finally said to Elisha.

"Without Midnight, his black Bentley, and the red carpet?" Elisha double-checked. I hesitated and then said, "Yes, without him, but I still want a badass black Bentley and the royal red carpet. After I walk the carpet I'll let my girls get in the whip with me. So make that six crystal flute champagne glasses."

"Cool. I'm surprised you let it go that easily," Elisha said.

"Midnight is not the only cool one. I'm a 'word is bond' kind of bitch. I already gave my word and my loyalty to you that if you handle my special request I'll do the show. So that's our agreement. I'm waiting to see if you can honor that."

True, I didn't ever explain the details of the situation to my girls about the trade-off I had to make. I did not feel like I owed any one of them a damn thing, not even an explanation. That night in my cell during lights-out it dawned on me that this was the reason I was spun out over Midnight, whipped and fixed and maybe even a little obsessed. He was the only man in my whole wide world who I wanted with my whole heart, who I put in my full effort for, who I showed my whole self and even revealed my bare body to, who I could not draw to me. I just couldn't move him. He was the only man who nothing anybody said mattered to him. He was so solid, his mind so made up that no one could move him unless he had already planned to move. Beside the power that moved within him, he could not be forced. It caused everyone who ever seen him to want him even more. Even my girls, although none of them would ever admit it, felt it, saw it, wanted a taste or touch or to really have him all to themselves. But they knew, from when he first walked through our Brooklyn block with Santiaga, he was not a man within their reach, not within their capability, not a dick they could pull, suck or just hop on and have their whole body, every part, in a state of involuntarily continuous overwhelming orgasm.

Now I could feel the frenzy in my pussy, after not having felt it in a very long, long time. It was throbbing. That's the type of heat that moved with Midnight. Just the mention or thought of him could even arouse a dead bitch! My breasts were hot and my chest was heaving, my nipples erect. I was dolo in da dark and just about to cum, so moved by his image in my memory that it made my whole body quake.

Suddenly, I felt a shot through my chest and I was being pulled. I'm a dead bitch back on the move again. I'm fast-forwarding through the dark. It felt so good. From orgasm to feeling high. This was a higher type of high though. The difference similar to on the one hand smoking straight weed, and on the other hand smoking weed with cocaine sprinkles on it. I was never a cokehead, but hey, when you drink or smoke with friends or lovers, you never know if they spike the Kool-Aid or punch or put sprinkles on your weed. Now this cocaine-blunt feeling had me enjoying the mysterious ride and feeling even lighter than a feather.

When the action stopped, I floated down softly and landed in what felt like grass. I wasn't certain, though. I couldn't see nothing. Then, *blat dow!* Bright blinding sunlight! I threw my hands over my eyes and took only short peeks until they adjusted to the shocking shine. While my eyes were still covered, I could smell a certain unrecognizable scent. I eased open my fingers. I was standing in a field of flowers, all of them green-stemmed, tall, and yellow-faced.

Hold up now, I'm a city bitch. So I'm like, *What the fuck? Where am I and why am I here?* I dropped my hands. I could see everything clearly. There were blue-headed, red iridescent-feathered birds with long curved beaks soaring above me. There were also uniquely orange-colored birds with straight long beaks and a crown of feathers on the top of their heads. They were flying around the field. Some landing in the trees—trees that looked like a memory that I didn't want to remember right now. It was from my eighteen-years-young trip to the Florida Keys. Yes! Palm trees, but these had sacks of strange fruit hanging from them that were not Florida coconuts. There were exotic butterflies fluttering up way too close to me. Some were several shades of orange only. Some of them were polka-dotted and multicolored and in all types of unexplainable shapes. I started laughing. I'm used to pigeons and moths and mosquitoes and cement and sidewalks and gravel!

In the far distance there was a tall, wide, and long white wall that somehow glistened as though it had been covered with diamond dust, causing the shine from it and the power of the sun to collide and my eyes to squint. I never saw a wall like that. Someone had to be hiding something behind it, I thought. Looked like money to me. So I began walking in that direction. As soon as I did, I stopped short. I got psyched that I have legs and can suddenly fully feel them. In fact, I can walk, see, hear, smell, and even taste the air. Ah shit, air! That means I can breathe. I'm alive!

After I walked for what felt like forever, I realized that fast-forwarding through darkness was a swifter mode of transportation. Walking for me now was somehow played out, a thing of the past, a tiring non-necessity. Finally reaching the white wall that had sparkled from afar, I could see the detailing of it. It was about fifty thousand square feet long. It was solid as though made from huge shiny white rocks. And every ten feet there was a parallel indentation perfectly carved into the wall. I walked to one of them and turned and stepped inside of the indentation. It was as though someone had carved out a space for a six- or seven-foot person to just stand outside but inside the wall. Crazy! I'm thinking, *Why would a man be standing inside of a solid rock wall?* I stepped out from it and counted twenty-one indentations before I couldn't count any further because that was how long the wall ran. Then I thought, *Maybe armed guards stay tucked in there.* This wall must be protecting a mansion and each security guy stood in each indentation. But what type of hustler needed fifty security dudes outside of his crib? Maybe they were not even regular security, I suddenly thought. Maybe they were spaces for soldiers who carried M-16s. Yo! Maybe this was Pablo Escobar's joint or Tony Montana or El Chapo or . . . I laughed, excited as I now walked alongside the wall looking for the entrance.

Sterling silver, that's what the incredibly sturdy, solid, wide door that was embedded inside of the white wall was made of. I stepped back to fully check it out. I looked up. On top of the wall sat white doves. They stared at me but didn't fly off all nervously like how birds tend to do when even being looked at by human beings. I took a good look at them and walked towards that badass door. I was glad that I don't have that bird fear that one of the chicks on lockup had. She would have been terrified if she was here.

When I reached for the heavy metal knocker, my arm went right through the door as though it was not solid sterling silver, even though I am one hundred that it is. My body followed. Once inside I was still outside, meaning I looked up and I could still see the sky, not a ceiling or a roof. I was standing in what seemed to be the front yard. Beneath the beautiful trees were seven sterling silver outdoor chair-and-table sets with designer cushions, and two sterling silver benches. Beyond the trees at the center of the yard was a huge multiple-level fountain that seemed to be made of the same rock that the wall surrounding the house was made of. In addition to it sparkling, it was gushing water that looked clean enough to drink or bathe in. I walked towards it. I inhaled to see if it smelled any particular way. Clean water, I thought, should not have any smell whatsoever. I leaned in and stuck my hand in the flow. But when I drew my hand back there was no water or trace of wetness in my palm. I thought about it. I'm not even thirsty or hungry. I had not seen food since prison breakfast this morning, which I didn't eat 'cause it was my release day and I was gonna be eating way better food from then on.

But hold up. That could not have been this morning. I was released into a winter storm in the winter season. Where I am standing right now it is obviously summer, not even spring. It has to be August, the hottest month. I can feel the hot breeze and everything is fully blossomed. I grabbed myself. What am I wearing? It better not be the white three-quarter hooded mink coat and the thigh high boots. It isn't. I am wearing the, I'm *rich bitch* Chanel, winter-white brocade, tapered, sleeveless mini with the pleats that gently hug my hips. Of course I am. I had ordered the mini to rock beneath the mean mink and to highlight the red python boots. *Wait a minute . . . the red boots are gone.* Now I'm not wearing no shoes. *No shoes!* Un uh . . . I walked around to the backside of the fountain. About seventy-two feet away was another door, which looked like it was made of pure platinum. Super wealthy, I get it. Dripping with dough! Caked up! Nothing but cheddar, gwop to the ceiling, raining paper! Overwhelmed, I didn't bother knocking, just breezed through, which I now know I can do. I'm thinking. If I look around, I can find a pair of shoes and make them fit. I'm not worried about them being cheap or worn shoes. Evidently I am in a wealthy place. No wealthy bitch would have a cheap shoe collection. Furthermore, every wealthy bitch would and should own tens if not hundreds of shoes that have never been worn yet. I'm not gonna be caught dead and barefoot in someone else's mansion. I started laughing but then stopped real quick, remembering how my laughter just might start doubling, tripling, and mutating.

This is not a mansion. It's a . . . palace. Has to be. It has the highest ceiling that isn't a ceiling. It's a dome. The design of the dome is so dope I want to fuck the architect just to congratulate him on doing what I plan to do in my fashion and decorating business. Design some shit that no one else had. That no one else has ever seen. That mostly no one could ever afford, except *my clients*. My clients, who needed to be filthy to afford *my commission*.

The sunlight poured through the dome's platinum-framed glass skylights. It lit up the wide, long space, making for nice shading. Some spaces had natural spotlights from the sun. Other spaces had shade. Why weren't there separate rooms, separated by walls, though? Why wasn't there any furniture? Instead there were intricately woven carpets. Must have taken four hundred weavers to inlay the designs. It was open space, no bedrooms or kitchen. But there were sinks, on both the left and right, front and backsides of the building. *It's a high-end nightclub, no, a ballroom,* I thought. Then I canceled the thought right away. People can't dance freely on carpeted floors. No owner or boss would want liquor spilling on hand-woven rugs. And I didn't even see no Hermès flats, slippers, or shoes, so I walked right out of the back of the palace.

Crossing another yard, I reached a black wooden door. It was not just any door. It was made from ebony, and the grain was not anything that would be sold in anyone's local furniture store or super mart or Home Depot. It had inlaid hand-carved designs. I could tell from the way there was no knob or outward handle that it slid open instead of swinging in or out. I didn't slide or swing it, just walked through the solid wood, same as I had walked through the solid platinum and the solid sterling silver.

A premium gymnasium like a private Madison Square Garden for some boss that obviously decided to have everything on his property that most had to leave their little apartments and houses to drive outside to get to. The gym floor shined so perfectly. I bet the owner must have 'bout forty slaves he orders to get down on their knees and hand-wax it every night and buff it every morning. I laughed picturing that. This the type of gym every hood needed. Where niggas could run a full court and the bitches could watch and cheer them on and eventually call dibs on the players they liked. I know some chicks would like to run a game and handle and dribble the ball themselves. Not me! I remember Brooklyn's infamous Hustler's league, and even the Harlem Rucker. I lived for that excitement. I loved the fashion show that framed it. I liked that crowd that poured in from every direction and even flooded down the block and caused the cops to shut down the traffic in the surrounding streets to watch the best ballers ball, showcasing amazing moves and skills. I lusted the whips that had pulled up close and parked and double and triple parked creating a show within a show! Bitches all done up so nice, the best players played even harder.

I looked up. Seven flags were hanging from seven metal poles lodged in the walls close to the high ceiling. I only recognized the American flag. It was number six in the flag line up. I was glad to see it. I had been starting to think I was somewhere unfamiliar and too far away from where I am from.

The sound of hydraulics and the back door of the gym slid open. A bunch of bare-backed young men walked in barefooted wearing boot-cut black pants. Bare feet was starting to feel like the theme of this place, but I still wasn't with it.

"Line up! Take your spaces." What I *am* with though is the twenty-one to I'm guessing possibly twenty-three-years-young deep black-skinned fine-ass nigga leading the pack. I don't know what they about to do. Not one of them has a basketball in their grip or kicks. The blackest one, who I have both my eyes on, positioned himself at the forefront of the rest. He called out the orders as he faced the other lined-up teen-young to maybe age twenty dudes. His eyes are serious. Not the eyes of some sheltered palace dweller or suburban sweetie. He's muscular but lean. His jaw is etched and sketched. His teeth are as white as the sparkling wall that surrounds this palace. His hair cut is sharp and clean. Man I'm feeling him. I know he's too young for me but he is not a child. He is a man. And I know the trend is now for these young niggas to prefer slightly older women who are still more beautiful, more refined, more sensual in the sheets and more independent than the young bitches who ain't figured out their power the way I figured out mine at sixteen. And I can still pull dick. I know that. And to this day, no nigga can tell my true age unless I decide to tell him. I won't.

"We all know what this is," the leader said, his voice so *ooh*, it made my pussy pulse.

"Whoever wins the fight competition gets to fight the fight master tonight. I doubt y'all could take him down. I've tried a few times." Everyone laughed. "It hasn't worked out for me. But I'm confident that I can take down every one of you."

"Ahh . . . yeah right . . . whatever man . . ." the young men on the line up roared.

"I like that!" the leader said in response. And when he smiled he had me so open. "Men are supposed to be trained and confident, sure and solid. Now let's see if you can back up all that back talk. Give me two lines of ten. Partner up. After this spar, the last man standing will fight me!" He said it like a threatening invitation and challenge. He spoke so confidently I'm sure it convinced the other guys that they had had no chance of beating him.

"Ansar, I'm hoping you're the last man standing. Heard you have designs on my girl," the leader said, jaw locked and straight faced.

"Whoa," the men sounded and then went silent.

"She's not yours until you marry her," the one who must've been Ansar replied. "And since you're moving too slow and no one can touch her before marriage, I'll take her from you, and marry her so I can touch her." He said it like he meant his words also.

"Let's skip the sparring and bang it out right now," the leader said and rushed right into the ranks to face Ansar. The other nineteen men broke the line up and swiftly closed in and began circling around the twenty-one-years-young leader and Ansar. The moving circle was blocking me from seeing. But I could hear the blows and the *whoas* and *ohs* and the advice being called out by the crowd. They were fighting with their hands and feet, I realized. Not a Brooklyn confrontation that ends in one second with no muscle involved. Just the strength to pull the trigger and the eye to hit the target.

The imperfect circle would spread out as the men would step back, sideways or forward, however the action moved them. I don't know who the bitch was they were fighting over. But I felt a strong feeling like I want niggas to fight over me *just like that*. I want to see muscles moving, and fists swinging and bodies dropping over me. I miss that effect that a woman like me always caused many men to have.

All of a sudden I wanted a mirror more than anything. I want to see myself and check my hair. I'd position it properly over the scar and perfect my look. I need to confirm exactly what I look like right now. I want to check every inch of my body as well. I want to recapture that baddest-bitch mojo and come back with full and pull that leader for myself for a tryst. He don't have to marry me to give me that good feeling that I'm sure he and I both want to feel. We don't have to waste any time. And time is not what I have going in my favor.

I dashed to the side room that I figured was the restroom for the gym. Once inside I could see that it was for men, with seven urinals and one long horizontal cement sink, with seven silver faucets, soap dispensers, paper hand towels and an automatic hand dryer. Three stalls for taking a dump and three stalls for taking a shower. A steam room and a sauna but . . . no . . . mirrors!

Angry, I dashed through the men's room wall and ended up in another yard, filled with white roses, facing a separate house a short distance away with a gold door. *A gold door,* I repeated in my mind as I walked. Goddamn! How much is the owner worth that a property could be built with multiple buildings, secured behind a great wall made from a mountain. Doors all made from precious metals and rare materials as expensive as the buildings and beautiful outdoor spaces, pavilions, and furnishings. I got the feeling that here there was no regard for budget whatsoever.

Close up on the door now, I quickly dropped down. On the right side I saw a computer or flat TV screen. I was sure that the owner could see me through that security screen. I didn't want anybody to see me before I could fully see myself. Squatted low and facing my own toes, I was relieved that I still had the pretty pedicure that I allowed one of my girls on lockup, who was the meanest in that toe art, to design the night before my release. I ran my fingers over my feet, surprised that I didn't track in any soil or grass from that long walk through the field. I was happy that my hands and feet looked top-notch still.

I glanced to my right. In an alcove in the wall was a men's shoe rack, three levels high. Seven velvet-lined slots on each row, for seven pairs of shoes. Maximum capacity, twenty-one. My eyeballs zoomed into each slot recognizing what only the Queen of Queens could recognize. Of course, because a broke bitch would never even know what she was looking at. A connoisseur of kicks, I saw on the two bottom rows sat side by side a collection that only wealth and fame could get hands on and feet in. The red-and-black Jordan's Banned were autographed by Michael Jordan himself. That's big. The only kicks that could sit beside those were the autographed Kobe Bryant Mike Zoom Colby white-and-gold striped. Next in the lineup was LeBron James 8 South Beach. In the other velvet slots were men's black Gucci kicks, Prada high-tops, and an assortment of Air Force Ones, some custom designed and unavailable at retail.

I am impressed. Were all of at least fourteen of the young men in the gym caked up, and these were their kicks? Were the remaining seven of the young guys broke bastards with no shoes? I laughed and had to say to myself, "*You got some nerve! You barefoot bitch!*" Or was the whole rack of twenty-one pairs of shoes all for the feet of the owner? Amazingly, in the top slot was a pair of Aubercy diamond-studded shoes, next to a pair of Louis Vuitton Richelieus, next to a pair of Berlutis, next to a pair of Isaias, next to a pair of Tom Fords.

Tom Ford! He is my fashion designer hero. For the only years that matter Ford was the creative director of Gucci. He made Gucci lingerie, clothes, eyewear, footwear, and accessories so fucking sexy that any nigga or bitch anywhere in the world wearing Gucci from head to toe fucking slayed the scene, ruled the room, rocked the party, and shocked the streets. The Santiagas, we "pulled a Gucci" plenty of times. Our whole family Gucci'd out from under, inner, and outerwear and accessories. On those days and nights we stole the light and walked above the heads of niggas who were on a budget and could only cop one Gucci piece, like a key chain, belt, wallet, or a money clip. While I was locked up, Tom Ford and his man Domenico De Sole left Gucci and opened up their own elite Tom Ford line of every fashionable thing imaginable. His designer handbags were proof of his fashion supremacy. On lock when I saw them in my mags, I thought they killed the Birkin, even though Birkin was trending. Real fashionistas recognize real. When Ford and Domenico left Gucci, they took the stitch and the style, the sense and the allure, the quality and the reign over all, with them. In fact, when they left, it was the same as when Princess Diana "left" the boring-ass royal family, or the same as when Santiaga "left" the streets he ruled. Or like when Notorious B.I.G. "left" music. Or like when Jordan and Allen Iverson and even Dennis Rodman left the court. The game just wasn't the same no more.

"That thing" is something that can't be bought or sold. You either got it or you don't. Hell, "that thing" can't even be stolen. How a bitch like Simone like them apples? *Oh fuck, don't think about her. I don't want to get angry and disappear.* The point is, even if some new him or her or this or that arrives on the scene and tries to step in the shoes of the ones who got "that thing" in their blood, body, or look, in their profession, talent, or skill, in their hands, feet, or voice, or in their sports music, or whatever! The newcomer, even if he or she or it is a great imitator or knockoff, can never ever reproduce the same level of feeling or sound, movement or hustle, fashion or flow or perfection.

I felt a little sad for like six seconds squatting there at the golden door. *Snap out of it,* I reminded myself, a mirror and . . . I glanced to my left. In the left alcove I saw a six-thousand-dollar pair of Jimmy Choo's Avril crystal shoes sitting on top of a shoe rack, packed with designer women's footwear. I stared. The crystals sparkled even though they were not in the sunlight. However, my fashion eyes were redesigning them, flooding each shoe with princess-cut authentic diamonds tightly and properly placed leaving no opening to see the shoe fabric. And on the back that hugs the ankle, six small emeralds. That would have been even more Fuck the worldish! I laughed. *I'm a dead bitch redesigning a pair of six-thousand-dollar shoes into a pair of six-hundred-and-sixty-six-thousand-dollar shoes.*

Not funny. I picked up the pair of crystal-flooded Jimmy Choo shoes. I stood up and placed them onto my pretty feet. At first they didn't fit. Suddenly they did. *I must've wanted these pretty bad,* I thought to myself. Before I couldn't grasp anything into my hand, not paper, or envelopes, or even water. I pranced through the left side of the sealed-shut solid-gold-at-minimum plated door without knocking, ringing, or activating the security screen or alarms. I walked through same as if the pure gold door was made of nothing but air.

A circular scene was what I was seeing now, sexy curved walls instead of flat and straight lines, boxes, squares, and rectangles. It was all quarter circles, semicircles, ovals, and even walls that seemed to swerve. I was blown away by it. There was no drywall, plywood, or paneling in this palace, or even the other buildings that seemed to be all part of one to-fight-or-die-for empire. Even the clay potted flower and plant shelves as well as sitting spaces were indentations carved into the walls so sturdy and solid I imagined they could withstand a bulldozer.

Whoever's place this is, they're in love with the sky. They must've told the architect no ceilings, just domes, and clear not stained glass, so they could watch the sun rise and set or the moonlight pouring down stars. I was so fucking impressed.

I searched for family photos and paintings. I could tell this circular building was lived in. Everything about it screamed "occupied," even though it was cleaner than the Board of Health. Instead of pictures, the walls were covered with tiny pastel-colored ceramic pieces so perfectly placed that even when the walls curved, the pat-

tern of the tiles and flow of the art didn't break. It was so precise. It
was kind've crazy, I thought. This property existed behind a fifteen-
foot-high white solid rock wall, but on the inside of the buildings,
there were no walls separating one room from another like we are
accustomed to having in our houses and mansions. In this circle, the
kitchen was at the center of the huge wide space. It was so doped
off that it could have been mistaken for a . . . a . . . what?

Fact is, I didn't have shit to compare what I was seeing to. The
dangling utensils and steel pots and pans were outdone by the immaculate collection of tiny to massive all-glass pots on the stovetop.
There was even a glass frying pan. I had never seen cookware like
this before. One refrigerator freezer was as wide as three family refrigerator freezers. Two stoves and ovens, a total of ten burners. A
flat griddle for pancakes and a waffle iron for waffles, and blenders,
and cappuccino machines and graters, slicers, choppers, and toasters
and even a deep fryer, a dough mixer, pasta maker, and an old-
school popcorn machine, with the butter bin designed like the one
in your favorite movie theatre. Ceramic dishes and deep bowls and
water and juice gourds and deep-welled decorated ceramic soup
spoons. How many servants did they have? How is a lived-in space
so perfectly clean? I started to doubt my own eyes, was searching for
crumbs or dust or something spilled, even a droplet of water. Found
nothing. Figured I was just bugging and reminded myself, *the mirror the mirror the mirror*, which led me to walk down the corridor in
my crystal pumps that I wore like they were stilettos.

I got startled when I had almost reached the next door, which I
was sure had to lead to some bedrooms that had to have walls and
privacy, bathrooms and showers—and yes!—mirrors. A beautiful
all-black green-eyed cat stepped out of one of the indentations in
the walls. It looked at me like it was a person seeing another person.

I'm not a pet lover though. I never had any intention of pick-
ing up anything's poop or of living with animals like we family. I'm
from the projects. We see roaches we smash 'em. We hang sticky
paper so all flies get stuck to it, their legs pulled off until they die. If

we even think for one second there's a mouse in the house we trap it, snap off its tail, and trash it when it's finally dead. Let my project building maintenance man think there's some rats. He gets the whole cleanup crew to spread out the pink poison in the dirt. Then they rope it off, put up the tape so kids don't play in it, like a murder scene.

So I didn't stoop to pet the pretty creature. But I did see its diamond collar and that made me pause and take a closer look. When I still didn't pet it and instead walked off, it followed me. I wanted it to go away. Cat looked sneaky, like it knew stuff a cat shouldn't know. Or like a detective that would watch me too closely and then report back to some higher-up cat authority that would come tryna do me something, a ferocious den of lions, where the Lion King held his throne.

When I finally reached the door, I forgot the cat, that was still there paused at my feet. The door was made of pure pearls. My eyes widened and my lips parted. I'm not the type that would ever buy a string of pearls, or get all excited if a nigga bought it for me either. But I felt enticed by the designer's mind that thought to make a door made of pearls. I reached up to feel the surface, wanted to press my body up against it. But instead I passed through it, same as I had passed through the other incredibly precious doors. Soon as I did I was whisked away, fast-forwarding for what felt like only five seconds but moving at a speed that prevented me from seeing what was on the way. When I stopped whizzing, I no longer had any vision. I was angry about it. Felt cheated. I knew I was just about to find a mirror, a big one. People who cared about their look more than mostly they cared about anything had to have mirrors. People of wealth all worked hard at at least one thing, *image*. So, they have to check and recheck and be certain before they allow anybody to see even one small detail out of sync. This was the kind of sensational property that I'd rather lose my hearing in, if I had to choose and lose something, but definitely *not my eyesight*.

"Kush, what are you doing in here?" I heard a woman's voice say.

Who was she talking to? Then I heard the cat purr. She must have been stroking it. How did the cat arrive the same time as me? Was it whizzing through space like I was?

"Chee, there's only one wildcat allowed in this bedroom and it's not Kush," I heard a man's hypnotic voice say. He sounded *real* familiar.

"Kush knows she's not allowed up here. This is the first time this has happened. One of our daughters may have left the door open by mistake," the female's voice said. *She must be Chee.* "I'll let her out. But I think she has a crush on you. Look at how she stares into your eyes," Chee said.

"Oh, now even the cat has a crush on me," the male said smoothly without laughter.

"You know I know *every time* a woman is attracted to you. I've always been right. Have I ever been wrong?" she asked playfully. The cat purred, the sound much higher and closer to my ear, so I knew she must be holding the cat in her arms. I heard her walk away. I wanted the male voice to say something so I could be sure. But with Chee, whoever that is, gone from the room, he wasn't talking no more. I could only hear the rustle of his clothes, an expensive business dress shirt, I figured. Then I heard a slight clink. Cuff links, I imagined he removed his and laid them on his glass-top dresser drawer or night table. Next I heard one jingle, his belt buckle, I believed. Then I heard his zipper. Oh hell, yeah! Soon, I heard the sound of him removing his pants and then his boxers. He must've felt good being undressed. I could hear the rhythm of his breathing change and his breath escaping like being naked was more comfortable. I stood still listening to the sound of his breathing. Then I heard the sound of his feet on what sounded like a marble, uncarpeted floor. A shower switched on.

Yes! Let's shower together, I thought to myself and felt even more excited. I heard the sound of a door closing. It was a glass shower! Of course it was. There would never be a cheap pole and shower curtain in a palace bathroom. And I could tell it was not the sound of the bathroom door shutting because the volume of the sound of the downpour of the water didn't decrease much at all. I threw off my Jimmy Choo's crystal heels like they were Payless. I wiggled out of my Chanel mini inch by inch. It was tapered so lovely, that is was like a second skin. There was no room to remove it, as though CoCo wanted a bitch rich enough to afford it and bad enough to afford it and bad enough to wear it right, to die with it on. When I was finally able to shed it, I tossed it who knows where. I'm not wearing a bra, panties, or a G-string. I like my titties free and my pussy raw.

Now I am naked and tip toeing into the bathroom guided by the sound of the water and the warmth of the stream of the steam. I figured hey, since I was able to pick up the heels and properly use my fingers, it meant that now I can even hold his balls in my hand, feel the ridges of his dick; the depth, the width, the texture. I started feeling around like Helen Keller, blind but determined to get to the shower glass door and inside, body to body. Ooh, I'm in. I can't feel the warm water though. Am I really in? Did I open a linen closet and walk in there by mistake instead?

I'm getting pissed at my misses, and at my circumstances. I move around. Still can't tell if I'm in the shower or not. Then I smell a new scent, like flowers or some gourmet fresh-baked dessert or an expensive perfume. Something extremely alluring. Then I hear the shower door close. Did he get out? *No, that would be too quick,* I thought. But maybe I had again lost track of time and how to count it. I was sure of one thing though. I could now hear two people breathing One of them was not me. I could hear lips locking and tongues sliding. I could hear wet sudsy skin rubbing against skin.

"Oh huh, oh huh, oh huh, oh huh." Her breathing was accelerating. Soon she was moaning softly. Then suddenly she screamed pure pleasure like a celebration. He started talking some sexy shit to her. I could tell by his tone. But, he was speaking in some other language that I have either never heard or never noticed. She replied in the same other language. It was all soft sexy talk while the intensity of the downpour of the water was the soundtrack to it. I'm trying to control my anger. Wished I could find and snatch the shower head and turn the temperature of the water to freeze, spray that bitch and cause her to flee. "Speak English like you two motherfuckers were speaking it five minutes ago," I screamed. My scream was not like her moan or her scream though. Hers was on some ecstasy level. You know what mine was.

Eventually the shower water went from heavy downpour to a trickle. The door-closing sound happened. They were out of the shower now. I could just feel it. But they were still in the bathroom area. I could feel that too. It was obviously a large space. Duh, what else would it be? I should have been calling it a spa. To name it a bathroom sounded like a cheap insult. I heard the rustle of a towel. Then, a top was being opened and a tube being squeezed. Or something like that.

"That feels so good," she said.

"Put your hands up," he said.

"Am I under arrest?" she replied so softly that you knew her ass wasn't under no fucking arrest. Niggas getting arrested either don't say shit or say something foul.

"Your turn," she said on some sexy shit. They were kissing again. I was ready to leave. "I like it better when you do it for me," she said softly. I could hear their bodies moving but not leaving the bathroom area. It dawned on me that it didn't matter that I was ready to leave. A dead bitch doesn't control the action. I don't even know where I am or who I'm with. Picture a grown-ass Brooklyn bitch who don't know even that!

"Draw the curtains," I heard him say. The sound of their voices and bodies was back in their bedroom.

"Why? No one can see in." She paused. Then I could hear the curtain fabric dropping down. "I always thought that's the reason we have no neighbors." She laughed.

"I don't even want the birds peeping at my wife," he said calmly.

"Impossible!" she said excitedly.

"Impossible what?" he asked coolly.

"Impossible that you could still love me that much," she teased, then added, "After I have given birth to seven of your sons and two of your daughters."

"What fool would not love a woman even more than he loved her before, after she pushed out nine of his children?" he asked her and he sounded serious. But she was still playing.

"Um let me see," she laughed. "Maybe a guy who has three other wives, two of them younger than me. One from Sudan, one from Oman. Then there's the first wife from Korea . . ." she teased.

"Come here," he said to her, and the sound of the way he said it turned my rising anger to intense desire as though he was saying, "Come here," to me.

"And one from Japan," he said and kissed her. I'm feeling burnt. "Who flies freely in and out of all of those countries and follows me all around the world wherever I go," he said.

"I do not!" She laughed, and I definitely knew she was lying.

"Who follows me even when she's seven months pregnant, no matter how far I go? A girl so pretty, smart, loyal, loving, helpful, that I built her a private palace. A queendom, and I put it right here in the UAE, a perfect peaceful place. Made it of everything precious to show her how precious she is to me. But the pretty pilot won't stay put in her palace unless I am right here beside her. So now, to please my second wife, the pilot, the wildcat, I moved all of my wives and all of our children and even my friends and their wives and children to where she is, so I could be right by her side."

My vision clicked on. I thought it was cruel. She had her naked body pressed against his body. Her hands clasped at the back of his neck. I walked up behind him and pressed my body against his back. I put my hands on each side of his waist and tried to pull him away from her and on to me.

"True," she said softly. I could tell she was about to re-seduce him. "And . . ." she said playfully then kissed him. "After you do 'that thing' to me one more time," she giggled. "We can talk about how two of our sons are about to fight over the Santiaga daughter."

Santiaga daughter! That's me! I thought. I ran around to face him.

And over her shoulder, I could see clearly what I had already sensed and known. I tried to swipe her out of his grasp but my hands had no impact. I tried to yank her long black braid, choke her with it. My hands couldn't clasp it.

"Hey, what are my heels doing up here? I left them outside on the rack," she asked softly. I couldn't tolerate any more. I screamed at the top of my lungs, "Midnight, Midnight, Midnight!" but obviously he couldn't hear, feel, or see me. It didn't matter anymore. I overheated and instantly, I dissolved.

Furious on several levels, I was back to being a ball of heat. The bitch he had was perfect. She knew it. He knew it. I knew it. She was golden-skinned, my same complexion, 'round my same height. Her hair was black and long. She wore it in one thick braid down the center of her head. It was real, not purchased, same as mine. Her silver-gray eyes gave her the advantage. They looked stunning like the sterling silver door lit up by the sun. And I could tell she had him hypnotized. Like me she had that diamond-cut body, unbelievably tight and lean especially after pushing out seven boys and two girls. A pilot, well what the fuck? Who's gonna beat a bitch in a jet or better yet a helicopter? Men like foreign cars and like foreign bitches even more. I hated that. Four wives? And they all cool with that? They're fucking up the game. What am I supposed to be, wife number five? Picture dat, never, ever, ever.

I had thought that after my victorious prison release, emerging out a snitch-free, time-served, real million-dollar bitch, which even though Midnight wasn't scheduled to be there, he would without a doubt be watching me on his wide-screen TV, then I could get rid of his wife. Not kill her of course. Just replace her, because I'm obviously the better choice! How am I supposed to dispose of four bitches? Who come to find out are all from separate faraway places that nobody ever heard of, been to, and where nobody would ever want to go. What the fuck is Oman? Sudan? UAE? UAE! I was tryna figure that out the whole time we were all three in his bedroom. He said that's where we were standing in the palace he built for Chee.

What is UAE? Is it United African Empire? Ah hell no! When I was whizzing through the darkness it was a longer journey than the other two times it had happened to me. But it wasn't long enough to have traveled all the way to the African jungle. And when I arrived, there was no safari! And, I didn't see no broken-down huts or bald-headed ashy babies with flies chilling on their noses, their fingers so weak from starvation that they couldn't even swat them away. I didn't see no braless pygmies lined up to get one bowl of cereal from some foreigner scooping it out of a metal trash bin because they pitied them.

So that's that. It definitely wasn't Africa. Yeah, I heard of Korea before because they the ones who owned a lot of markets in Brooklyn and who shined up the fruit and stacked it in neat rows before any other grocers started doing it that way. They were the originators or champions of the open-twenty-four-hours salad bar. They was also the ones who was quick to say something slick to a nigga shopping in their store and set off a whole heated situation.

Of course everybody in the whole world heard of Japan. The Japanese got sushi. Any real top bitch has not only heard of it, she's been served it, and has tasted it. Plus the high-end Japanese restaurants flaunted wicked architecture. Even their interior designs was doped off with separate grill stations at each customer's table and a personal Japanese chef doing a knife show as he prepared steaks and shrimps and shit like that.

However, Chee definitely didn't sound like a Japanese bitch. She didn't look like any Japanese bitch I ever seen while chilling at Benihana. She was above them. See what I'm saying? And, once those foreign bitches, who got our same look, start speaking in different languages, showing the fuck off, how a hood bitch gon' keep up? How she gon' shine?

I was cool hugging his back. I had somehow blotted her out. I just wanted to get my moment, my feel, have my way with him without him being able to resist. I had always wanted to suck his collarbone since I was thirteen. Press my nude body up against his. Trace my prettiest finger lightly over his incredible jawline. Hold his face in my hands and feel the pleasure of his thick lips. More than that, he was the only man worthy of me marrying him and whose children I ever wanted to push out and keep and say these are his and my babies. Babies who were not a burden, but a treasure. But when I looked up while hugging him, her hands were dangling there on the backside of his neck. I could see her unusually precious pear-shaped diamond wedding ring. That sent me over the edge. It was the same as if she had stolen my life, was wearing my jewels, was living in my palace, was the mother of my sons, and was loving my man and apparently he was loving her back even more. Of course he was. They were both standing there glistening from the oil I'm sure he had massaged onto her skin. Her wet silky freshly braided long black braid, that after I put two and two together, and from what I had just overheard, had been braided by him. That infuriated me. But when she asked about her shoes, the Jimmy Choo's crystal pumps, I felt stabbed. With one simple question she had highlighted for me that *hey she's right. This all her shit not mine.* The silver, pearls, platinum, palaces, gold, and diamonds were all hers! Worth more than all those precious jewels was the man she had wrapped around her finger. How am I supposed to deal with that? It was as though she had hit the local number, the lotto, and the mega!

My mind switched when she said, "Our sons are about to fight over the Santiaga daughter." At first I thought, *Yeah that's me.* Then I sobered up and figured out what should've been pretty clear. Midnight had adopted my twin sisters, Lexy and Mercedes, when Santiaga got locked down. So one of them girls had caught the hearts of two of Midnight's many sons. That's stepbrothers in love with their stepsisters. I don't believe in step-anything! Only real blood relations matter. And the fact of the matter is Lexy and Mercedes don't share one drop of the same blood with Midnight's real children.

So Midnight's sons were fair game for them. Since Santiaga's daughters all know a real man when we see one, 'cause we are the daughters of the realest man, of course one of them or maybe even both of them peeped that that twenty-one-years-young leader of the bare-backed young men in the palace gym was pure fire. Undoubtedly worth scratching a next bitch eyes out over or even putting a knife in her ribs. Who else could the young leader have been other than the son of Midnight? The king of men.

Wait a minute. My math mind was merging with a memory. When I was seventeen years young I definitely had asked Midnight if he had any children. He told me no. Why did he lie to me? He couldn't have a twenty-one-year-old son now if he was not already born when I first asked him at age seventeen. Maybe I'm wrong with the number twenty-one that I guessed, from what my eyes saw, was the young leader's age. Now I felt greasy for wanting to jump on his son's dick. But not too greasy 'cause I didn't know. And I did fifteen on lockup. I'm allowed to feel a lil' anxious. But why were Midnight's two sons fighting over one twin? They each could have had one to themselves. Hey, my twin sisters both look the same! Or maybe not anymore . . . Maybe one of them had gotten fat or sloppy. I doubt it, though. Maybe one of them was extreme fashion, and several cuts above the other. Maybe one of them had become an undesirable bookworm. But the fact that Chee was even the mother over my twin sisters, and she had all of the answers and info about them that I didn't know and she had raised and seen them while I was locked in a cage, was another knife . . . , this time, through my throat.

Experts of art, fashion, and design, like myself, have eyes that are swift to see, survey, and size up the look, the authenticity, and value of all. Of course I had seen through the sheer white ceiling-to-floor curtains that were pretty but not powerful enough to block the sun. I saw their doped-off backyard replete with everything that hood niggas and average everybody else has to go to the park to enjoy with a million other strange motherfuckers doing the same.

Aside from the swings and the seesaws, the outdoor brick-oven kitchen and the barbecue pit was to cry for. The collection of off-road vehicles, motorcycles, and exotic whips were lined up in the distance as well. That choked me, strangled me. To think that my father, Santiaga, was locked up in the box in an eight-by-five cell with no way out, while his man who he put on was wearing his crown, fathering his daughters, living his lifestyle and then some, was way too much.

I got even more heated because I did not know how everything went down between Santiaga and Midnight exactly. Santiaga didn't say in his letters. I'm not stupid. So of course I know Poppa couldn't say it in writing and also couldn't say it to my face because we were both prisoners serving time. I do know that Poppa still trusts Midnight and that Midnight still looks out for him. That meant that Midnight never flipped on Santiaga. Poppa was swift with his revenge over anyone who did. Even from behind bars, Poppa he could make that type of shit happen. Still I couldn't figure. Why was Midnight, who I saw back when I was seventeen years young on the exact day he left New York to move down to Maryland, rich? No not rich, filthy rich . . . when on the day he left all he had was one suitcase in the backseat of his black Acura, which I saw with my own eyes. Seeing him and Chee's monopoly over everything and everyone, his wealth, women, property, possessions in great detail, was suffocating me. Now was I supposed to hate him? I already loved him. The fact that he landed on his feet and blew the fuck up like a real motherfucking hustler made me love him even more.

The real headbanger that happened in that master bedroom was when I realized that there had been mirrors in the palace, placed in the usual spots where mirrors belong. I had even looked into those mirrors one by one. It wasn't till the end when I saw Chee's vanity table, packed with perfumes and oils, lotions and creams, then looked up and saw Midnight and her in front of me, and looked back and saw them behind me, that I realized that I was staring into a mirror, but a dead bitch ain't got no reflection.

5.

Must be in my casket now. I'm still. I'm laid out on my back. My face and neck are numb, paralyzed even. The back of my head feels mushy. I'm cold, no longer a ball of heat. I'm stiff, feeling no space on my left or right, over my head or beneath my feet. I don't know if my limbs are all swelling or if the casket is shrinking. I can hear my own ribs cracking. I don't know if I am still blind or if this is just the darkest darkness I ever saw. My eyes are glued closed. I can't scream when I get furious. Someone stitched my lips shut. I feel something tiny crawling on me. Or maybe I'm imagining it. I'm outraged that I can still imagine. If I'm in my casket blind, deaf, and dumb, why isn't my mind shut off? I want it shut off completely. Who would ever want to be buried deep in the cold dark earth while being 100 percent aware? Not me, but that's what I am now, nothing else besides thoughts and imaginings. I was never a daydreaming, fragile, action-less vulnerable bitch. Now the tiniest bugs and worms and insects, and whatever else creeps and crawls below the earth, are looking at me like I'm food. On lockup, we had bitches who we treated like food. No one dared to treat me that way.

I'm thinking now, the whole rest-in-peace thing is a sham. I'm dead but definitely not resting and definitely not in peace. I began to think about people who I knew who got dead in my lifetime. One of my closest, tightest Brooklyn fly girls, from way back when we used to say shit like *fly girls,* was named Nique. We were best friends before I ever met Natalie. Nique was a crazy cutie, a goody two-shoes girl who loved school and was a cheerleader. Because we were both dimes, even though we were extremely different from one another, our looks and mutual popularity pushed and held us together. Only murder could separate us and it did. Nique was killed by her own moms who believed that Nique was fucking her man. Nique wasn't. Nique wasn't fucking nobody. And everybody except the donkeys know that fucking and raping ain't the same damn thing. The night before her moms killed her, I found out from Nique that her momma's boyfriend was all the time chasing and cornering her, tryna touch, feel, and fuck Nique even though she said no, hated him, and fought back. Her moms stayed stuck on stupid. But I think the crazy bitch was just pretending. She would tell Nique to try and get along with him even though he was not her real father. She would be telling Nique how nice he was and how good he was to her. She even said if it wasn't for him, their lights would've been cut off 'cause she couldn't afford to pay all of the bills on her own. I think she was on the low trying to convince her daughter that since the asshole was paying a few essential bills, why not overlook "the situation."

But even she couldn't take her own advice. She must've caught him in the act of lusting or violating Nique. So she mercked her own fourteen-years-young daughter. I was also fourteen, when I lost my fly-ass best friend. The Friday after Nique's murder, me, Natalie, Simone, Reese, Zakia, Toshi, and Asia all went to school to rep for Nique. We had the wildest, illest "Rest-In-Peace Rally" our high school ever had. We made the whole student body stand up for Nique. We made the cheerleaders cheer for her, the band play for her, the drum line drum for her, and the thugs to feel for her on that day. Now I know it's all bullshit. I'm wondering if Nique is still laying in her casket umpteen years later, still getting violated by creepy-crawly things same as when she was alive, 'cause now that she's been dead for years, she can't move, and her legs and arms are swollen and her casket is shrinking and her ribs are cracking, and the back of her head is disintegrating same as mine.

Before my death, this was my point to the prison chaplain, who along with the prison social worker and the prison psyche were all the biggest frauds. Furthermore, they existed not to cure or correct or inspire us. They were not qualified to do any of that anyway. They were a trio of broken-down bitches barely holding their own lives together, strategically placed and meagerly paid to take out their misery on the prisoner bitches who they stupidly thought were beneath them. Point-blank they were there to interrupt the gangs, crews, cliques, and families we formed to protect and provide for ourselves, instead of obeying any of the bullshit they was all peddling that, put together, all added up to nothing.

I was one prisoner who they couldn't access. I was one who didn't ever and never ever would confess or confide in them. When they talked, I'd think of other things, listen to music in my mind. I'd give 'em the glare of the blank stare and the torture of silence. They said I needed an exorcism, whatever the fuck that is. They couldn't send me to church by force. So they tugged at my team. They even targeted my cellmate, a bitch named Veronica. She wasn't one of my original Brooklyn crew. She was from Queens claiming Queensbridge. That was a reputable hood on my hood map but wasn't the reason I put her on. I put her on with my team because me and Veronica was locked up in the same small cell, sitting on the same toilet, spitting in the same sink. She was watching even if she pretended not to be watching me. She could clock my movements, intercept or read my kites and letters, and count my contraband. I jumped her into the gang so she would understand our routine, participate when we breaking the rules, and maintain the confidence of the crew because of the threat that she would also be held responsible if we got caught doing the shit we do.

Next thing I know, Simone da Beast said she saw Veronica coming out of Chaplain Kaplan's office. She left it up to me to find out what my cellmate was doing in there, what Chaplain was asking her, what Veronica was saying, and who she was telling on.

"Heard you was chopping it up with Chap," I said casually. It was lights out and we was both laid out in our bunks.

"Something like dat. I didn't say nothing in case that's why you asking about it," Veronica denied instantly.

"Nah, I know you ain't no snitch. You know better," I said softly.

"So what about it then?" Veronica turned the question back on to me.

"Chap's the one I don't trust. What did she ask you?"

"She was doing her job, talking about Jesus and saving my soul."

"Why you was listening to that shit?" I asked her.

"I'm doing fifteen same as you. That's a long time. I'm scoping out the benefits." Then she added, "Chaplain got a jar of caramels. I heard another mate talking about it. She was like if you listen to Chaplain's Jesus stories, Chap will let you chew her caramels," Veronica said, then laughed.

"Chap got you open with a piece of candy?" I said, letting Veronica hear how ridiculous she sounded. "So all you did was listen?" I asked, still measuring the threat.

"Yeah. I figured if she got caramels, she got some other shit in her stash. So I listened a long time."

"And what did you get out of it?" I pushed. Veronica went silent for some seconds.

"Chap has a few steaks in her stash. I ain't taste nothing that good in a while. She threw butter on her beef. I got hooked. After I started chowing down while listening to what Chaplain was saying, it all started to make sense to me. She was talking about sins in a slick way. Like not asking me about confessing my sins but just telling me about what sins are; like lying, cheating, stealing, murdering, coveting other people's stuff, having sex without being married, sleeping with someone's husband or wife, shit like that. She was telling me how to confess, pray and apologize to the Lord for my sins and say certain prayers and then I'll receive blessings from doing that."

"That bitch is lying," I said swiftly. "First of all, me and you is both serving 'mandatory minimums.' Do you know what the word *mandatory* means? It means that that shit is nonnegotiable. No matter what you do in here on the inside, even if you kiss the warden's ass and the chaplain's ass, and the social worker's ass, and the psych's ass, and all the C.O.'s asses, *you ain't getting out till you hit fifteen years' time served.* You can pray to the warden, the judge, the jury, Jesus, whoever! You ain't getting out no earlier than fifteen. *Don't let her run that psych on you.*"

"True dat, but Chaplain was talking about if human beings don't give our lives to Jesus, and apologize to the Lord for our sins, and stop living sinfully, the only place our souls will go is to hell." Veronica sounded like she was going for Chap's talk.

"That's pimp talk," I told Veronica. "Chap's a pimp and so is Jesus. Hell, even a pimp on the street only demands that you give him some of the money you pull in while working your body. Jesus demands that you give your life to him! Check it out. Chaplain stole some steaks from the staff café. She fed it to you, an inmate. Both things, stealing and contraband is illegal. She's a lying bitch who pretends everybody else should tell on themselves. She don't tell on herself. Chap even got a girlfriend. You know C.O. Baker, the one with the close-cropped boy haircut who works in the other building but we see her on the yard? Her and Chap are lovers."

"So what?" Veronica said passionately.

"I agree, so fucking what! No big deal, right?" I was 'bout to show her. "A lot of chicks on lock got their girl lovers. You know why? Because that's what they want to do. That's who they picked and that's their choice, right?" I asked.

"Hell yeah that's right," Veronica agreed.

"But meanwhile, Chap doesn't want to let you do what you want to do, choose what you want to choose. Chill with who you want to chill with. Chap says you gotta confess your sins and stop or else you going to hell. But Chap ain't confessing her sins and even if she was, she damn sure ain't stopping her stealing, smuggling, or her relationship with C.O. Baker who I know through the vine is actually married with some other woman! All that shit is a sin, even according to Chap. But not according to me. So what's up with that? And if there really is a hell, and Chap knows she's going there 'cause she's still sinning and not stopping, it must not be too bad of a place to go, or she must not really believe in what she saying in the first place." I wrapped up my campaign to snatch back my girl Veronica so she wouldn't break our crew or eventually flip and betray us.

"I never thought about it from that angle," Veronica said after a long pause. "But according to Chap, Jesus died for all of our sins."

"Let's say he did. Whoever he is anyway. I don't trust people I can't see, didn't grow up with, ain't from the same hood or at least from the same circumstance. But let's say he died so we can sin, which sounds like mean pimp game. Then why is Chap sweating you then? Jesus threw away his life, washed your sins away, hers and everybody else's. That means everybody is free to do whatever the fuck we want to do. Jesus, whoever that is, took the fall for everybody? That's what Chap said. Chap's still doing what she wants to do, even though she knows she's sinning. So we all even-steven. If everybody minds their own fucking business and does whatever the fuck they want to do, and don't try to judge, block, stop or control anybody else's life or choices, it's all good, right?" I could see in her eyes that my reasoning was working on her. To seal it, I asked her, "So who you suppose to be praying to if Jesus is dead?"

"I didn't ask Chaplain all dat," Veronica said, suddenly sounding aggravated.

"Now you won't have to. There's nobody to pray to. Nobody is listening. Don't you think Chap been praying asking dead Jesus for a better job than this fucked up place? Even if somebody was listening, *mandatory* means exactly what it means. Besides, Chaplain

is right in here with us, New York State prison. She ain't no different 'cept she got a fucking jar of caramels and stolen steaks and we
got commissary and gotta pay for what we want. We work in here.
She works in here. 'Cept, she gets a little iddy-biddy paycheck. So
the difference between her and us is about three hundred dollars
a week. You gon' bow down to a bitch who every other word out
of her mouth is a fraud game, who in one week only brings home
three hundred dollars? Veronica, you locked up for hustling, making three hundred dollars every three fucking seconds!" Case closed.
I won her over. I could feel it.

Veronica never answered me that night. I know she wasn't
sleeping. The next day when we had fifteen minutes to shoot the
shit, our girl crew was talking. Simone had told everybody about
Veronica's trip to the chaplain. Asia said to all of us, "If Veronica wants to start going to church and chilling with the chaplain
leave her ass alone. It ain't got nothing to do with us. Most of the
hustlers and even the rappers who we know and love be rocking a
Jesus piece. It don't mean nothing. It don't stop shit from happening. When I was on my knees sucking Rojo's dick, that diamond-
flooded crucifix was swinging side to side right above my head. He
wasn't thinking about Jesus, his wife, or his kids! That nigga was just
moaning like a bitch!" We all started cracking up, even Veronica.
Next day she was back to confidently doing what we do, with us.

My casket plus my memory of my girls caused me to miss
lockup, which I never ever thought was possible to miss. Back in
Brooklyn I was used to living with my Santiaga family and running with my hood girlfriends. When Santiaga moved us to our
Long Island mansion, I spent all my time trying to get back to my
Brooklyn hood, my bitches and my niggas. On lockup I got ganged
up eventually and was used to rolling in a crew of my girls. Even
when planning my release after fifteen years I had thought to live in
the same house with my crew. That's why this casket shit is bullshit
to me. Why am I alone? If hell really existed, which I never really
thought about unless some sucker from the group home or the

prison bought it up, same as I don't believe in the boogeyman, or ghosts, or anything like that. Same as I love the haunted house and horror flicks 'cause that shit is all just entertaining bullshit to me that could be enjoyed and laughed at after having a few blunts and beers. And if this is Hell that I'm in right now, why ain't the place packed? Where is everybody else? I'm game for hell long as I'm not the only one in it. If this is hell bring all of the other motherfucking dead sinners so we can have a party. I can only exist where the action is at.

6.

It can't be only me here, I thought. But it was. It could have been six seconds, or six minutes, or six hours, or six days, or six weeks, or six months, or six years after my death. I could not tell how much time had passed. All I know is what's happening to me at the moment. I'm no longer laying flat in my casket. I'm sitting, same as I would be sitting back on my Brooklyn block on a bench or stoop. Really though it feels like I'm sitting on a curb close to the open sewer. The stench is like a beating, a continuous foul smell that only changes from stinky to the stinkiest. The odor is so foul that even after I suspected that the smell might be coming from my unwashed rotting body, I could not confirm it. Must be the stench is traveling in waves of steam coming up from the sewer. I want to get up and walk away from the smell like any sensible bitch would, but my legs cannot move. It's dark, completely black. There has been no sunshine here or even one speck of light. Not even artificial light, like from a light bulb. That meant there are no days and no seasons. There is no sunrise, and no sunset. I *could say* it's like nighttime all of the time where I am now. Even that would be a lie, though. Down here there is no moon and no moonshine and not one single star. So it is unlike nighttime because there is no night shine. Instead of the rotating earth, and the alternation of days and nights, instead of a moving sky or clouds or even rain, snow, or hail, thunder or lightning, there is none of that, just deep blackness. There is only the threat of the unexpected. The stench is the only permanent thing. Could be six months' worth of odor from my period blood, my poop, my urine, and my sweat combined. Even the thought of that stinks. The odor randomly intensifies ranging from high to higher to the highest foulness, as though it is being controlled like how the knob on the stovetop can lessen or increase the degree of a flame. There is no flame to be seen, though, because that would be a form of light and would upset the theme here. But at certain intervals a heat rushes beneath me that causes me to want to leap up. Yet, I cannot. It's like here where I am, it will be cold as a freezer, then suddenly it would feel like someone was frying my ass as it sat on the curb, and the soles of my feet as they rested on the street. I'd rather whoever runs this place to decide on one temperature and stick to it.

There is no music here. I ain't heard a jam or joint in I don't know how long. But, there are plenty of strange sounds at varying volumes, some soft, like the hissing that comes and stays for what seems like a long while. It is a hissing that makes my skin crawl. Then suddenly it disappears only to be replaced by the sound of cracking, like ninety-nine niggers cracking their knuckles at the same time. If that ain't enough, next it's the high-volume sound of bones breaking and the screaming that follows the breaking. Sounds like a whole city of screamers, as though all of the boroughs of New York including Brooklyn, the Bronx, Manhattan, Queens, and Staten Island, more than eight million people, are screaming at one time. The screaming sound is the weirdest to me because I am the only one here. When it comes around I try to ignore it even though it is too loud and impossible to ignore. I just use my determination, go inside of my own thoughts and think about some other shit that I prefer. Once the screams cease, I'll hear something like grinding. It is kind of like the sound of that annoying drill that the dentist uses. It's like a million people getting dental work done at the same time. That shit is annoying and even harder to ignore.

Someone was trying to break me, I know. But Winter Santiaga is not easily broken. Number one, I'm not afraid of the dark. Number two, I don't like the noise but I've heard the sound of a hundred bitches banging on their cell doors at the same time. Number three, I've heard screaming when the task force forces their way down the tiers and into each prison cell and starts attacking chicks for some trumped-up bullshit reason. Number four, I remember when the prison toilet system failed and instead of all of our shit getting flushed down, it squirted up and into our faces, then flooded our cells. So I'm well familiar with overwhelming stench. Number five, I've heard Simone sharpening chicken bones by dragging each bone back and forth on the cement wall till they were each good enough to stab or puncture somebody who wouldn't bow down to our crew. When it wasn't bones she was sharpening, it would be anything that could be continuously scraped and grinded until it was razor sharp so that she could sell it to some other bitch who wasn't one of our enemies, wasn't one of our crew either but was simply a customer who needed to defend herself, which was an everyday thing. As for number six, the hissing, I'm *not* accustomed to the hissing. If I could choose to dead one sound, that would be it. Sounded like six hundred jealous bitches whispering at the same time about someone whose look or style they simply couldn't match or touch or tolerate. Come to think of it, I have heard that envy-inspired, whispering-hissing sound before plenty of times.

"How long you just gon' sit there," I heard a sexy-sounding male voice say. It had the rhythm and the accent and cockiness of a New York dweller. It was the next unexpected thing happening in this unknown place at this very moment.

"Mind your fucking business," I replied, all matter-of-fact.

"Hide your fangs, honey. Nobody down here shows all of the cards they are holding when the game is just getting started."

"Whatever." I rejected his talk with that one word.

"What's your name?" he asked me.

"Don't ask me shit," I told him.

"Find out if I got what you need before you dismiss me," he said calmly.

"I know you don't," I said dryly. "Nigga you got a palace? A glass shower? Water that actually makes me wet? A king-sized bed, silk sheets, and a whip with navigation to drive me out of this disgusting dark place?" Which I knew he didn't, otherwise he wouldn't be here.

He laughed. "You're real pretty," he said, dragging out the word *real* like it wasn't a short one-syllable word. "But I see you're the tenacious tough type, like to play hard to get, make a nigga prove himself to you about sixty-six times, and that still ain't enough."

"Can you see me?" I asked. I was excited. Him saying and knowing how pretty I am piqued my interest.

"Pretty eyes, and pretty dark eyelashes, pretty skin and beautiful hair, sexy lips and sexy body curves. I see you clearly," he said calmly. "I especially love the scar. Makes you stand out. I never trust a bitch who doesn't have a few cuts and scrapes. It means she never lived, never did nothing real."

I felt myself opening, but immediately closed down on him. *He's suspicious.* I thought he was trying to gas me. *Don't go for it, Winter*, I told myself. "What am I wearing then," I asked him in a tone that was all doubt.

"Easy question," he said calmly. "You're the only one down here wearing white . . ." he said strangely. I didn't see nobody down here at all before he showed up. So what the fuck was he talking about?

"Mink and the python," he said. I was caught off guard. I couldn't feel or see my mink or my red boots. I couldn't see myself. I couldn't even see him. But, I was starting to like that he could see me, that he acknowledged my look and style and perfection. On top of that, his presence confirmed that it was not me stinking! It must be this atmosphere 'cause no nigga is gonna pull up and kick it to a bitch that smelled like trash mixed with old rotting pussy.

"What do you want?" I asked him with less stress in my voice.

"That's the question I am supposed to ask you," he said confidently.

"What you selling," I asked, knowing full well ain't shit free.

"Exactly what you want and need," he said, then added, "Things that you need to have down here that money can't buy. You gotta just know somebody who knows somebody . . ." he said, sounding like an old Trick Daddy joint.

"How would you know what I want and need?"

"Let me take a stab at it," he said. "You need light," and as soon as he said that a six-foot flame shot up across from me that caused me to lean back. I was so freaking happy to see something, anything! But I played it cool while I let my eyes adjust to the brilliant flame so I could use it to check and see exactly what he looked like. Could be his voice is sexy masculinity, but he was not. I wasn't gonna just let some fat, bald, old, short, pussy guy push up on me in the dark and expect me to flow with it just because he made a fire. The red flame turned blue. The blue flame emitted black smoke. Out of the smoke walked a six-foot-tall more-than-handsome black beauty. A chiseled man, who flicked a flame off of his muscular left shoulder. It fell to the ground and became a lamp that allowed me to look him over even more carefully. I surveyed him with my game face on. All that time sitting in darkness I had not needed my game face. Now it was on and popping even though I didn't visibly react.

"Stand up," he said, extending his hand. I didn't give him my hand. I didn't want him to know my handicap. My legs didn't move anymore. So I remained seated. Suddenly the entire black atmosphere, minus the flame lamp, turned green. I was so accustomed to the blackness that I stared for what I guess was a minute at the green gas-like substance replacing the black. I was thinking, *If it's not blacker than night here, then it's supposed to be either bright like sunlight or blue like the sky.* I recalled the sun and the sky. It had not faded from my memory. So the now-green backdrop threw me off. To break my stare, he leaned in, and grazed my legs with his fingertips. Instantly, I could feel them. Yes! I can feel both of my legs! I extended my hand. When our fingers interlocked, he pulled me up into him as smoothly as though I had not been sitting there paralyzed for six months or six years.

"And you need a man. Not just any man. You need me," he said. I could feel my pussy pump even though he was spitting a corny movie line.

"Let's go!" he said. Of course I'm game to get the fuck out of here no matter where we are going next. Long as it isn't here. We started running hand-in-hand. I was thrilled that my thighs were moving and I could feel my feet hitting the pavement. I was even more excited to have a companion. I don't trust him, but he gave me the gift of light and made my legs work so fuck it. I'm giving him the benefit of the doubt.

Suddenly a strong wind of the prettiest perfume I ever smelled came breezing through like a powerful hurricane that made it more difficult for us to run. It pushed us both back a bit. The expensive and enticing scent completely replaced the foul severe sewer odor. As we ran against the force of the perfume wind, a sexy lavender sky appeared overhead. So sexy I stopped to watch. He pulled my hand and said, "Don't stop if you want to ever get out of here." But I had to stop. I haven't seen colors in what felt like a hundred years. The lavender sky opened up and began spilling some sparkling stars that were like diamond raindrops. The stars formed into the outline of a feminine figure. I was caught up by the design of it all. Then the unexpected happened. Although I shouldn't have been surprised, I am.

"Come on. Don't pay her no mind. She's my ex," he said about the sixteen-years-young vibrant dime when she walked out of the diamond rain.

How can I ignore a bitch made up of stars? That's some new shit. Besides, she looked like me at sixteen. I could see that Santiaga beauty blood running all in her. Had me confounded. Was she Mercedes or Lexy? No, why would any one of them be down here? Maybe one of them did die and that's why the two Midnight sons were fighting over the only twin left alive? But if one of the Santi-aga twins had died, wouldn't I know it? I am their sister, so of course I would know. Unless they were planning to tell me after my prison release to keep me from feeling pissy going into my big reality-show debut. *Yup, that's what happened,* I convinced myself. I knew that a bitch like me who did more then a decade bid only really had word of mouth, gossip, and rumor from the streets to rely on. No details about what was actually going on with my own bloodline behind closed doors, except for Santiaga, who was locked same as me.

"She's the police! Don't be fooled by her. She fooled me one time," he warned. He didn't have to tell me twice. We ran off for what felt like a long distance. He jumped into a black Jaguar. I heard a female voice calling me back. It wouldn't have mattered to me none. The police always say some shit like, "It's the police! Freeze!" But in this case, the powerful feminine voice had called out only one word, "Winter!" The volume and intensity of her voice, and the now repetition of my name and just the fact that she even knew my name, sparked my curiosity. Although, it couldn't and didn't stop me from jumping in. He pulled off.

Since the Jag windows were tinted, I instinctively turned to look out of the rear. I still couldn't see anything. The atmosphere had turned completely black again. I could hear whipping winds that howled like a wind war. The winds were so forceful that they rocked the ride from side to side even though it was speeding forward. He didn't react to the rocking or the darkness or the deafening wind-whip sounds. Instead, he was leaned back in his driver's seat like a real hustler riding dirty. Chilling so hard as if it was just another day in his neighborhood. He turned on the radio without reaching. Music finally! It was the provocative and arous-ing instrumental track to the song "When Doves Cry," by Prince. I pictured him in my mind. Prince was not the style of man I would want to fuck. But he is king of those guitar strings. Fur-thermore, he is hands down definitely one of the rare ones, who got "that thing."

"You tryna burn a hole into the side of my face?" he suddenly asked me. I must've been staring. I was digging his carved-up arm and the way his strong hand held the steering wheel. Of course I was checking him out thoroughly and examining his whip. Couldn't believe he had the new joint. I had read about the Jaguar XJ. The timing caught my attention. Both me and the car released in 2010. The dash was mean and the controls were embedded in his steering. He's shifting gears smoothly while enjoying the sounds. As Prince's music was ending he lowered the volume with the press of his thumb while reclining. The high speed of the ride decreased and soon we came to a smooth stop. We were sitting there in the blackness. I heard the radio jock say, "And this cut is by the Scissor Sisters. It's titled, 'I Can't Decide.'" I never heard of them. How could the DJ try and follow up Prince with some unknown performers singing an unknown song?

"My place is down this hill. Before I downshift, I want to make sure you want to be with me. If not, you can get out," he said calmly. But I thought it was strange. It was total blackness outside. Why would I get out? Where would I go? And without him, would my legs go back to being paralyzed after his touch had caused them to feel alive and move properly?

"Nigga what!" I said, instead of telling him the thoughts in my mind. "When I ride with a nigga, I ride with a nigga," I confirmed. He leaned my way, reached up and pulled down my seat belt, then locked it into place. His gesture got me feeling even more open.

"That's what I thought," he said, smiling some. "But it's good to double-check. When the action starts, I don't want you pretending that I forced you," he said.

"I don't let nobody force me," I said. "That's not the type of bitch I am."

"So you ready to handle me?" he said, smiling again. He knew his teeth were perfect and his smile convincing.

"I don't really know you like that, but I handle whatever comes to me," I said in my first sexy tone.

"All you need to know about me," he said, "is my stroke is strong and my dick is longer than my tail."

The Jaguar dropped, angled, and then sped downhill like a rocket instead of a car. My heart was racing. It felt good. Reminded me of the drop on the Kingda Ka roller coaster at Great Adventure. When I was teen young I'd choose the fastest, steepest, wildest-drop roller coaster and ride it repeatedly the whole day. My cousins and them would be like, "Come on, let's try something different." I'd be like, "Nope, I already know how this ride makes me feel." They'd leave. I'd stay. I was straight riding alone. Told them I'd meet them at six at the haunted house. In his Jaguar speeding down I was thrilled. Most drivers would be cautiously riding the brake downhill. He was all gas pedal. I was curious and turned on. I couldn't wait, *My dick is longer than my tail* . . . kept repeating in my mind. I could feel my pussy pumping.

"You are probably hungry," he said as he carried me over the threshold of his front door. It was not a palace or a mansion. It had more of a weird warehouse feeling. Or maybe more like an old fire station that he bought and redecorated. That was genius to me. Inside was as dark as outside of his building. Maybe that's why he held me in his arms. He didn't want me to trip or bump into walls in an unfamiliar location. I dig that. He put me down on my feet.

"Stay there," he said. I didn't reply, just waited. The area suddenly lit up. It was a flame, though. A torch on top of a metal pole that was cemented into his hard-top floor. *That's crazy.* I laughed. Fuck the utility companies and power bill. And since this was an old fire station with high ceilings, no worries about an uncontrollable fire burning down the entire spot. Only thing is, with a flame, I could only see but so far. I hoped he didn't want to do what we were about to do in the dark. I like to see my man's muscles moving, the expression on his face and in his eyes, especially the desire as he admires me, my look, and my body.

"We'll fuck first," he said. "Fucking is better when both parties are thirsty and starving to death," he chuckled.

He's bold, I thought, *a take-charge type of nigga*. Usually I'm in charge. But I liked his rough style. He approached, removed my mink and dropped it right on the floor. He picked me up again, then sat me on the mink and began carefully removing my red python boots and sat them together to the side. He began massaging my legs. Ooh, that felt nice. He tore my Chanel dress right off of me as though it was made of silk and not the thick luxurious brocade. I like that his desire for me makes him too impatient to search for a zipper, a string, or a set of buttons. He got a Jaguar and a strong house so I'm telling myself to disregard that he ripped up my six-thousand-dollar custom Chanel made just for me.

"I should shower first." I said softly like I was some shy bitch. Hovering over me, he ignored me for some seconds as he pressed his nose into my armpit and inhaled deeply. He moved to the next pit and inhaled deeply. He moved to my bare pussy and inhaled deeply, his nose creating an extra sensation when it grazed against my clitoris.

"Shower, but don't get too clean. I get high off of the funk," he said, exhaling.

"Oh yeah," I said, sultry like. The reality was, though, I had never heard no line like that. "Well, you got some real get-high?" I asked him.

He smiled and said, "Why, of course. I'm the master of smoke." He stood and went into a clothing closet and pulled out a bag from a coat pocket. He lit the blunt so swiftly I never saw him strike the match or click the lighter. I didn't give a fuck. He got high off the funk. I get high off the blunt. He passed it to me. I'm puffing la . . . finally.

"The shower is down that hall to the left," he said, pointing. "But don't wash too long. Leave your pussy as is. I'll clean it with my tongue," he said.

I leaped up, the ripped mini offering him more than a glimpse of my juicy. But it was a glimpse that he would have had to catch through only the flicker of the flame. I ran straight. Knew he was watching. Let him see my booty bounce. Then I turned to the left, turned on like a motherfucker. In the warm downpour of the first water that I could actually feel while cleansing my body, my feelings towards this nigga began to multiply. He had brought feeling back to me after death. Said he preferred his woman to have a few scars. He made me able to walk when I had been stuck seated by the sewer inhaling something fouler than sewage. He fastened my seat belt, carried me into his home, gave me my first after-murder blunt, and now he had made it possible for me to shower and not be some strange invisible waterproof bitch.

When I finished showering, I couldn't find no towel in his dark bathroom. So I stepped out cautiously, dripping wet and butt naked. When I did, there were now twelve flames up high each atop of a metal pole. I didn't see him, though. However, I could see his fucktastic gymnastics bedroom, that was out of this world. It was not expensively designer decorated. It was not made of sterling silver, platinum, gold, or even pearls. It was made only of sturdy steel. What made it dope, though, was its uniqueness. This nigga had a huge bed covered by a black silk duvet, black silk sheets, and six black silk pillows that were not too fluffy. That was all high-end normal, but what made it ill was the bed was enclosed by a network of monkey bars! The same monkey bars we had in city parks, except his was much wider and taller and more intricate. The mattresses sat in the middle. The bars ran high up to the high ceiling overhead and to the left and right and front and back and side of his bed. It was elaborate. In big city parks, the monkey bars were made for a bunch of kids to go climbing and swinging all at once. But his bars were higher and stronger and apparently made for one man, him. I walked around amazed by his setting and slowly searching for him. I was turned on by his hide-and-seek. The heat from the flames soon dried off the droplets of water from my shower. My skin was warming. When I rounded the back of the bars I looked up. He was hanging up there naked. No, he was doing chin-ups on a metal chin-up bar and his dick was definitely longer than his tail. Now all I craved was to feel his strong stroke that he guaranteed he had.

He must've felt my feelings. "Grab hold of both my ankles," he said as he lowered his body overhead where I was standing. I did. He restarted his pull-ups with me holding on like crazy beneath him. After six pull-ups, my fingers began to slip. He jerked his body sideways, which threw me down to his bed. I loved the feel of the fall. Beneath the silk duvet, his mattress was not soft. He leaped down swiftly and flipped me over facedown. It felt like under the silk bedding there were rubber thorns. Next thing I know, this nigga got his nose pressed deep into my ass. Both of his hands were pulling both of my butt cheeks open. He withdrew his nose and hands and then laid on top of my back.

"You overdid it," he whispered in my ear. "The asshole is too clean." I ignored him. I was concentrating on how good the weight of his body felt on my back and the rubber thorns felt pressing up against my front. He put his hands in my hair, massaging my scalp. All niggas do that with a bitch like me. They are each amazed that my silky long black hair is real and grown up from my scalp. Most chicks catch fever if a nigga even thinks about putting his hands in her hair upsetting her glued-in, stitched-in, laced-in, braided-in weave.

Massaging my shoulders, my feminine diamond-cut back, my tight waistline, and my rump, he eased off of my body. Without leaving his bed he slipped some kind of cloth around both of my ankles and my body jerked up feet first. I was in a dangling upside-down type of headstand. With both of his strong hands, he pulled my legs apart until I was stuck in an upside-down split. When he had me in the position he obviously planned to have me in, he buried his face in between my thighs and began "cleaning" my pussy with his tongue. I didn't notice it when we was in his black Jag, but his tongue was unusually long. It was sweeping into each area of my most intimate space. I was trapped in the good feeling he was making me feel. Then he sucked where he had been cleaning and held the suck until my insides bursted in his mouth. It felt so incredible. *He knew he was good at it.* He pulled his face back and said, "I promised to clean it."

He reached up, released my ankles, and I fell to the mattress again in the midst of multiple orgasms. It created such a thrill in me. I was out of control of my impulses. He leaped down beside me on the mattress and looked into my eyes. I wanted him to tongue-kiss me. He didn't. He plunged into me with that hard, strong and thick, long flesh pipe. It was the strongest stroke. He was right. It was the best feeling. Each pump created such intense pleasure it felt like even my eyes would pop out of their sockets. Cumming continuously, I ran out of breath and energy even though he was doing all of the work. He flipped me around. Next thing I know he pushed into my asshole before I could say "No! I don't get down like that." It was either before I could say no, or was I really with it? Was I so overstimulated that I just let it happen? Wanted it to continue?

Several strokes later, the twelve flames went out all at once. I couldn't feel him pumping anymore or the weight of his body pressing down against my back. I was in complete blackness once again. Shocked, I couldn't feel my arms, my legs, or my own pussy anymore. The feeling was not even numbness. Even numbness would have been a feeling. It was as though my arms and legs no longer existed. My body felt like it was just one long flowing thing without a sturdy spine. *I need to get to a mirror,* was my instant thought. Then I remembered that a dead bitch doesn't have a reflection.

But hadn't he made me come back to life though? Didn't he give me limbs that feel and a pussy that pulsated? Didn't he say he saw me clearly and even described what I looked like accurately? So maybe I will see my reflection *this time.* But how will I find a mirror in the dark? And even if I find one, I still won't be able to see. How could my body move forward without legs and arms? Before I could formulate the answers to my own questions, I was crawling

without legs or arms, fingers or toes. But clearly I was moving forward searching for a mirror. I smelled something I had not noticed
before. I lifted my head a little and felt light-headed. I was realizing
that now I was hungry. I had never been hungry since I was shot
dead. My mouth involuntarily opened widely, then snapped shut
solidly. I was chewing meat, soft bones and blood. I was swallowing, satisfying my hunger on the floor, in a corner, in the dark.

A doorbell or a ringtone, I couldn't tell the difference. But I heard
his voice answering. He wasn't on the floor where I was. He wasn't
even on the bed where he and I had been seemed like seconds ago.
His voice was coming from way up high. He must have been sitting
at the tip-top of his monkey bars or maybe he decided to do a few
more chin-ups. How could he do more exercise after that thorough
sexual workout?

"UBS, what's up?" I heard him say rough but gently, affection-
ately. His tone caused me to feel pissy because he wasn't speaking
to me.

"You'll never know what's up, you filthy bottom-feeder," a
female voice answered back. Seemed like he had her on speakerphone and I swiftly figured it was his ex.

"I know you love me. You're always prowling around my territory," he said coolly.

"The devil is a liar every time," she said, passionately but calmly
at the same time.

"What did you call me for? I know not just to disrespect my father," he said strangely.

"Your father can go straight to hell," she said hatefully.

"That's funny," he laughed genuinely.

"What did you do with my mother?" she asked oddly. I thought
it was bizarre. Ex-lovers heated over their parents! "You and I need
to make a deal this time," she said desperately.

"Too late. It's over. If you don't want to come to my playpen,

talk face-to-face in my bedroom, you and I will never have any deal
to make, or anything to discuss," he warned and invited her at the
same time.

Next I heard the sound of fireworks, like on the Fourth of July.
I suddenly saw explosions of sparkles. That bitch must've been real
mad. But if she wasn't here in his bedroom and she was on the
phone, how did the fireworks happen?

"You sent your bullshit army of UBS to my crib?" I heard him
ask her.

"Why don't you step outside and check? Maybe I'm right here
at your front door," she said. Next I heard him swinging down
on his bars. Was he that excited to see and welcome her in, when
me and him just finished fucking *and I'm still here*? I crawled till I
bumped into one of the metal bars. I wrapped myself around it and
crawled upwards. I paused to listen for where he had swung to. But
I never heard his feet land or him walking across the floor towards
his front door.

"You must be scared of my little *bullshit* army," she said, after
having not said anything for what I guess was some seconds. Now
she was baiting him to open up his firehouse door. I was glad he
didn't. "Or is it that you're in there staring in one of your six mirrors, worshipping yourself?" she asked. She sounded bitter and a
little bit crazy. Her words were followed up by a piercing, whis-
tling sound and then a loud boom shook the firehouse fortress that
seemed unshakable. It was like a bomb had been thrown through
the roof and had exploded in the air.

Instead of causing the firehouse to collapse into nothing but
rubble, like how places on the TV news reports looked totally de-
stroyed after a bombing, it lit up the entire inside with sun-bright
light, much brighter than when the flickering torch flames were the
only way to see. When it did, I could see everything that I could
not see before. He was squatted on the bottom rung of his monkey bars, still nude and his feet perfectly balancing his powerful
body on the bar even as the house shook. And in an instant, I could

see his reflection through the wall-to-wall mirrors, which I had not noticed framed his large warehouse "playpen." Strange thing was, I could see another reflection as I crawled his way. I was on my belly. When I moved, it moved. When I lifted my head, it lifted its head. When I stopped to stare at it, it stopped and stared back at me. Unexpectedly, because it was not something anyone would ever imagine is desirable or even possible, I, fully awake and with my same Winter Santiaga mind and thoughts, had turned into a red python.

7.

Another wind war, I could feel it coming before it hit. I'm super sensitive to the ground, could always hear the vibration of feet or anything that impacted the earth that I crawl on. I could hear the howling and his house shaking and things being tossed and slung and flung around. I could hear chains rattling and fireworks going off. I could hear the clash, not of fists but of forces of the wind.

After a nasty breakup of any couple, the war begins. I knew bitches who keyed their ex's ride, or punctured his tires, or banged in his rims with a hammer. I knew bitches who beat the new bitch's ass, who her man had replaced her with. Or even stalked her, then choked her, stabbed her, shot her, or mercked her. I knew even live-er bitches who, instead of killing his new bitch, killed him. I knew bitches who ran up his credit cards, crashed his car, cut up his clothes, pawned his jewels, and even burned down his house. But when a man or woman who used to be lovers, living together, working together, eating together, showering and fucking together, and one betrays the other, betrayal makes the matter more meaner than murder. 'Cause you can just kill someone if you want to, no matter who you are. No matter who they are or where they hide. They bound to resurface eventually. Let down their guard eventually, and that's precisely when they can get got. But ex-lovers, who more than just creeping and fucking other niggas or bitches, where one betrayed the other, told a life-changing secret tat he or she had confided with, sold him or her out to his or her sworn enemy, called the cops on him or her for any damn reason, flipped on 'em in a court of law or was way-worser, like working as an undercover police, a bitch-ass informant, spying and telling on his or her lover, murder ain't enough get-back. A betrayed nigga or bitch wants to be the one who delivers the hurt over an extended period of time. Not a quick stabbing or gunning down. A betrayed lover wants to witness his or her traitor in severe loss of either: wealth, status, or something or someone he cherished. A betrayed lover wants to see the traitor in actual excruciating pain. He or she wants to taunt and torture first and then deliver the last blow that leads to the traitor's complete and final downfall.

I know. Bullet was the main one who betrayed me. He's at the top of my payback list. He was my nigga for many months before I got arrested. Yeah, he was a hustler. I fucking loved that. His fuck game was strong. I loved that too. Once he and I first hooked up, I never fucked around with no other nigga but him. I'm a loyal bitch. Loyalty runs through the Santiaga blood. But he never fully acknowledged my loyalty to him. He never gave his loyalty to me. It wasn't about me thinking, expecting, or believing that he was out fucking some random bitches while we was together. He didn't cause me to feel or think that he was. It was that he . . . I don't know. He loved me with his mind and body but never gave me his heart. He treated me like a suspect, who was bound to turn on him or turn him in. I wasn't. I'm the one bitch that wouldn't . . . ever, Santiagas are born snitch-free.

Bullet put our Manhattan condo in my name, and every purchase he made for both of us in my name. Back then, at the time, I thought that meant he loved me. Of course I did, he provided. In turn, I covered for him here and there. Held his coke, concealed his weapons, and carried his cash here and there quietly whenever he told me to. I was trying to earn my way up and also in, to his heart. I thought we should be on some Bonnie-and-Clyde shit. But fuck Bonnie and Clyde. We should be on some Winter-and-Bullet shit, stacking our chips and styling and fucking and eating and chilling and staying together.

Turned out, he put everything in my name not for love or for providing for a top bitch and daughter of legendary hustler and entrepreneur Ricky Santiaga. Instead Bullet was on some Brooklyn scheming. He made it so that if everything or anything went wrong, he could drop all the legalities and blame onto me without losing any street credibility because it wasn't like he snitched on me. He simply left a paper trail and documentation all in my name that told the fictitious story of me being the hustler and him being blameless, unarrestable, and scot-free. On the day of my arrest that led to my conviction as a drug dealer sentenced to serve fifteen years on a mandatory minimum, which at the time I had never even heard of, my nigga Bullet had a car rented with a credit card in my name. In the rental car was me and the product, I was 'bout to ride round trip to Virginia on a run with him, a big and necessary business move.

Simone, who for some reason can't get the fuck out of my mind or life or death story, saw me sitting there on our Brooklyn block in the rental waiting on Bullet. I didn't see her, though. Simone had bullshit beef with me that she swore was real. So, soon as she saw me that day, it was on. Bitch threw a brick through the rental window. Bitch dragged me out the car swinging. We thumped. My nigga Bullet saw the rah-rah from the distance. He started rushing over. He fired one shot in the air to cause the commotion to break. Seeing him boosted my confidence, but the gunshot distracted me from keeping my eyes on her. Simone took advantage and sliced my face. Bullet held my bleeding face in his hands. He sat me back in the rental car. He tossed the gun beneath the seat. He walked around to the driver's side. I was relieved that he had rescued me. But the furious fight and the gunshot drew out the cops.

The cops swooped in and Bullet, instead of jumping into the rental car and speeding away, walked off calmly as if he never was with me. Never even knew me and never intended to get in the car with me at all. I was arrested in the rental car that was in my name, with the weight stuffed inside teddy bears, and the weapon tossed beneath the seat. They cuffed, fingerprinted, mug-shotted, jailed, grilled, and investigated me. They asked me for names or just one big name. I gave them nothing. I rejected their bullshit tricks and game. The name is Santiaga, royalty not rats. I wasn't mad at Bullet for being a hustler, obviously. I wasn't mad at him for renting me the condo or even for taking me on his big business run to Virginia. I was down for him. I wanted to go. I didn't like being left out of the business or the action. It's that that nigga Bullet didn't come for me. He didn't add a dime to my legal defense. He didn't send one of his men to make sure I had all that I needed. He didn't put one cent on my commissary. He didn't write me one letter, slip me one kite from his peoples on lock. He didn't check for me and to me that meant he never loved me. That's why he's on my payback list. He betrayed me. I never betrayed him, not even once.

So I understand this little sixteen-years-young-looking one, oddly named UBS, who is tight and at war with her ex. He seemed more my age than hers. But I knew that once a bitch blossoms, gets curves and titties and hungry between the thighs, whether or not she's twelve, thirteen, or sixteen, whether or not the law says she's a minor, she is bound to hunt and chase down a man she chooses for herself. A young sexy bitch, I know, can make it impossible for even an older guy to resist her powers no matter who he is. He could be handsome or ugly, paid or broke, married or single, hustler or preacher, politician or teacher, doctor or lawyer or even a goddamn judge. I accept that. As long as it's not the other way around, some old guy hunting, cornering, and chasing her young ass. Fucking and raping are never ever the same thing. He says she betrayed him. He said she's the police. She seemed too young to be anybody's police. And in the, I guess seconds I had seen her, she didn't seem like a cop. But I ain't from down here. I don't know how shit goes 'round here. Everything is unexpected. It's like I'm stuck in the world of the unseen and unknown and can't control or predict the action.

But now I am not alone down here. Of course I choose him. He chose me in the first place. He was the greatest sex I ever had. The wildest feeling I ever felt. He was the only man who ever caused me to let go of Midnight, who *never fucked me at all*. I like a man who *gives a bitch what she wants*. A man who *doesn't make a bitch feel lonely*. Wife number five! *Oh hell no*. That would never, ever be me.

My new nigga is my forever nigga, from now until the real lights-out. Even though he only fucked me once on the same night we met, I was able to exist inside of that fucking memory. And unlike Bullet, who left me because I was cut and bleeding and would obviously wear a scar, and who set me up to take the fall, or either didn't set me up but reacted only to secure himself, my forever nigga is different. When I became the red python, my forever nigga kept me, adored me, even allowed me to crawl all over his beautiful body no matter what time or where he was at the moment. Even if he was busy I could wrap myself around his neck. He is a thousand times smarter than Bullet. He knew I was poisonous and quite deadly, but apparently he was 100 percent certain that I would never ever bite him. This nigga kept it real. He still brought home and fucked other bitches. I'm sensible enough to know that if he couldn't fuck me in my condition, he had to fuck someone. He didn't try to sneak or hide any of them. He even let me watch. After the sex, he showed me his loyalty. Threw them random bitches right out. I remained because we lived together. He fed me. He shared his monkey bars, which I used to stay fit. He even talked to me even though I could not speak back like a human being. I could only gesture. He told me that I was the sexiest serpent ever, and that I would make a mean-ass belt, handbag, or pair of heels or boots, but that he would never ever allow anyone to swipe me from him or hurt me in any way.

But on the day of the most recent wind war, he wasn't home. I was hanging there on the bars waiting for his return when the firehouse was attacked. As our firehouse rocked I promised myself that if the bitch UBS came in here, which she had not been able to do any other time while he was alert and home on watch, I would bite her with full venom.

Unexpectedly, without her entering our house, I was sucked and pulled into a vicious vacuum-type current and fast-forwarding through blackness once again. As soon as the fast-forwarding stopped, and while my mind was still whirling, I was immediately mugged by the odor. *Oh no,* I thought. *I'm back in the sewer location.* I'm in the sitting position on the curb next to the gutter. Now I had arms and legs and fingers and feet. I touched my face. I could feel it. I even had my silky hair back. I was a human, Oh shit! I would have celebrated, but instead I was coughing from the stench. I reacted, wanted to jump up and walk away from it. However, I could not move my legs. I hated that. Thought it was foul play. Rather see my enemy face-to-face and have the opportunity to fight and change the action. I don't like the feeling that someone is trying to control my story, my life, and even my life-after-death story.

I was uncertain how many days I sat there alone in the over-whelming blackness. However, I could count the number of unexpected events and the ways in which it affected my body. *My body,* I repeated to myself. Was it even mine? How could it be when I could turn into something other than me? Some inhuman thing that I never chose to be. But it had to be my body, because even after I got shot dead, my mind never shut off. My thoughts continued. They were my same thoughts. I was thinking the exact same way I have thought about things for as long as I could remember, and I have a great memory. No matter what other thing I became, no matter alive or dead, I was certainly throughout it all, me. And, I still was.

I'm the crippled version. My arms and hands work but my legs don't. I wasn't gonna start crawling on my belly like I had to when I had no other choice. I wasn't gonna make my way across the street from the curb I was sitting on, using my knuckles to carry the weight of my legs like some monkey. I wasn't about to be on some Special Olympics–type vibe and walk on my hands. Besides, where would I be going? It was black where I was, and black across the street from me. Reminding myself to exist in the moment and not get caught up in bullshit depression. No matter who you are, depression is a fucking waste of time that people with no action and no brain to tell them how to get the action started or flip an inactive situation into something brand-new are enslaved to. Having that thought reminded me not to get hung up on the what-ifs, or what would or could or should have been. I'm a motherfucking survivor no matter what!

So I endured the things I had become immune to: the blackness, the breaking of bones, the waves of heat that scorched my ass and the soles of my feet, the chorus of millions screaming different words and sounds but all at once, the sounds of ninety-nine niggas cracking their knuckles, the scraping and grinding and even the hissing. The hissing had become my only form of music down here. For serpents, hissing is like rhyming.

I wasn't prepared for the add-ons, though: a swarm of tiny flying-insect-type things. I called them that because they reminded me of the aggravating existence of mosquitoes. But I couldn't actually see them. I don't know if they were mosquitoes or not. But they came through suddenly in a violent swarm attacking my face and eating me. When I would touch myself, there would be rashes on me, which was something I never had. I never even had the chicken pox or the measles when I was a kid. I tried not to scratch because the scratching only satisfied me for what felt like a few seconds. Then the rash would feel moist and spread further. I don't know if it was blood or what oozing from the rash. This was disturbing. On the low, I was waiting on him to find me. I was 100 percent sure he was out there searching for me. I wanted him to show up, but not while the rash was on me.

Then there would be coughing spells. Felt like it lasted for days. All I could do was cough and could never catch my breath. Next were the sneezing spells that always came after the coughing but never both at the same time. When I would sneeze, which was continuously, if felt like my organs were going to fly out of each of the openings in my body. That's how powerful the sneezes were. There were no tissues. There was no one to help or who would even complain that I was sneezing germs onto them. Instead my fingers felt the mucus accumulating on and around me. It was a good thing that I was back to being a dead human. It meant that I was never hungry. If I had been hungry in that situation, the mucus would have been all that I had to eat.

I was sitting in my slime when the green-colored atmosphere began to devour the blackness. My eyes were attempting to adjust to the new existence of color that contained light. The greenness somehow eliminated the foul odor, silenced the screaming, and the grinding, cracking, breaking, and hissing. Although I was happy about the presence of color, I was worried that he was about to show up to come get me only to see my rashes and scratches and my lap filled with mucus that had oozed down over my feet.

Instinctively, I touched my face, wanting to clear and clean it up a bit if that was even possible. When I touched my face, it was not slimy anymore. It was not bumpy. It was not wet. I moved my hands over my whole face. I could not even feel my scar. My hair felt soft, no more grease or residue or dead insects from the swarm. I pulled it to my nose. It smelled like it had been washed with expensive shampoo. My mood was shifting up. I was excited. I leaped up. My legs were working. The feeling of being able to really feel returned. As it did, the lavender sky appeared overhead. It opened and spilled out stars that were absolutely everywhere, like diamond raindrops.

"Ah-hum-doo-lah-lah," she said. Or at least that is what it sounded like to me. It was her, the Diamond Rain girl who I had seen once before. The one who he said is the police. "Soo-pan-ah-lah," she said, and I was already getting tight at all of her foreign talk. "I apologize for being too late," she said, switching to

English as though she heard what I had just thought. Immediately I switched to my game face. I thought she had caught me slipping and read my facial expression. I had been so long fucked up, sick and paralyzed by the sewer in the blackness, that I had no reason for game face. Now I was back in pocket and even feeling like I got superpowers. I must. I'm standing up, feeling myself. My skin is flawless like how it was for the first eighteen young years of my life. She began speaking to me in a tone as though I knew her.

"I'm not from this realm. I even have to get permission to come down here and an army of my UBS to back me up," she said. But I had thought UBS was *her name*. Maybe not. Above her, the sparkling stars continued to decorate and light up the lavender sky. I could see and understand clearly why he liked her. That aggravated me. She obviously had something that the rest of us bitches don't have. Not even the exotic foreign ones. Never met a bitch that came from the stars—stars more mesmerizing than flawless jewels. And somehow she controlled the color of the atmosphere. Probably she could keep a nigga fully entertained with just her little light show.

"And if the trip down here is not exhausting enough, the battle is," Diamond Rain said. I looked her over. She didn't look like a bitch who had been fighting her way here the way she said she had to do. She didn't have no scratches or knife swipes or burns or bullet holes and even her clothes were neat and fresh. The belt around her waist had slots stuffed with what seemed like big bullets. They were not exactly the same as the bullets I seen plenty of times in Brooklyn. But they definitely appeared to be ammunition. Around her neck was a diamond chain.

She's stunting on me, I thought. But the illest thing about the chain was her piece. I had seen the jewels of the hottest hustlers— my father at the top, of course, and his crew, celebs, and dealers at VIP parties, as well as low-level cats from our hood that were on the come-up. I had never ever seen any hustler or celeb with the piece she had hanging on her necklace. It was a grenade. *This must be part of her psych game,* I deduced. She came with her pretty face and sleek body, nicely dressed, but wearing warrior armor in a way that it was on display to make the next bitch she was 'bout to battle back off or bow down.

"If it was so much trouble, why did you come here then?" I said without any excitement at all. She looked sad for a second, then brought back her smile. Maybe her smile is *her version* of her game face.

"Is that all you have to say to me? And do you really want to say it that way? Why not start with the good words and good feel-ings?" she asked, then threw her arms in the air. She held them there and made her pretty un-manicured fingers dance, and then spun around rhythmically like a belly dancer. I'm thinking, *What the fuck?* A knockout combo: bullets, bombs, and hula-hoop hips.

"You must like my hilab," she said, striking a pose..

"Hilab," I repeated.

"Yes, hilab means the scent that announces me. It remains only while I am here and trails me when I leave this realm. How come you don't even mention it, when before I arrived down here, you were choking on odor?" She placed her hands on her hips gently, not like a commander or authority. Of course I smelled her beauti-ful scent. But one bad bitch don't really need to be complimenting another badass bitch for her look and her style. Real bitches already know and don't need compliments from anyone except their nigga. So I ignored her.

"Or maybe you like the lavender sky? These are all gifts that the ONE has allowed and given me Alhamdulillah." She said the foreign words again. "And I am so grateful to share these gifts with you," she added.

"Bitch, we ain't friends," I said. I wanted to cut out the bullshit niceties and get to it. "Did you come here expecting me to help you catch him? Or are you down here just to fuck with me?" I asked her.

"Him!" she said and collapsed into a squatting position so that now she was looking up to me. I was like, *That's right bitch, look up to me.*

"He is evil. He is the enemy!" She stressed each word, raised her voice, but still had the happy face and delight. I didn't like the mixture.

"I see you're still salty over him," I said. "But a real bitch lets go after she gave it her best fight. So let go. Besides, you disqualified yourself. You betrayed him," I blurted out so she would understand that he confided in me about everything and that I was aware of their past relationship and that I was even aware that *she was the police.*

"Soo-pan-ah-lah, this is why we are shown that whoever the ONE leaves in error can never be corrected by anyone else except the ONE. Because of love, we UBS still try. And because the ONE is the Most Merciful, we are granted three trips of mercy to strive to correct the misunderstandings and wrongdoings of the ones we love," she said, mumbling some foolishness. Then she stood up. "Please forget him. He is a liar. Every word he says is false. If you believe in him, and follow him, he will lead you to an even more evil destination than down here. You will be completely ruined in his company."

"So you're not a cop. You're a C.O. who showed up to correct me." I laughed like, *Yeah right, beat it bitch!* Then I told her, "After a breakup all bitches talk just like how you are talking now."

"Blot him out! It is not about him! It's about you and me. I don't know exactly what lies he has told you. But I have never ever had any romance or relationship with him."

"Bitch, stop lying. You keep coming here. You came to his house a bunch of times tryna shake him. You bombed his house and did all types of crazy shit. I know. I was with him the whole time. Bet you didn't know that. So you're busted!" I told her.

"True, some of our army of UBS were there attacking his house of evil," she admitted. "I was not with them. Although I sent some of them. While others of them fought him for their own reasons." It felt like she really wanted me to take her side. To believe her words.

"You don't recognize me?" she asked after some seconds. "I

know everything about you, Miss Winter Santiaga. It really hurts that you don't recognize even one speck of me," she said softly. "But I forgive you. You don't even know who you are, or where you are, or why you are here, or the meaning of what you have done in the past and what you continue to do in the present. So why did I ever believe that you would be able to recognize even a speck of me?" she said as though she pitied me.

"I hate bitches who try and talk slick and who beat around the bush. Get to the point. Talk straight," I threatened her.

"*Straight*, that's a good word," she said, delighted all of a sudden. "Can you handle straight?" I was starting to heat up. Seemed like this young bitch thought she was a cut above me. Seemed like she thought she also knew a bunch of shit that I didn't know or that she thought I couldn't possibly figure out. So I took a good close look at her. She looked like a reflection of my younger self. I thought about the first time I saw her. *Maybe she is Lexy or Mercedes, one or the other.*

"I can handle whatever. But I control the action," I finally answered her in my big-sister tone, because I am the first daughter of the Santiaga household. I'm not going to have my youngest sister talking down to me as though she is my teacher, *even if we are both dead.*

"You said you know everything about me, right?" I asked her. She smiled. "Everything," she said like there was nothing to it.

"What am I wearing?" was my first question. I didn't know the answer myself. I was checking to see if she could actually see me and what she saw. My look matters the most, I know. If I am looking shabby to her I know it changes my leverage in this conversation.

"Ah-hum-doo-lah-lah, you are the most beautiful-*looking* human to me, of course," she said strangely. "I used the *mercy* I was given to remove your scar because you seemed uncomfortable wearing it," she added, and I didn't like her flipping shit like I owed her something. She probably removed my scar because she knew her ex-lover lusts women with scars.

"Don't try and be slick. You still have not said what I am wearing," I reminded her. Suddenly she started spinning round and round like she was trying to make herself dizzy. Then she started saying words like she was singing a song.

"Gucci Gucci Gucci, Louis Louis Louis, Fendi Fendi Fendi, Chanel Chanel Chanel, Hermès Hermès Hermès, Birkin Birkin Birkin, Louboutin Louboutin Louboutin, Jimmy Jimmy Jimmy Choo Choo Choo, and good Lord Tom Ford! Okay! You are wearing it all." She dropped to the ground in a squat, then collapsed into a lying-down position. Then she closed her eyes. I guess all that was her attempt to stop the dizzy feeling she caused herself. I liked seeing her throw a tantrum and lose her cool. And I liked it even more that she knew the names of some of the top designers. And she was pretty and nicely dressed, her hair covered with the trademark intricate delicate designs of a colorful Hermès scarf. Her sporting Hermès forced me to forgive her fashion-wise for covering her hair! And she was rocking her mean-ass saddle bag by wearing the strap like a sash across her front and the pouch on her ass. I liked the reversal. Quality fabric, expensively stitched leggings compliment only a sleek body type, like hers. Big sloppy bitches or even little sloppy bitches in dollar store cheap leggings is a crime. Diamond Rain's fashionable leggings were also like riding pants that rich bitches wear on horseback. Oddly, she wore black leather ballet shoes with the ribbons criss-crossing up past her ankles. It wasn't my style. I guess her coming from the sky caused her to dress to travel light. She looked dope. I was willing now to give her that. Her fashion outburst had chipped off some of the ice between us.

"Lexy or Mercedes?" I asked, looking down at her.

"The cars or your sisters?" she replied, opening her eyes. So she knew those were my sisters' names without me having to tell her. She passed that little test.

"Which one are you?" I asked, still keeping it brief.

"Neither Mercedes nor Lexus are dead. Miss Winter, you are dead," she said, sitting up and turning the mood very, very serious. "I am not Mercedes or Lexus. If I were either one of them, you would not ever have been able to see me or them, because you are no longer in the realm of living humans." I didn't need no clarification.

"So fucking what? You're a dead bitch just like me!" I shot back. She leaped up. "Otherwise you wouldn't even be here."

"I am not a 'dead bitch,' as you say. And I wish you would change your manner of saying things. It would be to your benefit."

"So why exactly are you here? You said that I'm dead, yet you say that you can see me. At the same time, you said that I cannot see the living and you say that you are not dead, but clearly I can see you. What are you then?" I asked forcefully.

"Very good," she said, and I didn't like her slick compliments or how she spoke them softly with a smile.

"First things first, Lah-il-la-ha-illah-huwa," she said.

"Speak English or fuck it all," I threatened her.

"You must never follow up sacred words with niggardly words," she said. But I was tired of her foreign shit.

"English is only one of thousands of languages in the universe. UBS are suited to speak all of the languages in existence as part of our mercy, Alhamdulillah. Our mission is to be relatable. We introduce dead humans whose souls are lost and roaming in error to the path of cleansing. We show them how making prayers to the ONE is a means of protection for themselves. And also, it is absolutely the only path out of this area." She pointed out beyond the green towards the looming darkness that I had been stuck and sitting in. Then she continued.

"Our prayers and praises to the ONE are always only in the language that the ONE revealed the Truth in. So when we are speaking to dead humans in their language, we will often add in some words of prayer and praise to the ONE. This is the proper way of speaking for all of us servants. And, Miss Winter, you and I and every soul are each and all servants of the Maker of all souls."

"Servants!" I cracked up. Thought the bitch was pretty but crazy, pretty crazy!

"Miss Winter, for you to get permission to leave this realm, you will need to stop mocking Faith and stop blocking the Truth, which your soul already knows to be true. Down here, the biggest wrongful error any soul can commit is to pretend that it does not understand when it does understand and has understood all along. This is a bigger wrong than murder or suicide in this realm. Do you understand what I have said so far?" she asked me as she stared into my eyes. I just stared back at her. Didn't say shit.

"So I am here to help you place everything in the right order. We have already established that there is only ONE God who is the Maker of all souls. If a soul does not feel and acknowledge this truth, *every other thing and choice* it makes will be completely out of order, all confusion and chaos."

"Is this some fancy Jesus talk? Are you down with those crazy Seventh-day Adventists who go around knocking on people doors who they don't know like they ain't got no damn sense? Back in Brooklyn, one of 'em got shot dead for knocking on the wrong door talking shit." I laughed.

"Shot dead . . . same as you, Miss Winter," she said, and I felt an anger and a chill.

"Jesus, peace be upon him, was a servant of the ONE. Jesus was not a partner, an equal, a son or a relative to the ONE. The ONE has no partners, no children, no equals. No one and none of us compare to the ONE who created time, created the sun, moon, and all stars, the universe and all souls, spirits and living things. Jesus was given many, many MERCIES from the ONE, Ah-hum-doo-lah-lah. MERCY is something only the ONE can grant permission for and give. MERCY is the reason you can walk today and see, hear, touch, feel, and talk. In this realm, when you see the atmosphere turn green, it is an indication that the ONE has provided a MERCY happening at that moment. And because the *devil is a liar*, him and his army of demons shows up and spreads mischief and confusion among the population of lost souls such as yourself, Miss Winter. The demons prey on the weak-minded and convince them that it was they who healed you, gave you feeling, healing and mobility, sight and sound. Demons show up when they perceive the green color in the atmosphere. The same way that sharks show up when and where they perceive blood.

"The demons cannot and did not and could never give you anything good or useful at all. They cannot heal you or answer your prayers or save your soul. They cannot protect or preserve or prolong your life or alter or interfere with your death and the return of your soul to the ONE. They are only evil demons lurking, luring, and striking at the right time to utilize the MERCY that the ONE has allowed to further mislead the many lost souls. Once you or any lost souls falls for it, Shayton, who is the devil, and an evil whisperer, who makes millions of evil suggestions through his army of demons, whom he calls his sons and daughters, will mislead you to great harm. The key is, Miss Winter, without your permission, cooperation, and acceptance, the demons cannot cause anything whatsoever to happen to you. You must resist and rebuke them. Humble yourself to the ONE who created your soul and all souls and gave you life."

Young and sharp, she spit game like a real motherfucking pimp, a lady pimp. She was doing double talk, meaning she was talking about my forever nigga without admitting that that was what she was doing. She was throwing shade on him in such a way that she was twisting his character. She was so devious she wanted me to flip on him and to believe that I made the choice to do so and she had nothing to do with it. He had done so much for me. She wanted to flip it and make it seem like he had done nothing good at all. She was redesigning and packaging my forever nigga as a powerless predator. She was like those crafty detectives that tried to get me to give up info leading to Bullet. They came at me from so many different angles all at once. I didn't let them in. I didn't let them win. I wouldn't let her win either. Did she think that I preferred a life of being a boring-ass praying servant to any fucking body? Oh hell no!

"Miss Winter, I have only seven Earth minutes remaining in my MERCY to you. I want to leave you with the information that you will need in order to cleanse your heart, mind, and soul and make choices that will not destroy you any further," she said, interrupting my train of thought. She shifted her saddle-bag strap. Now the pouch was hanging in front of her. Her hand rested over it.

"You are extremely far away from Jannah, which is Heaven in your English language. You are so very far away in terms of actual physical distance and in terms of spiritual distance, which prevents your soul's return to the ONE who created you. If the ONE chose to do so, you could be in Jannah in an instant. But you have not *earned* a place on any level in all of the peaceful beautiful heavens, which is so vast that no mind can even imagine it. There is no pain, debt, deafness, blindness, paralysis, burning, screaming, breaking, cracking, hissing, plagues or viruses, crimes or torture or illness in Jannah. There are only good souls and good interaction, and beautiful rivers and elaborate comfort and most of all there is great PEACE." She lifted her arms in a victory gesture. Guess she thought she had won me over with her talk.

"On the left hand, this realm where we are right now, in the absence of the ONE's mercy, Ah-hum-doo-lah-lah, has not even a molecule or grain of Heaven. The same way you are Brooklyn born, the County of Kings, in the State of New York, in the country of the United States of America and all of those names accurately describe your prior location on Earth, this place where we are standing right now is first known as the Last Stop Before the Drop, the County of the Ungrateful, the State of Ignorance, and the Land of Arrogance. Population is around five hundred million, give or take a thousand or so souls depending upon their choices, prayers, and actions," she said.

"Five hundred million!" I laughed. "You almost had me," I lied. "But I'm the bitch who sat here on this curb for what felt like six thousand years. I was dead *alone*. There was *no one* here but me. Five hundred million, yeah right!"

"Winter, *you are able to lie.* I am not. So everything I say will be the truth. It is a condition of my permission to access my second mercy to you."

"Everybody lies," I said. She paused and didn't reply.

"Yes, you are right. Everyone who resides in the Last Stop Before the Drop *is a liar.* Including you. However, I mentioned that I am not from here—"

"Then what the fuck are you doing around here? Why are you sweating a nigga who is not from your hood?"

"Who!" She balled her hands into fists and set them at each side of her waist. "I see that you don't even know his name. How could you? You don't even know anything about him really. Down here the real name is the name of the soul. The nickname is the name of the action. So even though you don't care and never asked because you can only care and think and feel and concern yourself about yourself and him, the name the ONE gave my soul is Siddiqah. It means 'believes in the words of Allah and Allah's books.' My nickname is Bomber Girl, 'cause I bomb the devils every time that I am not bowed in prayer or out on a mercy. I am a servant dispatched to destroy devils. Now your guy, the name of his evil soul is Lucifer 66. He is the sixty-sixth 'son' of his 'father,' Shayton, the head devil who is condemned to the Eternal Fire and likes nothing more than to invite lost souls to join him in his eternal misery. Lucifer 66's nickname is 'Dat Nigga,' because a nigga is a spirit, soul, or person who refuses with all of his or her will and might to learn, grow, and change. Also, he is called Dat Nigga because he is a top recruiter for Shayton, an expert at luring souls. I really can't believe that after your gruesome death and your periods of loss of eyesight, hearing, touch, feeling, mobility, and health that you are *still* talking and thinking about him," she said to me all indignant. "Yes! Of course you are! He is the same one who you ran away with and left me for on my first mercy." Then she laughed. "Me and twenty of my UBS chased after you. We were fighting fiercely and outnumbered by his sixty-five jinns. They still couldn't defeat us, but definitely did slow us down considerably until we were too late to retrieve you. You had already *willed to* remain with him. We can defeat evil jinns, but we cannot defeat *the will* of a dead human's soul."

"All bitches talk greasy about their ex-boyfriends and baby daddies. Sometime a bitch be telling the truth, and sometime a bitch be lying for a thousand different reasons," I said, folding my arms in front of her. She needed to know that I could and should teach her, instead of her trying to lead me around.

"*Let me put you up on game,*" Bomber Girl said, spinning on her ballet shoes. She was somehow sounding like me. She stopped spinning, landing close up in my face wearing an aggressive expression that was more familiar to me, but that she never had with me before. I liked this expression because I could see her anger in it. I was like, *Yeah bitch, now you showing your real face!*

"Blah blah blah blah blah!" I spit and then talked over her talk. "Wow, how could a teenager talk so damn much! I see why Dat Nigga cut your ass off. No man wants to hear all of that bullshit. It's a real downer! How could he even keep a hard-on with you talking all of that shit. Fucking you must have been a nightmare, a total wet blanket. Fuck you if you think that I'm a stupid, dumbass, clueless, whatever! I know what a soul is. Soul is the feeling in the music, or the look in the fashion, or the style in the jewels, or the rhythm in the streets. My soul was created by my momma, who pushed me out of her big coochie after my father went in her, repeatedly." Then I laughed a little.

"Funny you should mention Momma," she sang softly in a melody like they were lyrics to a song, withdrawing any trace of her anger. That got me thoroughly heated.

"Don't say *shit* about my mother. This may be another fucking realm but where I come from, you don't say shit about anybody's mother unless you want to get knocked out, stabbed, or shot dead," I warned her.

"So you do have some emotion, concern for, and memory of your mother. I did not think so. After your body was shot dead, the

Most Merciful ONE allowed you three visitations of your choice. You did not even think about or ask about or choose to visit *your own momma*. Honestly, you would not have been able to have visited her, though, because she is no longer of the Earth's living and the three visitations are granted to say goodbye to the Earthly living ones whom you cared about the most and whom you would miss the most as your soul exited the Earth realm immediately after your death."

"Are you a fucking mind reader?" I spit. "How would you know if I thought about my mother or who I visited after my death?"

"I cannot share with you just yet how I know."

"Well shut the fuck up then!"

"Here," she said, suddenly handing me her saddle bag. I didn't like that she was giving me some type of hand-me-down even though it looked brand-new. But it was Gucci dope style. So I took it. It was heavy. I learned from living in the streets that if anybody hands you a bag, you better look in it right then and there. Know what you're holding! So I looked. In it was a book so heavy that no one in their right mind would ever open or read it. Even I know an author should have some fucking consideration and keep it brief. That's why I love magazines. They're less wordy, more art and photography. They are constantly updated, so they keep up with the flow of fashion, the movement of models, celebs, and caked-up people, and display the finest furniture, newest technology, awesome travel destinations, elite products, and the flawlessness of jewels. I handed the saddle bag back to her.

"The BOOK is an English translation of the 'Book of Guidance,' the most important words revealed and written to the living. On its pages are the answers to every question you have and any one of us has ever had. Keep it in case you have a change of heart. The answers and the straight way will be right at your fingertips. There is a tiny dictionary in the bottom of the bag in case you don't understand a word, just look it up." She handed it back to me. I didn't take hold of it.

"Bitch, you said I was dead. Why do I need a Book of Guidance with all of the answers to questions for the living?" I knew I trumped her, showed her how smart she isn't.

"Because the soul is eternal. You need to know what the difference is between good and evil, right and wrong. Once you read these pages, you will be able to distinguish and understand and most importantly self-reflect. Don't you care to know how come you are here at the Last Stop Before the Drop? Once you read, you will see the error in your choices and feel responsible for your missteps. Then you will *will yourself* to pray. Sincere prayers are the only path out of complete darkness."

"Beep-beep." A red G wagon rolled up, fully AMG kitted and rims glistening. It parked a short distance away. It had me mesmerized. Of course I had seen a Benz G Wagon before, but never a red one. It was so mean it seemed to glow. The tinted windows dropped down. "What are you waiting for? Get in!" Lucifer 66, Dat Nigga, said. He was calling for me. My forever nigga showed up *just like I knew he would.*

"Momma Lana Santiaga is not down here with you. She is in Heaven," Bomber Girl said quickly. She thought she knew my weakness and tried to stab me in it. She stepped in close to me, trying to block him from my line of vision. She placed the strap of the bag over my shoulder. Maybe she thought that heavy-ass book would make it impossible for me to speed off. "Excuse me, Miss Winter," she said, downshifting her tone now that I obviously had a better option. "Before you decide which path to take, I want you to know who I am and why it *might* matter to you." In my mind I was like, *You are a non-fucking-factor.*

Real bitches like bad boys. I'm the realest bitch, so I strutted right over to my forever nigga and hopped in. Through the blackened window, I could still see the spark of the Diamond Rain girl. Then *poof!* She suddenly exploded and disappeared. She left a trace of her hilab. The lavender sky and green atmosphere all faded to black. As me and him sped into the complete darkness, I opened the saddle bag, admiring the grade and texture of the leather, as well as the detail of the stitching. I decided to keep it. I lowered my window and tossed that heavy-ass book right out.

There was a foul breeze rushing into the rugged whip. Still, I kept my window down. I needed the air. I was concentrating on reducing my temperature. I had to prevent myself from suddenly turning into a blob of heat, especially before I got the dick-down that I was anticipating like a motherfucker. The only interruption to my thorough excitement about being back to human, and my pure enticement with him, was my fury with that little bomber bitch, who stood there with her bullet-lined waistline and a hand grenade around her neck. Yet, she tried to come off like she was some kind of fucking innocent angel. She needed to be armed and she knew it. Without her ammunition and weapon, I would have never hesitated to whoop her ass for mentioning Momma and reminding me of shit I worked hard to forget.

"I'm gonna need a drink," I told my forever nigga. "Something strong," I added.

"I got whatever you need. Whatever I ain't got, I'll get it," he said solemnly, and I loved it.

"What did UBS say that got you upset?" he asked me calmly, to which I replied, "Don't ever ask me about any other bitch. And when *I'm with you*, don't say no other bitch's name."

8.

"I got an idea," he said in a more like a thinking-to-himself tone. He pulled the G wagon to a stop. I don't know what he was thinking but we were still surrounded by pitch black. He opened his car door and got out. "Stay right there," he commanded me. I wasn't going anywhere without him anyway. And as far as I know, there is nowhere to go. I was *still tight* 'cause the teenage bitch's voice was revolving in my mind. For some bullshit reason, I couldn't push it out. "Funny you should mention Momma. *Funny you should mention Momma. Funny you should mention Momma.*" Her words and her voice were on a loop in my head.

Bomber bitch was forcing me into deep thought when in fact I think that, dead or alive, there are subjects and topics and things that a person should never *have to* think about. A dead person should be dead and without thoughts. I am dead and thinking about *precisely* the things that I never want to think about.

Bet all of the assholes who committed suicide were shocked and angry as hell when they found out that *dead is not dead* and they would be the same person after death, with the same thoughts that they had thought they were ending, getting rid of, silencing.

Now Momma was dead center in my mental line of vision. In

that freeze-frame she was Brooklyn Momma, before the move to our luxurious Long Island mansion. Before some nigga who was jelly shot her in her face and permanently altered her perfect look. But most importantly, the picture of Momma in my mind was before she ever toked a hit of that crack pipe. I knew, after having fifteen years on lock to just sit and think about it, that for me to accept my mother, aka Momma, aka Lana Santiaga, aka the Baddest Bitch on the Planet, after her crack breakdown would be the same as rejecting myself. No! It would be the same as destroying myself. Brooklyn Momma was the voice in my head. She was the image in my eyes, my pattern, my fabric, my fashion. She was all of the ingredients mixed together that made me, *me*.

Momma was the most. She was the beautifulest, the livest, the baddest, the funniest, the finest, everything. *I didn't need no books.* Momma was all show-and-tell. She told me and showed me while she was telling me all that a bitch needs to know.

"Ooh now, that's not cool," she would say when I shitted in my diaper at age two. That's how way back my earliest memory of Momma goes. It is my first and earliest memory of anyone or anything, including myself. After Momma said that, she taught me how to pee and poop, where to pee and poop, and how to clean myself thoroughly and smell like a lady always should smell. "Come in the bathroom," she would wave me in. "Always close the door while you do your private business. And remember your private business and your business-business both ain't nobody else's business!" She would talk to me like I was an adult, and then laugh at herself. But I knew she meant it and I understood her perfectly. "No potty," she would say, kicking the baby toilet into a corner. "Sit on the real seat like I do," she would say, pointing. I would be trying my best to balance my little body on the adult toilet with the humongous hole. "Now tinkle!" she would say, like it was a magical thing, not just pissing in the

bowl. While I tinkled, Momma would turn away and look at herself in the bathroom mirror while singing a song, which relaxed
me. Momma had the dopest music collection of original singles
and albums. She knew every song ever made from the oldest to
the newest. In my first memory, she was singing "All I Need,"
an old joint that she loved. She was doing Marvin Gaye's part
and Tammi Terrell's twisting and turning her body while fixed on
her own reflection. She was singing so passionately I wondered.
*Is she singing to Poppa? Or, is she singing to me? Or is she singing
to herself?* After that first memory, I remember Momma singing
"Everybody Is a Star" to me in the scented bubble bath as we
bathed at the same time in the same tub. Momma was musical and Poppa had the whole house wired with speakers in every
room, including the kitchen and the bathroom, so that Momma
could be happy at home.

All fresh and clean, Momma is carrying me wrapped in the
thickest, softest white terry-cloth towel to her bedroom. Both of
us sitting on her king-sized bed, Momma would oil and powder
and dress me. She'd comb through my silky hair like each strand
was a thread of pure gold. "All good!" She would leap up and rush
into her clothing closet, to the top shelf where she kept her collection of eye-catchers, show-stoppers, high-fashion hats. She
would carefully select one and put it on my little head, drowning
me in it. "Tilt it like this! Lay it to the side!" she would cheer, as
my little fingers attempted to adjust the hat to the style that was
the only way a fashionable supastar like Momma would approve.
Soon as I caught the right angle, Momma would be clicking her
Kodak, or pressing out Polaroids of me that would end up on her
wall of photos of everything Momma *loved the most.* That was us,
family.

By the time I was six, Momma would play-dress me in her
real clothes, with real bitch accessories, so that I could walk down
the runway that Momma made in the apartment corridor which
she lit up with colorful lamps and lights. I'd be killing the red car-

pet while the overhead speakers would be pouring out the sounds
of Rod Stewart's "Da Ya Think I'm Sexy." I worked the runway
to all Momma's music picks, which could be anything 'cause she
knew everything musical. Donna Summer's "Hot Stuff," Grace
Jones's "La Vie en Rose" or "Slave to the Rhythm." Momma loved
Grace Jones. Momma loved anyone and everything that she loved
to the fullest. She was the loyalest woman on Earth to anything
or anyone who she chose. Momma marked time and her favorite memories through music. She loved to tell me her coming-up
stories. When she would be narrating them to me it seemed she
was more excited hearing the stories she was telling, even though
she knew them all already, and had told them to me or Poppa
more than once before. She never sat still when she was saying
her stories. She was all movement, demonstrating, gesturing, and
reenacting. She told me I was born a product of two songs, Betty
Wright's "Tonight Is the Night." She wouldn't sing the whole
song, just certain lines to highlight and prove that this song was
her story. Momma said Betty Wright's song was the soundtrack
to her fourteen-years-young first love, first intimacy, first sexual
experience with the one and only Poppa. She'd be acting like she
could feel herself giving up her virginity right while she was telling the story. She squeezed her eyes tight in anticipation, clamped
her legs together like she was really nervous, and even had
sound effects like *ooooh* and *wooo* and *oh yeah!* The other record
that made me happen, according to Momma, was Rod Stewart's
"Tonight's the Night," 'cause he was cool, sexy, and smooth, and
only Santiaga was sexier, smoother, and cooler than Rod without
having to sing one note.

Momma had more style, got more looks, and had more wigs
than the Supremes. She could rock it long and silky to the back of
her thighs, or wear blunt cuts, short beautiful bobs, or her own hair
in swirls of finger waves. She threw me big birthday parties, which
could not be called just "parties" cause they were major events that
niggas from Bk to Bx fought to get invited to. Many of the peo-

ple who showed up I did not even know, even though the celebration was for me! After the huge crowd went home, when only
family remained gathered in the ballroom, Momma would emerge
dressed up on some karaoke-type vibe. She'd be Tina Turner and
somehow lured Poppa into dressing like he was Ike. He didn't sing
though, he just laid back and let Momma mesmerize him with her
high energy and vibrant personality. No matter how she freaked it,
Momma was larger than life and glowed more than any worldwide
superstar.

That's right. Momma taught me how to talk, by always talking to me and singing to me. Come to think of it, hip-hop was
Momma remixed, sampled, looped, slowed down and sped up with
a dope-ass beat beneath it. Momma is the reason why I love hip-
hop, memorized it like I memorized Momma, and moved my hips
to it, up until this day, dead or alive.

Momma taught me how to walk, whether it was on her
homemade runway, up and down the project steps, or on the
stoops, cement streets, or curbs. Momma taught me how to stand,
style, and strike a pose. Momma taught me body and style language. How to talk without ever saying a word. How to capture
and wear the prettiest, most stylish meanest fashions, so I would
never have to tell a next bitch anything. She would just stay the
fuck back or back the fuck off because she knew beside me is not
where she belonged. Momma taught me how to choose friends,
and be so badass that they would choose to bow down to my
look without me asking or having to be snobby or shitty about it.
What to share and not share. What to give away and never accept back. What to keep and never allow anyone to touch, beg
for, or borrow.

Momma ranked and ruled everything, even her own real-life
sisters who were my aunts. She didn't say "So-and-so is number one, and this one is number two," or anything like that. But
I could see Momma's words through her actions. Barbara, aka
Aunt B, was her oldest sister. Momma had her babysit me from

time to time. Aunt Barbara was appointed and paid to be baby-sitter to all of the family's kids even though she hated children. The fact that we all could feel that Aunt Barbara didn't want to watch even her own kids was proof that Momma, even though she was the youngest sister of her family, was boss. Barbara did what Momma "asked" her to do. My Aunt Lori cooked the dinner meals for Momma. Momma would speed down the hall to her apartment, pick up the prepared foods, run back, set the table at our place and pretend like she cooked everything herself. Aunt Lori knew better than to mention it. And she never did. Me and Poppa knew the deal, of course (and so did Momma, really), but we went along with it because Momma was so cute in all of her ways. Momma's sister Lilah got down on her knees and scrubbed our toilets and bathtub. She was our Brooklyn project apartment housekeeper. She waxed our floors on her knees without a mop. She vacuumed the carpeted floors, and she made our beds, and did dishes and windows!

In addition to paying her sisters, Momma treated them to spas and clubs, hair salons, concerts, sports events, and parties and Broadway shows. Places they could never have afforded on their own dollar. Momma's brothers all worked for Poppa. Momma made Poppa commander over them. Usually men don't like that type of thing. But for baby sister Lana (who kinged and hooked the hottest hustler), everybody would do it her way, *because she was her*. Besides, Poppa made them capable, decent, and most importantly, hood wealthy. All of my cousins, my same age and of course older, kissed my ass because I was Lana's golden child. So I learned how to rank everything and put everyone and everything in its proper place where it belonged, beneath me.

By thirteen, I was nine-millimeter dangerous and I knew it. I didn't need no more instructions, homemade runways, or private concerts. I had watched and listened to and loved Momma so much *I was Momma*, the young version. And, because I was naturally a Momma-Poppa combo, I was considered an upgraded version, a limited edition of Momma. Poppa gave me that light-skin-and-long-black-wavy-hair look and pretty eyes with the long lashes that I didn't have to buy from the cosmetics counter or wigs or weaves from the hair store.

Still, deep-brown, flawless-skinned, brick-house-bodied, long-legged, forever-young-faced, sultry Momma topped all, any-and everyone everywhere we went. I would see boys to men of all ages' eyes dance back and forth, up down and all around as they tried to choose between us. For me, Momma was the queen and obvious best. My most luxurious, stylish, lovely one. She was hands down my most incredible possession. And Momma was *my mirror*.

It was great becoming best friends with Momma. Having someone in your teen-young years who is not trying to stop you from living, feeling, running wild a little bit, just for the experience and for the hell of it, is diamond class. She wouldn't expect anything stupid that other parents expected, like for me to be all in love with and enslaved to going to school, earning stupid-ass best-attendance awards or even getting good grades and studying. *We had plenty paper!* Poppa earned it. We spent it. We had no reason to take the long bullshit route that lower-ranked, less-prepared families and people had to take. We weren't mad or mean to any of those people. Many of them were our friends, neighbors, family, and workers. Besides, like I said, they bowed down, voluntarily.

Brooklyn Momma would smoke a blunt, and might sneak some lines of cocaine while running with her sisters. She would throw back a glass or two of champagne at our huge events, parties and celebrations. Still she could be overheard reminding all in our close family circle, "Crack makes us rich. Crack makes them crackheads!" Then she would laugh her laugh that would trigger anybody listening to laugh along with her. "Seriously though," she would say while they were still laughing and she had switched her mood. "Crack is wack, don't let it bring you down!" Momma used to tell me when choosing my friends, not to choose the children of the "customers," because customers are crackheads who can never ever be trusted. Besides, they are beneath us and they don't get the privilege to come into our family circle, apartments, or our luxurious world.

Crackhead Momma erased Brooklyn Momma, the phenom, who I thought would shine and live forever. Crackhead Momma caused Brooklyn Momma to drop down through all of the ranks that she set up. Crackhead Momma unlocked the doors and let in all that was beneath us. The crackhead was doing every single thing that Brooklyn Momma taught and showed me a real bitch should and would never do. Momma fucked up her currency. Her currency was her look. If she was my mirror, and she was, and smoking crack fucked up her look, which it did, what was that supposed to do for me, to me?

Seventeen and a stunner, surrounded by my Brooklyn friends I had, *since day one*. Friends who competed with one another to be the closest to me, friends who looked up to Momma and who wished she was their momma. Friends who either never met their fathers, hated their fathers or ain't seen that nigga in a decade, admired, sweated, and studied Momma because Poppa wifed her, gave her everything and stayed. Crackhead Momma gave these same friends of mine, who quietly worshipped me and eagerly bowed down, the advantage and the opportunity to talk behind my back. Laugh right up in my face. Step right up to my rank and act like we was all, all of a sudden equal.

In the Santiaga family, Santiaga and me stayed true to the game. Even my sisters Porsche, Lexy, and Mercedes all rebounded, landed on their feet, and kept it royal. I never ever said it out loud, but that's why I pushed Momma way to the back of my mind, and deleted her from my talk, mention, and memory. And even if there is a Jannah or whatever, and Momma is there in Heaven, if she don't look and feel and talk and act familiar like Brooklyn Momma, I don't need or want to see her. To see her would be to kill my own self. And I never ever been a suicidal bitch. Crackhead Momma was and is an unacceptable complete fucking embarrassment to me.

9.

"Crazy bitch bombed us," Dat Nigga said. Guess after the six stops he made on the way back here to our firehouse, Bomber Girl had the time to do her thing. Still I played dumb to test him and asked, "Who?" He looked at me sideways with half a smile and replied, "You asked me not to call out any other bitch's name in your presence."

"That's right," I said, feeling satisfied that I had reduced the Diamond Rain girl, aka Siddiqah, aka Bomber Girl, aka the young bitch, to being referred to by him simply as "that crazy bitch."

The young bitch had blown the sturdy front door of the firehouse right off its hinges. But because down here there is no alternation of day and night, no moon or sunshine, no traffic lights or street lanterns, it was next to impossible to see and measure the damage. Immediately outside where we stood there was only complete blackness. Facing the door that was no longer there, we saw only the blackness of the corridor leading into his place, which remained black every day until he chose to light one of his twelve flame torches that still stood cemented in the floor even after all of the attacks and wind wars that shook the house.

He picked me up. I loved being carried in his strong arms. Loved that he could do chin-ups lifting both of our body weights at the same time, effortlessly. "I have to unload the trunk. I'll make sure you are safe inside first," he said. Soon as his Timbs hit the floor inside of the corridor, I could hear the sound of broken glass beneath each of his steps. He stopped, uttered, "Crazy bitch" again, and walked until he had to dip low to enter in through his monkey bars and toss me onto the bed. "Don't move." He lit one torch on the left side, by me.

"Do you have a flashlight?" I asked before he walked away.

"I prefer fire. You know that."

"I'm gonna clean up every trace of her. I'm asking for the flash-light and a broom so I can do it right. I know you have both be-cause I know you have *whatever I need*." I smiled at him nicely.

I high-beamed the Lumen industrial flashlight, scanning the floor to see just how bad it was. The glass didn't appear like it re-sulted from some chaotic explosion. It seemed it had been pur-posely placed. It was as if someone had one of those salt-spreading machines that spit out thick salt during the winter storms to thor-oughly melt the snow and ice. Except it was as though someone had used that type of machine to spread glass everywhere instead. I peeped a pair of his kicks right by our bed. *Perfect, I'll put these on.* I didn't know the whereabouts of my red boots anymore. When I put one of his kicks on my left foot, I expected them to be way too big. I didn't expect them to have a pair of panties stuffed inside. I removed the sneaker and pulled them out. Knew they wasn't mine. I don't wear none. I smelled them. Smelled like pussy and his dick, a mixture. *I'll remove every trace of every bitch,* I thought to myself. I wasn't angry. It was my first time being back here for what felt like at least six months sitting by the sewer with paralyzed legs. As I began to sweep, beginning in the area of the bed that I just got off of, and clearing each way as I moved along, I began to discover all types of shit that belonged to other bitches. I put it all in a heap, lit the bottom of the straw broom with the flame on top of the metal-poled torch, and burned it all. When he walked in finally and saw all of his bitches' shit on fire, he didn't react. It was the perfect re-sponse to me. Meant he knew I was his top choice and got the respect that he needed to give and show me that I needed to never ever have to ask for or mention.

"Good job," he said as he was now able to walk in and around with zero glass crackling. He took back his flashlight and returned with a pair of soft furry slippers, which he slipped onto my feet. "Get in the shower," he said, "because I know you want to. But remember how I like it. Don't overdo it." I didn't say nothing back. Of course I remembered. Leave the ass half dirty, and he will clean my pussy with his tongue.

He had lit a scented candle in the bathroom that normally stayed unlit and in complete blackness. There was a tiny vase with six dead daisy flowers. I appreciated the gesture. I never seen no plants, trees, or flowers down here. He must have went through so much to obtain these. In the shower there was a new bar of soap with the paper still on it. I unwrapped it. I'm happy. Under the warm downpour my mind began to wander. As I instinctively slid my hand between my thighs to suds up my privacy, it occurred to me a lot of shit changed since I was a teen. Niggas used to love the bush. Used to call it the nappy dugout. Now top bitches get their pussies waxed for smooth access and to receive better head, no hairs left between his teeth or caught in his throat. I laughed. I missed having manicures and pedicures. I missed shopping and switching up my hairstyles at the salons of my choice. Even in lockup, I could always get my hair done if I really wanted to. I could get my v-waxed too, believe it or not. But there was no reason to. I didn't want to look good for a thousand locked-up bitches. Winter Santiaga is strictly dickly. I love to be top looker for the men to lust and the women to envy. Prison deads most of that freedom flow. But on the night before my release, I chose the top, most talented scrub girls, masseuse, hair and nail stylists on lock to doll me up precisely according to the designs in my mind. They knew it was a privilege. They knew it was a first and last golden opportunity. They each did their job as though they wanted to leave an impression on me that might pay off for them big time one day when they step out from the cage. Every inmate in there believed in their heart and bones that I was headed to becoming the realest and the brightest superstar.

"Don't you want this dick?" His voice jolted me. I threw back the shower curtain and smiled in great anticipation. "Turn off the water," he commanded me. I did. "Now, come here," he said and I could already smell the scent of the weed. He shut the door, closing us both into the small bathroom space. He pulled the lighted blunt from behind him where he was holding it hidden inside of his palm. He turned the lighted blunt around and put the lit-up side in his mouth. He held it with his teeth and blew the weed shotgun smoke into my mouth and I sucked in like a champion. I don't know if he laced his weed. But here at the Last Stop Before the Drop, the weed was three times more potent than any weed I ever toked.

Both nude and standing close together, I could feel our feelings as though they were filling up the air, replacing the shower steam that was there moments ago and mixing in with the smell of the soap on my body, the smoke in the air, and the scent of the weed. I felt his erection grazing my skin. He handed me a short glass. I wafted it and swooned on the aroma of Hennessy.

"Where's your glass?" I asked him.

"This is the last glass left in the house," he said as I swallowed. Ooh, my head was nice. I was feeling more than good. He relieved me of the now-empty glass, set it on the sink. He grabbed my hand, placed it on his dick. I held it gently like a tight leash. He led me this way as he walked out backwards into the blackened corridor without tripping on his steps.

Back in his playpen, all twelve torches were lit now. He laid me on top of the dinner table. There was no tablecloth or cutlery, plates, or food. I was nude on my back. He placed the linen stirrups, which now hung over the table, onto my ankles. Then he spread my legs eagle, squatted down, and stood back up holding the Hennessy bottle in his left hand. I was like, *Hell yeah, that's my shit!* My pussy trembled when he poured the liquor inside of my most intimate space. The shocking coldness caused me not to say nothing. In what seemed like seconds he was lapping up the liquor with his long tongue. Wonderama!!! Oh, what a feeling. He kept the licking coming. His stirrups kept my legs spread all the way open. I came so hard my body jerked up into the sitting position on top of the dinner table. I wanted to thank him, give him head as passionately as he gave me. I leaned further forward to remove the stirrups. He kicked the table out from under me with his powerful legs. I was now hanging upside down. My head was close to the floor. He walked behind where I was hanging and buried his nose into my ass and began whiffing. Whiffing turned to him spreading my cheeks and licking there, which no man had ever done. I was helpless and overwhelmed and overjoyed. He then slid his body beneath me. Must have sensed that I wanted to please him. It was quite a maneuver to give upside-down head. But, I locked my lips around the tip and my hands around his pole, like how I held onto the moving pole of the merry-go-round horse long ago.

He spanked my ass six times. Even that felt good. "You were the sexiest with the scar. What happened to it?" he asked. It was the first time I was proud of the scar. And in the momentum of pleasing him, my lips locked around his joint, I even wished I could bring the scar back. He removed the stirrups, broke my fall, and carried me with one arm like I was a beach ball or a basketball he was about to play with. He sat me on his weight bench in the straddle position. He adjusted the back of it to recline partway. He moved a pin to steady it, and it clicked into the locked reclined position. He fucked me in such a way that my back could not move and there was no resistance. When he stroked, he would hit the target each time. It was more than the friction of our flesh or the dimensions of his pipe that thrilled me. It was the choreography of a sexual encounter with him. It meant to me that he knew exactly what he wanted me to feel and how he needed to design it to deliver the highest sexual high.

"Stand up," he ordered me off the bench after a full stroking, but my legs were still trembling and a bit wobbly from the orgasms and maybe the weed-Henny mixed somewhere in it all. He yanked me up. Pushed his right hand's pointing finger in my pussy hole and thrust his thumb in my ass. He steadied me this way, held like how a nigga carries a six-pack, while his left hand adjusted the bench. He withdrew both fingers. He pushed me down face-forward on the same weight bench that was now locked into a position where my head was by the floor and my ass was up high. He spread my ass cheeks and plunged between them. "I really like you, bitch," he said as he stroked. "And your ass is the most comfortable to me. That's good," he said as he stroked again. "I'm an ass man," he added. The whole sexual encounter was perfect, minus those four words, *I'm an ass man*, which, come to think of it, he said in the heat of his own passion. Still, I didn't like it.

It didn't seem to matter though. The twelve flames that he had lit when I was showering all blacked out at once. The weight of his body was off of me. Somehow now I was on the floor instead of his weight bench. I got immediately worried. I didn't want to be back crawling on my belly with no legs and no arms. I wasn't! Whew! *I had legs* and I could feel and move them, all four of them. My tongue was hanging out and I was panting from the athletic sexual experience. I tried to shake myself into a reality. Clear my weeded-Henny head and figure myself out. I laid on my belly. My front legs extended in front of me and my back legs tucked beneath me. Still panting, I couldn't seem to close my own mouth or keep my tongue from hanging out. I wagged my tail. After I did, I didn't need no lights or mirror to confirm it. I felt it. Now I, Winter Santiaga, with my same mind, fully awake and aware, was a real, bona fide bitch! I had turned into a fucking dog.

10.

"I heard she's back," a woman's voice said before he even saw her. She was coming through the black hole where the firehouse door used to be. I heard her coming with my dog ears. That's why I tucked myself behind the huge medicine ball in the far corner.

"Is that why you broke all six of my mirrors, all of the glasses at my bar, and blew off the front door with your succubus temper?" he asked her in a neutral and calm, manly tone. He obviously already knew the answer. I was listening carefully but a bit confused. She definitely did not sound like that teenaged Bomber. And what the fuck is a succubus? Was that her name? I thought niggas in da hood had wild names. In this realm, the names were even stranger.

Succubus didn't answer. She just strolled further indoors. I didn't peep. I wanted to listen to their convo and have her believe that the two of them were alone. That way she would say whatever was on her mind and fully expose herself. There was only silence between them though. She kicked off her heels. One landed by me. I had an impulse to fetch it. I shut that impulse down immediately. *She's a cheap-shoe bitch*, I could tell. Her worn red pleather pump was pitiful. The heel laid to the side like it was too cheap and she was too heavy for it to hold her up on level ground. Then I heard her bare feet on the monkey bars. As she moved from bar to bar, I suddenly saw her peering down at me from the top. I collapsed on my four legs, laid on my belly, and played dumb. She shifted her gaze to the bed, which was now covered by a red silk duvet and red pillows rather than the black ones he had when we first met. She swung down like a monkey. Her feet were big, like bitches who had to special order their shoes because they wore larger than a size twelve. Only bitches who play basketball can be excused from the embarrassment of that. Succubus smelled the silk blankets, then pressed her face into the sheets. I didn't care that she was inspecting them. Our incredible gymnastic fuck didn't happen on the bed. She laid down.

"Don't let me catch her. I know she's around here somewhere. Iblis saw you speeding through his block in your father's whip with her riding shotgun. He told me she was the same bitch he saw you with who was wearing the white mink. He said you been supposed to deliver her to your father. So what's the deal? You turning soft all of a sudden?" she asked, but it was like a jab, not a question. My tail started wagging. I had to think really hard to control it. I was happy that I was the topic. I was now confirmed that his love for me was real. The streets be watching. Tongues start talking whenever a nigga gets a top bitch. Her presence cancels out all the other bitches who were getting dick from him here and there but were never allowed to be a live-in or definitely not a wife. *A wife*, I thought to myself. *This nigga needs to queen me. When I get back to my normal self, I'm gonna make him feel so good that he'll cough up a ring for my married finger without me having to suggest it.* Top bitches ain't ever gotta suggest anything. And no bitch could claim top status if she ever-ever had to ask her nigga to marry her instead of him asking her based on his thoughts and feelings that sharing or losing her to any other man was completely unbearable to him. Real men ask that top bitch to marry him because she is who she is. At least I am.

"Stop messing with those tools and come lay beside me," she said in her bossy tone. I thought she was too ugly to be bossy. She should've been begging.

"I'm 'bout to fix the door you blew down. Get up and you'll pass me the tools when I tell you."

She leaped up. They walked down the corridor together. I stayed put.

When they finally got around to fucking, which she actually had to ask for more than a few times, I didn't mind. He didn't set a shower for her, no scented candle or soaps or blunts or Henny, and not even dead daisies. He butt-f'd her on his floor and that was that. There was no choreography, passion, or concern. I saw him glance at me when he collapsed on top of her back. I wondered if he was saying sorry, or more like, "She's nothing to me." He didn't need to reassure me, though. I observed, and I could tell through his actions and inaction. The residue from her stinky ass clouded the room. Made me wanna pass out. When he was done, she wouldn't leave. He locked himself in his bathroom for what seemed like a long time. When he came out fully dressed he gave her numerous hints.

"I got shit to do. I gotta make my runs. No! You know you can't ride with me." She wouldn't give up and leave and go back to wherever she came from. So he left her bare butt right there on the floor. He slammed the front door. I heard the G wagon turn on and pull out. She was staring at me. I turned away. I must have fooled her. She got up. The stinky bitch didn't even take one step towards the bathroom. She never showered. Instead she searched around, went all through his belongings until she discovered a set of keys. She stuffed them between her tits and climbed all the way up the monkey bars. Once she was up top, she glared down at me and said, "What the fuck you looking at?" I turned away, walked a few steps, and sat looking in the other direction. Then I heard keys turning in a lock. I heard the sound of her disappear. When I turned back and looked up towards the high ceiling direction over the monkey bars where she had just been, she was gone.

Since I could not distinguish night from day, I could only count the amount of times I saw Succubus. When she wasn't around, there would be random bitches coming to play in his play-pen. I was the only permanent one. He petted me quite often. It felt good too. Then I would lay on my back and he would stroke my underside. Oh, how exciting. One time when she saw him pet-ting me, she became jealous.

"What's with that fucking mutt?" she asked him.

"Easy, she's a full-breed Lhasa Apso. Isn't she beautiful?" he asked, but I thought he shouldn't have said the last part. "And look how clean I keep her white fur." He rubbed salt in Succubus's anger.

"You're rubbing her. You should be rubbing me," she said, and left in a hissy fit.

After she left, some young pretty chick arrived. "Ooh, you have a pretty dog. When did you get her?" She approached me. I gave a low-grade growl. She squatted and petted me. Then she picked me up. Right away, I bit her. She screamed and let go. My forever nigga looked at me and smiled. "You think that's funny?" the pretty bitch asked, all pissy.

He answered back, "Nobody told you to touch her. It's good that you have blood. It's nice to bleed every now and then." He said it casually and didn't tend to her wound. He fucked the pretty one out of her anger. It was athletic and thorough. I felt excited because I was watching and could clearly recall how incredible each move-ment felt. It aroused me and mixed with a jealousy. I am unaccus-tomed to feeling any jealousy ever. I ran and jumped on the bed and wiggled in between where they lay after their sex. "Do you normally let her onto your bed?" she asked. He didn't answer back. "Once you do it becomes a habit. You should train your dog," she said. But the torch lights all blacked out at once. I could not see or feel him or her anymore. I leaped off the bed and searched around but in the dark, found nothing except the bone he left me in the corner and the dish of chicken chunks.

After that I began sleeping in his bed each time he laid there alone. In the dark I would lick his face first and he would kiss mine. I didn't want our first kiss to occur while I was a dog. I also didn't want our first few kisses to be closed lipped. I wanted and craved a deep tongue kiss in the mouth when I was in my best human form, in the heat of our most incredible lovemaking. After the pecks on my face, he began petting me. When I rolled over so that he would pet my underbelly, he did. Then the unexpected occurred. He slid his thickest finger in my dog pussy hole and made me feel so overwhelmed I howled. After that time, I couldn't wait for bedtime. He would caress me better than when he caressed me when I was a woman. He would again penetrate me with his finger. In my dog state, it really felt like a satisfying dick. I would thank him by licking his balls and eventually his anus. It was all done in the dark where no one else would ever know our secrets but me and him.

But the next day, Succubus used the key she had made for the front door to enter. I was seated on the bed waiting for bedtime, whenever that would occur, I didn't know for sure. He was out for a while. Succubus lit two torches and the flames revealed what I had caught whiff of on her arrival. She had a dog in her hand. She placed it on the floor and said, "Now this little bitch will learn her place." Was she talking to me?

He came home. "Why did you bring that mutt up in here?" he said as soon as he walked through the door.

"Your bitch looked a little lonely," she replied dryly.

"Put him back in the basement," he said, as though he knew the dog.

"She stays up here. Why can't he?"

"I don't want puppies," he said.

"It's the closest you and I are ever going to get to having babies," she said oddly.

"You talk too much. Take him down now," he commanded her. She left. *Babies,* I thought to myself. *She's a dead bitch just like me. We can't have babies, and she should be glad.* I loved the fuck-arama without the pregnancies and all of the complications that go along with it. From their conversation I could see that she thought she was top bitch, although I can't imagine why? There had been plenty of women in and out of his playpen. All of them looked way better than her. She was a no-action bitch. For some reason, though, I thought further. *How come I never see any of the other females twice in a row?* Meanwhile, this Succubus showed up all of the time? What was she doing to make all of the rest stay away after that first freaky, unforgettable sexual encounter? Wouldn't every single one of them want a second and third go-round? I did! Why didn't he snatch back her key to his place? Especially because she used it like she was a co-owner, or paid rent here and was a resident. Why bother to let her in when clearly he didn't like her? He didn't even fuck her right. He never ever broke down and whispered in her ear a confession of his attraction to her, or highlighted her irresistible qualities. She didn't have none! I laughed, but it came out like barking. I didn't like the sound of that, so I stopped.

"What's the count on your side?" A male voice had entered our darkness, sounding like he was on speakerphone. I didn't hear no ringtone, or no doorbell, or door opening, though. He wasn't in here before he started talking either. And, I never saw my nigga's house phone or cell phone even during the few times that the firehouse was well lit.

"Two thousand six for the week," my nigga answered back.

"I'm at 1,566," the other guy said. "And if you keep dipping into your stash soon I'll catch up and surpass you," he added.

"Keep trying," my nigga said confidently. "Iblis, what's the week total citywide?"

"Six thousand houses reported in to Father. Average house 1,100, plus top twenty earners average recruitment 1,468."

"Aight cool. What did father say?" my nigga asked.

"Why ask when you already know. He's greedy and never satisfied. You the top earner. It doesn't matter what he says." Iblis paused. "Yo! Who's that pretty thing you sped through the block with two times? First time she was in your Jag wearing the white mink. That's how I spotted her." My nigga hung up. My head swelled. Even in the Last Stop Before the Drop, the County of the Ungrateful, the State of Ignorance, and the Land of Arrogance, Winter Santiaga was still turning heads and the streets was still watching.

I heard a key turn in the lock what seemed like immediately after my nigga left out. Now that I had overheard the stats on his hustle, I didn't even get mad that he was leaving me behind fairly regularly in the dark firehouse. Besides, it was warm, and the silk blankets on our bed were soft and comfortable even with the rubber thorns below them. I heard a chain rattle. A flashlight beam flashed on. When I finally saw Succubus, she was holding a long leash with no dog attached. I wiggled beneath the blanket. She started searching around for me with her thin beam of light. It was hard not to make any doggy sounds. The breathing and panting and wagging are endless. When the light beam landed on me, I wiggled out from under and darted to the floor. "You got the nerve to be on the bed under the goddamn covers!" she shouted. I dodged the beam, scattering here and there. The sound of my nails skidding on the floor was giving me away. She started using her chain as a whip and trying to strike me with it. Instead of running away from her, I charged her and bit her left ankle. My teeth penetrated deep in her. "You fucking little bitch, I'll kill you," she threatened. She wielded the chain whip so hard that it landed on my back and stopped me dead in my tracks. The pain was great. And it took everything I had not to whimper. Pausing was my biggest mistake. She grabbed me by my hind legs and dragged me backwards. After she was satisfied that she had burnt my face and underbelly, which was scraping against the cement floor, she raised me into her arm. I tried to bite her again. She took both of her powerful hands and forced my mouth closed, then clasped it shut with thick rubber bands. She hurled me against the wall, which was completely extra unnecessary. On impact I felt smashed. Then I slid down to the floor. I was out cold. That must have been the exact point when she leashed me, dragged me out of the firehouse, and drove me away. But I don't know if she drove me out, or if she put my bloodied body into a trash bag. Maybe she threw the bag into a large trash bin and then it was picked up and dumped elsewhere. After I had high-speed hit the wall, I really don't know what happened to me next.

11.

My mind clicked on before my eyes opened. Good thing I had no expectation to see light. Even in my dreams there is no light. It's good that I had let light go. I'd gotten comfortable with only the flame and the dim visuals it allows me to see. Because, when I woke, there was only blackness and no vision at all. I laid there panting. So I knew I was still a dog. My wet and cold nose was assaulted by a series of smells, each distinct, but somehow mixed together. It was not the scents of humans. I know the difference. And it was also not the odor that I was well familiar with that oozed out of the open sewer where I often found myself seated, legs paralyzed and alone. I could feel that wherever I was now, I was not alone. Normally this would be a good thing. However, I sensed a threat.

The side of my body that hit the wall when Succubus threw me was paining me. Testing my abilities, I tried to stand up on all four of my legs. When I did I ached and felt lopsided. I attempted to walk, but I was slow and gaining only inches, which is less than even a new toddler would gain when taking her first steps. In what seemed like an instant, my nose hit metal bars, which caused me to inch backward. When I had taken a number of steps back, my tail hit metal bars. So then I knew. I had experienced this before. I was in a fucking cage. I could hear lots of others breathing. Also some cooing. Some screeching. Some squeaking. Some braying.

Some hissing. Some snorting. Some howling. Some mooing. And I also heard hooves hitting the ground. They were all different languages. Yet, I could tell all of the sounds were sounds of captured creature's, anger, and complaints. I only understood English and barking. So I began barking. It was a genuine, "Where my dogs at the moment." Many canines returned my call, including the howling of wolves. However, when they did, I could tell that they were extremely far off from where I was caged. All they were barking about was how fucked up this shit is.

Succubus ain't slick. She was the same as the authorities. She put me wherever I am right now, to keep me in an unfamiliar territory with no allies. Other dogs would be the natural attraction for me to go to, to gang up with, and not turn into food. I was only happy about one thing. I didn't hear no roaring. That meant wherever I was, there are no lions, tigers or bears, at least not yet.

For what seemed like a very long time, there was no action. Even in solitary someone comes through and slides in a tray of goop for you to eat and water for you to survive. C.O.s hated us. Yet they had a job to keep us alive. They were responsible for the count. But who's running this situation here? If there was no feeding, it meant they planned to slaughter us. Or worse, let us die of starvation. The last possibility was they wanted us to attack each other and decide who was food and who was not. Survival of the fittest, like my niggas in Mobb Deep rhymed about on that hot-ass track.

Suddenly I could hear what sounded like two hundred cows mooing. It felt like a funeral song. I got worried that they must know something. I just woke up here. I didn't know what the hell was going on or what to expect. Then I reminded myself that I was in the realm of the unexpected. *Don't expect shit.*

Just when I felt my body getting dangerously weak, after what felt like about six days of nothingness, an alarm went off that caused every animal of every kind to panic even though none of us could do nothing about it. After it damn near blew out my dog ears, which were supersensitive to sound, it stopped. Then the abusive sound of some type of heavy machinery entered the area. Next, a sprinkler system clicked on and my cage was being sprayed with what I believed to be water. I was like, *Is this their idea of giving us something to drink?* Instead of just standing there with my fur getting soaked, I opened my mouth so that some of the water would land on my tongue. It worked. But I was so vexed that this was how it was being handled. Next I heard a machine that sounded like a snowblower. I know because upstate New York where I served my prison time, some winters brought on six to eight feet of snow. I thought the snowblowers were way worse than the snow pile.

When the sound of the blower reached near to my cage, a bunch of pellets shot out like bullets. I squatted low down to avoid getting pelted. But, there was nowhere to go. As the loud noisy machine moved slowly down the tier shooting pellets in what I guess was each cage, I stuck my nose to my cage floor to inspect what had been served. It was like corn and rocks.

I was tight. Even though I was a dog, Dat Nigga always fed me real food, the way a human would enjoy. I'm not normally a food lover. When I was alive, I never really concentrated on eating. Even when I was at the table with family, for me it was more about them than what was on my plate. I kept a badass bitch body figure, a tight waist and had no desire to ruin it. I wasn't suicidal. So I was never starving myself or forcing myself to vomit. But, I was never ever pigging out either. *A real bitch gotta look right.* I don't want nothing in my body that fucks with my look. At the same time, after I got shot dead, I wasn't hungry ever and never ate anything. Still, I felt alive, was thinking and having a whole bunch of shit happening to me that I could never have predicted would happen to a dead bitch. As a serpent, and then as a dog, I was the opposite with food. I wanted and needed it. I would strike to get it, even if that meant chewing it alive and swallowing.

This wack-ass feeding system was so disruptively noisy. It caused nothing but a chorus of animal reactions, resistance, and complaints mixed with chomping, cracking, and chewing. I still didn't eat the corn or the pellets. I knew if I ate corn and all of the rest of the animals were served the same thing, there would be a shitting frenzy to follow. I wanted to vomit just thinking about the odor and the aftermath of thousands of creatures having a shit blizzard and nothing to do but sit in it because nobody would show up to clean it. Dat Nigga was good to me. He let me go off in a far corner and do my thing. He didn't come walking over there and he never watched. When I was done and had walked away from my own shit pile, he would go and clean it up. I wouldn't stare when he did. He wouldn't look my way when he did. He never made me feel like an animal. This circumstance I was in right now was nothing even remotely similar. I sat down, all four legs collapsed. I was thinking about him now as a means to blocking out all of the noise and fuckery. Would he come and get me? Did he know where I was? Would he beat Succubus's ass until she told him where she put me? Would she ever tell him? Would she tell him too late, after I was already dead? Oh, wait a minute. I *am* already dead. Um, how did this work? I definitely don't know. Can a bitch die twice?

Since I couldn't count the days, I counted the feedings. Six feedings after my first feeding, which I assumed was once a day, I broke down and began chewing from the pellet pile. I had swept the corn to the side with my tongue. So there was a pellet pile and a corn pile and a little iddy-biddy shit pile behind me. My underbelly was wet from the piss. I hated that. My fur was matted. I could feel it. I hated that too. I was heavily hoping Dat Nigga would walk through and free me. At the same time, I didn't want him to see me in this condition. He had kept me clean and combed and loved.

Suddenly I heard a rumble and felt the ground moving. All of the animals began wailing. They heard and felt it too. I never been in an earthquake, but that's the word that came to me when the ground shook. When the walls shook and the cages began to rattle, I was like, *Hold up. It's Bomber Girl.* Never thought I'd be happy to see the young bitch. But, since she had bombed the firehouse, even though she said it was not her, and even though it was way before Succubus knocked the door down and broke the mirrors and everything made of glass, it felt just like what was happening now, to the tenth power.

After the shake-up, a male voice made an announcement that sounded like it was being propelled everywhere through a megaphone.

"Lah-il-la-ha-illah-huwa," he said. I was like, *Oh no, speak English!* Then I heard the sound of a heartbeat being amplified. Somehow, the beating heart seemed to calm all of us animals. It reminded me of the rhythm of roller skating back when my teen crew used to chill at the Skate Key or the Rink. We even had a jam titled "Heartbeat" that hip-hop producers and beat biters sampled all of the time. The soft sound of one flute began drifting over the rhythm of the beating heart. It was so soothing. I'm not accustomed to flute music, but I wasn't mad at it either. Next I heard a long and high-volume hissing. It was not part of the music. The serpents must be here somewhere in the mix. But it sounded like they were all on the move. I heard cage doors opening way off in the distance. I stood up in anticipation forgetting my weakness and my pain. Suddenly, the sound of the cymbals that a drummer creates with the tap of even one drumstick joined in, making the flute sounds more legitimate. It was working, whatever it was. Various groups of animals seemed to be on the move, following the sound of the music. My anticipation was moving back and forth mixed with fear. Fear of being left behind. Fear of being last out of the cage. What if the walls caved in from the heavy bombing and I got buried alive, dead?

Once the sound of cages being unlocked reached much closer to me, which seemed like forever, with that sound came some light. It was the first light since my dog captivity. My eyes shut to readjust. The light was giving my eyes a burning sensation. Once I opened them, I saw young men wearing lights like a headband.

They were dressed in khaki jackets, had a sash of bullets laid across their shoulders, and a grenade belt around their waists. Were they a part of Bomber Girl's UBS army? She had the bullets around her waist and the grenade on her necklace. Maybe the male and female soldiers rocked it differently. I don't know. I do know that I could only see young males running the tiers, opening the cages and setting the animals free. They were all guided forward towards what I guess was the exit. But I didn't see no lavender sky or green atmosphere. I wondered who these guys really were? Who was freeing us and why? *Was it Dat Nigga's crew?* It had to be! He was going to war over me! He sent his army to find me! He had to let all of these creatures out until they located the right one, me! My tail was wagging like crazy. I was excited. Finally a nigga who went full throttle for his bitch the same way bitches go full throttle for our niggas! Usually they don't return the favor. I began barking. Wanted to alert his boys that *hey, I'm over here in the corner in the last cage* in the last tier.

Once my cage door got opened, I leaped out. Soon as my paws hit the ground my piss squirted out everywhere. I couldn't contain myself. I started shaking my whole body trying to free myself of anything matted in my fur. I used my toenails to comb through my hair. Without a doggy bath, it would be hard for me to look right. However, I gave it my best effort. Once I did, I had to run to catch up. When I did, I was in a herd of creatures, all running out of the barn warehouse, or barn factory. No matter the type of creature, we were all mixing together, pouring out of each tier and all into the total blackness that was the usual atmosphere of the Last Stop Before the Drop. Animals who would normally be fighting or eating one another were not fighting or preying. There were so many creatures, I couldn't see all the way to the front. I didn't know where I was going or who I was actually following. My Brooklyn mind flashed me a warning. What if this was a trick? What if they were leading us all to the slaughterhouse? What if we were all about to become food? Should I turn back? Should I dodge left or right and break through the ranks? What if I did? What then? I was torn. I didn't want to help myself get got. I didn't like the feeling of anyone outsmarting me. But, I had some impatient pigs behind me pushing me forward. Then there were the donkeys trotting in front of me. Some chickens fucking up the order and flow just running wild in the ranks. So in order not to get trampled, I didn't stop or even pause long enough to look all the way to the back. I kept moving in the long march to the unexpected.

We were all tired and thirsty and filthy and angry. We were all creating such a sound on the ground that it seemed to shake the area. We were all following the sound of the music. My legs were not all the way healed yet. The flute faded out. The cymbals silenced. The heartbeat remained. Then suddenly what sounded like a drum corps of more than a thousand drummers began drumming some driving beats that seemed to give me and each of us a second wind of energy and pep to our movement. We all rushed forward. Then what seemed to be six hundred to a thousand of us, suddenly jerked stop. On the way to wherever we were going, I was already thinking, what happens if so many creatures stop moving without warning? Now I was experiencing the answer in real time. The donkeys in front of me fell back. When I saw them coming. I gathered up all that remained in me and leaped on top of one of them as soon as it landed. Good thing I did, because the pigs behind me fell forward. I dug my nails into the donkey's skin. He was kicking and sounding off. I ignored him. I just needed to buy enough time to see what was happening up ahead before he shook me off. I saw it! The green atmosphere. Bomber Girl said that when I see the green atmosphere, that meant mercy. So we weren't being driven by some dope-ass beats into a slaughterhouse. I was relieved. How cruel it would have been if I was executed without Dat Nigga knowing what happened to me. He'd be out searching forever. All I needed to do was to have enough energy to follow the herd into the green and out of the blackness.

I jumped down off the donkey and landed on a chicken that

padded my impact. It flapped its wings like crazy. It then flew up a little bit and fell back down before it could ever get airborne. I was not falling. I was determined. The others must also be determined because they were each squirming or shaking or digging or pulling themselves out of the creature pileup, and getting back onto their feet.

Slower now, I kept pace in a parade stranger than the West Indian parade that marched and moved and drove down and through Eastern Parkway in Brooklyn causing everyone alive to either stand aside and watch or just join in. It brought everything that was not moving with it to a halt. So did this parade of creatures do the same.

As my row finally, after what seemed like a long way, was in range of the green atmosphere, something amazing occurred. The donkeys up ahead of me entered the green as donkeys and immediately turned into human beings once they exited the black atmosphere. I rushed forward trickling pee for the last push toward the green. *Bam!* I made it! I was myself. Everyone in front of me who entered the green were human again. I turned around to watch the pigs arrive. As soon as they did, they turned back to humans as well. I kept looking around, wild-eyed! I was inhaling and exhaling hard. I was glad, though, that I was not panting and my tongue was properly in my mouth. I tried to calm myself down, engulfed in a dense crowd of about six hundred mostly women, who were also trying to calm themselves down. We were all doing a type of body check. Eyes working? Check. Arms working? Check. Legs working? Check. And on and on and on and on to the beat y'all.

The all-drum corps was doing it. They were in a line up to the left, right, and now rear of where all of us women were standing. In front of us was a huge stage. It was a setup like a rock concert or better yet Summer Jam. The sound system was stacks of six-foot-tall speakers. There were microphones setup as though there was going to be a performance. But on the stage were only young males, uniformed like the ones who set us free from the animal warehouse factory. Once the shock of those six hundred or so of us who were animals moments ago wore off, we started milling around. So there were rows and rows of women milling around. I don't know if they were each looking for somebody in particular, or were just pacing out of nervousness. I was standing still, expecting the unexpected and observing.

I don't know why I was so surprised to see all different types of women weaved and woven into the herd. There were so many white women. There were as many Chinese women, or maybe I should say Asian, because I have no idea what countries they came from. I just call them all Chinese because they all have similar slanty eyes. There were Spanish women, Indian women, African women, African American and Caribbean women, and women of every complexion, color, language, country, and category that I didn't even know about, or that I left out of mentioning. I guess it would be fucked up if the Last Stop Before the Drop, the County of the Ungrateful, the State of Ignorance, the Land of Arrogance was a place that was reserved for only hood niggas. Wouldn't it?

Why are we gathered here? What do these young men want from us? Did Dat Nigga tell them to line up each one until they identified the right one, me?

Drowning out the sounds of all of the different languages being spoken at one time, my eyes scanned, surveyed, and zoomed in and out like a lens. Quite naturally they would land on the African American women more often than any other kind. They are most familiar and expected to me. I was looking at what each woman was wearing, the fashion and styles, and tallying it up. Then my mind began to wonder, were all of these women wearing their death-day clothes? I noticed that I was back in the white three-quarter-length mink and the white mini and red boots that I had lost track of what seemed like years ago. I wondered if these were all murdered women same as me. I also wondered why none of our garments had bloodstains and why my dress that Dat Nigga had ripped open in a lusty heated rush was back on my body fully intact. The teenage

Bomber Girl would say, "It is because the ONE is Most Merci-ful," or some words like that, which obviously had a much heavier meaning to her, and no meaning to me. I would be satisfied if Dat Nigga came for me and at me with even more fever and ripped it open again.

"Remember me?" A bitch walked over to me and sat down like we were buddies. Of course I remembered her. She was the pretty bitch who I bit when I was a dog. The one who petted me without Dat Nigga's permission. The same one who got a thorough dick-down from him. The kind he gave to me. I hated that. I even hated that I hated it. "Did you sit over here to bite back?" I asked her. But that wasn't my real question. I wasn't scared of her. My real question was how could she see me as a woman and know that I was that dog that got her good?

"I was in the cage next to you," she said. "When we got set free, I saw you walk out right behind me. I was a rat. I thought about turning around and biting you then. I changed my mind because getting out of that awful place was my first priority. Besides, you looked injured. I knew my bite would kill you." She said it like she wanted some type of award for giving me a pass instead of taking her revenge. When I didn't thank her like she seemed to want me to do, she cut the nice routine and spoke her mind.

"I thought you was a mean little bitch and I was mad as hell that you bit me. Especially after I was really nice to you. But I wouldn't kill you for that. That wouldn't be fair," she said, and still paused waiting for a compliment or a word of thanks. She seemed to need to be acknowledged for her niceness. I didn't say shit.

"If I could, I would kill Lucifer 66, though. That was the sec-ond time I let him fuck me. The first time I turned into a goddamn monkey. We had fun, I swang on his bars and all. But monkeys are smart, I started to think about how and why I turned into a mon-key. Then I figured it had to be because of him somehow. You know like how when you and I were alive on Earth, and some nigga we fucked gave us herpes, and you had to go through your mind and remember all the niggas you fucked and try to figure out which one did it?" she said and then paused. She was really talking to me like we were some type of friends.

I looked at her. *She is younger than me*, I thought to myself. *I'd say she's about twenty-five-years-young right now.* I hated that when I was twenty-five I was locked and only seven years in on a mandatory fifteen. When I know I did absolutely nothing wrong. She interrupted my thoughts and said, "The point is, when I was alive, I would never let no nigga make a fucking monkey out of me. And if some nigga gave me herpes, I wouldn't be like, 'Oh maybe I did this to myself.' I would be trying to figure out which nigga gave it. But I would be sure that one of them niggas did. With Lucifer, I second-guessed myself. Maybe I was in denial 'cause the dick was so good. I didn't want to believe it. When I went back for more, we fucked like crazy. Then I turned into a disgusting rat. You were there. That's when you were a pretty puppy. You looked for me on the bed. I had already darted. I was so angry at myself for letting it happen again. I was even thinking thoughts like, 'I'd rather be a monkey than a rat!' Now that I'm back to my real self, I'm not fucking with Dat Nigga no more. He better not even look in my direction. How 'bout you?" she asked.

I didn't say nothing back to her. Maybe she wanted me to agree. Then I would stay away from him and she'd run right back to his side. I did not know that she had been with him twice. She must have showed up when I was stuck by the stinking sewer for what seemed like forever. If she was fucking with him while I was away, it didn't matter. That means he had her before, but still showed up to get me from the curb where my legs were paralyzed and I was sick with some virus and rashes and horrible things. He showed up. He got me and kept me. For some time I stayed living in there with him. *I was there when she came for round two,* I told myself as I sorted it all out in my mind.

"I guess you will go back to him then," she said. "Did you see the range of animals in that warehouse we was caged in? What if you go back and Dat Nigga turns you into a snake?" she asked, pushing her face too close into mine.

"If I was a snake and you was a rat, I guess I'd have to eat you. Chew you up, swallow, and shit you out," I told her calmly. She got the message, leaped up, and kept it moving.

12.

Immediately after the drumming ceased, a voice said, "Please take a seat" over the loudspeaker. And as it did, two sixty-foot canvases rolled down, framing the stage where the voice had come from. One was green and had pretty, gold foreign lettering that of course I could not read. The other was white and was written in English. RALLY OF THE SONS.

Just then, an eighteen-years-young or so blond-haired young man, all blue-eyed and wearing the same khaki uniform as the guys who let us out of our cages were each wearing, stepped forward. He gestured for all of the women who were on the yard same as me to take a seat. He then started speaking in some foreign language. I was like, *Not this bullshit again*. As I watched, I could see women who were igging his "take a seat" request, by either standing still or walking while socializing in packs. The blue-eyed boy shifted to a different language. It must mean that when he gave the orders in a language each woman could understand is when she or they finally sat their asses down.

I was already seated. I wanted all of the bitches to cooperate, to make it easier for Dat Nigga's army to find me. Eventually, whether or not their language was called out, all of the women caught on and sat down. When we were each seated, some of the young men all in the same uniform began moving up and down the rows of us, handing out a tiny paper package.

"You each are being given an earpiece that will allow you to hear and understand all that is happening in your own language. Please place it in your right earlobe."

The silence that was complete once we were all wearing the dot and seated was a silence that gave me the chills. Then a handsome young black guy, maybe seventeen or so, got on the mic and began speaking.

"The Most Merciful ONE has allowed all of the UBS gathered here to free each of the women gathered here from the clutches of Shayton and from the House of Evil, which is his franchise. The male UBS who surround you, as well as the UBS on the stage where I am standing, are your sons. We have put our mercies together in a unified effort to conduct a raid that would free our mothers. The ONE has rewarded our effort with success, Ah-hum-doo-lah-lah.

"We are here today because of love. If we did not love you, we would not be here. Love gives us the courage to fight a war on your behalf. Because we do love you, we also forgive you. Each son here is fully aware that each mother here chose to follow in the footsteps of the devil, and to join hands with evil. We forgive. Our only objective is to use our deep love for you to show your soul a path to a better, cleaner, more peaceful existence and to ensure that you don't become an eternal occupant in the Eternal Fire, which is more painful than anything that you have experienced so far here in The Last Stop Before the Drop.

"Your sons know that each and every woman here has never made even one sincere prayer during her entire lifetime and existence on Earth as a human being. This is why your souls are confined here in the Last Stop Before the Drop, the County of the Ungrateful, the State of Ignorance, and the Land of Arrogance. Because we love you even though you chose evil over your sons and daughters, we forgive."

Suddenly every other bitch began crying. I mean crying real tears. What the fuck did this all have to do with me besides nothing? I ain't got no damn kids. So none of these sons were mine. Why was I here?

"Mommas, please clear your tears. We are here to comfort you and assist you to a better path. Mommas, there is no reason to be confused anymore. Quiet yourselves and listen to the guidance Allah has placed in each of your souls, our souls. All of the males who are surrounding you today, and who are standing with me stage front are UBS. 'UBS' stands for 'unborn souls.' This means that we each were once in your womb. You each chose to abort us. We sons gathered today are only a handful of more than a trillion unborn souls who were murdered in the womb. We forgive."

Instead of getting quiet, the bitches were in a bit of a frenzy. Me, I was tight that Succubus had thrown me against the wall and locked me up with all those animals and got me mixed up in this situation that had zero to do with me, I went to get up. My legs were locked. I was furious. This was bullshit. Why were my legs locked? Was I the only one? Was the reason why each of these women had remained seated and still because their legs were also locked?

Next, a young Chinese male in a uniform stepped to the mic. His haircut was kind've mean. I never ever thought of any Chinese man as handsome. I never paid not one of them any attention whatsoever. The one on the mic was a good departure from the rest of them. Maybe the young ones were learning how to get in the groove with that fashion flow. If they wanted to be relevant, they better.

Come to think of it, I never been anywhere social and laid back with anyone Chinese. Like everybody in my hood, I have been to the Chinese restaurant. That's not a place where I would listen to or have a conversation with a Chinese person, though. I'd just tell them my order. They wouldn't say shit back either, not even thank you. They cook it, put it in the Styrofoam container, staple it shut, then push it into a brown bag. They take my money first, then shove it forward. So even though my Brooklyn hood had the same

Chinese takeout spot for all of the years we lived there, we didn't know not one of their names. We didn't ask. We didn't care. Niggas would push through the doors and bark out their orders. "Wings fried hard, shrimp fried-rice, none of that bok-choy shit." Then when it was time to pay, a nigga would put his money on the counter and say, "Come on man, give me more napkins and soy sauce packs. Don't be so fucking cheap." That was the summary of the whole relation of hood niggas to Chinese people who been in our hoods forever but remained strangers to us.

Forced to listen, the Chinese guy said, "I am able to forgive because I know that my mother was never taught of the existence of the Most High. How could she know that there was a need for sincere prayer to the ONE who made her soul and the souls of all living beings? How could she break away from bowing down to every other powerless thing, a statue, her boss at work, her husband at home, her parents, her dead ancestors, a community leader, a politician, or bowing down to fear of the police, military might, the criminal syndicates and the gun? These people may seem to have some form of power. But, they do not have power over your soul. Only the ONE, Maker of all souls, is All-Powerful. Only the ONE could have protected you from all of the evil you faced on Earth. But mother, you never asked the ONE. You never made one prayer. You asked all of the wrong people and things who you were taught to worship. But if you worshipped idols, money, men, governments, leaders, history, ancestors, material things, this is the reason you lost your protection from the ONE who made your soul and gave you life and who is the only real protection you have. It's time to stop. I participated in the raid on one of Shayton's many animal warehouses today, as an expression of my love and loyalty to you, Momma. Also to say that it is not too late." He was pleading and begging passionately. The women cheered. Not only the Chinese bitches. All of the women who had the ear plugs. So we all heard his talk in our right language.

He let the cheering die down and closed out by saying, "But

soon *it will be too late*. I cannot force you to do anything. None
of the UBS can force a decision on you. It is a requirement of the
ONE, the Most Merciful, that 'each soul is responsible for itself.'
The ONE has mercifully placed within each soul *willpower*. You
have to will your choice into existence. You have to separate yourself from evil, even though it is so familiar to you. Then bow down
in sincere prayer to the ONE who created all souls. Lah-il-la-ha-
illah-huwa." He ended his talk. I remember Bomber Girl said that
they mix some prayers into whatever language they are speaking in
because it is a reminder and a better way to talk. He was applauded
wildly.

The Spanish male youth looked like any Puerto Rican from
Brooklyn. He was handsome. Not as handsome as Poppa Santiaga, of course. This guy was obviously no gangster or hustler even
though he was strapped. He seemed very emotional. He held the
mic with two hands and put it too close to his mouth.

"*Madre,* don't worry, Momma. We love Jesus. And we know you
love Jesus. Your sons forgive like Jesus taught us forgiveness. I am
here because I love you, and because I want you to know that yes
Jesus was a real man. The Most High created the soul of Jesus. From
even before the birth of Jesus, the Most High gave Jesus many gifts,
mercies and blessings. Of course, who was the mother of Jesus? It
was Maryam, I mean Mary. The ONE also gave Mary many gifts
and many mercies, Ah-hum-doo-lah-lah. I'm sure Jesus was very
grateful to have a mother like Mary. I know I would be so grateful
too, Momma.

"The truth is, Momma, there is only ONE GOD. The ONE
GOD has no partners and no children. The men who the ONE
GOD created and gave mercies of great abundance to such as
Jesus, Moses, Abraham, are called Prophets, not sons or daughters
of the ONE GOD. I am saying this so that when you bow down
to make your prayers, you pray properly and sincerely to the ONE.
Many mothers are here today because they don't have anything
in the right order. While on Earth, they were sometimes saying

good things but living evil lives and making wrong choices. We forgive. Think of it this way. You are asking for help, but you were asking the wrong person. Jesus walked the walk that the ONE assigned him. Jesus was a servant to the ONE. I am a servant to the ONE, so are you momma. Jesus, while he was among the Earth's living, forgave and forgave and forgave. The One and Only God, however, is the Most Merciful and only All-Powerful, Maker of All souls, including all Prophets, like Jesus, peace be upon him." The Spanish guy ended his talk. This time he was the one in tears.

The Indian guy had an outburst when he grabbed the mic from the Spanish dude. "Maa, I wanted nothing more than to taste a meal that you prepared for me with the same amount of love that I have for you. Maa, there is so much that we UBS are not saying. They are hard words to hear. But I've learned that the truest words are hard for most to hear. But without the truest words, I fear that you will be part of the endless punishment, the Eternal Fire. I cannot bear to exist knowing that this is the end of your story. I cannot survive if you cannot survive. It would be unbearable. Maa, you see we are UBS, the meaning is 'unborn souls.' All of the sons standing here today, the reason you do not recognize us as your sons is because you and each of the women here has aborted us before we could have the chance to be born. We were sucked and scraped out of the heaven that was your womb. Still, your sons and daughters who you chose to murder rather than give birth to still love you and we forgive!

"You know that idol who you place on the mantel is nothing. It is powerless. It cannot save you. And the time that you spent hating all of the people around you who worshipped the ONE and who refused to bow down or praise your idols, it was all time wasted, hatred wasted, and it hurt your soul instead of the souls of the ones you hated. It became the reason that you are here, One Stop Before the Drop. So Maa, please, leave it all behind you now. Please let's meet in Heaven, *InshAllah,* and I am still wanting to taste the dal and rice and paratha you prepare for me."

Overwhelmed by his own words, he threw the mic down. It made a disturbing amplified noise and created a feedback.

I thought it was foul play, saying that we cannot be forced to do anything then breaking our legs so that we have no choice but to listen to all of this blah blah.

"Why ain't y'all looking for your fathers!?" a lady who was obviously an African American shouted. The sobbing thousands turned their faces towards her. I don't think the UBS on the stage could even hear her. "Nine times out of ten, your bullshit-ass fathers are the reason we aborted you!" she yelled, stirring up a commotion. One of the UBS from the side came forward. He handed her a mic so she could be heard by who I guess were the leaders on the stage. She repeated her words. Now six hundred bitches were in an uproar cheering her on. "And yeah, I might have aborted a couple of y'all. But what about the kids I did keep and raise. Raising them is how I figured out I better abort y'all." She laughed, and her laughter was amplified across the wide field. A white woman jumped up and took the mic after a small tussle.

"I think we have more women here today than sons as you call yourselves. I think us women should all stick together. We need to push back against anyone who wants to tell us what to do with our bodies! Our bodies, our lives! And why would we need to worship some so-called God who wants to punish us for making our own damned decisions! He is just another man telling us what to do! Our bodies, our lives! Our bodies, our lives!" she chanted, and soon most were chanting along with her.

"I reject that! I reject that!" she screamed. Then the chanting of the crowd switched to "I reject that! I reject that! I reject that!"

One of the handsome Black sons stepped forward and spoke. "The focus of the raid that happened Earth hours ago was on our mothers. We sons used our combined mercies to make it happen. Most of our mothers have already received our mercies. And once we utilize the third mercy it is our last chance to have any contact with you at all. Our strategy was to each use one mercy to address a large group of mothers all at once. We believed that if each mother saw how many women had fallen for the same evil and made the same choices, it would cause you to stop, think, reflect, and then choose the right path, which wasn't happening when we engaged you one on one.

"We sons also love our fathers. UBS are eighty-five percent love. For the UBS gathered here in this section, fathers are not the focus of today's mission. However, there are one trillion UBS. One trillion of us who have been aborted by our mothers who we forgive. The three hundred and fifty sons gathered here today are only a handful. The majority of UBS are right now bowed in prayer asking for mercy for their parents' souls.

"This battalion you see here are the UBS working the west side of the Last Stop Before the Drop. There is another UBS battalion on the East side addressing fathers the same way we are addressing you, with the same truth that we are sharing here. Fathers will have only one way out of the Last Stop Before the Drop same as you. They must humble themselves to the ONE who gave them life. Same as you! There is no other way for all men, all women, and all civilizations. All of the pain that each of us from various nations have experienced. All of the evil, racism, hatred, and hurt. All of it was a test and a punishment for humanity's rejection of the ONE who created all. For humanity's lack of gratitude. As punishment to the arrogant, the bold, the niggardly, the spiteful, the forgetful, the worshippers of all that should never ever had been worshipped.

"And, there are five UBS battalions at war in the air right this minute with the devils who are fighting to win back your souls," he explained, and that set off a loud clamoring of chatter among the women.

I don't know if they were excited the way I was. It was just confirmed that Dat Nigga was at war. He was fighting his way back to get me. That's the only reason he hadn't showed up yet. Probably all of the women here had somebody they were waiting on to come get them. I am sure that none of their men are as loving and reliable as Dat Nigga.

"Time is running out. We will conduct a roll call of all the mothers. When you hear your name, by the mercy of the Most High you will have the strength and the ability to please come forward to meet your unborn son or sons. Once you are in the presence of your son or your multiple sons, because some of us are actually brothers, you must decide if you will walk on the straight path and make a sincere effort to change for the better. If you choose good over evil, right over wrong, we sons will lead you to a beautiful masjid, where you can shower nicely. A wide peaceful space where you can self-reflect fully. A place with sincere teachers who will share with you from the Book of Guidance. We will distribute you clean new garments, and you can prepare your sincere prayers in a safe place, as mothers and as women, not as pets or animals or prisoners. And within the mosque, there is continuous light, warmth, and welcome."

I listened carefully to the most important parts. When they call my name, my legs would unlock and then I must make a decision. However, they were not going to call my name or even know it. I was just at the wrong place at the wrong time because Succubus put me there. There would be no way for any of these other bitches' sons to know who I was, or to have known that I was locked there in the creature factory, warehouse, whatever.

After hundreds of names were called out, I heard my name. My legs unlocked. I did not walk to meet any bogus person who claimed to be my son. None of these dudes were any of the women's here sons. If a bitch aborted you, that's it. And apparently there's at least a trillion women who agree with me. There's a trillion UBS, which equals a trillion abortions. Truthfully, as good as I am in math, my capacity of understanding stops at billion. I don't know the name of the next set of numbers after billions. I don't know where in the number line trillion falls in. I got common sense, though. So I know it's a whole lotta motherfuckers!

Before my name got called out, which I never expected, I had already charted my way out of here in my mind. Now that my legs were mine again, I was on the move. If I cut through the left side of the endless gathering of women, I could stand closest to the perimeter of it all. If Dat Nigga shows up, and I knew he would, he would be parked all the way on the outside a short distance from wherever the UBS were doing their thing. He liked to keep a low profile, even though he always pushed a high-profile whip.

"Ms. Winter," I heard a male voice calling me. I didn't answer right away. I was thinking about if it was to my benefit or not. I kept weaving through the enormous crowd. Figured whoever it was I could lose him easily. I felt him following me, though. I didn't look back. After swerving and zigzagging, I felt his hand grip my right arm. I turned. Don't like nobody touching me without my permission. It was a young guy, maybe sixteen or so. Instead of a sash of bullets, he wore a colorful strap that held his drum close against his body. And a backpack on his back. When he smiled his teeth sparkled. The whites of his eyes were like beams of light. I had never seen those type of lighted eyes. Well, only once, Midnight's eyes were like this. He was the only other one. But, I was trying not to think about him anymore for obvious reasons.

"Siddiqah said you would take this path out of the gathering once your name was called," he said very politely like he was trained to speak a certain way to adults. I don't even think of myself as an adult. I missed turning into one from eighteen forward. Fifteen years on lockup since then. So, I feel like those years don't count. I'm really like nineteen right now. A nineteen-years female who died young.

"Siddiqah?" I repeated, like it was a question. He ignored my pretending to not know that it was the name of Bomber Girl.

"Yes, Siddiqah. She really loves you," he said. I wasn't used to dudes who talked openly, frequently, and freely about love the way these UBS dudes did. I assumed he was one of them, but since his outfit was a little different, I wasn't sure. It's a strange mixture, these nice-physique young men with sharp, handsome looks and strong voices, but who keep using words like *forgiveness* and *love*. They got that rough exterior thugged-out look. Bullets and bombs, cooled-out uniforms and even drums gave them masculine sex appeal. But then their manner of speaking and word choices, topics and style doesn't match up.

"She sent you a gift," he said as he removed his drum strap, rested his drum on his kicks, and reached for his knapsack behind him. He pulled out a package wrapped in paisley tissue paper. As soon as he pulled it out the scent of her hilab went rushing up my nostrils. It was a beautiful extremely relaxing scent. I imagined it was her knockout potion. Once you inhale enough of it for long enough, you somehow give her anything she wants. Ha-ha. It was a delightful thought, except when I thought about whether or not she had ever used it on Dat Nigga.

"Here. Take it. She wanted you to have it." He held it out for me to grab hold of. I didn't. Instead I asked, "What is it?" When he unwrapped it and held it up so I could fully see it, it was so amazing that I instinctively pressed my face into the expensive fabric. Then I took hold of it.

"She said to show you the label because that would be so important to you." So I checked the label, but I did not have to. It was designed by Tom Ford, oh my. A regal black layered pleated Chiffon *I Rule the World* dress. It is delicate, elegant, and feminine. He pulled out a next item wrapped in white wax gift paper. He didn't bother handing it to me. He began carefully unwrapping it instead. He handled it as though there was something alive inside. Or something precious. It was a Burberry tapered trench. The color was pearl. And I loved that it caused me to think of that pearl door in Midnight's house. I had the urge to put it on and return there just to lean up against that pearl door with this designer trench on and nothing else.

He unfolded the coat carefully and was holding it up by the fabric shoulders.

"She asked me to help you put it on."

I removed the white mink. Now that I had worn it unexpectedly to the Rally of the Sons, it was time to put it in storage. Only a broke bitch replays her fashion. No matter how expensive or limited edition it is, once you flash out in it and exhaust that one appearance, one event, day or night wearing it, lay it to rest.

He pulled out a wide, taut fabric shopping bag and placed my mink in it. He sat the bag down and helped me to put on the pearl trench. It fit. It fit perfectly. He pulled one more thing from his backpack. I laughed soon as I saw it. It was a pair of high-top black Prada kicks. Not what I would ever imagine matching up with the mean-ass dress and the bad-ass coat.

"Siddiqah said she saw the most incredible pair of heels that seemed to be made for only your feet. But then she said she bought these kicks instead. They are more suited for you because you like to run away, according to Siddiqah," he said, looking into my eyes with his lighted eyes. I turned back towards the stage. The line of mothers going to meet their unborn sons was crowded. But there were many women who remained seated. Perhaps they were like me, wanted to leave what was done, done.

"She's not here at this event. She's on the south side fighting the devils." Me and him stood silent for a bit, even though we were surrounded by more than a thousand people chattering and milling around, and of course the boom of the speakers as more and more women's names were being announced. Instead of saying thank you, which would have made me feel like I owed him something for delivering it, and owed her something for giving it to me in the first place, I asked him, "Are you her man?"

"We are both UBS, Siddiqah and I. Because we are unborn souls, we cannot have the kind of man-woman relations that you and our father had."

"Our father!" I repeated.

"Yes, his name is Sean D'Costa, but you know him only as Boom."

"I know your father?" I said.

"Of course you must. Siddiqah and I are twins. You are our mother, Boom is our father. You killed us both when you were eighteen. But we both love you and we forgive you." I dropped the shopping bag.

Beep-beep. A midnight-blue BMW 7 series pulled up and sounded a powerful horn. It caught more than my attention. But the young drummer didn't turn back to see who it was. He was still staring at me.

"Ma, let me help you put your kicks on," he said. I was like *Ma!* Still, I squatted. He moved his drum to the side. He removed his jacket and laid it on the ground for me to sit on. I sat. He removed my boots carefully by holding the back of my thigh and the back of the heel at the same time. A careless rough nigga would of yanked them off recklessly. He wiped my feet with his hands even though they were somehow already clean. Then he loosened the adhesive strap and the Prada laces and put the right kick on my right foot. It fit perfectly. "Hold out your other foot," he instructed me. As I did, I saw Lucifer 66 get out the BMW, looking irritated and impatient and staring straight at me. He was standing outside of the green atmosphere beneath the blackness. He was not far off, but too far for me to throw my voice and let him know to give me six minutes and I would come right over.

"You good now, *InshAllah,*" the drummer said, and stood up. He folded down my red thigh-high boots and placed them in the shopping bag, buffered by the wrapping paper. He was preventing the mink from getting soiled. He was thoughtful and charming like Poppa. He was not deep-black skinned but he was beautiful like Midnight. He stepped back to admire me while handing me the shopping bag. "Perfect. The trench looks cleaner, more modest, nice quality. Besides, with the mink everybody knows it's you. Sometimes it's better to slow it down, play it cool." He said and smiled a million-dollar smile. Because I was looking at the young drummer, I didn't see Dat Nigga running forward so fast he seemed

to be flying. Apparently some other UBS dudes did. They intercepted Dat Nigga like they were missiles and he was the bull's-eye.
His body blew backwards with such force from the impact of the
hit that he flew over his car and must have landed there. When
he dropped down it must have shook the ground because out of
the blackness arrived tens and tens of soldiers, who came so swiftly
they had to have been there all along, camouflaged.

The young drummer snatched up his drum and began drumming furiously. It was no longer music. It was a war call. UBS who
had been guarding the women flew up and turned into globs of
light. They attacked without hesitation the soldiers moving through
the black atmosphere who could hardly be seen because they were
all black against a black backdrop. Obviously the UBS could see
them, though. When they hit one it exploded. And in what would
be called the sky, but is nothing like the Earth's sky, explosions
were happening everywhere. The UBS were so fierce and aggressive
though, they never let one black soldier into the green atmosphere.
Instead they blew the black blobs up in their own black territory.
Half of the six hundred women were way across field from the lineup to meet their sons and to decide which path they would travel
on. I was where the action was. A whole bunch of bitches still seated
in the field were just staring up like they were watching the fireworks display at Universal Studios. I calculated that the ground was
safe except for the falling flames that landed creating patches of fire
on the black side. I picked up my shopping bag, dashed from the
green side to the black side, passed the BMW. I had to rescue Dat
Nigga, who showed up to rescue me.

He was laid out on the driver's side of the BMW. He seemed
knocked out or dead. Flames shot out of his chest from the spot
where his heart should be located. I grabbed the white mink out of
the shopping bag and threw it over the fire. When it didn't put it
out, I picked it back up immediately and used it to swat the flames.
After I got rid of the flames, I tried to drag him into the whip. His
body was way too heavy. I smelled her hilab. Stars suddenly rained

down and she appeared standing over me as I tried to drag my for-ever nigga. "Help me lift him," I said.

"Are you pretending that you do not understand?" she asked me, with her hands balled into fists and seated on her waist. I didn't say shit back.

"Just admit that you have been making some awful choices and fleeing from the ones you should embrace. And embracing the ones whom no one should ever embrace. Just will your existence to change. Make one simple sincere prayer to the Most High, say 'Lah-il-la-ha-illah-huwa' and ask for mercy on your soul!"

A ride-or-die bitch doesn't kick a nigga when he's down. She never abandons her guy. That's why I was in the driver's seat speeding into darkness in a 7 series. I flipped it in my favor. Siddiqah helped me pull Dat Nigga into the backseat. In exchange, I told her I'd think about how I wanted to use my willpower. She reminded me that the third mercy was her last. "If you don't see the light on the third mercy it is the painful end to our relationship and to your salvation, I believe," she warned.

I didn't have directions or navigation to the firehouse. But I knew how to drive. And I remembered to just speed through a long black tunnel for a long time till we reached a steep hill. Downshift and speed down. So I did it.

13.

I am not a dumb bitch. But, I am not easily won over by anyone. I am not religious. I'm not even like the fake bitches who also say they are not religious but then claim that they are spiritual. People should keep it one hundred. If you don't believe in God and don't want to jump through hoops and follow a bunch of boring-ass rules, then don't. Don't try and front it off like there's something else to it when there is not. That's why I hate phonies. People who dress up in some particularly poorly designed outfit claiming that they are part of a religion and start talking a whole bunch of shit about this and that. That's why I hate preachers. They want to do the same shit that they be telling everybody else *not to do*. And *they do it too!* People should just admit that so-called evil *feels better*. Everything religious people say we should not do is the exact things that give us who do it that good feeling, that excitement, that joy and relief. What could be wrong with a bitch who likes to style and stunt, fuck whomever she wants to fuck, throw back a few glasses of Henny, puff a few joints, party at a packed party, fight when she's mad, fight back when she's violated, and change her mind about all of the above whenever her mind changes? I say that's how everybody really wants to live. Even though I don't know everybody. The proof is in the action.

These were my thoughts as I sat parked outside of the firehouse, my nigga knocked out in the backseat. Or blown up or whatever. I couldn't carry him in. He was all muscle and strength. I thought a cold glass of water thrown in his face might wake him up. Then I thought again and something just told me not to put even one drop of water on the man who I met as he walked out of a six-foot flame. Who preferred fire over light. *Who never* stepped into the shower with me like lovers do, and who described himself as the Master of Smoke. If you put matches in water, they won't work anymore. A wet cigarette ain't shit. The fire department uses water hoses to put out huge fires. Water deads it completely. So I canceled out throwing water in his face to wake him up.

My scheming mind booted up. *Maybe I should use this as an opportunity.* I needed that flashlight. I jumped out the car, ran to the door, and remembered I didn't have no key. Then Succubus flashed in my mind. She was the one always walking in whenever she wants because she has a set of his keys. Me and that bitch gonna thump. One of us is gonna die. She's big-bodied, though. That's putting it mildly. I was remembering once when she had her oversize size-12 feet, only the toes though, the rest of her foot couldn't fit, jammed into my furry slippers that Dat Nigga bought specifically for my feet to welcome me back on our night of pleasure. The bitch's ankles were ashy and her flesh heels were like leather, probably from dragging her bare feet, the parts that couldn't fit into any regular shoes or slippers, on the ground. How a bitch gon' seduce a nigga like that?

I ran back to the driver's side. I checked on the car-key ring that he had laid on the middle front-seat island. I thought maybe his house key was there. It wasn't. I opened up the backseat and ran my fingers over his pockets. When I grazed over his thick dick that was inviting even when he was knocked out and limp, I got excited. Had to take a deep breath and remind myself to focus. *Found it!*

Inside the always-dark corridor, I could locate the closet—by memory, of course. My eyes were useless in this deep darkness. Instead, I searched with my hands. Once inside of his closet, I searched with my hands on the closet floor first. Felt a lot of shoes and kicks, even found a set of keys in what felt like a boot. I didn't need them. I already got the house key. Standing up, I ran all of the inside and outside pockets of each of the jackets, sweaters, and coats hanging in the dark closet. I came upon six blunts, a couple of chains and locks, strings and ropes, and even almost sliced off the tip of my finger on what must have been an unsheathed and open, small but very sharp knife. Glad I didn't grab it too hard. Instinctively I sucked my fingers. From the taste I discovered that I didn't shed any blood. There was not even a small cut. There should have been. I knocked a bunch of shit off the top shelf. It was too high so I had to jump to reach it. Everything came tumbling down on my head. Finally found the flashlight on the floor.

Of course I was working up a plan. Now I had some weapons in case she showed up. Or anybody, really, who ain't him. Brooklyn taught me to always have a weapon even if it's only a small sharp razor, tucked beneath my tongue. I could whip her with the chain, like she did me. Strangle her with the twine, or stab her with the knife. Anything I did to her after she separated me from my man and moved me into the animal factory and caged me in could not be considered an overreaction by anyone reasonable. I put all of my weapons in my saddle bag, which I located. I threw it over one shoulder and wore it like a sash. I was starting to see the reasoning behind Bomber Girl and her UBS keeping their ammo on display: first as a warning; second, so they would never be caught with their guard down; third, keeping it within reach.

I searched high and low with the beam of light from the flash. I couldn't find one lighter, one match, or a flame from a stove to use to ignite a few of his torches. More importantly, I was keyed up to puff one blunt to help me think and relax with a nice head.

On the wall I found a metal panel. On closer inspection it popped open. When I shined the light on it, it reminded me of the fuse box in the projects. I flipped a switch thinking it might be a way of turning on a lighting system that he never wanted to use, but that I could really use at the moment. Instead I heard something draw open. The direction the sound came from was not where the front door was located. I followed the sound with my one beam of light. While walking towards the sound, I fell into an opening on the floor that was never there before. It felt like I fell twenty feet or deeper. I landed in some type of prickly-feeling stuff that might have saved a dead bitch like me from experiencing my second or third death. I lost count. I felt around searching for my flashlight, hoping it didn't break when I fell.

"You heard that?" a distant voice that I had heard at least once before asked.

"Maybe 66 is back," another voice that I had never heard before replied.

"Yo, yo, yo, yo!" the familiar voice called out from the distance. *It's Iblis,* the nigga who called my nigga on some business-type matter, what seemed like a while way back. Oh yeah, he was Dat Nigga's brother, I remembered. They discussed their father who had built some type of empire and who they both worked for. I thought to myself, *Maybe I could get him to help me pull Dat Nigga out of the backseat.* He must know how to heal him. Since they're related, they must be made the same. *Should I approach them? Should I wait till they walk over to where I am? Or, should I hide?* My mind was racing back and forth.

"Ssh, that ain't him," Iblis said.

"I didn't think so. Heard he got bombed the fuck up on the east side," the other voice said. "That was after he lost a whole team warring with those fucking pesty-ass UBS on the south side," he added. Then Iblis said, "Yeah, bro lost his soldiers in that battle earlier today. They can be replaced. He survived. He probably messed up after that though, when he went east looking for that sexy bitch he rides through with. Heard she got him open," Iblis said. Their flame torches that they must have been carrying began piercing the blackness of the atmosphere down here where I am. Their voices were drawing near. I sensed a threat even though their talk was not threatening.

"Open ain't the word for it. Look at this place! Brother is losing his touch. His whole barn house got raided right when it was time to feed the fire! Your father gon' sacrifice him."

I figured out it was hay. I had fallen in the donkey bin. I was in the animal warehouse factory, where Succubus caged and abandoned me. I never expected that it was beneath the firehouse. We always entered the firehouse at ground level. This had to be an underground level that extended way beyond the perimeter of the firehouse. Did my nigga run it? Why didn't he simply walk to the underground, which apparently he could reach from his playpen, so he could find me? I was gone for at least six feedings, which should be six days. Would he not know to look down here first? Did Succubus deceive him? Did she tell him that I ran off on my own through the front door and couldn't be found? Would he fall for some bullshit like that? No, of course he wouldn't. Especially not if he really loves me.

I wanted to get up, crawl or walk or run away. I was froze with indecision. I knew to make any move, even a small one, would cause the sound of the hay rustling beneath me. That sound would be distinct enough for them to know exactly where I was. I wasn't confident that if I just introduced myself as his brother's woman, that all would run smoothly. I opened my saddle bag quietly. However, the slight shift of my arm from right to left caused a slight sound. Those two had been stopped talking. I knew they were on alert. I buried myself beneath the hay, thinking, "*Okay they know where the sound is coming from. But if they don't see a donkey, they'll walk right by.*" Soon I felt their presence had arrived in front of the donkey cage.

"The sound definitely came from here," the unfamiliar voice said.

"Must be a serpent," Iblis said and threw a flame into the hay. The stall caught fire. To beat burning, I threw the hay off of me. I was backed in and trapped by the quick heated blaze.

"It's that sexy bitch who put a spell on our brother," Iblis said.

He pulled opened the iron gate, walked through the fire, unfazed by its mounting intensity. He removed his jacket, wrapped it around me, and carried me out.

"Okay, you can put me down now," I told him. He was holding me too tightly. We were out of the blaze. The other one was spraying it down with the hose that had been hanging on the opposite wall.

"Bitch, say thank you." Iblis threw me down, lifted me back up by my trench collar, cocked back his hand, and slapped me as though I was a man. Before I hit the ground again, I went straight in my saddle bag and pulled the knife, leaped up, and pointed it at him. He laughed. "What you gon' do with that?" he asked. The other brother began laughing and dropped the hose. I lunged at Iblis. He jumped back, but not with fear. He jumped back playfully, as though this was amusing. I ran through the opening. They both ran after me. Iblis grabbed the saddle-bag shoulder strap and used it to pull me back. Once in his clutches, he wrapped the saddle-bag strap around my neck and began to choke me with it. The other brother watched with joy in his eyes. Right before I passed out from strangulation, Iblis let go. "Maybe we should taste it for ourselves," he said to the other one.

The other brother did not even wait for an answer. He grabbed my pearl-colored Burberry trench that I had received from Bomber Girl and pulled it off of me. Iblis threw me down and tore off my white brocade mini. "I'll take the front. You take the back," Iblis said, dropping his pants and pushing way up deep inside of me. He was stroking hard and licking my face with his long tongue. I turned my face away. When I did, I saw it laying there. It must have been in my new coat pocket somehow.

Iblis raised up off of me. "The bitch wasn't worth it. Maybe the back end's better," he said, and flipped me over. The other brother was already out of his pants, erect in anticipation of going in my ass. I reached with what little strength remained in me. I grabbed the grenade, pulled the clip, and I bombed 'em both.

"Siddiqah really loves you," Young Drummer had said before he said anything else to me. The truth is, I didn't believe him. I didn't even care. But I spent three decades of my life without being raped. Rape and fucking is not the same thing. Now, I have been raped as a dead bitch, which somehow made it worse and more disrespectful. Now I can say that I loved her. Why? Because she did something almost no one in my lifetime could do. She made me feel something. By her placing the grenade in my pocket, is what only a real bitch would do. Instead of blah blah blahing me to death, she took action. She planted what she knew I would need to survive. And ultimately, whomever truly loves you or anything, protects it by any means necessary.

14.

I made my own torch out of the fire that was shooting out of Iblis' chest as he lay knocked out in the same way my nigga was knocked out when I discovered him on the ground by his BMW. Since my flashlight turned out to be broken, I used the torch to escape from the massive underground animal warehouse. It was a long trip. I had to walk all the way around since I had no way to zoom back up twenty feet into the playpen. There were no stairs beneath that drop. I'm sure there was a reason. I felt horrible about the rape, but felt good about leaving both bodies down there on the ground without any pants or underwear. Her grenades were strange weapons, I thought. They didn't cause the body to shatter into tiny bits and pieces. Apparently they only killed the target they hit. Bombs I've seen in films blow up everything until nothing is left but ashes and dust. But I had exploded both niggas without hurting myself at all.

When I finally made it back to his BMW, Dat Nigga was gone. I got worried that he had healed so swiftly without any real medical care. Does that mean that even though he got bombed, he could in a matter of what I guessed was two hours or so easily recover? And if it did mean that, would his brothers Iblis and the other one also wake up and walk away in two hours from when I bombed them? If so, what would Dat Nigga do about them niggas who violated me? Would blood be thicker than water? Or would he step up like

a man is supposed to? For me, that would be the measure of everything moving forward. If he defended me and punished them severely, me and him was locked and loaded forever. If he fronted
and gave me the same feeling I had about Bullet, I was out! I didn't
know where I would go to, but I would be damned if I let a family
of brothers use me as their fuck hole. I stood looking around into
the blackness. But it was futile because when you look around in
blackness all you see is black. I felt a little vulnerable because now I
was naked underneath the pearl three-quarter-length tapered coat.
I wasn't wearing underwear in the first place and I had burned the
rape dress before I left from down there. I had on my saddle bag
and my Prada kicks with no socks, which was not how I normally
rock my footwear.

I looked again into the whip window. My shopping bag con-
taining my new Tom Ford black Chiffon pleated dress, my white
mink, and thigh-high boots, which I had left on the front passenger seat, was gone. *Maybe nothing is wrong,* I reassured myself. *Dat
Nigga is inside the firehouse.* He had carried the shopping bag inside
with him of course because he knew it was mine and that I must be
the one who at minimal rode in the BMW with him to reach home,
or if he thought about me the right way, he'd know that a loyal action bitch like me saved him. He'd realize that he didn't drive himself home. I was the driver who drove him to safety. *Yeah, that's what
happened,* I reassured myself, took three deep breaths, and walked to
the firehouse front door. I smiled. He had left it unlocked for me.
The moment I went in, I could see that the torches were lit in the
playpen. Of course he was home. I dropped my guard some.

Succubus was in there. I saw her walking away from the front
door wearing my white mink by draping the hood over her head
since she couldn't fit her body in it or even push her man arms into
my sleeves. I knew it was her even though I could only see her from
behind. No one else would wear a coat, no matter how badass and
designer expensive it was, with a big-ass smoke hole in it, where I
had used it to put out Dat Nigga's chest fire. And no one else would

almost break their ashy ankles wearing red python boots like flip-flops with the butter leather folded down because her calves were worse than her feet and were way too bulky to fit inside the tight lean design.

When she turned back to see who walked in behind her, she was holding a blunt loosely between two fingers. She lit it without matches or a lighter, just using her fingertip it seemed. Right then, I was like, *Oh, she's one of them.* She took a long toke of the blunt, then held her hand out, offering me to hit it. I hated her but loved the blunt, so I walked up close and took a few pulls.

"Which one are you?" she asked me after a long pause taken for us both to feel the hit of the weed. I felt the buzz and the insult she was throwing at me as though I was any random bitch walking into the firehouse.

"I'll give you a hint," I told her. "That's my mink you are wearing and those are my boots. You keep them. I don't want them back. They're yours." I spoke calmly, my words pushing through her like a knife. She kicked off the boots first. I could see her black toenails. Damn! Not one bad nail, all ten thick, black, and curved like claws. She flung off the hood. The mink dropped to the floor. I didn't know whether it was the weed or the tricks of trying to see through the glare of the flames, but her eyes seemed to be red. Not the whites of her eyes. The actual eyeball seemed like beams of red light.

"No, you take your shit with you back to wherever you came from. He's gone."

"Where to?" I asked.

"His father picked up his body in his body truck. He'll be fed to the fire tonight. May already be burning." She said like it was no loss to her. Like Dat Nigga was trash being picked up and thrown out by the sanitation man who happened to be his father.

"Body truck?" I repeated.

"You heard right. Dat Nigga and his soldiers caught a bad bombing by those pesky UBS who ain't from down here and who ain't supposed to even be in our territory. Shayton, that's Dat

Nigga's father, in case you don't already know. But you strolled in here like you think you live here. Like you think you know so much, so you must. If you really know Dat Nigga at all, you must know who his father is. He runs the Last Stop. Anyway, Dat Nigga's father was out collecting the bodies himself, which he doesn't normally do. Must have known Dat Nigga got hit. He collected his son and threw his body in the back of the body truck." Her red eyes were peering into mine. The expression on her face was like, *How you like me now, bitch?* I was hurt about losing Dat Nigga, but since I knew that she was trying to raise a reaction out of me, I kept steady with my game face on.

"Where are you coming in from?" she asked me suddenly, switching to disguised friendly small talk. I want to get at her and let her know I'm not some random bitch.

"I'm coming from the same place you left me at, after you slammed me into the wall," I said, pointing downwards. She busted out laughing, ran and grabbed one of the torches, and used it to highlight the bloodstain on the wall right where she had thrown me. "Oh, you were that stuck-up little dog," she said. "Now that I think about it, even now, *you still look like that little bitch.* You must have let Dat Nigga butt-fuck you and that's how you turned into a damn dog!" She cracked up even more. I didn't have a rapid comeback. My mind suddenly went to review mode and I was seeing the face of the pretty bitch who had said that it definitely was Dat Nigga who had turned her into a rat. I didn't believe her. But now Succubus was saying essentially the same thing. Then my mind clicked.

"Yeah, I was the one who turned into the dog. But I was also the dog who saw you get butt-fucked right here on the floor. After you begged him, that's all he gave you! So if you're not a lying bitch trying to blame Dat Nigga for turning me into a dog, why didn't you turn into the fucking pig you are?"

"You stupid little stuck-up bitch. You must have thought that you and Dat Nigga was gonna get married and live happily ever after here in his house. Stop dreaming! First off, you're a dead human. Duh! That means you *can't* ever live happily ever after." She laughed. "How could you be so fucking dumb? It's the dead humans, the women and the men, who come down here and let Incubus fuck them in the ass. It's the Tyrant who forbids ass-fucking. It's the Tyrant who turns the dead humans into all types of animals as a form of punishment. Your stupid little ass is supposed to wake up and figure it out. Then you supposed to kiss the Tyrant's ass because it's the only way out of the Last Stop Before the Drop!" She folded her arms across her chest. I was still heated at the one thing in particular. This ugly bitch Succubus thought she was smarter, slicker, and better than me. I was like, *Fuck that.* I couldn't let her get away believing she has the upper hand or that I would ever trust anything she had to say.

"Incubus didn't fuck me. Dat Nigga did. It was the best sex I ever had. He loved me and that's why you're tight. Even a dog could see that he didn't give one fuck about you. That's why you had to beg him. That's why you didn't get no thrills. He couldn't even fake loving you."

"Dat Nigga *is* the Incubus, you dumb bitch. You down here ready to throw him your soul when it's obvious you don't even know who he is." She turned the hand torch towards me like she was going burn me with it. I took three steps back. Getting burnt was not an option. I've seen burnt bitches before on lockup. Their burnt faces turned pink and swollen into blisters and bubbles. Then the doctors have to take skin from their ass and stitch it over the pink. Then the face turns into a monstrous mismatched patch of pink and ass skin. That would never be my look. If it was, it would be the only means of turning a bitch like me into a suicidal bitch.

"And you're delusional. You seem to think you are the only one, or the true love of Incubus. Did you see how many other animals were down there with your dumb ass? All of them were either as dumb as you or even dumber. All of them came back for seconds and let Incubus ass-fuck them, fully aware from the first time they turned into some filthy creature how it would turn out all over again. That's why you're back here, isn't it. Is it your second time? Or is it your third?" she asked, but I didn't say nothing back. She laughed. "See, you came back for the third strike, didn't you!" she gloated.

"Your ass is right in here in the same house where I am right now. So who's the dumbass?"

"You!" She laughed so hard her face appeared to switch back and forth from its normal ugly, but human appearance, to some type of dangerous fanged beast. "The Tyrant made all of us. You must know that. Even an ant and a tick and a worm is aware that there is only ONE. That same ONE who created good also created evil. The same ONE is the ONE who created every living thing. I was created to do exactly what I am doing and I hate it. But bitch, this is who I am. That's why I did not turn into a pig as you suggested. The Tyrant, who is the best knower of all things, is not out to punish me for being the succubus that he created me to be. The Tyrant is using me to wake your dumb ass up. But you have such a sturdy brand of stupid that you can't awaken. The Tyrant made you look so attractive that you worship only yourself. I don't give a fuck about you worshipping yourself. All succubuses and all incubuses worship ourselves. That's how this whole thing popped off. The Tyrant who created every goddamn living thing ordered Shayton to bow down to Adam, the human. Shayton refused. The All-Powerful Tyrant casted Shayton out of the Heavens. So Shayton hustled up and built up this whole empire down here."

There was nothing separating me from her except the flame dancing atop of her hand torch. "Incubus never loved you. He never loved me either. He butt-fucks 'cause that's how Incubus get down. We all do it naturally and prefer it that way. But ass-fucking is sodomy. It's forbidden to humans by the One. That's why y'all suffer when you do it. But y'all all too dumb to understand. And y'all are too much just like us to care. That's why I love Shayton. I think he was right not to bow down to Adam. What the fuck for? You humans are the weakest dumbest pieces of shit." Then she torched my hair. Jealous bitches always go for the hair first. That's how you know they want what you got. They're jealous of you. Now I was on fire.

I dashed to the bathroom, slamming and locking the door behind me. I threw back the shower curtain and turned on the water. I snatched down the showerhead and put out the hair fire before it had burnt off all of my hair. I stood stroking my hair and shivering from the cold water. Half of it was gone. I wanted to check the mirror to see if it had burned evenly, or if it had left bald spots. But as usual, it was dark in the bathroom. I couldn't see in the mirror. And even if I looked in the mirror, unless I was in an animal's body, I couldn't see my own reflection.

"Dumb bitch! Come back out here. Let me school your dumb ass some more," she said, steadily banging on the door. I was still stroking my hair. It was no longer long enough for me to gather it into a ponytail. I couldn't finger-comb it up into a bun. With a rubber band, maybe it could gather into a pigtail. I was so fucking angry, I wasn't game to be no afro-wearing bitch. I didn't know of any hair salons down here. I couldn't really hook myself up right, without a mirror or reflection to confirm my look.

I guess it's okay. Succubus said that Dat Nigga was dead and gone, fed to the fire. Only good thing is I would never want him to see me in this condition. I was still not sure what parts of what she was saying were true. I could not let her be the one who decided whether he loved me or not or whether or not I would continue to love him.

I picked up the scented candle jar, remembering the sweetness and thoroughness of his love for me. I stuck the jar underneath the downpour of the shower water. I turned the shower off. Now there was only the sound of her banging. Quietly I unlocked the door. She must have still heard the lock click though, 'cause she stopped banging. I snatched the door open and threw the jar of cold water right onto her face. Her head began disintegrating. Her neck was sending off curling black smoke. Her bulky body fell to the floor. Fire sprung up through her chest. I looked down on her. "You look better with no head, you ugly bitch. Tell Shayton to come back through and throw your stinking ass on his body truck. I may be a dumb dead bitch, but I'm a fucking survivor."

I walked out wearing my Prada kicks, the wet pearl Burberry trench coat, and clutching the saddle-bag strap. I jumped into Dat Nigga's BMW and sped off. For better or worse, I am the real wife of Dat Nigga. So of course I inherit his whip.

15.

The ride was all uphill. It's crazy how it's so fun going down, and such a slow drag driving up. When I reached the top of what was the steepest road I've ever known, I felt relieved to begin driving through a straight tunnel. Even though it was all blackness, I enjoyed that there was no posted speed limit, no cops to be seen anywhere, and no traffic. Felt like Heaven to me.

"Well, then negotiate," I heard my middle sister Porsche's voice in my head. And that's exactly what I planned to do. I didn't know anybody down here except Bomber Girl and Young Drummer, and both of them were not really locals. So there was no guarantee that I would see them again. But she said that she had one remaining mercy. It felt like she was on my side. But she hated Dat Nigga, and was probably the one who chased him from the south side where they were battling, all the way to the east side, where he came to pick me up. She may have even thrown the bomb that killed him. Yeah, I had caught feelings that she had provided me with the bomb that saved me from the second rape and got me out of the animal warehouse factory. But I still don't like her religious talk. I'm never planning on bowing down after a whole lifetime of others bowing down to me. Furthermore, I couldn't feel this so-called god they called the ONE, the All-Powerful, All-Knowing, who allegedly created every living thing. Fashion is like life. If fashion had one designer creating, how boring would that be? Fashion and life both have to have many designers and creators wrapped in a passionate competition with one another, to push and rule the culture and the look of absolutely everybody and everything. So why should I believe in one God who had a monopoly over it all? The same God who threw Shayton the devil out of Heaven, because he craved that same type of competition I'm talking about? I respect Shayton, tossed all the way to the bottom. Instead of defeat, he built an empire! He filled his city with his houses of evil. He put his sons to work. He even had his own sons competing with one another. Competition, that's how it should be done. That's how Poppa and Brooklyn Momma did it. Everybody know not to let men get lazy. Put them to work. Make them grind and force their own come-up. Then the reward is them having the choosiest bitches and finest whips and gear, food prepared like they want it, VIP spots everywhere they go, the livest parties and all that they earn from their hustle and flow. That's my religion, if I have to have one. Ass-kissing is for those who don't mind getting shit on their lips and stinking all the time. I laughed.

Reality is though, back when I sat on the curb by the sewer paralyzed and had no other choice than to sit and listen to Bomber Girl's talk, I should have presented her with my counterproposal. Now I would.

First step in my plan was to drive back to the exact spot where the sewer was. For some reason, she had showed up twice at that same location. Her arrival had overpowered that extreme odor. I also noticed that the rally of the UBS was also in that same location. The march of the animals also led to that same location. Therefore, I deduced that there had to be something to it. I should go there and Bomber Girl would show up. I would unveil my plan once I figured it out. She would be the one to do what I told her to do, to get me what I want.

The stench let me know I was in the area. It was so powerful that even with all four windows sealed, I could smell it racing up my nose holes and could even taste it on my tongue. I drove through it for a while, unable to see or locate an open sewer. I stopped because it felt like I had driven far enough and maybe should have stopped a little further back. I pressed my face up against the window. It was all black in every direction. I thought I should get out and search around on foot. However, I reminded myself that I am naked beneath the pearl trench. I burnt my white silk rape dress. My badass, *I Rule the World*, black Chiffon, never been worn, oh my! Tom Ford pleated dress was swiped by Succubus. Even though her fat ass could never ever fit it. Even if she stopped eating entirely for sixty days. Naked beneath the trench would have always been some sexy shit to me. However, after the rape I was feeling a little more cautious than I had ever felt, dead or alive.

I should sort it out, I said to myself. Once my plan was solid, I would blow the car horn and use that loud sound to call Bomber Girl while I remain locked inside of the vehicle in case anybody different showed up bent on violating me.

I was in a world where—no, I was in a realm was what they called it. I was in a realm where there was no money. The hot commodity is the soul. Apparently, anybody can sell their soul to get something in return. Or a hustler from the Last Stop can sell the souls of others like Dat Nigga, his father, and their team did. Souls must get a high price. Shayton and his sons and team all had whips and trucks and sturdy houses and business locations, warehouses and factories. They had a full franchise going. Dat Nigga kept his potent weed stacked. He had a full bar of whatever liquors were craved or needed for every occasion.

Hmmm . . . Winter, just because the soul is the hottest commodity at the moment, it doesn't mean you can't jump in there and create a new commodity and make it hot, I told myself. Obviously, anybody who knew how to hook up utilities, lights in particular, would become a trillionaire in this realm that was always dark except for a flame or during a time of what they called mercy. But mercy was imported. It didn't come from down here. Them UBS can speak all those languages and got a great starlit light show. But let's face it, they needed spaceships like the Jetsons rocked on the Cartoon Network when I was young. Then Siddiqah wouldn't be complaining about the distance between Jannah and the Last Stop. I laughed.

The food industry was booming on Earth. However, down here it seems like the incubuses and succubuses don't eat. They definitely don't drink water. Come to think of it, the dead humans, me and my kind, don't eat or drink water either. I never saw or asked if the UBS eat and drink. But if they so religious that they can't even fuck, well they probably don't eat or drink either.

That left the food industry with only one business option, pet food. Or should I say animal food, because those warehouses housed all types of creatures who were definitely not treated like pets are treated on Earth. That led me to believe that animals down here have short lives. That means animal food was not a real come-up.

Thinking further, since there are no lights or cameras down here, and the predominant color is black, that means the death of fashion. Hold up! There must be a black market because Dat Nigga wore Timbs and butter leathers, had silk and satin sheets, and fine fabrics. There has to be a textile industry or some way for hustlers to travel to Earth and bring back the fabrics, shoes, kicks, and whips and products they wanted to peddle that we had a stockpile of on Earth. All of my thoughts kept leading to Shayton. To be a player, *I need to make a deal with the devil*, I said aloud to myself.

The same second I said that, a storm of rocks thundered down from every direction onto the BMW. Not pebbles—heavy, jagged rocks, the size of, say, golf balls. Instinctively, I put my hands over my head, but I knew if they hit my hands, they would break both of my wrists. The pounding lasted for what seemed like a long time. Fearing that there would be nothing left of the car if I just sat there with my hands on my head, I turned the ignition on and pulled off. The rock storm followed me.

I tried to dodge it by suddenly driving to the left, then the right, then speed-reversing. Then slamming on the brakes. Then I'd take off again. I did this over and over until, *What the fuck?* While

speeding forward, the car started jerking, then put-putting. *Nooooo!*
I said to myself. *I'm out of freakin' gas.* Eventually, the rock storm
ceased. What remained was a car that must have looked like it
drove through an ambush and got sprayed on every side. The windows were still intact, though. That impressed me. However, they
could no longer be called windows because I could no longer see
out through them. They had a gazillion glass dents and cracks.
Whatever. Wherever I ended up when the gas ran out, was still all
stillness, stench, and blackness.

Once I calmed down some, I realized I had a massive headache. Even though none of the rocks had landed inside of the car,
my headache was so severe it felt like some of them had went right
upside my head. There was a pounding that I was unfamiliar with.
All of my blood vessels seemed about to burst, but I had no aspirin
or medicine of any kind. I reclined back in the seat to rest my head.
I comforted myself by thinking, *Don't worry bitch, you ain't got no
blood.*

It seemed like the headache lasted for no less than six days. It
might have been six weeks or six months, though, of continuous
head pain so severe that I couldn't think. I couldn't pursue my plans.
I was at a standstill. Ever since I had gotten shot dead, I wanted my
mind to turn off. Now it was so painful that I was without thoughts.
But that wasn't what the fuck I meant when I wanted my mind to
shut off. I reminded myself that at least I wasn't in a cage. I wasn't
an exotic snake or a pretty dog, and I could still feel my body and
each of my limbs.

It wasn't until my headaches stopped completely that I recalled the six blunts I had in my saddle bag. Damn, I could kick
myself. Why didn't I think of the weed as the medicine that could
of wiped away six months of pain? I would have puffed it so preciously, like how prisoners cut one cigarette into sixteen pieces
and smoke it pinched between their fingers no matter how tiny
the piece becomes. I could have made those potent blunts last for
the six months, now that I think about it. I opened the saddle bag

for the first time since I sped from the firehouse. I pulled out one blunt and held it so preciously. I searched through the bag looking for matches. Then I heard voices that I was sure was in my head. They were laughing at me, in the same manner that Succubus had laughed at me repeatedly.

"I fucking get it!" I screamed. "There are no matches in the fucking Last Stop Before the Drop, the County of the Ungrateful, the State of Ignorance, and the Land of the Arrogant. Only the Incubus and his crew monopolize and make the flames. There will be no sun, moon, or stars or even a trace of clear or bright light unless one of the UBS comes through with a mercy from the ONE who created us all," I screamed and then collapsed on the steering wheel. "And why do I fucking need to say all of that shit?" I asked myself aloud. Then the voice of Siddiqah came to mind. *You must never follow up sacred words with niggardly words.* I sat up, unlocked the door, and hopped out into the blackness. My legs felt fucked from six months of sitting in the driver's seat with migraines that halted my clear thinking and movement. I pushed myself to stand firm and screamed through the darkness, "Siddiqah! Siddiqah! Siddiqah!" like a hundred times. I fell back against the car and waited for what felt like six days. Then I screamed out, "Bomber Girl!" a hundred times. I waited for what felt like six weeks. Then I felt furious that she didn't respond when I had given her more than enough time to travel down here even if she was coming from Jannah. "Hey, you fucking young bitch. Get your ass down here right this fucking minute!" The cursing didn't work. I figured it wouldn't. I couldn't control myself, though. I had been so long waiting outside of the car for her, worried that if I remained inside she might see only the vehicle and believe that Dat Nigga was inside. Then she would drop a bomb on him and kill her own mother by mistake. "Own mother," what the fuck had I just said?

The odor was nothing to me now. That's how long I had been there alone in total and complete darkness. The quietness was so airy I even wished I could hear the sounds of the screaming and hissing and bones breaking and teeth grinding and even knuckles cracking. I even wouldn't have minded if a few enemies showed up and I had to fight them. That would be action. For months or even for a year there had been no action. Complete silence unless I was reacting to the inaction by screaming. There was no one and nothing else here but me.

I climbed on top of the hood and laid down. After six days or so of lying there on the hood, I had no further expectation to see anyone else ever. Of course, that's precisely when I heard something slowly approaching. It sounded like one person on a bike and a couple of others on foot. I got excited. I sat up from my lying-down position. It was painful, like my body, bones, and muscles were all attacking me for having been lying down way too long. Then a multicolored huddle of grandmothers showed up. They stepped right out of the darkness. One of 'em had a red wheelbarrow. I was suspicious of them. I saw their cheap wooden crucifixes hanging around their necks on an even cheaper string. They were all wearing long gray garments and Payless . . . no dollar-store plastic sandals. *Just my luck*, I thought. *Why in the hell after all of this long, long lonely time are these old bitches the only ones who showed up?*

"Are you alone, my sweet darling?" one of them asked. I didn't answer. Thought it was a weird first question.

"Oh, my dear, you look like you need Jesus!" another one of them said in like a tone of pity. I threw myself back down onto the car hood with my arms stretched out wide. I was officially exhausted.

16.

There was some light in the convent. Not powerful, like natural sunshine, or bright, like a 125-watt light bulb. It was, however, more light than a flame could cast. From a BMW 7 series to a wheelbarrow. That's how I traveled here. Pushed by a group of grandmas each taking a turn. They insisted that I was feverish and needed treatment. When I finally sat up, they pushed me back down. Two of them rolled me off of the car hood, two of them caught me in the wheelbarrow. Man, were they shocked when my pearl trench unsnapped from all the gymnastics. They stared at my nude body as though their own bodies was not made with the same woman parts. Then off we went, my dead husband's car left behind in the black space, riddled with a thousand rock dents and windows that if touched might cave into ten thousand separate pieces of glass.

I went along with it. Of course I could have overpowered the old ladies. Hit them with some of the rocks that surrounded the whip, then run them over with their own wheelbarrow. But I figured they must have something to provide that I could flip into something more. Even if I only learned my way around town, met some other people, located a gas station. That would be better than standing, sitting, and laying around.

"Rest until you heal, or, at least until your temperature goes down. Once you're stable, we can have a nice talk," one of them said. I didn't reply, just laid there like even talking was too painful for me. Even though at the time, I wasn't feeling any pain whatsoever and didn't feel fever hot.

I was back in a little room the size of a cell, but this time with no cellmate and no bars or prison door. Just cheap, hollowed-out fake wood and a knob that didn't lock. I sat on the thin twin mattress with one sheet and one blanket and looked around. Somehow someone must have thought it was inspirational to see some guy hanging on the wall, his feet and wrists bound, head bowed, and blood trickling. I got up to remove it. It wouldn't come off. It was plastered in place. No other pictures, not even of the ocean or the sky or some flowers in a field. Who in their right mind would think that the gruesome statue on the wall was all that was needed to decorate a room? The whole little place looked lonely. One wooden chair, one table for one, as though whoever lived in here would never have a guest and should never expect one. On the table was one empty glass and one metal pitcher filled with what I guess was drinking water. There was one little dresser with one little lamp on top of it, with one dim bulb. I opened the top drawer. There was one black book with too many pages, but less pages than the book Bomber Girl wanted me to read. In the bottom drawer was one pair of suspicious cheap white paper slippers wrapped in Saran Wrap. Had they been worn before? That's nasty. There was one sewing kit wrapped in a cheap plastic dollar-store case and one pair of white socks. I closed it. There wasn't even one window, which suggested that there was no hope for the alternation of night and day or the existence of a sun, moon, or stars. From my interior-decorating skills, which I sharpened by reading magazines for fifteen years on lock, I believe every room, apartment, house, home, or palace—the manner and style and way in which it is built, designed, and decorated—says something. Like a cell, this one room in this one convent had only one message. *Make a move. Get the fuck out of here* as soon as possible.

The door opened, no knock. "I'm here to wash your body," the grandmother said after some hours since my arrival, I guess. She walked in carrying a basin of water with a bar of soap floating in it. Beneath the basin was one neatly folded towel, one washcloth, and some clothes pressed and packaged in clear plastic wrap.

"I can take care of it myself," I assured her. She was gripping the basin like it was something of great value, walked past me, and sat it on the single dresser.

"Stand up," she said with a trace of aggression that wasn't in any of the old ladies' manner up until now. I stood. She tugged at my coat.

I resisted. "I said I'll do it myself."

She yanked it off of me. "No one can wash their own back properly," she said. "That's why we all need help. May God help us all."

"I'll take that," I said, holding my hand out for my trench.

"A place for everything and everything in its place," she said. I was starting to think the bitch was crazy. She went to the door and opened it slightly, then handed my coat to someone who must have been standing right there on post.

"Do you have any candles?" I asked her.

"Yes, but why?" she asked.

"They're more soothing to me than a lamp. Especially when I don't feel well, like right now." I made a painful face. "The light bulb is making my headache worse."

"Let's get you all cleaned up. I'll tuck you in. Then I'll come back with a candle."

"Great," I said. It was my first step to getting what I wanted in this place. Not what they wanted me to have or wanted me to do or wanted to do to me. I let her wash my body with the warm water. I didn't need no grenade to get *her* off me if she tried something slick. I was catching chills being wet and bare bodied, with my bare feet on their cold floor.

"Goose bumps," she said as though she was excited. She started patting me dry with the towel. "All finished. Cleanliness is next to Godliness," she said, handing me the wrapped garment. Soon as

I took it from her hand, I had a flashback to when I first got my prison uniform.

"I'll get dressed while you get the candle," I told her. She walked to the door and ordered whoever was posted outside of there to bring back a candle. She closed the door and sat down on the bed that was supposed to be mine temporarily. I unwrapped the garment. It was one cheap, plain, long, gray, ugly thing. I rushed and put it on to stop her from watching my body the way she was watching it.

"Come sit." She patted the bed. "Now let's pray together." I was like, *What the fuck?* I was just restraining myself from throwing her weird ass right out until I could get my candle. "We will say the Lord's Prayer. Do you know it?" she asked doubtfully.

"I don't. You go ahead and say it. I'll listen," I lied.

"I will, but I would like you to repeat each sentence after me. It's the best way to learn it for yourself and use it when you are praying alone," she said.

"Sure, whatever," I answered sharply. I was mad at myself for not fully controlling my reply. I meant to conceal my anger until I receive the candle.

"Our Father who art in heaven
Hallowed be thy name
Thy kingdom come
Thy will be done
On earth as it is in heaven
Give us this day our daily bread
And forgive us our trespasses
As we forgive those who trespass against us.
And lead us not into temptation
But deliver us from evil
For thine is the kingdom
And the power and the glory
Forever and ever amen.

I repeated each sentence after her. The door opened, no knock again. It was a young woman. *Finally, not another old bitch*, I thought to myself.

"Excuse me, Mother Maria. Here's the candle." She placed it on the dresser in exchange for the dirty water basin. I could hardly contain my joy at seeing that candle, even though it had a very faint flicker through the thick glass jar it sat in. I kept my jaw locked shut. Yeah, I had a bunch of questions I needed answered. But not at the risk of causing the grandmother to say even one more word or to remain in my room for even one more minute. It didn't work. The old lady sent the young one out with the basin. She turned, reached out, and touched my hair. Instinctively, I leaned back.

"You have quite a lovely head of hair. The Bible says that a woman's hair is her glory. The Lord made your hair glorious." I just looked at her from the leaning position. "But it seems that your ends are singed. Did you have some experience with fire?" She smiled. I straightened up. "You requested the candle. I wouldn't like for you to harm yourself," she said, hiding her suspicion of me unsuccessfully.

The young woman walked in carrying a basin filled with clean water. She placed it onto the dresser top. "No, nothing like that. I had a straightening comb that got too hot and it singed my ends. But I plan to clip them and wash my hair," I said smiling politely, even though I was running real low on patience.

"What is your name, my dear?" she asked me. No one had asked me that question since I was shot dead and had arrived at the Last Stop Before the Drop. They all either knew it already or didn't ask at all.

"Brooklyn," I said without even thinking.

"Brooklyn, this young lady, who is named Petra, and who has graciously brought you the candle you requested, was once in your same position. I will let her share the rules of the convent guesthouse and our expectations." I thought the grandmother was going to walk out and leave us two young women to talk. She didn't. The young woman sat down beside me. The grandmother stood directly over us. I was like, *Oh my fucking god!* Petra started speaking like a programmed puppet. "Welcome to the Sisters of Grace Convent, which has been in existence for more than one thousand years, here at the Last Stop Before the Drop. Although you may feel uncomfortable at first, our goal is to make you comfortable and prepare you to protect your soul in the name of Jesus." She was talking, but I could feel her uncertainty about what she was saying to me. She lowered her eyes and continued.

"Mother Maria has washed your body for your comfort and cleanliness, but also to check and test whether or not you are an evil spirit in disguise. Evil spirits are powerful and they can make themselves appear to be anything male or female of any type or complexion. As powerful as the evil spirits are, they all fear water. Had you resisted being washed, Mother Maria would have thrown the water on you instead. If you were an evil spirit, you would have been exposed," she said, speaking softly.

I was like, *Oh shit, so the nice-old-lady thing is a scam.* All the while, the grandmother had been processing me like a suspect—no, better yet, a convict—while pretending that she was simply doing some charity for my benefit.

"Also Mother Maria was studying your body, checking your skin for signs of the Beast."

"The Beast!" I reacted. Then I got mad at myself for saying even one word.

"The evil spirits each have certain markings on their bodies," the young woman explained.

"You had some marks," the grandmother chimed in. I was alerted by what she was accusing. "But they were the markings of someone who has been hurt by the Beast, who is not a beast herself. So you are in the right place," the old woman assured me.

"Tomorrow, when all of the souls we have collected are gathered in the sanctuary, Mother Maria and many of the other sisters here at the convent will teach you how to prepare to give your soul to Jesus," the young woman said. "It's the only way to get saved and protect yourself from the powerful evil that resides down here," Petra cautioned.

Then the grandmother pulled a card out of her long ugly dress pocket and handed it to me. I looked at it suspiciously. "The Lord's Prayer is written on the card. If you would have been an evil spirit in disguise, you would never have been able to listen to the Lord's Prayer being spoken aloud, nor would you have been willing to repeat after me. Pure prayers are like water to the evil ones. It causes them great agitation. Pure prayers plus water makes them dissolve long enough for you to flee from them," she said strangely. The image of Succubus after her head had dissolved flashed into my mind. Then I saw the rapist Iblis and the other one who was with him, whose name I did not know.

"Brooklyn!" The grandmother called my new name out sternly. "I can see from your expression that you have had an encounter with evil. We all have had such an encounter. Some more than others. Have no fear. The Lord Jesus will protect you."

"You mean the One, right?" I checked.

"No. We believe in the Trinity, meaning the three. The Father the Son and the Holy Spirit," she said.

"The Three?" I repeated. Siddiqah, aka Bomber Girl, said the ONE. Now the old lady is saying the Three. This shit is like three-card monte. You gotta watch the mouth, the hands, and the meaning all at the same time. Keep watching closely until you can figure out which shell the pebble is under, or where the truth is actually located, to win the bag and escape.

I agreed with her three-Jesus talk by head nod. I agreed with everything they said for one reason. I had to hurry them out without being obvious. Soon as the door closed, I pulled off the bullshit gray garment. It was an insult to my royalty and fashion. I used the towel to seal the opening beneath the closed door. Took the chair, jammed it beneath the doorknob. Grabbed open my saddle bag, reached in, and pulled out my blunt. I smelled the beautiful scent of it. Licked it lightly like it was an old-school rocket lollipop. I put it between my teeth. Next, I stuck my whole face into the candle-jar hole and finally lit my joint. Couldn't believe it took me six months or six years after bombing Iblis and beheading Succubus to get my hands on a matchstick, a lighter, a candle, and a flame!

A few pulls and puffs of the most potent weed I ever smoked in my life-and-death-time led me to think about Dat Nigga. This was the weed he provided for me. I thought about what Petra and the grandmother had said. Water and prayer causes an evil spirit to dissolve and disappear long enough for a person to flee from them. It sounded like that meant that there is a way for an evil spirit, as they called them, to recover after dissolving. That meant I may have another battle coming up with Succubus. It was good to know. I would not let anybody else blindside me like Simone did. I toked and laughed a muffled laugh. Simone was built stronger than Succubus though. Succubus's weaknesses, water, and prayers were very easy to use against her. If Simone was like that, I could of got rid of her in the prison shower. I cracked up. Then I started feeling sad and moody. I thought on the other hand, I was glad that I bombed the rapist. The thought of them being able to come back alive was too nasty and unfair an advantage for them to have. But then I thought about Dat Nigga, who also died from the blast of a bomb. *I wish he could come back to me.* But then I thought, *If I am only able to have it one way—all bombed stay dead—then I'd rather bombs bring permanent death.* Because how could I stay with Dat Nigga, whose own brothers had violated me? The only way that would be possible was to either inspire or require Dat Nigga to murder his own brothers. That's the only way him and I could live together peacefully. If he's a real nigga that's exactly what he would do anyway. My father Santiaga had murdered two of my mother's brothers in prison.

Back then I knew that if Santiaga killed them, they needed to die. They must have done some real pussy-ass shit or treachery to end up in that predicament.

Naked and beautifully buzzed, one leg cocked up and my back against the wall as I sat on my bed, I finally felt at ease enough to plot my next move.

17.

This time, Petra knocked. Good for her. She couldn't have walked right in anymore. I had removed the towel but left the chair in the jammed locked position. I guessed this was their morning, although I still didn't know how anyone down here tells time. It felt like I had stayed up all night. Who knows? I did know that it was time to put what I had stayed up scheming on into action. I removed the chair and opened the door gently.

"Come on in," I told her nicely.

"I can't. I have to wake up all of the other girls in time for the gathering in the sanctuary," she said, but then she looked at my hair. "You changed your hair. It looks pretty."

"I washed it. Thanks for the clean water."

"That was for your face!" she explained.

"I used the water in the basin to wash my hair and the water in the pitcher to clean my face and hands. Don't you all have a bathroom and shower in this big place?" I asked.

"The water in the pitcher was for you to drink. I see you are very creative and like to do things your own way." She stepped inside after saying she wouldn't. She looked around. "And you have hemmed your dress and embroidered your name across your breasts. Um, that should be fine for today but you will have to do as each soul must do. Nobody here really stands out. We are each here for the same purpose." She turned to leave after her careful inspection.

"I see you are barefoot. Your socks are in the drawer with the slippers. Please put them on before you come out."

"I only have one sock," I lied.

"Really? How could that be?" she asked, but I did not reply. "Okay, I'll get you a new pair." She left.

I had used one sock to do my hair. It was some old-school Brooklyn shit. When I was like twelve years young, we used a tube top like a headband and folded the hair around the tube top to create the hairstyle that I have now. If you know what you are doing and do it right, no one can see the tube top, headband, or in this case, sock. Of course I did it right. I preferred to rock a bun or a ponytail, but Succubus had torched half of my hair. Only a few inches of it had grown back so far.

She returned with the socks in a jiffy! "You never answered me about the bathroom," I reminded her as she tried to hurry out.

"Of course we do have a few bathroom and shower facilities, but everybody's first night here is the same. Each body gets washed and examined by the nuns upon arrival. It's for all of our protection. You'll get the tour after the gathering in the sanctuary."

"Do you work here?" I asked her.

"Yes," was all she said back.

"How long have you been working here?"

"One Earth year. Now I do have to go."

It was good enough information for me for now. Really, I was just testing her, seeing how either secretive or flexible she was. I did want to know if this was her job though. That grandmother Maria, who they call Mother Maria, had said that Petra used to be in my same situation. Now I know it is possible to upgrade from being a charity case to having a job in this convent. If I could get one, I would use it to collect information, gain access, and buy time to set my *real business* in motion.

Once I get to know all of the women here, and all of their stories, talents, assets, and traits, I could use it to get whatever I wanted out of each of them. I was accustomed to shaking down new prisoners on lockup. I would find out where they were from, what crimes they were convicted for, how much they had in their commissary, if they had any relatives or visitors who would be coming upstate on a regular. Plus I was checking if they was about the streets and the hustle, if they could get people to bring shit on a visit that I ordered and would buy from them. Of course other details, like are they related to any cops or corrections officers in the prison where we were locked.

I was gonna play it the same way here. I stayed up all night memorizing that boring-ass Lord's Prayer. I even ended up having to crack open that dictionary that Siddiqah had stashed in the inside pocket of my saddle bag. I didn't like the flow of their prayer. It used weird words that as far as I know are never spoken, like *thy* and *thine*, and *hallowed*. I looked up *hallowed*. The dictionary said it means "sacred." Then I had to look up *sacred* just to be sure. The definition of *sacred* was a bit strange. It said, "Pertaining to God, secured against violation." So the line in the prayer, "Hallowed be thy name . . ." which I thought meant that the name is hollow, which would mean empty, actually means "Sacred is your name." Seems the asshole who wrote the prayer should have just said it plainly unless he just didn't want anybody to understand on purpose. Not everybody is going to take the time to look all these words up. And besides, the prayer starts off talking about "Our Father . . ." I was like, *Whose father? Not mine!* Maybe that works on people who ain't got parents or memories.

If I could pray to Santiaga, my prayer would be the sincerest, most influential words in existence. No one who heard them would dare say they didn't understand. They'd feel each word pumping in their veins, thumping in their hearts! Then there was a line in the Lord's Prayer like, "Give us our daily bread . . ." To that line I was like, *Every fool dead or alive knows that no one just gives you shit.* They would've been better off saying, "Give us jobs so we can earn some paper and feed ourselves." Even though I didn't like the prayer, I could recite it. I planned to impress this old chick in charge and pretend to gobble up all of their gobbledygook. They would in turn let me keep this rent-free room, get me a job assignment, and access. After I got paid and soon as I was set up right, I'd bounce like I was never even here.

"Who wants to volunteer to lead us in the Lord's Prayer today?" Grandma Maria said. My hand shot up like I was an eager fifth grader. She chose me. I walked from the rear of the sanctuary in my Prada kicks and upgraded altered dull gray garment. I pretended not to hear the comments as I whizzed by. All eyes on me. The key to grabbing control of a scene is to be so good at whatever you do that everyone there wants to be you. Once they want to be me, that's when they become either my customer or my victim.

I tripped. The gathered gasped. I almost fell on my face but caught myself before humiliation. When I regained my footing I looked back. All of the women's faces were feigning innocence. I knew one of them stuck their foot out.

"Are you okay?" One of the grandmothers walked over to escort me like I was some cripple.

"I'm fine," I said, controlling my anger. When I reached the front, I found myself facing about 150 or so women who were all seated on long rows of wooden benches. Also there were the ones who remained standing on both the left and right aisle. I saw Petra standing. I assumed then that the other women who were standing were also young corridor captains and staff. The grandmothers were up front. I saw their eyeballs roaming over my overnight version of their garment. Grandmother Maria—'cause I'll be damned if I call her Mother Maria; she ain't my goddamn mother—had her eyes fixed on my feet. I wasn't wearing the cheap Chinatown-type flat slip-ons that came with the garment or the paper slippers. Of course I have to draw the line somewhere even when I'm scheming. I will never, ever be a cheap shoe-wearing bitch. But just then when I looked down at my own feet, I saw a scuff mark from almost tripping. That got me pissy. I played it off.

"Our Father who art in Heaven . . ." I announced and projected. I was so confident. The type of confidence that comes when you don't know none of the people who surround you, and they don't know you either. I would impress, use, and discard. "Hallowed be thy name . . ." They all repeated after me. That's when I saw one mouth that wasn't moving. She was standing there in the aisle where I almost fell. Her arms were folded across her chest. It was the pretty young bitch who I bit when I was a dog. The same one who was getting fucked right by Dat Nigga before she turned into a rat. The same one who came and sat next to me at the UBS Rally of the Sons. I was careful to not let my expression acknowledge her. Game face on!

"Thy kingdom come," I said. I even began giving eye contact to let the grandmas see clearly that I was not reading from a card or a paper. I learned it by heart. I'm useful. Hire me. "Thy will be done . . ." I said at full volume, "on Earth as it is in Heaven."

Once I completed the prayer, a long line formed in each aisle. I was surprised to find out that it was a line for hugs. Women who wanted to hug me for leading the prayer so well. I was like, *Hey bitches, just sit back and clap.* I'm not all touchy-feely. Especially not with a bunch of broads. I hugged each of them. Over the shoulders of those embraces, I took note and read the faces of the ones who stayed back. I respected them more. I would make a few of them my team. And I now see that one of them was the white woman from the Rally of the Sons who got a whole bunch of bitches to rebel against the sons on the stage.

The corridor captains walked to the front when my fan line ended. Grandmother Maria announced, "Glory be to the Father. We welcome each of you. Assembled up front are our six corridor captains. I will allow them each to introduce themselves. We will break down into groups and your captain, who was the first face you saw this morning, will escort you on the tour of our convent, a transitional home to thousands of souls. This is the place where you will each engage in prayer, cleansing your mind and heart. God is good. We are like a spiritual car wash." She laughed at her own humor. "Except you women are not cars. The sisters standing beside me are not car-wash attendants. But, God willing, you can understand what I mean." Each of us guests tolerated her dumb talk and lined up in front of our corridor captains.

"You were up there pretending to be sweet," the pretty younger bitch said. Then she laughed. "Now we are even. You bit me. I tripped you." She was obviously on my same corridor. Her and the white woman from the rally were both standing with me in Petra's convent tour line.

"Ladies, please pay attention during the tour. If you don't, it makes more work for me because you will ask me the same questions that I have already answered for the group," Petra said in an even tone.

"How long have you been here?" I asked the pretty bitch. She pulled up her long gray sleeve and checked her Lady Rolex. My eyes widened.

"About six Earth days. Long enough to know I'm not gonna stay. But not long enough to figure out where I'm gonna go. You stitched that yourself?" she asked as she placed her finger lightly over the embroidery.

"Bitch, did I tell you you could touch me?" I spit.

"That's the real you." She laughed. "Not the bitch up there talking about 'hallowed be thy name'!" She cracked up.

"Ladies!" Petra raised her voice as a means of scolding us without scolding us directly. "I am about to open the doors to our main prayer hall. You must be completely silent. Inside, there are many praying for their salvation. This is the place where you also will pray for your own salvation and where you will spend the majority of your stay at the convent." Trying hard to be quiet, she opened the door. She was right. It was a sea of women, some sitting with the black book in their laps. Some counting a string of beads for some strange reason. Some on their knees facing a statue of that guy bleeding and bound to a cross.

Petra led us in single file through the perimeter. She pointed to the colored-glass window once we reached the front. It was so dim, I could only see the colors but not the detail of the designs. It had faces, though—not beautiful faces but big-eyed people with pitiful expressions. I guess they thought these were scenes that would move a bitch like me to prayer. If I cared enough, I would teach Petra and the other corridor captains and the grandmas a lesson. The key to convincing anybody of anything is by showing them something that is or looks like what they would like to become and who they would be comfortable being. Why break your back praying when this guy at the front is all defeated? I didn't want to end up in his position. Neither did any of these other chicks here, I'm sure. And the chubby pale ladies pictured on the colored glass, I wouldn't trade places with them either.

"Bible study will begin as soon as the sand at the top of the hourglass reaches the bottom." Petra pointed at it. The tour was over. In addition to showing us the entire facility, Petra had pointed out that there was a six-foot-tall hourglass placed in each corridor to assist the welcomed new souls, who are often confused about time, to keep on schedule. She also handed out small palm-sized hourglasses to those of us who had not received one yet.

"Your Bible is in your top dresser drawer. Bring it to Bible study. And for those of you who are eager to learn—like Brooklyn, who learned the Lord's Prayer overnight, and who was able to recite it so nicely—you may begin reading your Bible before the Bible study session. Okay, relax until then. See you soon." Petra walked off.

"Brooklyn, is that your real name?" the pretty bitch asked me. "I was born in Brooklyn."

"What section?" I followed up swiftly. Didn't believe her automatically.

"East New York," she replied. "Where all the action's at." She smiled.

"Do or die Bed-Stuy," I smiled. That was like throwing an ace on her king.

"You smoke?" I asked her.

"You copped! I ain't had none since Dat Nigga—" she said, then stopped herself.

"He's dead. So you and I, let's bury it," I offered.

"You killed him!" she whispered.

"Never that. I had love for Dat Nigga. He had love for me too," I said. Something inside of me had to let her know that even though she was pretty and younger than I was, when it came to Dat Nigga I was top bitch over every other bitch including her. That had to be understood and acknowledged before we buried the tension between us.

"Love, huh?" was all she replied.

"What room you in?" I asked her.

"Twelve," she said. "You want to come in?"

"I got the smoke. You come by me. I'm in eighteen."

"Cool, give me five minutes though. I'll come way before that boring-ass Bible study. I'll need the buzz to keep me from feeling like killing myself in that class," she said.

18.

I looked at the candle. It was still burning, but the melted wax was mounting up. I wondered how much time I had left before the flame burnt out completely. I knew I can just request another candle when it did. However, I was in the rhythm of expecting the unexpected. Therefore, I was looking at this lighted candle in the tall jar as the only one I would ever have here at the convent. I needed it to smoke my weed. However, I wasn't gonna react to a fear of not having a candle, a match, a lighter or a flame, then rush and smoke it all before the candlelight expired. That would be too dumb and too painful. I'd be left facing the reality of this realm without it.

She knocked. I opened the door. She slipped in. I closed the door and dropped the towel on the floor and kicked it into place. Grabbed the chair and tucked it beneath the knob.

"You can sit on my bed," I told her. She was standing holding a book. It had no words or art on the cover, just heavy black-inked parallel lines, like the person who placed them there was pressing the pen too hard. Every four lines and there was an even heavier fifth stroke crossing the four straight lines out. It was obviously a count. There were more than sixty sets of five. I guess she wasn't lying when she said this is how she keeps track of time in the Last Stop Before the Drop. She placed it on my dresser and sat down. As soon as I picked up the blunt, stuck my face to the candle-jar hole, and blazed up, her eyes danced. I purposely passed the joint right to her. She pulled and puffed. She held on to it. Didn't pass it back right away. I was thinking, *Good*. The weed was so powerful, she'd be open in seconds.

"Name?" was all I said.

"Call me whatever you like. We're both dead anyway," she said casually.

"Well damn," I said. Even while expecting the unexpected I didn't expect that reply.

"What? Are ya still in denial? I was too, for about ninety days," she said matter-of-factly.

"How do you know it was ninety days? How do you keep track of time when there are no mornings, afternoons, evenings, or nights? And no sun, moon, or stars?" I asked her. She picked up her pink book and waved it back and forth. Then she picked up her left hand where she wore her Lady Rolex. "I know the time and date of my death. My watch still works. Each twelve hours I make a mark in my book. Every two marks represents twenty-four hours. There are twenty-four hours in a day. So, I do simple math," she said casually, while really enjoying the weed. I was replaying her response in my mind. I felt relieved that she must have had that watch on at the time of her death. That means Dat Nigga didn't buy it for her. Now I had less reason to hate her.

"What about the time you spent as a monkey?" I asked her in a nonoffensive tone, because I really wanted to know. How did she count the time accurately as an animal?

"Ha-ha . . . I'm glad you put me on to this powerful weed. Only a friend would do that. Otherwise, you reminding me of my time as a monkey would make me think you want to be enemies," she said, instead of answering my question.

"Well, we may be dead, but the way I see it, as long as you have your look and your body, you have life after death. I can see you, and how you look. You can see me too."

"I can see that you have a candle. Light is the hottest commodity in the Last Stop Before the Drop. The evil spirits have got the flames.

The UBS have got the stars and the mercies. That's their light. The churches have got some light, but it is very dim, like it's on the verge of shutting off. Have you noticed?" she asked, blowing out a straight stream of smoke right into my face. I did notice that she was clever at dodging questions, flipping ass and changing topics. "Where did you get the candle?" she asked. "You must have paid a lot for it."

"Paid," I said coolly. "Is there such thing as money down here?"

"Not our type of money. But you know supply and demand is always the setup. And no matter the world, there is always world trade. You must have sacrificed or traded something for it. Dead humans whose souls are stuck in the Last Stop Before the Drop are not allowed to have light." She pulled hard on the blunt. This time the smoke curled up. "That's why if there is a dead human with light, it's either borrowed or stolen," she said, and I was listening carefully.

"But I ain't seen no police, no courts, no judges or prisons. That means there's no consequence for a dead human, as you call us, having light just because someone said we are not allowed to have it," I told her, but really, it was a few questions tucked in one statement.

"Just because you ain't seen something doesn't mean that it is not there," she said strangely. I charged it to the high taking over her mind. "Besides, Shayton got this whole hood on lock." She gestured with her finger, moving it around in the air in the shape of a circle. "He hates police. So there ain't none. He runs the red market, travels in more than one world, and comes back with all the shit everybody down here ain't got. Since him and his whole team is all evil, they monopolize the flame. They don't sell or trade matches, lighters, flashlights, candles, or anything that can result in souls being able to see. To the evil ones, those items are considered contraband because they won't allow anything that rivals their flame game. The soul is what they are *really after*—that's us, by the way. They feed the souls to the Eternal Fire."

"How long did it take you to figure something like that out?" I asked her.

"A much shorter time than it took you!" She busted out

laughing. "You still haven't figured it out!" She threw salt in the wound she had just cut into me.

"I must have figured some shit out," I said in controlled anger. "You smoking my weed. Apparently you ain't got none. I got a 7 series BMW parked out in the blackness somewhere close. I got the hottest commodity, a candle, without paying shit for it. I had a flashlight, which you say we are forbidden to have." I looked at her cheap convent-issued slip-ons. "And I got Prada kicks, eight hundred American dollars a pair, a saddle bag, and everything else *you don't have*."

"I have a flashlight underneath my bed in my room," she said, all cocky. "And *I said* it is forbidden for dead humans to have light. That doesn't mean we can't figure out how to break the rules. I went to University of Pennsylvania. I should be able to figure out a bunch of shit. I got a super-high IQ." Then she added, "And I got an iPhone, a bottle of Chanel No. 5 that cost more than your kicks, a Rolex, a corkscrew, and a switchblade." She smiled.

"A college bitch," I said aloud, but really I was talking to myself. "But you can't be as smart as you think. You couldn't figure out how to stay alive." I trumped her. "And you can't make or receive no calls down here on your cell. And no matter how expensive your Chanel is, it's still not strong enough to cancel out the odor that saturates this atmosphere."

"True dat," she answered, flossing her verbal versatility. "Now let's you and I take my flashlight and go get your 7 series," she challenged me. She was calling what she thought was my bluff. I jumped off the bed. Just as I got ready to say, *Let's go,* someone tugged at my door. I put my finger over my lips to tell the pretty bitch to keep silent.

"Who is it? I'm not dressed," I said through the door.

"Open up or I'll blow your whole cover," a female voice said. She sounded familiar. I waited for her to speak again.

"I smell it. Open the door or I'll call the captain, the mother, the father, the grandmother, a team of ghosts, and the goddamn devil!" she whispered in forced high-voltage words.

"That's that crazy white bitch. She lives across the hall from you. She's like a fucking protestaholic," the pretty bitch said, then laughed. "*Every day,* she'll start screaming if she doesn't get what she wants. Might as well open it and find out what she wants." I removed the chair and slid the towel away with my foot. I opened up a narrow slit for her to speak through without yelling and exposing us.

"Give me one pot stick," she demanded and thrust her hand through the narrow opening. "That's all it takes. Then I'll go away."

"What do you have to trade? I'm not giving you shit for free just because you want it, even if you snitch me out," I told her calmly.

"What do you need?" she asked. I had a list in my mind already. So I called it out.

"Gasoline, battery-powered radio, batteries, matches, and a lighter. Some scissors, spools of thread, fabric. Should I continue?" I asked her, my tone like a boss and filled with doubt about her competence. She stepped in even closer like a fiend and started sniffing as though she could catch a contact high from the narrow opening in the door, while Pretty was still on the bed puffing.

"How much did she pay to get on?"

"Stay out of my business," I told her. "Put up or shut up."

"I can get gasoline. These nuns gotta a lawn mower, a pickup truck, and a bus in the garage."

"Where you get it from and how you get it is your business. Let me know when you got it. Then we trade. But it has to be in a gas can so I can use it."

"So that's two pot sticks for gasoline and a gas can with the spout."

"No, get both and you get one. Get one without the other and you gets none!"

"Can I get a drag now to hold me over?" she asked, reminding me of the crackheads from my Brooklyn block. Back then everybody knew you have to talk rough to them. Get everything they owe you up front or anything you want and need done first before they get even a crumb from the rock. They're fiends and liars and thieves. Never trust 'em. I narrowed the door, crushing her arm. Then I opened it wider so she would know to pull it back and go get my gas.

When I shut the door all the way, I turned around and looked at Pretty. I was like, "Hold up. What do you have to trade for the blunt you haven't passed back to me once." She laughed.

"That's not the type of deal we made. You have to state the terms of the contract beforehand. I have to hear or read the terms and decide if I wanna sign off on it or not. You invited me in here on some type of friendship vibe. Now you wanna flip the script after the crazy white chick showed up begging."

"True dat. I know that's how it should be done. So moving forward, it's all give and take. I won't need to tell you that twice. Just know that's what is," I said.

"Cool, I agree," she said. "That's mine and your verbal contract. That's valid." She handed me the blunt that was three-quarters gone. "I owe you one. You helped me get nice before Bible study. Now I won't have to kill myself." She laughed. "How 'bout, *if your car is real*, tonight we head to the club?"

"My *car is real*. After I get the gas, you bring your flashlight and we out," I told her.

Sister Claire was standing up teaching the twelve of us seated at Bible study about herself first and the other ones she called "Sisters" and then attached a name behind it. I thought the bitches were too old and too damn ugly to be called sisters. Grandmas would've been more honest.

"All of us sisters have taken an oath of poverty, chastity, and obedience," Sister Claire said. *An oath of poverty! Come on now. There's not a poor nigga on Earth or even down here who would do something like agree from the get-go to be poor and stay poor! That's some mean deception she's spitting right now.* I already didn't trust none of these nuns. Now I was confirmed about it.

"So Sister Claire, are you telling us that none of the nuns in this convent have never had any sex?" the pretty bitch asked. Sister Claire remained silent for what seemed like a few seconds. Then she calmly answered the pretty bitch back by criticizing her on the low.

"I want to welcome you and thank you for coming to Bible Study today. You have been here at the convent guesthouse for seven days now. This is the first day that your soul was moved to join us. Praise God, I'm so thankful to have you. You are right. An oath of chastity means that we refrain from sexual intimacy completely. Once the oath has been taken, from that moment on we restrain and forbid ourselves and protect ourselves from doing so."

"Thank you for welcoming me," the pretty bitch said suspiciously politely. "So that means some of y'all have been sexually active up until the time before you took the oath." She stared strongly into Sister Claire's wrinkled eyes.

"I cannot speak for each of the sisters. And I am not sure what you are going after. But for myself, I entered the sisterhood at age nineteen. I was chaste when I arrived and I remain chaste to this day. I am sixty-nine years old," she said, and I definitely believed that no man had ever touched her. Seemed obvious. She probably looked just as unattractive when she was young. So she decided to control the action by shutting herself in a place with only women. She already knew the boys wouldn't sweat her. She wanted to reject them before they rejected her homely ass!

"Thank you," Pretty said. "I was only going for the truth, Sister Claire. And you told us that we could ask any question. So I did. And I noticed that you and the other nuns are wearing a ring on your finger. How can you be chaste and married at the same time?"

"Our hearts are captured by the perfect man, Jesus. We are each married to the Lord," she said with seriousness in her delivery. I jumped out of my chair instinctively.

"Miss Brooklyn?" Sister Claire said as though it was a question. But I wasn't going to tell her that I leaped up because I had once told my cellmate that Jesus was a pimp, and that she, Sister Claire, had just confirmed that it was true. But man Jesus's pimp hand ain't strong. I mean he got way more wives than Midnight. But the whole stall of them is beat. None of the nuns were the type of bitches that a real pimp would possibly push out on the hoe stroll. I laughed at myself. Then I plopped down in my chair without giving any explanation for my behavior. Come on! She had to know. Sixty-nine years with no dick? Or even a thick finger and a strong lick! And on top of that, all the beat nuns are all married to the same dead man.

"The garment I am wearing is called a habit," Sister Claire said. "Yeah, right perfect name for the garment. A bad fucking habit," I mumbled for only Pretty seated next to me in the semicircle to hear.

"The covering on my head is simply called a veil," she said. I was like, *No it isn't. A veil would hide that gruesome face. You wearing a cheap scarf.* Then she grabbed the rope around her waist and said, "This may resemble a belt to you ladies. Actually, it is called a cincture."

Pretty leaned over and whispered to me, "It's an emergency rope for the day she finally figures out she should just hang herself." She laughed.

"I am sorry if I am not as interesting as you two beautiful souls," Sister Claire said to me and Pretty. "But down here, and everywhere really, it is the inside that is most important. Not the physical look." She was speaking softly with a fake calm. I would have respected her more if she yelled or threw something or tried to slap some sense into Pretty. That would have been more honest. I'm only saying that because these religious people always be pretending that honesty is their big contribution to the world.

Before Pretty could say whatever she was planning to say back, the crazy white bitch busted in Bible study mid-session. She caused all of us to lean back or bend forward. She smelled strong and toxic, like gasoline and paint. Sister Claire started coughing. Sister Constance, who was silently observing how Sister Claire conducted the Bible study, stood up. She cleared her throat and said, "Miss Bridgette, please let's go out together."

Some of the other ladies started saying "Ooh, ooh, ooh," as Sister Constance walked out with her hand on Bridgette's back gently guiding her. I didn't say shit. I know wherever a whole bunch of bitches is gathered and stuck living together around the clock, there's gonna be a bunch of lesbians! It was the same way in prison. I don't judge them, though. They mad moody. I mind my business. Don't get in their way, unless they get in mine. If they get in my way, then I treat them like any other bitch. I didn't know up until then that the white bitch's name was Bridgette, which they pronounced like *Breegeet*!

"Perhaps we should refocus," Sister Claire said. She slid one foot forward and started showing and telling us about her horrible sandals. Only thing I was thinking is whether Bridgette would get busted about the gasoline. Did she stash it well? Or would she confess to stealing it 'cause her stinking ass gave it away? Or would she deny it and come up with some clever excuse?

Sister Claire introduced us to not only the names of her clothing, but to the characters in the Bible that she was set to teach us about by reading selected chapters aloud. A whole discussion broke out when she said Mary was God's mother but that Mary was a virgin. Some of us laughed. Some just sat around looking nervous. Probably the quiet nervous ones felt bad about catching sexual feelings when they turned teen, and for fucking and enjoying it. They probably was the ones also pretending to be virgins, and that's why they suspected Mary of being in the same boat! I don't think people should feel guilty for fucking. That's like feeling guilty for peeing and pooping. It just something natural we all gotta do! On top of that, Sister Claire said that Mary had a man named Joseph. What nigga gon' let his girl tell him that she's pregnant but she didn't have sex with him or no other nigga? That's why these type of classes and the people who teach them is all bullshit. I could gather up a crew of hood bitches who got way more exciting but believable stories than the ones in this Bible class.

Sister Claire looked flustered. She began distributing one sheet of paper to each of us. "I can see my mistake," she said. "I can feel that some of you have been so hurt that I was rushing to what I wanted you to learn instead of starting at where you are at. On this paper are the definitions of the following most important things: love, mercy, forgiveness, confession, healing, atonement, and of course Faith. We will begin tomorrow's Bible study discussing love. So let's each take this list to your respective rooms. Think, meditate, pray about what these words really mean. What does each of these words mean to your particular life experience? How can these words, once understood, be used to cleanse the soul? Also, please use each of these words in a handwritten sentence. Write it on the backside of your paper."

When I pushed my bedroom door open, Bridgette was standing inside of my room. I got ready to punch her in her face for breaking in. But then I saw the gas can and it was a real one. I walked past her and lifted it. It was full. "I thought you got caught," I said to her.

"I did." She said it all casually. "It doesn't matter if you get caught doing wrong at a convent. Here for these nuns, *it's all about forgiveness*," she said in a high-pitched mocking voice. "They want to save us no matter how long it takes. We are their welcomed guests. These old ladies are nonjudgmental, spineless, and *so fucking gullible* and I love it. That's why I am staying here." She paused. "Pot stick please. I delivered your gas in a gas can."

I looked at her hard. I didn't trust her. What if the gas in the can is not gas, but paint, which she also smells like? Or something else? "I'll give it to you after I see if the gas checks out. When it does, our deal is complete."

"That wasn't a condition!" she screamed. "That was not a condition!" she repeated even louder. "That's not right!" she yelled. "We had a deal! I have a witness!" She got hysterical.

"Look bitch, you can scream all you want. The rest of my 'pot sticks' are in my car," I lied. "And . . . you already gave it away. Even if the sisters here find out that I purchased the gasoline that you stole from them, they'll forgive me. You should've kept that to yourself. Now go take a shower, comb your hair, and be ready in thirty Earth minutes." The protestaholic left reluctantly. I closed the door.

The pink notebook was still on my dresser top, with Pretty's death count scratched on not only the cover, but the sides and back of the book, now that I picked it up and took a closer look at it. I opened it up out of curiosity.

"I am the preacher's daughter. Unless you are also a preacher's daughter, you have no idea what it means or how it feels or what it involves. Even if you are a preacher's daughter, unless you are the bishop's daughter like I am, you have no idea the hellish life I've lived. This is my death story about my life." I didn't turn the page, but I could tell that the worn pages were filled with her heavy handwriting. I closed the book wondering why she brought it to my room in the first place? And if she left it here by mistake or on purpose. *Well, it doesn't matter,* I told myself. I got no time to sit around reading her story. Dead or alive I'm an action bitch who lives in the present tense.

19.

Pretty was riding shotgun. She couldn't stop laughing. I mean she was cracking up. It turned out she was the happiest-acting person I encountered in the Last Stop Before the Drop. Bridgette, all clean and fresh but rocking her gray garment and a cloth bag she called "her satchel," was in the back savoring her one pot stick. She didn't offer or pass it around. I didn't care. I got four more to myself. Besides, the car was filled with smoke. Bridgette's slow toke of the potent spliff was giving me a light, relaxing buzz.

"You said you push a 7 series. You left out that it's *all fucked up!* What happened to your whip?" Pretty asked while still laughing. "Don't drive too fast," she warned. "The glass fitting ta break out and cut us all into little pieces." Pretty's still laughing.

"Just tell me when to turn left or right. Bridgette got us the gas. I'm driving you bitches around. You make sure we get to the club."

"I'm navigation. I got you," Pretty said, and finally stopped laughing.

"Club, what club? You didn't ask me if I wanted to go to a club or not," the protester protested.

"You can cop at the club. They got *more* than weed. They got everything," Pretty said. That shut Bridgette right up. With the promise of more weed, she started pulling like a vacuum cleaner on her pot stick.

"I'm wearing the convent dress and the sandals!" Bridgette

laughed at herself. She was feeling comfortable now and her tone was less hectic and aggravating. "No big deal," she reassured herself aloud. "I'm white. Once they see my natural blonde hair and fair skin all of the doors will open *for me.*" She sang her words like a song. She believed it, too. I wasn't mad at her. I'm top bitch. No reason to stop other bitches from dreaming.

"What age were you at your T.O.D.?" Pretty asked.

"T.O.D.?" Bridgette repeated.

"Time of death." Pretty turned to face Bridgette in the backseat and clarified. Pretty seemed too comfortable discussing the death topic that I don't think no one at the Last Stop Before the Drop really wants to mention or face.

"Twenty-four. They say the good die young. I guess that's one thing 'they' say that's true," Bridgette said, sounding like she was trapped in some memory.

"How 'bout you?" Pretty turned front and asked me.

"Bitch, how 'bout you!" I said, turning the question back on her.

"Twenty-four," Pretty said.

"Twenty-four, me too," I lied, figuring they was probably both lying also.

"I hear music!" Pretty screamed, all excited.

"Hell yeah, it's Pink! 'Get the Party Started!'" She was singing the song but was obviously tone-deaf.

"Follow the flames. We're in the right area. They mark the path to the club entrance," Pretty said, excited, and they did. "Turn left! Don't pull up to the front. We gotta park this shit *on the darkest side of the street or in a dark alley.* Then we'll walk over like we just stepped out of a Rolls," Pretty suggested, and laughed.

The beats shook the building that was lit up by a massive torch with live flames shooting out into the blackened sky. Beneath the torch was a glow-in-the-dark red cage where what looked like a twelve-foot-tall red-skinned man with ram horns and a 144-foot-long tail paraded back and forth between the bars. Me, Pretty, and Bridgette weren't saying shit. We was all looking up at the red beast whose body was all muscle like the famous muscle dudes in the muscle mags that some chicks on lock enjoyed. I didn't get off on those types of magazines. I thought that weightlifters all had shrunken dicks, and that wasn't a good trade-off for more arm and chest muscles in my estimation. But this red beast had a big, hard, erect, foot-long red dick.

The line to get in the club snaked and wiggled because everybody on it was dancing to the most incredible indoor and outdoor sound system.

"Something wild is happening in the front," Bridgette yelled. This time she had to yell. The music was overpowering all. Shaking the ground and even making my eardrums vibrate. "It's 'Paparazzi,' Lady Gaga's song! Maybe she's performing!" Bridgette screamed. "Let's do a train!" She threw both of her hands onto my shoulders and pushed me forward.

Pretty ran in front of me. "Put your hands on my shoulders. We're gonna push!" she said. I did and we were choo-choo-training our way through a moving, dancing mob of hundreds. I didn't give a fuck about seeing Lady Gaga, but I loved the action and the reaction. Some moved out of our way willingly. Some got tight and pushed back. The crowd was so thick that even when we got pushed a few times we couldn't fall over. Our bodies would just press against some other bodies that were also pressed against some other bodies! We'd rebound and keep it moving. It was mad fun! Pretty ducked low like a football player anticipating a tackle. So we ducked and pushed our final push to the forefront. Pretty's high heel broke upon arrival. She didn't care, just started laughing.

There was no celebrity performance. We did all of that pushing only to find out that we were on the request line that led to a circus ring with a thick red rope dangling down in the center of it. No, it was not a rope—it was the tip of the red beast's tail and dangling from it was a microphone.

"I'm next," some guy screamed.

"We're next!" some other people screamed. The crowd mashed

forward. Some people raced in front of where we were standing try-ing to figure it out. They started beating the shit out of each other. The last man standing grabbed the mic and shouted, "Maroon 5, 'Misery'!" The red beast roared. The track changed tunes. The whole outdoor crowd began to jump up and down, scream and do some version of a dance.

"Oh, I get it. Check it out, he's the fucking DJ," Bridgette an-nounced, pointing up towards the red guy. "Let's go next!" she screamed while jumping up and down at the same time. "I have a request!" she shouted. But the song and the crowd overpowered her for once. Then she took three giant steps forward, waved for us to join her, and squatted like a runner who was waiting for the gunshot to start the race. I'm thinking she must really want to hear whatever song she has in her head. I didn't care enough though to start thumping with some strangers over the microphone. And I wasn't about to start rolling on the ground. Even though I wasn't Fendi'd up or Gucci'd down, I was wearing that one outfit that I had left to my name. The tapered mean-ass three-quarter-length pearl-colored Burberry trench and my black Gucci saddle bag and my black Prada kicks. Yeah, I felt bad about it. And it was unlike myself to be wearing a threepeat-repeat outfit. But as I got dressed to go to the club, I assured myself that I wouldn't know none of the motherfuckers out partying tonight. It would be their first time seeing me. So my gorgeous look, plus my almost brand-new fash-ion, would seem fresh to them.

The Maroon 5 song was coming to an end. Bridgette took off running towards the mic. A lot of others seemed to have her same idea to jump-start. They started brawling. Bridgette was fighting some white dudes. They were fighting her in her nun garment like she was a man. Her blonde hair and blue eyes didn't tame them, like she said it would. One of the dudes grabbed the mic. He shouted, "Kings of Leon, 'Use Somebody'!"

The red beast roared. The track switched to another song I never heard before. Bridgette came back tight. She was finger-combing her blonde hair back into place. She reached into her satchel and pulled out a—*What the fuck?*—camel-haired canteen! She began squirting water from it and washing her face clean, right there surrounded by the dancing crowd.

"I have something I want the DJ to play!" Pretty yelled. She had her heel in her hand. "And I'm 'bout to beat the hell out of somebody!"

"Round two! Let's go for it!" Bridgette screamed, excited to now have Pretty as backup. Now I'm thinking, *If somebody hits Pretty, I'll have no choice but to start swinging*. Brooklyn always fights together with whoever we showed up to the party with. I didn't join Bridgette 'cause I thought the white bitch is straight crazy! I couldn't be responsible for her ass. There was no telling what she might do in any given scenario.

As the "Use Somebody" track neared its end, a deafening horn sounded and the music stopped. Suddenly, everyone in the crowd divided, leaving me, Pretty, and Bridgette at the top, unaware of what was happening.

"It's a trick. Let's stay right here. We got next," Bridgette said, still scheming on the request mic. But the whole crowd about-faced and began raising and waving their hands in the air. A motorcade came riding through, led by a rose-red Rolls-Royce. Twelve exotic car doors swung open. But the red Ferrari doors swung out and hung in the air. I felt my pussy pumping. As the must-be top hustlers from the Last Stop Before the Drop eased out of their whips, a herd of females ran into the circus ring where me, Pretty, and Bridgette had been standing all along. The red beast roared and rattled his cage, causing his tail and the mic to swing back and forth. Pretty dashed to grab it while the crowd, including me, was mesmerized by the car show.

Bridgette snatched back my focus. She started screaming at Pretty, protesting. See what I mean? Now she was mad at Pretty for beating her to the mic. Every clique knows there's no infighting in public. Now Bridgette wanted to fight with her own crew who she rode here with.

"Rihanna!" Pretty screamed into the mic. Just the name alone of that green-eyed superstar bitch jolted the crowd to roar louder than the beast. "'Rude Boy'!" Pretty shouted, and the mic amplified her request for all to hear. The crowd cheered the choice. The track began. Pretty moved her body with the alluring fluidness of a belly dancer and a Jamaican dance hall queen mixed. She displayed her ability to hump and ride and fuck the beat. Some of the crowd got caught up into her movements. Others was in a trance to the sound of Rihanna's voice. Others were doing their own-style freak-out. Although no matter how wild the crowd danced, pushed, swung, moved, they all seemed somehow to know not to cross the line of the hustlers as they approached the ring. I had my eyes locked in on the hustlers. I was concentrating so hard that my hips only swung a little to the badass sexual beats. I was wishing I had a Cinderella moment and some fairy bitch showed up with some diamond stilettos and an open-backed minidress made innovatively out of the baddest Hermès scarves—a dress I designed just for this night— and authentic, flawless, glistening jewels and rare limited-edition designer accessories.

"The three of you. The three of us. That makes six," the hustler who I had saw easing out of the Ferrari said not with his mouth but with his hands. He had cut through the line-up of cheering screaming females and stood directly in front of me as Bridgette and Pretty were still doing their dances to the left and right of me. He pointed at me, then Pretty, then Bridgette, and raised up three fingers. Then he pointed out himself and two other ballers to the left and right of him. I looked them over thoroughly. When I looked at the one talking to me with his hands, I got a bad feeling. That never happened before when I first met any person, no matter their status. He must have thought since I wasn't saying nothing back that I didn't understand his offer. He stepped in close to me and said, "I choose you."

Without warning even from myself, I vomited right in his face. Pretty stopped dancing and her jaw dropped open. The music stopped. The goop slid down onto his expensive attire. The two hustlers with him did a one-eighty and grabbed two other begging chicks from the crowd who were still eagerly waving their hands in the air and cheering to be chosen. Now I was doubled over.

I heard Pretty say to him, "She's sorry. She must have gotten carsick from our drive over."

"Either that or she don't choose you!" Bridgette said and cracked up. The nigga cocked back his hand and open-smacked Bridgette. I stood up but felt dizzy. Bridgette slapped him back, then pushed him. The crowd closed in.

"I wasn't talking to either one of you," he lied, pointing to me and Bridgette. "I was speaking to the young pretty thing," he said, nodding in the direction of Pretty. As he attempted to step close to Pretty, Bridgette cut him off. He then snatched Bridgette's arm and twisted it behind her back. That was a wrong move. If he knew Bridgette, he would've cuffed or gagged her mouth. That's her weapon.

"We hate! We hate! We hate! We hate men who beat women!" Bridgette called out like a rallying cry. She broke free and began screaming, "We hate, we hate. We hate men who beat women!" on the microphone. She was screaming confidently, as though she knew there had to be at least three hundred other women in the crowd who also hated men who beat women.

Soon a chorus of voices were chanting, "We hate, we hate. We hate men who beat women." Then some of the men who were in the request line began beating the hustler who had been twisting Bridgette's arm. The crowd began cheering for the guys that were mobbing and mopping up the hustler whose face I vomited in. But the beast must have gotten angry. He roared so loud flames of fire shot down from his mouth. Some of the fighters caught on fire. Some of the people tried to put the fire out. Instead of it going out, it grew larger and spread wider. Then a deafening horn went off, like a horn on an amplifier. The horn caused people to cover their ears and scatter. Out from the flames came a man who could only be described as irresistible. He was light-skinned. Usually I'm only powerfully attracted to men who don that deep-black-skinned color. This hustler was more the complexion of my father. He had silky black hair but cut it low, faded the sides, and was sexy physiqued and immaculate.

It was as though the crowd recognized or respected him. When everybody saw him, they stopped doing everything and anything they had been doing. His walk was rhythmic, yet perfectly calm and humble, like a boss who never needs to get agitated because he runs it. He didn't have the overplayed swag of the hustlers who had arrived before him. From his, *had to be bespoken suit*, because of the way it fit his muscles and the contour of his body, he pulled out a handkerchief and extended his hand to me. When I didn't react naturally or quickly enough because I was hypnotized by the gleam of his clean diamond cuff links, he began using it to wipe my mouth with his right hand while grabbing the mic with his left.

"I'm the owner of this club," he said into the mic with calm seriousness. "You are all my guests." He gestured towards the attentive crowd. They cheered. "I train my staff to exhibit superior customer service, unmatched guest relations and, below all, common sense. This fool here is my son. He's a son of a bitch and a demon." He placed his foot on his son's stomach as he laid beaten and broken on the ground in the ring. "Apologize," he said, pressing further into his son's abs.

His son's face turned even more hateful. "For what! She's the bitch who vomited on me."

The irresistible father moved his Gucci driving shoe onto his son's neck. "Apologize to her for making her feel sick to her stomach. Then apologize to the noisy one for your unnecessary violence. Then apologize to the 'pretty young thing' for making it impossible for her to accept your invitation," he said as he carefully lifted his shoe from his son's throat and downshifted the mic to him so that his apology could be heard.

"Forgive me, forgive me, forgive me," his son said hatefully three times. I guess that was the best he could do. He stood up. He dusted off the ash and soil from his attire. "Sorry, Father, for ruining the night," he said, like only a son apologizing to his father could say. An unrelated nigga would never have apologized even if he was 100 percent certain that he was dead wrong. Niggas would've just fought or shot it out till everybody, and possibly even the crowd, except for one, was all dead on the floor. His son dropped the mic.

The father caught it smoothly and stepped my way. "My taste is more immaculate than my son's. I choose you. You're the finest choice," he said, and his words were amplified for all to hear, no matter how far off they were from the club. I was publicly crowned. I was won over. He just confirmed my top-bitch status even though I wasn't donned and dolled up in my fiercest fashions. I was won over in that second. "What do you say? Do you choose me back?" He smiled as though he already knew my answer.

The crowd cheered, "Say yes! Say yes! Say yes!"

I saw Bridgette in the crowd screaming, "Say yes! Say yes!" with as much passion as she protested or cheered for anything. She could have been screaming *Toilet paper! Toilet paper! Toilet paper!* and she would still be screaming it with the same resolve, enthusiasm, and force. The thought made me laugh. When he saw my smile, he took it as a yes. At the same time, my eyes landed on Pretty. She was watching closely, not cheering or laughing.

"If . . ." I answered.

"Whatever your 'if' involves, I agree. If you say, 'Allow all of these people into my club for free,' I agree!" The crowd went haywire! Now it was a different type of pressure. It didn't matter. He had everything he needed to have to have me. Pretty dashed and grabbed the mic. "But what does she have to give if she's agrees? What's the terms of the contract?" she asked sweetly, with what felt like a deep concern for me. But the wild crowd booed her. Wall-to-wall boos.

The club owner waved Pretty over, like how a boss waves over a worker. Then he waved his hand one time, commanding the crowd to silence. "A gentleman only offers and never forces a woman to do anything that she does not approve of. These are the only words in my contract," he said to Pretty, but really to everyone. He extended the mic to her lips.

I intercepted the mic. "Deal!" I said calmly. "Free entry for all the clubbers and the drinks are on the house!" I added, snatching back the spotlight and feeding the momentum in my favor. The whole entire outdoor crowd went buck wild. Pandemonium!

"Go get my whip," he said to his son.

"What about my car? I drove the Ferrari here," his son said. His father just stared at him. The pupils of the father's eyes turned red. The son went to fetch the vehicle without further hesitation. His father signaled his suited men who I just noticed scattered about in the crowd. I liked the way he commanded the situation so smoothly and didn't panic or respond to the wildness that surrounded him. He pulled back the mic. "Music! DJ, spin 'All I Do Is Win!'" And when he said the track title, he did a one-step dance move, like I seen my father do back in the day at certain moments where he had to be too cool to dance. The red beast roared and the cut came on at his command. I loved it. His choice pushed out pop and put hip-hop back into play.

The rose-red Rolls-Royce rolled up. He flicked his finger. His son got right out. He waved his son off like a man swatting a fly.

"I have something to say," his son said. The father ignored. Instead he opened the front passenger-side door and waved me in.

"I need my girls to ride with me. That was the 'if' I was talking about," I said to him. He waved Pretty over. She was standing and watching me. Held her heels in her hand, walked over in her bare feet and climbed in back. I looked around for Bridgette but didn't see her in the dancing crowd that was lining up to enter the club. I should have known that Bridgette would run off somewhere in search of her next outburst.

"The fair-skinned one is already seated." He gestured. "She seems to like Olga, my secretary," he added slyly. I dipped and looked in the back. Bridgette in her nun garment was hugged up with some tall, but petite-framed, European-model-style woman, who on first glance I saw was wearing three-thousand-dollar heels. Bridgette shrugged her shoulders like, "Whatever."

Now we were rolling in the rose-red Rolls-Royce. He was driving. I was chilling while falling in love with the white leather captain's chairs with the deep red piping. The whole beauty of this vehicle had me melting. My girls behind me were holding crystal wineglasses as his secretary poured the drinks. She passed the first half-filled glass to me. I was like, *That's right bitch. Keep everything flowing in the right order and I'll let you keep your job . . . maybe!* By the time this night comes to an end, I better be wearing shoes double the value of the pair she had on. I'd make him prove himself to me, over and over again, not through his charm-filled words, but through action. That's the way I measure a man.

On the dash right in front of me was a thin pure gold case. I leaned forward and opened it. "Help yourself. It's my business card," he said, granting permission, but I was already on it. The card was all black and made of expensive fabric. Strangely there was no business address or phone number, or even an email address. It contained only a finely embroidered, slanted, capital letter *E* enlarged and positioned in the center of the card. I flipped it over. The backside was just pure black with one sentence written at the bottom edge in fancy tiny white lettering. It read, ONE NIGHT ONLY.

"Ask me anything," he said, sensing my curiosity.

I was imagining going into the club tonight, getting VIP seats, drinks on the house, a few celebrity sightings. I was thinking of all my favorite dead celebs that might be performing at the club. I laughed to myself. I wondered if the stars have to be dead to perform in the city called the Last Stop Before the Drop? Or if they could be booked from the world of the living and required to sign a confidentiality agreement like I learned about from preparing for my reality-show debut. As long as they never told one living human being about the realm of the living dead, and the fact that "rest in peace" is a sham, would they be allowed to perform at his nightclub?

The unexpected that I had not imagined so far was *way better* than the expected. I dropped the card into my saddle bag. I had so many questions. I didn't ask him anything, though. Wherever we were going next as we cruised through the darkness was better than returning to my little room for one in a convent with a bunch of ugly broke bitches who were determined to stay broke forever.

20.

Laid out on the spa table having our bodies gently scrubbed with loofah sponges and fragrant soaps, it couldn't be better. When we arrived curbside, we were greeted by an attractive older woman. She came directly over to the driver's window with a very attentive and familiar expression upon seeing him. When his window lowered, she spoke to him in a strange language. Even stranger, he spoke back to her in the same-sounding language. But his talk was way beyond simple greetings. He looked over to me, placed his hand on my arm, then turned back to her. I could only guess that he was telling her to care for me properly. He looked back where Bridgette and Pretty were comfortably seated along with his secretary. Then he turned back to the attractive older woman and spoke some more. She listened with a knowing pleasant smile on her face, then stepped to the back door of the Rolls. Olga eased out as though she had fully understood their conversation. He eased out too and to my surprise walked around to open the door only for me.

"I have to finish up some business matters at the club. By the time you ladies are satisfied here, I will have returned to escort you to Pharos."

"Pharos?" I replied, but really it didn't matter. I was down to go wherever!

"The Light House. It is my private place, my estate, where I welcome only the most selective special guests." He smiled, gave me his arm, and escorted me to the front of the establishment. Once I was standing beside my girls, he checked his goddamn hot-to-death, rose-gold Audemars Piguet diamond-flooded watch. I was swooning as he walked back to his whip.

"Take deep breaths," Pretty said, and laughed a little.

"This way, ladies," the older attractive woman guided. Olga followed first. We followed Olga. But Bridgette bolted forward so that she could walk beside Olga.

"What amazing language was that?" Bridgette asked Olga.

"Amharic," Olga replied. "It is the language of Ethiopia."

"My country," the attractive older lady stopped to say proudly.

Three young Ethiopian maidservants serviced us. Olga was in charge of assuring that we receive the "royal treatment." I was glad that it was just us three receiving the works. If Olga had also been laid out on the table, then I would have known that she was not really a secretary, but maybe is a secret side piece, hopefully not more.

"Do you think he's married?" Bridgette asked me, as our soaped bodies were being gently hosed down with warm water.

"No, probably just divorced. Didn't you hear him say outside the club that his grown son was a son of a bitch? He wouldn't say that about his wife. So whoever his son's mother is, either just some jump-off baby momma or tired ex-wife he's no longer interested in."

"Son of a bitch. Yep, he definitely did call his own son that," Pretty added.

"Well, I hope he is divorced. I hate a scumbag who cheats on his wife. I really hate it, hate it, hate it." Bridgette was getting revved up.

"Relax," the Ethiopian girl who was serving Bridgette said softly. Bridgette had raised her head up and tensed up her back muscles just by thinking about my guy's marital status.

"Me too," Pretty said. "I hate adultery. It hurts."

"Ahh bitch, you were fucking Dat Nigga same time I was," I said too quickly.

"That's not adultery," Pretty said. "You were not married to him. And as far as I know, based on what he said, he was not married to anyone either. If single people fuck each other, that's not adultery. That's called fornication."

"Fornication, huh? What no-dick-having, no-pussy-having idiot came up with a dry-ass word like fornication to describe coming so hard your thighs tremble!" I said, and we all laughed. I was glad they didn't front like they couldn't understand where I was coming from. And suddenly the Ethiopian maidservants were laughing too.

Our bodies washed, scented, and oiled, we were receiving mani-pedis simultaneously from the now six *new servants* who were serving us in the same building but separate salon room. I thought it was dope how it was one wide, one-story building that accommo-dated all of a woman's needs. I had a thought while seated in the comfortable elevated salon chairs. "How did you find out about that club? It sounded like you had been there a few times before. Yeah, and you even knew the way," I asked Pretty.

"Because I went once before," she said softly, as though she didn't want to discuss it.

"That wasn't your first time seeing that beautiful red God in the sky playing the music!" Bridgette asked. Then there was a pause be-fore Pretty replied.

"I didn't get that far to the front of the club. I was on the back end of the line two or three blocks over. That's how I knew the club just *had to be lit!* You know it's like a great restaurant. It could be small like a closet but if the food is exceptional, there will still be three miles of people waiting for a taste. Or a restaurant can be fine and fabulous, totally upgraded but completely empty because of who or what's cooking. Or who's serving and how they look and also how they treat the customers. Stuff like that. So I knew the club had the right formula. Everything working right at the right same time."

"So what happened once you got to the front of the club? Was there a different DJ than the one we saw tonight?" Bridgette de-manded to know. But I had already figured out.

"I met a guy while I was on that long line just enjoying the music. We could hear it even three blocks away. Well anyway, the guy pushed a black Lamborghini. He pulled up right beside where I was standing. He gets out and all the girls were checking him. Even the men were fascinated with his whip. And out of the sea of women gathered there, he chose me."

"Same like tonight!" Bridgette exclaimed. And because she was all reflexes, she caused the polish on one of her toes to get nicked. I didn't say nothing. I knew that was the day Pretty had first met Dat Nigga. She knew my feelings and my bond with him. So she was either nice enough or clever enough not to bring him up by name. And I know he rocked her bells, same as he rocked mine.

While our nails dried, we were served, in tiny little colorful clay cups, sips of the best coffee ever. I'm not really a coffee drinker, but I got a bit curious from the aroma, and was impressed at having a servant hold the tiny cup for me until I sipped. It was the first drink I had as a dead human. The fact that they offered it to us made me feel alive. I liked that. The pastry that accompanied the coffee was the size of a coin. I thought it was clever to offer guests the best cake they would ever taste in life or death and to only give them enough for them to leave with a delicious memory and a continuous craving. Seemed like you would have to return to this exact location to experience the exquisite taste. I'm sure that was the whole point. Beyond my sexual enticement, I was getting pretty pumped about the business possibilities this new connect would open for me. I could do what any of the women working here could do. I could do it even better. Upon arriving in the next salon in the same spa, I became skeptical about letting some Ethiopian girls, who were still foreign bitches to me, do my hair. Even though the hair salon was crystal clean, I don't choose beauticians by how sparkling their salons are. I choose based on reputation, hearsay, and technique. Once I choose a beautician bitch, she gets one chance to make one mistake. Then I'm out. Never again to return, and I'm telling everybody not to go there.

"Here, madame." The maybe twenty-one-years-young beautician

set to do my hair handed me a *Vogue*, a *Cosmopolitan*, an *Elle*, and a *Black Hair* magazine. I was so thrilled to see magazines period, I could've peed with joy! I didn't, though. I grabbed hold of them and knew they were going to be taken with me to wherever my next stop is. I looked at the date on the front cover. These mags came out after my death!

"Choose a style. I think you may be particular," she said demurely. "But we are particular too. And we do a great job," she said pleasantly, striking a confident pose.

"Better than the Dominicans?" I asked, just to fuck with her. But she didn't know who the Dominicans were. I flipped through the pages, taking my sweet time. I settled on a short cut that I saw on top model Linda Evangelista. Only the prettiest bitches have the confidence to pull off a short wild cut. With my skin back in flawless condition, my scar gone like it was never ever there, I was as cocky as Naomi Campbell and as sultry as Chanel Iman. So I went for it.

"You got a mirror?" I asked when my cut was complete.

"What for?" the young Ethiopian beautician asked, then smiled. Then she pointed. The mirror was right in front of me. And even though I was seated in her chair and she was standing over me, neither one of us cast a reflection. "Trust me, you are more gorgeous than all of the bitches in the magazines. I'm counting on your look to win me a promotion, a bonus and a reward, all three."

"The two of you . . . ." the dark-eyed, dark-haired older Italian woman who was introduced to us as the top hostess who runs the fashion wing of the spa building said, speaking to Bridgette and Pretty " . . . may select two dresses and two pantsuits. You are limited to salon rooms A and B. You, my dear, follow me." So I did. She was like an old beauty pageant winner who walked as though she still had her crown on her head. Traces of beauty were there but obviously terminally faded. She swung open a heavy door. Inside were the designer's top pieces from all over the world. As my eyes zoomed from left to right at each item, I thought of how I didn't really have enough places to go down here to wear these type of "fuck the world I'm rich bitch" styles. I smiled.

"Enjoy it while it lasts," she said, but sounded a lil' greasy, even with her thick accent.

"How many can I select?" I asked, ignoring her little swipe.

"For you, it is unlimited. Choose anything you like. I will package it for you." She didn't have to tell me twice. I was like a greedy fat bitch in the chocolate shop. I strolled calmly even though I was overjoyed and overwhelmed. I paused as though I had to think about certain items, when there was absolutely nothing to think about. *I'm taking it all.*

From the look on her face, I guess she thought I overdid it. "Everyone forgets. The nightclub is called One Night Only," she said strangely.

"Yeah, what about it?" I asked her sharply, letting her know I'm top bitch right now, not thirty years ago. Even if this is a one-night shopping event, that's even more reason to grab everything while I can.

"You chose fifteen dresses, six skirts, ten blouses, eight scarves, six silk robes, and—"

"And go package them. Do your job." I cut her off.

"Which one will you wear to the club?" she asked slyly.

"Depends on how I feel and how I want to look at that time," I said, which was my super-polite way of saying bitch mind your fucking business!

"So-fee-ah!" she called out. A younger woman emerged from behind a curtain. "Package these," the old bitch said. "All but one outfit will be returned either way," she added. I just ignored her, crossed my arms across my breasts, and tapped my foot like, *Run, bitch, hurry up!*

"You didn't select any undergarments," she said deviously.

"I don't wear any." I said it old-school, like, *How you like me now!*

*   *   *

Bridgette and Pretty came looking for me at the designer shoe shop. I'm glad they showed up, because I was never coming out on my own. Being in there was like a tongue tickling my clitoris. I was turned on by everything I saw. "Who owns this shop?" I asked the French hostess who served me, the only customer at the moment.

"Why do you ask?"

"Well, you have a pair of shoes in a glass showcase over there that are selling for more than one million dollars."

"Oh, *oui, oui*, yes, yes. Stuart Weitzman loves to design this million-, multimillion-dollar shoe collection. He is showoff with diamonds and rubies and gold and emeralds!"

"So, uh, whoever *owns this spot* is so caked up, he could afford a seven- or eight-digit shoe inventory?"

She smiled. *"You know him.* He is the one who made it possible for you and I to be here," she said as though she and I were sharing some secret.

"Oh word, he owns the shoe store?" I double-checked.

"He owns the entire building, the whole spa, and all of the businesses on this street plus more."

"How did you get this job?" I asked her. I knew it was bold and that she might tell me to mind my fucking business, the same way I tell people that all the time.

But instead she said, "How does a woman get anything she wants from a man?" Then she stared into my eyes as though she and I would finish off our conversation speaking only through our eyes. After a long pause, she said, "Whenever you want something from a man, satisfy him." She winked. "And don't keep him waiting." She nudged me to join Bridgette and Pretty, who were waiting at the exit.

21.

"It's a real lighthouse," Bridgette exclaimed, as the Royce rolled along the torchlit path to his estate. "That means there must be a river or an ocean close by." No one replied. The truth is, I had never heard of a lighthouse and had no idea what its purpose was. I just thought it was what he decided to name his property. And because we were in the Last Stop Before the Drop, the name Light House to me signaled that he was a very wealthy man. If light was a forbidden commodity, and he had plenty of it, that makes him king.

As we drew near, I saw it. It was a tower of light, the only thing that pierced the extreme blackness that was the atmosphere. Pierced but not nearly as powerful, like the sun that lights not simply a small area but the whole world. Upon arrival, we saw that his parking area was packed, as though we were arriving late to an indoor concert that had already begun. It was not wild and loud like his nightclub. There was no dance line, fight club, or crowd waiting to crash in. There was no red cage or red beast. Still, I knew there had to be a reason that we were all dolled up and smelling sumptuous. I was amped that my six-inch crystal Dolce & Gabbana stilettos were not being wasted tonight. And my new look and crystal mini and matching clutch were the most perfect eye-catchers.

"Olga," was all he had to say. She got out and escorted Bridgette and Pretty to the guarded entrance. As I placed my mean manicured nails on the passenger door to join them, I heard the lock click. "Not yet," he said smoothly. So I stayed still. He was silent for some seconds. "You are not afraid of me, are you?" he asked.

"I'm not afraid of nothing," I said, with calm, sensual confidence. I meant it, too. Let's face it. I'm a hood bitch who just served fifteen years on lockdown. I got shot dead. I endured the casket, the sewer, the stench, the paralysis, the screaming, the grinding, the breaking bones, the swarm of mosquitoes, the rashes, the mucus, the virus, the prolonged stays in deep darkness, and even the cruel cage in the animal factory. I've been a sexy serpent and a loved dog. I lost a love, the best sex I ever had. I was attacked by Succubus, who torched more than half my hair length. And I am still top bitch.

"For you," he said, and pulled out a red satin pouch. I opened the red drawstring. Diamonds spilled into the palm of my hand. He reached in and pulled up a diamond necklace, the likes of which I had never seen. It was diamond chunks, not neat small princess cuts or tightly arranged gems. He placed it around my neck and clasped it. He went for the dangling diamond earrings still in my palm. He held one up so I could admire it first. Then he put each of them on. I felt like I owed him a blow job right then and there. But I didn't want to ruffle his look or mine. Plus there was obviously a crowd of people awaiting our entrance. Even Bridgette and Pretty had gone in.

A gloved knock broke the spell I was under. It was his manservant, who gave only a hand signal after catching his attention. He got out and walked around to my door. When I stepped out, my stunner heels landed on a royal red carpet. I had not gotten to walk the red carpet on my reality-show debut. However, tonight I was having it all.

Red snow, no, red confetti, spilled out from overhead as soon as we walked through the doors of the Light House. It didn't affect my flawless look or new haircut. I was beneath his wide red umbrella that he snapped open seconds beforehand. I liked that he had a team of men that surrounded and served him. That was very familiar to me. We were inside a huge and high ballroom facing a crowd of people cheering for him. There was even a live band. Only the drummer tapping the cymbals creating a stripped-down simple soundtrack for each step we took.

"The Ruler, the Ruler, the Ruler . . ." they all chanted, the male voices overpowering the women's cheers. As I looked around into the crowd, other than the passionate expressions on the faces of the cheering, I was blown away by what I saw. There were two live all-white giraffes. One was posted in the left-hand corner and the other in the right. The stage on the back center wall was made of black opal and was designed as a shining black serpent, its glistening head raised up over the stage top. But more than that, there were short black pillars lining the perimeter. On top of each pillar was a live monkey. Stranger was the crowd. There were plenty of humans—or should I assume dead humans—all dressed for an exquisite party. Although none as exquisite as me and him. But there were also some suited beasts. Bodies standing upright but with three legs, their faces covered with hair except for their eyes and nose holes. Several guests had short- to medium-length tails. Some tails were thin and taut. Others were thick and hairy. Some short afro puff style. Faces of foxes on bodies of human design, all upright, not crouched or crawling on the floor. All had drinks in their hands or smoke in their mouths. There was a patch of human-looking people, except they each had only one eye. It was located on their chins. The spaces where eyes normally go left vacant, yet there were deep black eyebrows. There were dudes with six fingers. Some with eight fingers. There were women with elongated tongues that they couldn't keep hidden in their mouths. There were enough humans, though, plenty of white ones and every complexion after white to the deep blackness.

Maybe this is the reason he asked me in the whip if I was afraid. But I wasn't. I already figured it out. It was a costume party! Wish someone would have told me and Pretty and Bridgette. We didn't have masks or horror accessories and gadgets. I was on some supermodel shit. Bridgette and Pretty were also dolled, but not as expensively adorned and refined as me. Besides, I was the only one wearing the chunky diamond necklace that he placed only on me. That was a confirmation that I was queen. And the moment I had that thought, the entire crowd bowed down. It was a half bow, and only he and I remained standing for some seconds. The band began playing and all heads lifted. It was an old joint, one of Brooklyn Momma's picks. It was originally recorded by the Ohio Players, a cut titled "Fire." The live performance made the hot record sound more incredible than vinyl or wax or digital CD could ever sound. I could hear the strum of the guitar, the stroke of the bass, the strike of the drums, the lure of the trumpets, the masculinity of the trombones. My whole body was stimulated by sound.

The lights dropped out. Suddenly a powerful strobe caused colored globes of light to spin around the room. My eyes were adjusting to the radical change. Then I heard his voice singing the words to the song that I knew well. Poppa had sung this song to Momma once at one of our big events. He was showing every one of our friends and family that Momma was his hot-to-death, badass wife and that no one else could fuck with her look or style. And that no other man could say he had a similar or equal beautiful thing. While Poppa mouthed these song lyrics to Momma, she strutted in the spotlight that was aimed directly over her. She didn't say shit. Just showed everybody gathered her flawless dark-chocolate skin, her mean-ass walk, long-ass legs, thick thighs, tiny waistline, and all-natural cantaloupe-sized breasts. That's why, when the spotlight hit me, like it just did, I began to strut my strut, swing my hips and dip it low. All hell broke out. They all cheered for me. Even he cheered and applauded all at the same time, his approval magnified by the mic. When I was done showing my supremacy, I strutted to him and clung on to him from behind. I didn't love him . . . yet, like how I had loved Midnight for years, or Dat Nigga for the whole of my death life. It was more like I wanted to possess him and all that he possessed. I believe if a nigga has power and style, plus the look and the empire, the love will come slowly. He was older than me. I could tell. He had a son who seemed around the same age as Pretty. And although I was a few years older than Pretty at my "T.O.D.," as she would say, I am definitely not old enough to be Pretty's or any grown-ass adult's momma.

He began addressing the crowd. Each time he spoke, he used a different language. It seemed whoever was gathered there who spoke the languages he began speaking in would cheer from wherever they were standing. He had spoken so many languages, but not yet English. So I didn't know what the fuck he was saying. But I was still clung on to him as he spoke. In my head I'm telling myself, *Do whatever is necessary to hold on to this handsome, manly, older-man jackpot.*

"Thank you for accepting my invitation to the Light House. It is always my intention to maximize your enjoyment, whether dead or alive, man, woman, or beast. I make it my business to treat each and every person and thing equally. In my realm, no monkey will ever be asked to be less than a human. No spirit will ever be asked to bow down before Adam, a human, or a beast. I like to provide a precious option and alternative to the ONE. He may have created every living thing, from the tick to the whale, the ant to the elephant, the serpent to the giraffe, the lions and tigers and bears, all of the ghosts, jinn spirits, and the goddamn human beings, but I say we are all equal. You never need to say one prayer to me. If you bow down to me, it is because you wanted to, not because I demanded it. And it is because I have provided you with the freedom of the so-called Last Stop Before the Drop. Yes, it is true that there is only one exit out of this realm. It is to say those detestable words that there is no God but Allah. And you must wash your body first, and raise your hands to the air and praise the ONE. And if that is not already too much, you must crouch, then kneel then bow down, with your forehead pressed to the ground, and pray and beg for mercy. But I say tonight and every night and all of the time to every living thing down here, 'Welcome, just stay here in my realm with me.' You don't have to beg for Heaven. We are comfortable here. We are co-workers, co-earners, and we are friends. We trade favors. And most of all, you will never be judged by me. You are never required to bow down to me."

The crowd went wild. The black opal stage split in half and opened slowly. As it did, the band played "Atomic Dog" by George Clinton. Behind the band was an elevator shaft lit up like a glow stick. He grabbed my hand gently and I followed him onto the elevator. As the doors closed and all remained cheering, I thought how dope it was to have elevators in your house! He lived in a tower. It was like taking an elevator to the sky. He seemed to have everything. I loved it.

22.

The penthouse. I had been in apartments, condos, houses, mansions, and even palaces. But I had never been in a penthouse or a lighthouse. Now I was in the Light House Penthouse and it was incredible. The walls were painted in warm colors. The artist had an awesome idea to do every variation of red, beginning with the lightest pinks and blending in every other shade gradually until it reached blood red. The ceilings were high but the walls did not reach the ceilings. Instead they were freestanding and laid out in an intricate maze. I thought it was different and obviously designed by the mind of a puzzler. I could not distinguish the exit from the entrance. There were so many paths in and out. You would have to have lived here for a long time to know all of the routes. He knew. All I could do was follow him.

Left, right, left, right, left, left, left, and we ended up in a living area layout, facing an aquarium with a shark swimming in tons of water, alone. The floors were all white marble. The white leather rectangular sofa pieces had no backs but looked extremely expensive and comfortable.

"Are you afraid of sharks?" he asked me.

"I'm not afraid of nothing. That shark is in a tank. I'm out here with you," I said.

"I like a woman who is fearless. Not afraid of the same things that every other woman and most men fear the most."

"Did you put the shark in there to scare people away from your place?" I asked him, since it was our first stop on the path he chose through his maze.

"No, I'm a collector of the living and dead things that are feared the most, and that most run from or cast down or aside, or away," he said.

I didn't reply.

"What do you feed him?" I asked.

"She's female. Her favorite food is dead or living human beings. Right now she's digesting Bridgette. Only her fingers, arms, and breast remain. I had my tank attendant freeze the rest for next feeding," he said calmly. I was froze facing front. Had to get my game face on tighter before I faced him. When I finally turned to him looking calm and collected but burning on the inside, he busted out in man laughter. I smiled.

"Ooh isn't that impressive. You've mastered cool," he said. "I'll keep poking you gently until I find your soft spot."

"Do you mean my weakness?" I shot back too quick.

"No. I say what I mean. I mean your soft spot," he said and reached his hand beneath my dress. My pussy was bare. So he began stroking it with his fingers.

"Is this okay?" he asked. Just a breath escaped from between my lips.

"Your eyes say this is good," he said. And it was. He pushed in with a thick finger.

"Lay on the floor. I want to sit on your face," I told him. He pumped his finger six times in me, then pulled it out abruptly, and stuck it in his mouth, and licked the finger clean.

"Not all pussy is for eating," he told me calmly. "But your pussy taste like my favorite fruit." His expression was as though he was even more impressed by my bossiness. I opened his suit jacket and pushed it off of his shoulders. He leaned forward and helped me to free his arms from his sleeves. I undid his "yeah I'm fucking you to-night" Gucci belt. Then unfastened his suit pants. My eyes darted down. He was not as long and thick as Dat Nigga. But he was young, hard, erect, and well equipped to satisfy me. And I had a feeling this man craved a crazy bitch and a wild performance. So I would be dat. He was fully naked. I stepped in close and bit him roughly. He looked surprised. Then he looked excited. He put his finger to the spot I bit and drew back his hand and saw a tiny bit of blood. He smiled.

"Only because I know a gentleman like you doesn't beat women," I teased and taunted, then slapped the shit out of him and mushed his face down to my waist. "Lay down," I bossed him in a sexy command. He did. I positioned his head between my thighs, then squatted onto his face. All he could do was enjoy his fruit. His tongue felt nice down there. Nice enough for me to explode. When I did, I surprised myself and screamed out. I forward rolled over his head and collapsed on the floor. Now we were both in the lying position, head to head. We both jumped up swiftly. We both were on all fours facing one another. He smiled deviously like he was having more fun than he expected to have. He growled. I growled back. He smiled again.

"You thought I was a doll? Fuck that. I'm a tiger," I told him, and launched at him. We wrestled. He dragged me by my foot. I broke loose. Now we were both standing, glaring at one another. He used his foot to hook the back of my ankle. I fell. He flipped me over. I flipped back to the front like an acrobat.

"No ass," I yelled, my chest heaving.

"No ass!" He laughed like, *What the fuck?*

"A man is supposed to prefer pussy. You are a man aren't you," I taunted him. He leaped at me like a leopard. I cocked my legs open.

"That's right nigga, pussy hole." We humped in the sitting position.

"Well damn!" Bridgette gasped. She must've been quietly tiptoeing or running through his maze. Barefoot, she stopped short the moment she raced into the corner where he and I was going at it, humping seesaw style. He turned his head back to see who entered our space. I snatched his face back and held it. "We ain't finished," I told him, ignoring Bridgette.

"You're so exciting," he said. "You even like when others watch." Still pogo-ing and my adrenaline out of control, I was mounting to a next orgasm and didn't want to be interrupted or cheated out of it. Six more pumps and I threw my head back. "Ahhhhhhh . . ." I exhaled, pushed him off of me, and rolled onto my belly. After catching my breath, but still huffing a bit, I asked, "Bridgette, where you headed to?" Before she could even explain herself, I rolled my body over his, laid my belly on his back, and covered his eyes with my hands. I was concealing him. I didn't want her eyeing my new, nude jackpot fuck buddy. And even though she was fully dressed, I didn't want him eyeing her either.

"Nowhere . . ." she said as though she was at a loss for words. But it was out of character. She's never at a loss of words. "Olga gave us the grand tour. But there was so much to it, I decided to look around once more. That's how I ended up here." She explained herself. After a pause, she was back to her typical-style outburst. "It's a labyrinth!"

"Labyrinth?" I repeated. What the fuck was she talking about now? But it must not be a bad word or a protest of his place. When he heard her say it, he just smiled coolly.

"Yeah, like, there are so many different ways to arrive to each room. It's like someone is purposely trying to confuse us. Or as though someone is hiding something from us or trying to hide himself from something or someone," she accused.

"Hiding." He removed my hands from his eyes. He rolled over. Now my back was on the floor and his back was on top of me. His joint fully exposed. She turned away from staring at it. She better had.

"Excuse me. Not hiding. It's like the owner of this place has a security problem."

"The owner . . ." He sat up. I wiggled from beneath him and went for my clothes. "That's me," he interrupted in a cautionary tone to remind her who she was talking to.

"Okay! That's you!" Bridgette said in a too loud voice as she clapped her hands together once. She turned to face him boldly. The whole embarrassed shy routine gone from her performance. "I didn't catch your name although you know mine," she said, pointing at him. He did not answer. His silence did not cause her to pause. "Anyway, if someone were to come in here uninvited, they would never find you easily. And on top of getting lost looking, they would expose themselves by the shock at all of the animals and creatures embedded in the walls. They would have to gasp or scream or run. But then when they start to run, they can't find their way back to the front door." Her explanation caused him to laugh.

"Not exactly. Olga invited us up. So I took it as it was okay to come up here."

"Yes, it is just fine. You are invited. But maybe I have somehow terrified you with my taste and my animal friends?"

"Not me," she said, her eyes darting in the other direction. I knew immediately she was referring to Pretty. "Where is she?" I asked Bridgette as I handed him his shorts, pants, and shirt and gave a glare like, *Get dressed!*

"Well, that's my whole point. I knew where she was a minute ago. Now I don't. We saw a glass wall. Inside of it there's a serpent. She hates serpents. She's scared to death of them. So Olga gave her a room far off from ours."

"Ours?" I repeated.

"Yeah, well you don't look like you're headed back to the convent anytime soon." She smirked. "You look totally comfortable." She smiled. "And me and Olga are gonna be roomies. So that's what I meant by 'ours,'" Bridgette clarified. I glanced at him and it seemed from his expression he had had enough of her talk.

"Follow me. I'll show you the way back to Olga's room since you say you are lost," he said as he stepped into his pants and picked up his dress shirt. "C'mon," he commanded me. I liked the roughness of that order. I followed. "The maid will collect the rest," he said, and led the way.

Olga's room had one queen-sized bed. It was large, like a suite, and looked lived in like a permanent place. It was lovely. The walls were peach and the thick carpet that covered only part of the floor was bright white. Bright white marble floors and bright white carpet made her seem like the princess of cleanliness. She had a kitchenette and a glass eating table for two, a peach leather love seat and a glass desk with brass legs. She had a ledge on top of which sat twenty-four white candles in curved thin-glass jars. It looked like a master bedroom. I could see the entrance to her private bathroom.

"I return you safely to your roomie," he said, smiling. He grabbed my hand and turned to walk out. I was glad he did. Olga, who was seated on her bed in her silk nightie, with papers in her lap and expensive Cartier reading glasses on her eyes, needed to see him choosing me continuously.

Walking hand in hand and talking softly to each other, we were like seasoned lovers, and I was sure, based on the events, that it had not been twenty-four hours yet of us first meeting one another.

"Tiger," he called me. I smiled, remembering. "A tiger in the convent?" he smiled and said as though it was a question not a statement. "Come to think of it, I could not imagine you or either of your friends as nuns." He laughed.

"Don't get it twisted! I would never be no nun. Take an oath of poverty!" I cracked up at the thought of it. "Bullshit fashion, no jewelry or cosmetics!" I laughed again at how outrageous it was to me. "I mean, as you can see, I don't wear cosmetics. I don't have to. But why on earth would a bunch of butt-ugly broads not try and upgrade their look!" Then we both started laughing.

"I love that you are so decided," he said calmly. "A woman who knows who she is and what she wants. That's badass to me," he said, then stopped walking and backed me against the wall. He gave me a kiss on the lips. I opened my mouth, but, he didn't come into it. I wanted tongue, a deep kiss. I had not been tongued down in more than fifteen years. For me, the kiss is the seal. The lust and the fucking comes easily. It's a must. But somehow the deep tongue-on-tongue exchange is the most intimate for a woman.

"Tell me more," he said. His body pressed against mine. Mine pressed against the wall. He was massaging my butt. It felt good. However, I remembered what Succubus said about how, alive or dead, humans are forbidden by the ONE, who she calls the Tyrant, who he called Allah in his speech what seemed like only a couple of hours ago. I don't believe in or care what the ONE aka the Tyrant aka Allah said or says. But I did care about the punishment of being turned into an animal for exceeding the rules and butt fucking. I still couldn't figure out if it is the ONE turning us into animals for butt-fucking, or if it is the man who's fucking me. Either way, solely for the protection of myself, the business I plan to set up, the fucking I want to be able to continue to do, my ass is off-limits, closed, an exit, not an entry.

I squeezed my ass cheeks. Maybe it was an impulse. A way to express to him without words that I meant what I said when I told him *no ass* right before we romped in the shark space what seemed like a few minutes ago.

"Relax," he said. "I won't deny you anything. But anything you deny me, I'll supplement. Deal?"

"Supplement?" I repeated.

He smiled and pulled back a little, creating a slight space now between he and I. "Bargain elsewhere," he said. "Because I know you want me to have all that I need, even if you are not the one to offer it to me." I caught on. I was quietly moving the thoughts in my mind in a hurry. How much did I care if he gets it on with other women? I only just met him. He was a good time for sure. The business opportunity was most important. Maybe I should get what I want out of him business-wise and stop caring about anything else. *Come on, Winter,* I told myself. *You know how to fuck without feelings.* True, but could I knowingly share a man with another bitch even though I didn't love that man? If I could, how would that affect my status, my access, and my fucking leverage and control over a nigga? If I let another bitch get an inch, she would try to take a yard. That's basic instinct. When I was with Dat Nigga, I had to take a backseat while I was an animal. I couldn't fuck him as a serpent. I couldn't even do as much for him as he did for me when I was a dog. Ooh, a memory. He made me feel so hot and satisfied and loved as a dog. His long thick finger like a dick. The constant fingering and petting. Rubbing my underbelly. Me sleeping right next to him on his bed. Whew, my nipples were getting hard simply remembering.

"That's the first thing I saw on you. I hope you don't mind," he said, snapping me back into focus. *Winter, you're with this dude now, in his penthouse, amazed in his exciting maze.*

"What?" I asked lovingly.

"These." He pinched both of my nipples. "I saw these poking out of your tight coat. I thought, 'What a bold beauty. She's naked beneath her coat.' I started imagining you nude. It was sexual first. I hope you don't mind. I saw your most attractive eyes, nose, lips, and face secondly." We fucked there on the wall. It was beastly, and when we were both satisfied, he had passion marks all over his body. My body felt raw, like the whole thing was one throbbing nerve. My pussy felt greedy, like it had to have more . . . soon. Even my nipples were pulsating. I wondered if his balls felt to him the way my nipples felt to me. I had given him the right blend of licks and sucks and heat and friction everywhere.

23.

An alarm went off. It pierced through my deep sleep. It seems I only slept soundly in this realm after a long night of thorough fucking. And last night or whatever time it was, I was completely and thoroughly and repeatedly fucked. I sat up. I wasn't alarmed, even though the sound was annoying and overpowering. I feel safe here . . . with him . . . in his Light House. He was the commander in chief. That's higher than the CEO, at least in my mind. But he was not beside me, as he was throughout the night. He must be out giving orders, protecting his property.

I stretched my legs. I smelled my sheets before I stripped them off of me. They smelled like sex. I placed my pretty feet on the cold marble floor. The cold surged through my body, helping me to awaken even more. I walked over to his rack and pulled down one of my six new robes and nighties. I put one on before show-ering, only because of the ringing alarm. I walked to the door and pressed the button. The thin steel doors slid open. I don't know which is more impressive: the secure powered soundproof doors, or the high-powered alarm that was able to cut through the sound-proofing enough to allow me to hear it, but now sounded ten times worse. I could here Pretty's voice, Bridgette's voice, and run-ning feet.

"I'm looking for y'all!" Pretty called out.

"We are looking for you too," Bridgette called out from elsewhere.

"I'm right over here!" I yelled out. Then there was the sounds of running feet once again.

"Stop moving," Bridgette demanded. "Two of us have got to stop moving and one of us has to follow the sound of the voice."

"I'll run to you. Say something and stay still right wherever you are now!" Some time passed before I heard Pretty and Bridgette celebrating because they had found one another. Their celebration was beneath the sound of the screech of the alarm.

I plugged each of my ears with a finger to drown out the noise. I told myself not to close the steel doors until they showed up. I'm rhyming so they could follow the sound of my voice, even though I could not hear myself! "Throw your hands in the air. And wave 'em like you just don't care. And if you're feeling good and you love your hood, everybody say, oh yeah! And you don't stop . . . Ain't no party like a Brooklyn party and a Brooklyn party's nonstop . . ."

Pretty and Bridgette arrived gasping. Once they saw me they both put their hands over their ears. I pulled them inside and pressed the button so the door would seal and they could escape the deafening sound minus times ten.

"Is there a fire?" I asked, my ears and their ears all unplugged and the alarm muted.

"No, not a fire," Bridgette said, calming down swiftly as though nothing had just occurred.

Pretty still had a painful look on her face.

Bridgette started wandering all around the space looking at everything like a detective.

"This is the master apartment, a penthouse within the penthouse. So amazing. Oh, oh, oh bingo! I finally found it," she said once she saw his wheeled rack of treats, weed, pills, cocaine, cigarettes, cigars, and bidis. Plus there were chocolates, caramels, gummy bears, Pixy Stix, and Now & Laters below. She opened her satchel and started grabbing from the top shelf.

"Chill," I told her. "Put it all back. I don't want him to suspect me of stealing his shit. I'm trying to build up a trust. And as you can see, so far, the better my bond with him, the better it gets for you two. Besides, I am sure if you ask for it, he will give it to you easily."

"Okay, let's put it all back," she said as she began placing everything back in its slot. "Except let's blow one pot stick together. Like you said, he won't mind." She was already holding one of his novelty lighters and lighting up.

"Aren't y'all worried about the alarm? It's much better in here. But I can still hear that it's on," Pretty asked.

"Here, this is some awesome pot. Have some. You won't even hear the alarm. Even if you still hear it, you won't even give a fuck," Bridgette said. She was already buzzed. Pretty took a few pulls and I could see that it lessened her nervous feeling. "I've learned so much in a little bit of time." Bridgette said it like whatever she had found out upgraded her status in our trio acquaintance. She wanted us to ask her and to need to know what she had discovered. She handed the joint to me. I took a pull.

"The alarm, it's about a security breach. His son—you know, the one who you vomited on outside of the nightclub—is attacking the Light House with a bunch of other dudes."

"That's dumb," I said, still toking. "How's he going to win by attacking his own father who lives in a tower? He's just gonna get humiliated like he did at the club. Then he'll start apologizing like a little bitch."

"What does his son even want? You don't want him. I don't want him. So what the fuck?" Pretty asked me.

"He's scared. Scared people always come with a bunch of niggas to fight one man. That's the only way they can possibly win," I said.

"No, but his father has got a whole army. He's not just one man. So it should be a brutal fight to the finish," Bridgette said, getting amped back up.

I finally asked her, "How do you know he's got an army? And how do you know it's his son leading the attack against him?" I questioned in a "prove it" tone.

"I saw it in the security room. Olga rushed through the crazy maze as soon as the alarm went off. She jumped out of bed and I followed her. There was a screen and she could view what was happening everywhere in this tower. She got right on a walkie-talkie and commanded the Yoo-nicks to mobilize. I thought this was an army of men who were stationed somewhere close to the tower. But then I heard first, and eventually saw, multiple men in black, up here sprinting through the maze to go put down the attack. They're all living up here in one big area, dormitory style, one cot each."

"Or like jail," I commented but really was just recalling jail before conviction and imprisonment.

"Oh, this guy has everything that no one else at the Last Stop has got. And Olga seems to be his right-hand man. That's one of the reasons I'm sticking close to her." She laughed.

"Not because she has pot sticks?" I asked, mocking her.

"I wish! Olga doesn't drink or smoke. Picture that," Bridgette said.

"So that's why you were out last night searching the entire penthouse, *for weed*, but saying it was for something else," I checkmated her. I knew when she rushed up on me and him in front of the shark room, she was out doing what crackheads do, fiending. I mean, me and Pretty smoke of course. But there's a difference between us and fiends. Fiends behave in a certain desperate way. Back in Brooklyn, when certain crackheads had smoked up all their dollars and needed the next hit, they would wander around the streets looking all over the ground for anything to smoke that may have been dropped or partly used. One crackhead who was not looking where she was going, and was so desperate in her search, crashed right into a pole and busted her head.

"Well, my eyes are always opened and seeing and looking. But it's true that I was really worried about her last night," Bridgette said, pointing out Pretty with her head. "You didn't see her reaction when she saw a few snakes. And it's not like they could bite her. They are stuck behind the glass in the wall." Bridgette's facial expression revealed that she was low-grade chumping Pretty.

"You two obviously don't know the story of creation. The serpent is the evil one that started all of this shit. Haven't you ever heard of Adam and Eve, the first man and woman who God ever created? God gave them everything. He only asked both of them not to eat the fruit from the forbidden tree. The serpent is obviously a representation of evil. Why else would God give it no arms and no legs, forcing it to crawl around on its belly? It lives inside of holes deep in the earth, is cold-blooded and poisonous most of them," she said, her voice trembling.

"Well, the serpent came slithering and started speaking to Eve making hissing evil suggestions. Saying that God was really nobody important and that the fruit was there to be tasted. He kept hanging around her until she betrayed God and ate the forbidden fruit. And when she did, God punished her and Adam. Gave them knowledge they did not have before, and it caused them to be naked and feel vulnerable. Then Eve was given the task of having babies. After that, all women became the ones that must give birth. That's why birth is taken as such a huge burden by us women. It seems like everyone gets really upset when we become pregnant, including us. And don't you guys remember how many women were gathered at that UBS rally? Each of us who were seated there were mothers who killed our children. Some of the women there had killed two, three, six, seven, or more lives. I killed only one. I didn't want to do it. My father forced me. But I should have been stronger. We are mothers who rejected the task of bearing the burden. And that goddamn serpent started it all," Pretty said, and then she cried. Her tears caused me and Bridgette to go silent. Pretty seemed so sure of everything she was saying. Most of all, she seemed to have a lot of regrets.

"You get the last of the blunt. It will make you feel better," Bridgette told her. Then Bridgette remixed Pretty's story. "It was that motherfucker Adam who started it all. He must have bossed Eve around saying that she was inferior to him. And he must have bored Eve to death. That was why she was out alone talking to a damned snake. Where was he? And what was he doing? There are always at least three sides to every story. Sometimes there's like six or seven versions," Bridgette said excitedly and it caused Pretty to laugh a little. "So what's the deal about us knowing each other's names? The two of you know mine. I don't know yours," Bridgette said.

"She is called Brooklyn," Pretty introduced me to Bridgette. "And I am named—"

"Pretty," I said, interrupting her. "I call her Pretty," I said, introducing Pretty to Bridgette.

Pretty leaped forward and hugged me tight. I was caught off guard. In all of my all-girl cliques, crews, and gangs we never hugged like that.

"I think you are even more pretty, the prettiest," Pretty said to me before easing up her squeeze.

"You two keep leaving me out," Bridgette said, and leaped over us both, gathering us into a hug huddle on his bed.

"What's going on?" The sound of the secure door opening caused us all to sit up to attention. Olga was standing there looking like a jealous lover.

Bridgette jumped off the bed and ran over to her. "Nothing at all. Hey, the alarm is off. Is everything okay now?" she said and asked at the same time.

"How did you get the door opened?" I asked Olga straight-faced.

"I know all of the security codes in this tower for the sake of safety," she said, and pointed to her head as though she had memorized each one.

"What if something happens to you?" I said, like a veiled threat.

"I guess nothing better happen to me," she said.

"We are all women here. Let's not fight." Bridgette jumped to Olga's rescue unnecessarily. I just need to hammer into Olga's head that I am here now. I am top bitch. I will make sure I get those codes from him that she thought belonged only to her. I am ready to get my business straight and solidify my status and position.

"I want . . ." I told him much later when he returned. After I greeted him warmly and massaged him out of his war mood, I provided the list of things that could not be denied. "I want a business space here in the tower. I'd like to design fashionable clothing for everyone existing in the Last Stop Before the Drop. You'll see. I'm talented. I'm profitable. Invest in me," I said in my baby-doll voice, then put on my baby-doll look that I used to use on my father.

"Is this the doll or the tiger speaking?" he asked me with a smile.

"Both. The doll is the bait. The tiger is the moneymaker," I answered. He was sitting between my thighs, his back pressed against me. I was softly rubbing his chest, stroking his few chest hairs. I lowered my hand down to his belly and then held his balls softly in my palm.

"I'm a businessman for a very long time now. No one else negotiates with me this way," he said. I squeezed them and slid my hand up and began a soothing hand job on his already at-attention thickness. He groaned. "You're confusing me," he said, straight-faced but in a playful tone. "I keep everybody and everything in . . ." He groaned pleasurably. I tightened my grip a little. "Separate categories," he said, finishing his sentence. I cocked back my legs and stood behind him. Then I took one step over him, turned, squatted, and bent, then put my lips tightly on the head of his thickness. I did him better than a Blow Pop, a Bomb Pop, or a scoop of pralines-and-cream ice cream on a sugar cone. When he was fully satisfied, I was lying facedown between his legs. I placed my head by his balls, laid it gently on his thigh, and tilted to my side, so I could still convince him physically, if my words somehow didn't win him over. But I could feel I was close to getting what I wanted.

"I want a business space here in the tower, two talented tailors, a sewing room with top-of-the-line equipment. Fine fabrics, ten drawing pads, thread, and all sewing supplies. I want a music system in my design room. I want to be the only one who has codes or keys to my business space. I want to change the code on our bedroom space, and you and I will be the only two who know the code in here. I want my own secretary. I want to develop a partnership with you where my designs can be sold wholesale and retail, maybe in your spa building, but in other places as well. I'd even like to design an incredibly better garment for the nuns at the convent and the people who they believe they are rescuing. Because that's business too."

"Is that it?" he asked, as though my requests were not troublesome.

"Should I continue?" I asked and licked his balls immediately afterwards.

"Please continue," he said, but I knew he was not meaning with my list of wants but with satisfying his wants. His joint was poking me in the eye. So I licked and sucked some to build up the tension. Then I stopped to torment.

"For your nightclub, I think I would make a great promoter. I could bring in talent and stylize each night to draw the right crowd to match the music." I began sucking again.

"Stylize," was all he said and I could barely even hear that. He was in the sex zone.

"Yes, like the music the night me and my friends went was not the kind of music line up that I crave to hear. So if we have pop night, hip-hop night, R&B and soul night, rock night, jazz night, throwback night—you know, like that—then the crowd would come based on their favorite kind of music and performers."

"What about my mascot, the DJ. Did you like him?"

"I like only you," I told him, then took the last powerful pull. I'm no amateur and I wasn't ever going to be saying I like some next nigga when I'm with another nigga. Real bitches know better. That shit backfires.

After he busted, he said, "You've never been inside my nightclub. How can you be sure about being a promoter there without having seen it?"

"Well, let's go see it," I said.

"Today we will go walking throughout the landscape of my labyrinth, as your friend calls it. We will choose the best space for your fashion design business. However, allow me to caution you and give you a choice. This way we both live without regret," he said, sounding way too serious. "I don't normally mix business and pleasure.

Same as I never mix sex and negotiation." He smiled. "I find myself at a disadvantage, a position I normally never willingly place myself in." He kissed my forehead. "But let's say this tigress has captured me and held me locked between her jaws and I like it . . ." He was caressing me. "There still has to be rules that we stand by."

He was over me now. I was lying beneath him. "Number one." He penetrated me. It felt good. "I'll allow you to be a tiger, roam freely around my territory, like no other beast does in the penthouse. But you must be *only my tiger*. Pledge allegiance to my dick." He pushed in once more, then pulled out. He was teasing me with a very-too-slow stroking. "Number two, I will allow you to be the only one to know the security codes to your new space and to change the code here to my master domain, only for you and I to know. Number three, I will provide you with the inventory for your textile business and introduce you slowly"—he pushed in and grinded for a bit—"to buyers and retail markets I currently either control or access." He pulled out. I had already cum. "However, my nightclub, I have decided, is off limits to you. You can tell me your promotion ideas and suggestions. If they are good, I will use them gratis," he said.

"Gratis?" I asked.

"Yes, as a gift from you to me. An enticement for me to agree to all else. And number four, you will only own and control and profit from your fashion business. Everything else that I already have belongs only to me. Number five—"

"Is there more?" I laughed to lighten up the mood.

"Yes, it's always better to do things in groups of six," he said strangely. "Complete confidentiality in all of our affairs, personal and business. You will not discuss with anyone except me what we do or how we do it, or about our business techniques, contacts, and associates."

"But what about my secretary?" I asked softly.

"Good you brought it up now. After the negotiation, after we are agreed on all the terms, you cannot bring up anything outside of what we agreed."

"Is that number six, the last rule?" I asked.

"No, that's standard business practice. Once our contract is executed, it's locked in place unless we both decide it's in our mutual interest to reopen." He looked at me.

"That's fine with me. So I get to have my secretary?"

"Yes, we will form a three-way confidentiality agreement. She will have to be someone who is bonded to all of the terms of our agreement with the exception of ownership and profits. She will receive a salary and benefits."

"Okay, number six—let's hear it."

"Number six, anything you deny me, I will supplement, bargain for elsewhere," he said, sounding like he knew this placed him at an even greater advantage.

"That again. That's personal, not business. You're talking about bringing in other bitches to fuck in the ass?" I got tight.

"That's way too specific." He laughed. "When I say 'anything you deny me,' I will supplement, it means *anything.*" He sat up. His eyes looked completely alert. He was excited by clause six, I could tell. I was thinking. I needed to turn it in my favor at least a little.

"You may supplement. But you cannot bring any other bitches into this tower. I am queen of the Light House. You fuck those bitches in the ass in the streets. Or somewhere where I don't have to see it. And make sure that they don't ever misunderstand that they are *ass* and that's it." I had on a stern expression. He smiled.

"So you agree to rule six?" he asked me again.

"Yes, if you follow my attachment word for word exactly," I demanded.

"Exactly, word for word, our six rules. Deal!"

"Yes, plus don't forget my two tailors. Deal!" I said, and leaped with excitement.

24.

Someone was tapping on the steel doors to our master bedroom with what sounded like a sharp object. I nudged him awake. He jumped up like a person accustomed to responding to surprises and emergencies. He threw on his black silk robe and stepped to the door. I though his penthouse needed security screens in each room so that we could always see who was standing on the other side. It's fine to have a security room with cameras, but a camera in each room would be more convenient and up to date. Then I thought twice. Maybe, because we are dead humans and have no reflection in the mirror, we also have no on-camera presence? But I wasn't sure.

He pressed the button to draw open the door, unfazed about any enemy possibility.

"Have you changed your password?" Olga asked, without any polite morning greetings.

I pulled back my blanket and walked naked to reach for my baby-blue silk robe. I needed her to see me, a permanent feature. I put it on and struck a pose. Then I walked back and sat on the bed where she had no choice but to see me as she spoke to him.

"Yes, it's changed."

"What is it? So I can update my mental," she asked.

"We will meet in the penthouse office moving forward," he said. Inside of myself I was cheering. *That's right! Let that bitch know.*

"What time? You've been so busy. I haven't even given you all of the new codes since the security breach yesterday," Olga warned. He looked back at me. By the time he did, I had on my innocent expression and remained seated quietly.

"A family fool throwing a poorly planned tantrum is not called 'a security breach.' But it's good that you changed the codes. I'll get dressed and meet you shortly in the office," he told her, and reached for the button to draw the steel doors closed.

She said swiftly, "Your son is disappointed at the changes." Then she looked my way. "And this time I think he's right. He has a point. Oh, and I scheduled the three ladies' nightclub visit for to-night as per usual," Olga said.

"Cancel it. She won't be going to the nightclub at all," he responded solemnly.

"And her friends?" Olga asked.

"You can take the one who's rooming with you. The other has been hired as a secretary. You know the protocol. She won't be at-tending the nightclub events either."

"Secretary! She's been in her room writing a book, you know," Olga said, as though he should feel threatened by Pretty's dusty-pink diary. He wasn't. He pushed the button. The door closed on her tight face slowly. Victory! Now all I needed to do was to mesmerize him for long enough that she would be stood up while waiting for him in the penthouse office, wherever that was. After that, she would get it through her mind that there had been a change of power in the Light House.

Leaving the Light House for even a small thing like shopping for fabric was a major maneuver. I styled my hair. It was easy since I had just got the dope cut. Today I am Chanel. I'm wearing black lace, blouse and pants that Chanel tailored and stitched so mean that it concealed everything and revealed everything at the same time. I acted like I didn't know he could see my nipples through the small openings. I'm carrying a Chanel clutch. My feet magical in black Louboutins, which caused my legs to look longer. I put my chunky diamond necklace that he gifted me basically as soon as we met in his safe, which I now know the combination to. Why not? I'm wearing the new diamond set that he presented me with after a few more rounds in his Egyptian cotton sheets and on his white marble bedroom floors. I had received so much so swiftly, I couldn't wait to find out what more would be coming my way. Since I chose black, he also wore black. He was Giorgio Armani, in a mean tailored suit. What blew it up big time was his subtle but sparkling, silver bespoke Battistoni dress shirt and diamond cuff links. Waist and feet, black crocodile belt and shoes. His silver dress socks blew me away. He looked fucking smashing.

When Pretty emerged, she was in purple Pucci, not Gucci. She looked good in anything. Her purple open-toe high heels showcased her lavender French pedicure. We had discussed her role as my new secretary and that I would take the fashion lead. She would dress like a fashionable executive secretary whose outfits would elicit certain business advantages. She had her hair wrapped in a neat bun at the nape of her neck.

Olga showed up strutting like a supermodel, not a professional executive secretary. She already had the chiseled supermodel face, green eyes, and model body. She wore a white lace mini and white Converse. She seemed a little conflicted fashion-wise, but I'm not about hating on fashion, so fuck it. Besides, I was vexed that she wore lace same as I did. But hers was post-death Versace and mine is eternal Chanel.

Bridgette arrived last, her blonde hair swept into an attention-grabbing topknot. Her Betsey Johnson–designed light blue mini matched up nice with her blue eyes. Like Olga, she chose to wear kicks with her dress. I couldn't figure them out. But I could see they definitely liked each other. That's their business.

We traveled in a motorcade, one security car in the lead, one security car in tow. In between was Olga pushing his white Porsche with her and Bridgette inside. Him and me and Pretty rode his white Bentley that was the opposite of his rose-red Rolls. The Bentley had a white exterior and red leather captain seats inside with white piping. It was reeking with richness. Screaming, *fuck the world!* As soon as I found out that all of the cars in his underground garage were his, I chose this one, naturally.

I stayed looking out of the window for the drive. Speeding through the continuous blackness of the Last Stop Before the Drop, the roads and streets are the opposite from my streets up top. I started to feel a little sad. The only reason to rock these high fashions and flaunt these whips was to be seen in them. Diamonds glisten to catch eyes. In the blackness, if anyone was seeing us, I couldn't tell. It wasn't until we got close to the block that he owned that we saw faint light. The spa was lit up and the adjoining stores of all kinds were as well. On one side there were tall torches and flames. On the other, there were telephone-pole-type pillars with one powerful streetlight atop of each. Wondered why he had flames on the left and lampposts on the right. Thought if he had access to utilities, why not just light up both sides brightly? Maybe he preferred the dimness of a flame? I don't know.

All I do know is out of the left side suddenly something hit us hard. Rammed into the Bentley severely. I had been looking to the right out of my window so I never saw it coming. *Oh fuck,* I thought to myself as my head banged hard on the side window at the same time that the airbags blew up. *Why? Why? Why?* I thought to myself. *Every time I'm about to make it big, something fucked up occurs and snatches it away from me.* I was in a type of shock. I think I felt my head bleeding but my brain froze and would not order my arm to move so that my fingers could feel if there was warm moist blood trickling or not. I could not turn to the left or sit up straight, or turn to the back. I could not see if he was hurt or if he was saved by his airbag. But of course he was hurt. It was his side of the car that was impacted the hardest, I thought sadly. It turns out I had caught real feelings for him. Furthermore, under our contract, if something happened to him, I would not be entitled to anything except my fashion company, which was just getting started. And would I live in a tower without him? Impossible, his nasty-ass son who I threw up on would probably be there to seize all of his things, including the Light House. Yep, he'd show up before his father's body was even cold. But then I felt my body falling as though someone had opened the front passenger door where I had been chilling enjoying the drive. Now someone was pulling me out.

"Keep your hands off of her," I heard him say.

Good, he is not dead, I thought, excited on the inside. I didn't know if my eyes were filling up with blood and that was why I could no longer see. But I could hear. A scuffle occurred. *Oh shit, men are fighting over me.* They were so into the fury of it, however, that one of them dropped my body in the street right next to the Bentley. I heard fists breaking bones. I didn't hear Pretty. Was she dead? I felt my eyes crying. Or was it my blood leaking? My voice wasn't crying though. I could feel the heat of a pileup of men wrestling or dragging each other right next to where my body lay.

"She's my bitch! You knew! Iblis told me he told you."

"Son, I told you. Everything is mines."

"That's fucked up," another voice said. I heard the struggle of multiple bodies.

"Security, get these young fools out of here," he ordered. Next I heard what I guess was security trying to move the men who were attacking him. I heard a lot of sounds of injuries being given and injuries being received. Then someone picked me up from the ground. It was the scent of a woman. I could smell her Obsession perfume. She dragged me to the back, opened the door, and pushed me back in the Bentley. I was helpless. But my mind was still on. It never ever shuts off. I was thinking about the time that I was outside of the rent-a-car fighting Simone. Bullet came to so-called rescue me. He put me back into the vehicle. It was because I was seated in the rental car that I caught the charges and the responsibility for all of the drugs and weapons. Recalling, I tried to reach for the Bentley door handle to open the door. I would throw myself out of this vehicle if I had to. The ignition started just then. My arm would not lift high enough or follow my demands. The Bentley pulled off as though the driver pushed the pedal all the way to the floor. My arm fell. When it did, my fingers grazed Pretty. I could smell her Estée Lauder. But I still could not see. Apparently she could not speak. She didn't react to my touch or this crazy accident scene. Then I heard and felt something smash into the Bentley again. The half-million-dollar powerhouse vehicle spun some. Seemed we were being chased by another vehicle whose driver was fucking determined to crash us until we were all dead . . . again.

"You motherfucker, motherfucker, motherfucker!" Bridgette screamed out. I was like, *Oh no! The crazy white bitch is driving the car with me and Pretty knocked out in the back.* Just then we were hit on the left side this time. *Did the one who hit us on the right fall back and come up on the other side,* I wondered. Or were there two cars chasing the Bentley now? I was worried about crashing again. Could I survive another violent impact? Did Bridgette really know how to drive or was she in the midst of a wild outburst?

"You'll never catch me. Never, never, never!" Bridgette screamed. "You wanted to send me to the nightclub alone. There's nothing inside that nightclub building except a raging inferno! You wanted to throw me to the fire like I was trash. And you murder people that same way every night, every day! People who loved your club and the beautiful red DJ and the music! You have some fucking nerve. You are worse, worse, worse than the serpent in Pretty's story. You are the real son of a bitch. No! Not son of a bitch. Son of a motherfucker. You, your sons, and your whole goddamn man-empire. I will never, never, never, let you murder me and my friends! Not after us three bitches all survived death!" Then she smashed into something extremely hard. Or something extremely hard crashed into her. It was the last I heard of her and the last I heard of myself.

25.

"We forgive you."

Oh no. The frightening faces of three old bitches all crouched over and way too close to my face is what I woke up to. The last place I wanted to be on Earth or after Earth was the convent. What was I wearing? Please, not the straight gray garment.

"Back up," was all I said to them at half volume.

"Welcome back." One of them smiled at me with her crooked beige teeth.

"Where are my clothes?" I asked. I could now see that, yes, I was in their gray garment. "Where are my jewels?" I asked. "Where are my Louboutins?!" I screamed. These bitches had the nerve to put those cheap sandals on my feet while I was knocked out.

"All of your material possessions are in the box over there in the corner." Sister Claire pointed. "But, as you can see, none of your material possessions could defend you from your choices or save you in your time of need." I sat up. "Only Jesus could," one of them said.

"Bridgette, not Jesus," I said aloud. She was driving the car. "Where is she? Is she okay? How about Pretty," I asked.

"Who?" Sister Claire said.

"There were three of us. Where are the other two?"

"You took the longest to heal. The other two young sisters are each in their rooms preparing for the service. We will have to go prepare as well. But you have Sister Petra to thank. She saw your eyelids and your fingers moving late last night. We ran right over first thing, expecting you to wake."

"So get ready. We have already washed your body and returned your embroidered garment to you. Sister Claire just placed your sandals onto your feet. We are all eager to see you walk into the gathering. Everyone remembers you so well from your recitation of the Lord's Prayer." They turned to leave, one following the other. I looked around. Everything was same-same. Table for one, the pitiful guy plastered into the wall, a kettle of water, blah blah blah, minus the candle I once had. I slid over, then slowly stood. I lifted each leg one by one. I threw my hands up in the air and wiggled my fingers. I wished I had a mirror to check my face. Then I remembered, no mirrors here. No reflections either. I squatted to remove the ugliest sandals I had ever seen in my life-and-death time. I walked barefoot to the box of my "material possessions." Of course I would wear my real clothes to the gathering. No one would choose the gray garment.

There was no blood on my eternal Chanel. My black lace blouse was fine. If there was blood there, it didn't show up. I threw off the gray garment. I shook the precious lace pants just in case some soil had gotten on it from my being dropped onto the ground during the accident. But there was no soil. Gently, I put my lace on. I stepped into my Louboutins. Now I am sauntering down the corridor to the gathering simply to see Pretty and Bridgette. We need to plot to get back to where we belong. When I swung open the doors to the sanctuary, it was packed. Sister Claire, for some reason, wanted to point me out. I didn't need her help to get attention. My style already distinguished me from every one of them—the nuns, the nuns in training, their staff, and each of their charity cases.

"Welcome-back song," one of the excited-to-see-me nuns called out. Everyone gathered started singing some ridiculously corny song while she waved me over to the front where she was standing. There were no available seats anyway. Even the aisles were

jammed. To me, it was just confirmation of how bogus this whole
scene was. All these bitches been in here praying and not one of
their prayers were heard or answered, obviously. I was up front and
facing the crowd. Sister Claire placed her arm around my shoulder as Sister Maria and the other grannies were all giving me their
scary welcome smiles while singing their happy song. My eyes widened after searching the crowd for Pretty and Bridgette. I saw Olga
dressed down in Guess farmer jeans with the bib and all. Beneath
the bib was a simple thin short-sleeved white tee. Seated next to
her some homeless-type-looking man. When I examined the
man, hidden and crouched in the pew like he didn't want to be
there either, I realized it was the guy that I had vomited on. My
eyes darted away from him but landed in the left corner. Standing below the exit sign, it was him, my lover and partner, owner
of the Light House. I could tell he was doing his best not to stand
out in this bleak, dim, dank, condemned convent. But because of
his exquisiteness, he could not camouflage with the down-and-out
crowd of helpless, homeless, sick, injured, lost, and pitiful. He tried.
He was wearing sunglasses indoors. But, more importantly, he was
wearing them down here in the Last Stop Before the Drop, where
nobody wears sunglasses because there is no sun and no sunlight.
His brand of choice was Gold & Wood. Of course no one would
know that except me and him. The cheap and the poor can never
recognize luxury or trace its origin. His Ermenegildo Zegna suit
was so mean, I wanted to fly over and fuck him in the church. I had
never seen him don a hat. But he was there holding his hat in his
hand.

He must have seen me seeing him, staring and studying and
admiring. He lowered his sunglasses slightly. Our eyes connected. I
smiled, naturally. But when my eyes darted down to the pew beside
where he stood, I saw the impossible. It was Dat Nigga, alive and
in color, as they say. Boldly black and too big-bodied for the convent seating. Yet he was there. My jaw dropped open. I'm sure Dat
Nigga had watched me watching my new lover with an intensity

that he believed belonged only to and for him. My insides knotted. My feelings for my present and my past love conflicted, fought, and mixed even. How could this be? But why was I asking that question? How could any of this be? I am a dead bitch standing in the guest dormitory of a dank convent. I had already been murdered, whisked around for visitations, buried, trapped in a casket, paralyzed and swallowed by darkness, tortured and engulfed in horrifying sounds and circumstances. Converted into a serpent and then a dog. Stoned by a storm of rocks. Raised up and upgraded to a luxurious afterlife lifestyle, then crashed and killed a second time in a luxurious whip. If all of or even any of that is possible, why couldn't Dat Nigga—whose body I saw collapsed, whose chest I saw opened and on fire, who was picked up by his father in his father's body truck and "fed to the fire"—why couldn't he be alive again? But what to do? What was my next move? *Think, think, think . . .*

"There's a Nazi in the house!" Bridgette burst through the sanctuary doors wearing a wife beater and jean shorts, dragging a garden hose and shooting water like it was a gun shooting bullets. Everyone leaned, ducked, scattered, and panicked. She kept screaming, "Nazi. Nazi, Nazi, Nazi!" I didn't know what the fuck she was talking about. Last time I heard her voice she was screaming. Now she was screaming again. "Grab him. Lock the doors. Form a human chain. There he is!" She pointed her water hose at my Commander in Chief of the Light House. But he was too smart, too swift, and too smooth. He slipped right out. My eyes dashed to Dat Nigga. He was dissolving again under the weight of the water. But so was Olga and the guy I vomited on. And so were a few other randomly seated convent guests. The nuns began choking on the smoke from the dissolving ones. One of the trainees began saying the Lord's Prayer in a loud voice like it was a chant or she was in a trance. One granny started throwing white rocks that turned out to be huge chunks of salt. Bridgette dropped the hose. She ran over to Olga. But Olga was a pile of ashes. "Olga, I'm so sorry. I thought you and I were the same. You weren't a demon. You were my sweetheart. I'm so sorry, I'm so sorry," she kept repeating. During the confusion, I walked right out. My black lace blouse was wet. So was my face and hair. But my legs are working. Now I'm running in the Louboutins that he had provided. Going to get my man.

A mean black Suburban with black-tinted windows was idling. It was not raining but the windshield wipers were on. That was him. His vehicle was the only glistening vehicle in the convent parking lot besides a wheelbarrow, a lawn mower car, a nineteenth-century bus, and the remains of the rocked, smashed, crashed BMW. I ran right over. Heard the Suburban locks click open as soon as I reached. I opened the door and jumped in my seat.

"Put your seat belt on, Tiger," he said to me calmly, as though the whole riot-like scene in the convent had not just occurred.

"Brooklyn," I heard Pretty's voice. She was seated behind me. I was overjoyed! Then I fell immediately suspicious. Why was she in my man's car while I wasn't?

"How come you're here?" I asked her.

"Of course I'm here. You are here. And I am your secretary," she said, and sounded true. I relaxed.

"Shower together," he said to me and Pretty once we were safe at home in his tower. I didn't really get his instruction. He must have read my face. "The two of you have been through a lot over a period of time. I'm sure you may have some things you want to discuss. And you both are wearing the same clothes that you wore on the day of the accident. The shower in the guest room that your secretary is using is built for six. Enjoy," he said, and walked in the direction of our private penthouse within the penthouse. I was still stuck on him pointing out that both Pretty and I were wearing our now-old new outfits. Of course I knew we were, but it hurt a little to hear it. I wanted him to see me as beautifully perfect all of the time.

The shower was like a little glass house. Turned out there were six showerheads and three hoses. That worked, because I liked my water way hotter than Pretty did. "I used to have eczema," she said as she washed her body under the downpour of cold to moderately warm water.

"What's that?" I asked, standing beneath the hot water that I enjoy.

"It's like a skin disorder that come from being stressed and nervous. "

"You mean like rashes?" I asked.

"Really bad ones. The itch is so disturbing. But when you scratch it's impossible not to scratch too much or too hard. Then the rash bleeds. It's really ugly. My father sent me to the doctor for it. She said I was not to shower too often. Also, when I do shower, it should never be hot water."

"So what about now? Your skin looks perfect."

"That's because I'm dead. What a relief. I'm way less stressed now than I was before. Although during that car chase, I felt stress like the stress of being alive. Do you remember, Brooklyn, how everything happened that night?"

"No, bitch, you don't remember either. You were knocked out."

"I wasn't. I was experiencing a seizure."

"What the fuck is that?"

"It's like panic that causes me to lose my ability to talk. But I'm actually awake."

"Why do you have all of this shit when you look like you don't have nothing wrong?"

"Didn't you know? It doesn't matter how a person or thing looks. Although every single one of us loves to be, see, and stare at a pretty, beautiful person or thing. On the inside a beautiful thing could be all fucked up, like me. But I like you because you see me as beautiful and named me Pretty even though I'm all fucked up inside." She raised her left arm and flipped her wrist. "I saw you looking at the Rolex my father gave me. Usually it is right here covering up this," she said, pointing out a deep, crooked thick dark scar.

As I looked through the steam at her arm, I saw cut lines going all the way up to the underside of her elbow. "Those are from when I couldn't make up my mind," she said.

When we both stepped out of the bathroom, hair and body wrapped in long luxurious beach towels, he was bare-chested and seated in the center of Pretty's bed.

"Tiger, let's play," he said. "Is that okay, or will you deny me?" I was stuck, caught off guard.

"Pretty, what's up with all this?" I asked her. I was all cooled out before. Now I was gearing up to get pissy. She shrugged her shoulders.

"Pretty, that's a nice name for you. You are not as beautiful as Tiger. But I can feel the love between the two of you. I'm feeling left out. So let me ask you, Pretty, am I wrong? Are you not in love with my tiger?"

"I am," Pretty said.

"So you love what she loves. Is that right? That's why you were sitting in my car when I left out of the convent today. Not for me, but for her?"

"Because I knew she would go there to your truck. I didn't want to get left behind. So I snuck into the back. The door was unlocked," Pretty explained. I was happy to hear that she was not in the truck with my man. And it sounded like she had not been having an affair with him while I was knocked out from the accident. Those facts were in her favor. I already knew he's a fucking freak. Could I get mad at that?

"I told you not to have any other bitch in this house besides me," I said to him.

"You said not to bring any other bitch in this house besides you. I didn't bring Pretty. You did. I told you everything is mine. But I'm a gentleman. I never force anyone to do anything they do not agree to. So both of you tell me if you want me to leave. I'll get up and leave. If both of you don't mind, let's play," he said smoothly.

I looked at Pretty. "I don't mind," she said, and I was floored.

Now I was left looking like the wet blanket canceling out his good time. I'm top bitch. If she agreed, wouldn't that switch our positions in his heart, mind, and business?

"My tiger, if you agree, please remove Pretty's towel. She wants to play with you." I did. The towel dropped to the floor and she was naked. Her nipples were erect. "Pretty, please remove my tiger's towel," he said softly. She did. Now we were both naked. For some reason my nipples were also erect. Maybe it was because I was cold standing in a large bedroom in a high tower. "Both of you remove your hair towels." We did. "Pretty, kiss my tiger on the mouth." She walked up close on me. Instinctively I stepped back. She stepped up again. She closed in on my face and with open lips, she gave me the passionate deep kiss that I had craved from Dat Nigga but never received. I was kissing her back imagining that she was one of the three men of my heart, Midnight, Dat Nigga, or him, giving me finally what I want. I heard him pull back her bedsheet. He approached us. "Pretty, suck my tiger's nipples. Can't you see they are calling for your mouth?" Pretty began sucking my nipples. My pussy started throbbing. He stepped between us, used his left hand to finger me and his right hand to finger her.

Soon we were all three on the cold marble floor. He straddled me and began his stroke. As he stroked me, she was still there for some reason, kissing my face. I came continuously, and my cocked-open legs relaxed but remained open. He flipped off of me. Flipped her over and thrust into her ass repeatedly. She did not complain or resist. She moaned like she liked it a lot. I was conflicted. I did not want to be butt-fucked because of the risk. But I did not want her giving him anything that I had not allowed him. That would give her the advantage. I got up on all fours, doggy style. He was in the heat of excitement as he thrusted into her. When he glanced my way and saw me doggied there, he left her and pounced onto me with full adrenaline and lust. I was giving him what she was just giving him, but I was better. He was more lusty over me. I was top bitch.

Then the lights in the room switched off. I could not feel the weight of him on my back. In fact, I could not feel the weight of myself. It was as though I was suddenly tiny, really small. I called out to Pretty. But my voice was just a squeaky sound. I kept squeaking, thinking it was like clearing my throat and my real voice would come back. It never did. Pretty responded with only hisses. *Oh no, oh no, oh no!* I dashed. But my tiny legs couldn't run fast enough. Now, with my same mind fully aware, I was between the jaws of Pretty, whose worst fear in the world became real. Now, she is a serpent. I am a goddamn rat. She is eating me, painfully. I know she has no other choice. I know the hunger of the serpent. I had been a serpent. Now I am what on lockdown only I caused others to be, food. The only thing left was for me to dissolve inside the belly of the beast and be shitted out. Fuck it, a pile of shit has no mind. I would finally be able to be dead. I would feel the relief that Pretty felt after she killed herself. Wouldn't I?

She was thrown into the glass case with the others of her kind. I knew because I was still inside of her. My mind was still on. It wouldn't shut off. I could hear, but I couldn't see or feel a damned thing.

26.

The glass case was shattered after what felt like six months of time. Now, we are on the move. Pretty is. I am still inside of her. I can now hear more than just hissing. I can hear the sound of multiple footsteps running. Some are heavy human kinds of steps. Others are the pitter-patter of small creatures; others are the sound of things trotting, the sound of fluttering wings and sliding things, all creatures in motion.

"Reject the Nazi! Reject the Nazi! Reject the Nazi!" Bridgette was shouting again, although she didn't need to shout. Somehow she got her hands on a megaphone. It was the one thing no one should've allowed her. How did she get into his tower? "Pretty! Brooklyn, Pretty, Brooklyn, Pretty, Brooklyn, where are you, my friends?" she screamed through the device. We couldn't answer her. We could only keep moving through the maze, trying to find a way out. But then what?

"Gag the crazy bitch. She's ruining everything," I heard him say. But his voice was off in the distance. Seemed every creature and everybody and everything was trapped looking for a way out of the maze, while his security was searching in every direction for Bridgette and whoever was with her, if anyone.

"Ooch, don't you dare touch me. Don't you dare put your hands on me. You guys are workers. You should be on my side. Workers unite!" She shouted. "This guy is a tyrant. Join me! Reject the

Nazi! Reject the Nazi! Reject the Nazi!" she screamed. Then I heard something drop and hit the floor hard. "He's a murderer! He pretends to be a gentleman! He kills people in his nightclub oven every night! He lures them with his music! He makes them wait on long lines in huge crowds! They don't even know or suspect that once they get inside, he robs them of all of their clothes and jewels and feeds them to the fire. He's a grave robber! Poses as a businessman. Import/export my ass! He's an animal hater, posing as Dr. Doolittle! He's no Tarzan. And the Bastard! The Bastard! The Bastard!" Her megaphone must have dropped or got slapped away from her.

Now I could hear only her loud natural voice without the megaphone effect. "He has the nerve to name his nightclub *One Night Only*. Can't you understand? It's only one night because after one night in his oven you will no longer exist!! And another thing . . ." she said, and then her voice deaded. Pretty stopped moving. Other creatures were still moving. We heard a scuffle. Probably Bridgette fighting back, one woman versus his team of men. The exact kind of thing she hated the most. Then the scuffle stopped. I hoped they didn't kill her . . . again. I hoped she was just knocked out like how I was after the car accident.

"You gave her the security codes. This is all of your fault," I heard Mr. Light House say.

"No! It's your fault! You broke your own rules," I heard Olga's voice say. I was like, *What the fuck?* Wasn't she a pile of ashes on the convent bench? She was. But who am I to talk? Now I'm just a pile of shit inside a snake's intestine. Do snakes even have intestines?

"You broke the main goddamn rule," he yelled, losing his cool, which I had never seen him do when I was his top bitch. "You let a dead human have confidential information about our family. You put your own father at risk. I built this damned underground world. I let all of my children have more than enough. But my own daughter falls in love with this crazy dead human bitch. Then you give her all access to my tower. She already ruined my nightclub mojo. She's out there in her painted old bus screaming into the crowd.

Exposing the secret that makes every single night special. That's what you did! That's what my own daughter did to me!"

"No, it was that bitch who you let in here. You allowed her to change the security codes. You allowed her to put her own people on as staff. You gave higher status to a dead human than to your own sons. And you knew that that bitch was Dat Nigga's Bitch. You stole your own son's woman!" she said with hatred.

I felt like shit, for real. Was Olga his daughter? She looked white. Was Dat Nigga his son? Could a man as light-skinned as he is give birth to a man as beautifully deep black as Dat Nigga? Doesn't that mean that Iblis is also his son? Wait a minute. I fucked the father and I fucked the son. And I was raped by his other son, who is Dat Niggas's brother.

"You should have overlooked it. I am your father. I gave you a new body. Beautiful white skin like you always wanted. Green eyes and the face of one of those living humans in the magazines that you loved that I gave to you from my private collection. You were unattractive, tall and obese before. I had your hairy tail clipped and tucked. You had size-fifteen feet before. You were obviously a beast. I fixed that for you so that you would be comfortable with yourself. Didn't I do all of that for you?" he asked her, but not like he was looking for an answer.

"You did, Father. Thank you. But I couldn't stand you giving that same girl who Dat Nigga kept in his house and treasured like she was one of us the top position in your business, in your heart and in your eyes. How could she be more precious than me, your own daughter?" she demanded to know. Her voice sounded like she was aching, holding back from crying.

I was still stuck on realizing. Olga, who looked like a European supermodel, was Succubus, the ugly creature that tried to stuff her huge feet into my sky-high red leather boots. The beast that torched half of my hair. She was his daughter and she was Dat Nigga's sister. But still she had sex with Dat Nigga and basically begged him to fuck her in the ass! What type of unheard of shit is that?

"You complain about everything," he said to Succubus aka Olga. "You were jealous of my relationship with my head Yoo-nick. You demanded that I fire him! You said that you could do his job better than he could! Why do you interfere in the personal business of your father?"

"Because you always fall in love when you are personally involved with any man or woman. I thought it was a conflict of interest for you to be fucking him when he was the head of your tower security," she said, as though she had nailed him.

"Because I was fucking him, and because he is a eunuch and is unable to fuck anyone himself, he fought the hardest to please me and secure me," he said to Succubus.

"Humans—even if they are castrated—Father, are always more ambitious than they are anything else," Succubus said.

"So we are back to the beginning. If you know that, why did you, my dear daughter, fall in love with a dead human and give her the keys to my universe? I never made that kind of mistake. The sex was all my personal choices. I own everything. I never allowed one ambitious human, alien, or animal, dead or alive, to steal one item from me. It is only my daughter who allowed the crazy-ass, dead human Bridgette bitch, right here, to do that."

27.

I found myself in complete blackness once again. But I didn't know if it is the darkness of the insides of Pretty's serpent belly, or the outside atmosphere of the Last Stop Before the Drop. Pretty was not moving. She had not moved since the close of the argument between Succubus and her father. I don't know if there is a way that a snake can kill itself, other than hurling itself at a speeding vehicle and being run over. I knew if Pretty knew a way to commit suicide as a serpent, she would certainly do it. I considered that perhaps she had pooped me out and was somewhere moving along on her own. As a rat, I had felt the pain of being chewed and devoured. But, I never felt the pain of being squeezed through an anus. I assume that if I had been, I would have felt it, but I don't know.

Because of the stench, I thought that I was back at that sewer location alone. But then I knew that the stench might be the total result of what I was in this form. I wished that I had been better off. At this point, being beside the open gutter in complete darkness with limp arms and paralyzed legs would be a step up. But I didn't hear the familiar things that go along with that location. There was no screaming, grinding, moaning, groaning, hissing, or the sound of breaking bones or crumbling teeth noises. There was nothing but dead silence and only the sound of my thoughts. I remained like this for what felt like twelve months or maybe more. By then I felt a deep sadness that threatened to drown me. No one will ever know the pain of not being able to turn left or right, not having moving legs or arms, not hearing talk or being heard, or able to see anything, while still having the mind turned on and at full volume, until they go through it personally. I don't think any book could cause a reader to feel the torture that occurs after death. Nor could any rhyme, film, or song. Pretty was writing all of the time. Maybe she wanted to alert all of the ones considering suicide, or about to actually carry it out, that suicide was not the means to ending your life. It just removed you from the familiar world and dropped you into the unfamiliar realm. Both settings and circumstances as well as the people you knew and would come to know could be equal to the world that caused anyone to feel that suicide was better than living. Or, one could be even much worse.

The only thing I was happy about was that when I heard my own voice in my mind, it no longer was the sound of squeaks. Now it was the normal sound of my own voice. But since there was only my voice, and it was the only sound I heard, I couldn't tell if I was thinking or speaking aloud. At one point, I wondered if Pretty was right beside me, unable to talk while having or after having a seizure. Could a snake have a seizure? And if a snake did have a seizure, would that mean that it was a snake with no hiss? If so, a poisonous serpent with no hiss would be even more deadly. Still I had considered talking to or calling out for Pretty if she was somewhere nearby. Now I understood what Bridgette was saying about Eve being so bored she was out in the garden talking to a snake.

Six or so months after the twelve, my sadness had mutated to certifiable deep depression, the kind that I always believed only the losers had. But now that I am a no-action bitch, I am definitely a loser. On top of that, now I am suicidal. Worse than that, I am incapable of committing suicide, which is lower than committing suicide itself. I wish someone would walk by. Even if they don't speak one word to me, I wish they would step on me and put me out of this misery. Or a car would drive over me and keep going because there was no real reason to stop. Or that a heavy rain would fall and disperse and drown me—anything.

Bomber Girl came to mind. But that young bitch had abandoned me. She said there was one remaining mercy. She spoke as though I would see her sometime soon. She disappeared on the night of the Rally of the Sons after helping me to lift the heavy body of Dat Nigga into his car. I know that he was her enemy. I know that she didn't like helping me to help her enemy. Still, it's not a real reason for her to *cut me off*. She could have just said no and left me to try and pick him up on my own. He was my man. That would've have been fine. Besides, she had already bombed him, knocked him out, killed him . . . I think.

Speaking of the Rally of the Sons, Young Drummer, the dapper teenager who claimed to be my unborn son, where the fuck was he? My mind was pushing images of both of their faces together, which I had never done. They claimed to be my twins. The doctor in the abortion clinic sixteen years ago didn't say I had twins. Well, actually, she didn't say anything. She tried to make a suggestion. Soon as she started her talk I shut her ass right up and demanded the abortion that they advertised in the jingle I heard on the radio. I remember . . . everything, of course.

Now that all I can do is think, I wonder what they do with all of the dead babies that more than a trillion of us aborted? Do they get dumped along with regular food trash? Are they burnt or frozen, stored or recycled? Do they add something to them, mix it up, and turn them into something else? Hope they don't sell the babies like desperate crackheads do.

Might as well admit I killed them. But what would I look like walking around with a set of twins who I didn't even know who their father was? And according to Young Drummer, their father was Boom, a nigga I definitely did fuck but who I only knew for less than eight hours. And if I would've kept Boom's twins, Bullet would have been devastated. He had already been tricked by his ex all the way up until the birth of their child which turned out not to be his child. If I chose to give birth, when I pushed them two light-skinned babies out and there was no trace of his dark-brown face or red blood even, in either of them, what then? That would've fucked up everything. Or maybe it wouldn't have. Maybe if I would have kept the twins, me and Bullet would've never became a couple in the first place. Hustlers who have choices could easily overlook a bitch who has some other low-life nigga's kids, even if it's a top bitch like me. If he didn't choose me, I would not have been with him in that rental car preparing to do a run to Virginia. If I had not been in that car, I would not have been arrested and convicted on a fifteen-year mandatory minimum, which I didn't even know what that was till I started serving it.

It doesn't matter. The fact is that Bomber Girl and Young Drummer were unborn. Therefore I did not ever feel like a mother. Since I chose not to have them, they should never have thought of me as their mother. Why would they be down here fighting and trying to meet up with me who never wanted them in the first place? They both turned out nice without me or Boom. Young Drummer was masculine, cool, and handsome. Bomber Girl was lovely. Both of them apparently had places to live in Heaven, wherever that is. I'm starting to think that Heaven has to be better than the Last Stop Before the Drop even if it's not all that it's cracked up to be. Young Drummer was confident like any hustler's son who had actually been born. He was passionate on that drum but laid back when he talked to me. "Hey Ma, it's simple. If you want to get out of the Last Stop Before the Drop just say 'Lah-il-la-ha-illa-huwa.'" That's what he said to me when we talked on the sidelines of the Rally of the Sons. *Whatever that means. Wait a minute.*

"Lah-il-la-ha-illa-huwa," I said, and repeated it three times. I thought I was saying it in my mind. I hoped my mind could produce a sound that can be heard by whoever needs to hear a dead person when they finally have had a fucking-nough. I kept repeating it like I was Bridgette on steroids when she got fixated on saying something over and over again. I even hoped that I was saying it right. Soon it was all I would say or think. I just kept it on a loop in my mind so that I couldn't hear any of my other thoughts. I remembered what Bomber Girl said about not mixing curses with sacred words. Of course I remembered. I am not a dumb bitch, Oops! "Lah-il-la-ha-illa-huwa!"

Eventually, the green gas appeared bleeding onto the black atmosphere. In what seemed like only a few minutes, the green dominated. *It's a mercy*, I thought to myself. I was beyond excitement. And if I could see the green gas, it meant that I was no longer in Pretty's belly. And if I could see the green gas it meant that I had eyes. And if I had eyes it meant that I was a living thing, not a pile of shit. I was hyperventilating, trying to catch my breath. And if I could breathe it meant . . . I tried to jump up. I couldn't. But I could feel my arms all of the sudden. I start waving them around, like a person lost at sea trying to flag down a helicopter flying overhead. When my new arms got exhausted I dropped them and my fingers could feel the ground. I didn't want my fingers on the filthy ground, so I lifted them back up. I could feel my hair. "Ah-hum-doo-lah-lah, I have hair!" I shouted rhythmically. But what does that word mean? Why did I automatically say it without thinking? It didn't matter. I had a mouth to speak now and hair on my head and eyes on my face and ears. I began to cry uncontrollably. I got mad that I was crying. I tried to stop but like I said, I couldn't control it. I cursed myself out. Then I try and take it back because Bomber Girl said not to mix the curse words with the sacred words. *Where is she? I don't see her lavender sky.* Just as I thought that thought, a magnificent blue color appeared. I almost peed on myself. *Is it a blue sky forming?* Then I hear the sound of music. It's the soothing tapping of a cymbal that became rhythmic drumming. Three strikes of a larger-sounding drum and the blue color opened up and exploded. It was a blast of stars. The stars poured down like heavy rainfall, diamond rain. Except it was only raining where I am. A powerful cologne saturated the air. Out of the stars walks laid-back Young Drummer. Again, not what I expected. *But man was I happy to see him.* But I reminded myself at this point I'd be happy to see anyone or anything, even an ant.

"Hey Ma," he said. I didn't even argue. Normally I'd be like, *I ain't nobody's fucking mother.*

"Where is she?" I asked.

"Siddiqah would be so happy to know that your first question was about her. She is not here. She got herself listed."

"Listed?" I repeated.

"An official request that any UBS can make when they want permission to be born to new parents," he said.

"Oh," was all I could say in reply.

"It took her a very long time to decide. She loved you so much and dedicated her existence to seek Allah's mercy on your soul," he said, but still so calm and unaffected.

"So why did she if she didn't want to?" I asked, having nothing else to say really.

"Because we UBS know that it is perfectly okay to love our parents, to miss and to cherish, to pray for and yearn for them. However, it is never okay for anyone to worship their parents. Or to worship any person, living thing, place, or item. There is a razor-thin line between love and worship. The only ONE to be worshipped is Allah, the Maker of the sun, moon, stars, planets, universe, and all living things, of all souls, of all spirits, of all men, of all angels, of all women, of all Prophets, of all creatures. If any one of us gets it confused, and allow our love of someone or something other than Allah to turn into worship of him or her or it, we have gone astray, committed a grave mistake. Damaged ourselves, even."

"Damaged?" I repeated. His words led me to believe that Bomber Girl damaged herself by caring too much about me.

"Yes," is all he answered. After a long pause he asked, "Do you really want to know her story?" I widened my eyes instead of saying anything back. It took my total concentration for me not to say, *Yeah nigga, I asked didn't I? So of course I want to know!*

"After you threw the Holy Quran out of the car window, Siddiqah felt you would be dropped into the hell fire immediately. She was so troubled, she made the choice to make prayers for you all day every day for ninety Earth days. She was doing her regular five-times-a-day prayers and then doubling them and praying through the nights. She was so much consumed with saving you that she reached the borderline between loving you and worshipping you. Since she knew she was wrong for approaching the line of worship other than Allah, she began to fast and pray to correct herself. She begged for Allah's mercy. After seeking forgiveness for her error, and being forgiven because of her sincerity, that's when she decided to get listed.

"Once she listed herself, she prepared a gift for you. It was the pearl-colored coat, the dress, and the kicks. She chose what she thought *you treasured*. The grenade she secretly placed in your coat pocket was what *she wanted* to give to you, that she believed you would not want or cherish, but that you would definitely need because of your ongoing love of evil."

"How would she know I threw the book out of the car window? Did she see me do it?" I said, hood style. *Show me the evidence.* Then I felt bad about it.

"Just accept it, Ma. There are some things you cannot fight. In the realm of the unseen, Ma, you don't know anything or everything, like you thought you knew it all when you were in the world of the living. Even though you didn't know much there either." He said it so calmly and respectfully that I could not hate him, "Everything you have ever done in your living life on Earth and your afterlife at the Last Stop Before the Drop has been seen and recorded," he said, and I felt like I got hit by a sledgehammer. My game face switched on without me ever calling for it. Then I was feeling like, *Nah, that can't be true. Nobody knows what is done behind closed doors.* But then I looked into his eyes and studied his facial expression. I remembered that Bomber Girl said that UBS cannot lie about any sacred thing. He saw me, seeing him clearly.

"So I love you, Ma. But I don't worship you. I worship and fear only Allah, who knows all, sees all, hears all, and is the creator of every living thing within and beyond the universe." He held up his one finger. "And in the Holy Quran that you threw out, the

last and most important Book of Guidance ever revealed and written to humanity, were the answers to every question that you or
any of us have ever had. If you would have chosen to read it, even
slowly, word for word, line by line, paragraph by paragraph, or page
by page, day by day, you would have saved your soul a lot of losses,
pain, and suffering. But now I am here to ask you are you done
playing and pretending?"

"Pretending!" I said indignantly.

"Siddiqah told me that she already told you long ago that the
greatest sin in your afterlife is to pretend that you do not understand when you do understand," he said, and I was quiet. He started
playing his drum for some reason. When he did, he closed his eyes.
It was as though he was calming himself through his own music.
He was very talented at it. The way he blended the beats, separating
and combining, slowing down and speeding up and finishing softly,
caused me feelings.

"I'm done here," he said abruptly, and the silence that was here
before his arrival began to rise up. The thought that he would leave
and the blackness would come and swallow me and only I would
remain scared me.

"Your decision?" he asked. I could tell it was the last question he
would ever ask me. Same as I could tell that if my answer was not
yes or was not honest to him, he would disappear from me forever
the same way his sister, Siddiqah, aka Bomber Girl, had done.

"If by stop playing and stop pretending, it means—" I began
saying. He cut me off.

"Stop. Do not bargain with me. There is no God but Allah.
There is no judge but Allah. There is only one thing that remains
for you. Are you ready to stop playing and pretending and to begin
on the route, which is the only option and path out of here available
to any and every living thing?"

"Yes!" I hollered.

28.

I stood up easily. I knew now that it was because of the mercy and not because of any other person or any other reason that I could suddenly stand. He strapped his drum to his back and placed his drumsticks in a long side pocket. He offered me his hand. His hand was warm. Soon as I held on to it, we began to travel. Young Drummer didn't push a Rolls or a Bentley, a Suburban or a Porsche, a BMW or a Benz, but it was the best ride I ever felt. He was pulling me through the atmosphere. I could feel it. I was myself, still with my mind turned on. However, I could not feel the weight of my flesh. I wasn't worried. I didn't feel threatened. I no longer feared or anticipated being turned into some kind of animal that I never wanted to be. We were soaring inside of a green haze with a blue color above us and a relaxing scent. Outside of the green there was only blackness. But when I looked down, I could see the cityscape of the Last Stop Before the Drop, all of the buildings and roofs and vehicles that I could not see before. It caused me to feel like I was exiting from the Last Stop Before the Drop, the City of the Ungrateful, County of the Arrogant, and the State of Ignorance. I didn't think anything stupid like I was on my way to Heaven. I got that Heaven was reserved for those who lived life according to some certain standard. It definitely was a place occupied by those who didn't just do whatever the fuck they wanted to do. I still prefer to do whatever the fuck I want to do. I prefer unlimited freedom.

But anyplace but where I had been since I got shot dead and after my three visitations would be an improvement over the Last Stop Before the Drop.

After what felt like a long trip in terms of distance but not exhaustion, we were approaching a thin line that separated the total blackness from the light.

"We will descend here," Young Drummer said. I could feel myself moving down. Not the thrill of the sudden deep drop of a roller coaster. It was the sway of a swing, a very gentle landing. "Close your eyes," he said, and I did.

I could hear the sound of a waterfall. Once I could feel the ground beneath my feet, he said, "Look down first." I did. I could see the shadow of sunlight, lighting up low-cut green grass and a purple butterfly fluttering at my feet. "Don't look up yet," he cautioned me, then handed me a pair of sunglasses that I saw him ease out of his left pocket. "Put these on, Ma. You were so long without sunlight that your eyes will need to adjust. I have heard of situations where the sudden introduction to the sunlight after existing in the Last Drop and traveling here has caused some eyes to burn and others to bleed. So I came prepared for your safety." I put them on. "Now look up slowly," he said, releasing my hand that he had been holding.

When he let go I could feel the warmth leave with his palms. We were facing a huge fountain that was gushing water on seven levels. I counted. "Amal Nafura is the name of this fountain. In your English language, which you love, it is called the Fountain of Hope," he said while removing his drum and his drumsticks. He sat them atop a bench that faced the fountain. Then he squatted and loosened the laces on my black Pradas. Switching to his own feet, he removed his kicks and even his socks and placed them to the side. He then rolled up his fabric cargo pants with all of the pockets and cuffed them at his knees. He then rolled up his four-pocket safari-style shirt and cuffed his sleeves at his elbow. "Remove the sunglasses now and lift your head slowly. Introduce your eyes to the sun." His words moved me. *Introduce your eyes to the sun.* For me they had double meaning. I was seeing the sun in the sky that I had missed and yearned for, but over time had almost forgotten. I was also now seeing clearly a son, who I had never yearned for, barely knew, and whose existence I had rejected and easily forgotten. He saw me staring and said, "What are you waiting for? Remove your shoes." I did. "Tie you hair back." I did. He pulled a men's kerchief from one of his top pockets, stepped close to me, and used it to cover my hair. The nigga in me wanted to say, *Hold up! Don't even try it.* But I didn't. "Cuff your hands like this. Scoop up water and use it to wash your whole face. Rinse your mouth, clean your ears and nose, even inside of your nostrils." He demonstrated, and I followed his example. He scooped up more water into his palms. I did the same. He began washing his hands and arms up to his elbows where his shirt was cuffed. So did I. He then began washing his calves. So did I. He then began washing his feet. So did I.

"It is good to learn, isn't it?" he asked me. "So let's test it out. What are we doing right now?"

"We are washing ourselves hoping to get clean."

"What for?" he asked swiftly.

"Because we traveled a long distance and maybe we got a little dirty?"

"And what else?" he asked me, peering into me with his sixteen-years-young-way-too-serious eyes. I stood there thinking but nothing else really came to mind. Of course people wash up and shower to get clean. Maybe he wanted me to add that when we are clean we feel better. But isn't that obvious?

"What other reason do people wash themselves for, besides to get clean from dirt?" he asked again.

"I don't know another reason," I told him, frustrated.

"I am washing so that I can make a prayer. Before praying, each of us are guided to prepare ourselves by cleansing. People who are not playing and who are not pretending know in their souls that this is the right way to do before praying to Allah, the ONE, the Most High. We pray five times daily. The Book of Guidance, which is the Holy Quran that you tossed out of the window when you were fleeing with the devil towards an evil destination, also guides us to wash before prayer."

"All of this? Every time?" I asked. As if praying once isn't annoying enough, having to wash this way before praying each time and being expected to pray more than one time a day or week I thought was too much. Like some type of crazy cult or something. But I did not say this to Young Drummer. He seemed really involved in his beliefs, and I like to take it light most of the time.

"The nuns prayed a lot but didn't wash before each of their prayers." It slipped out.

"The nuns are still pretending," he said, and I was like *What!*

"They are pretending that Mary, who is the mother of Prophet Jesus, is the mother of Allah. They are pretending that Jesus is God. They are pretending that the Holy Spirit is also God and that the three, the father the son and the Holy Spirit, are mutual partners. This is false. Allah is ONE. He begets not, nor is he begotten. Allah has no parents, no partners, no equals, no children. And none is like Allah. Allah created Prophet Jesus, peace be upon him, the same way that Allah created Prophet Abraham, Moses, Mohammad, peace be upon them and all of the Prophets. And Allah created Mary, mother of Prophet Jesus. And what they are calling the Holy Spirit was created by Allah as well. All three of them are servants of Allah. None are equal to Allah. None are partners of Allah and none of them or you or I are children of Allah. And none of the Prophets, peace be upon them, nor anyone else or anything, can create a soul, a life, a living thing. And none of them created the sun, moon, and the stars or the universe. Allah created them all. Some say that science created the Earth. Allah created science and the Earth. Allah created Heaven and Hell and everything in between. Allah even created time. Allah is ONE." The way his words came out caused me to feel that they were not words that were false or that could be argued or joked away. And there was no trace of laughter or doubt in him.

"And if in between your last prayer and your next prayer, you have not used the bathroom, urinated, moved your bowels or passed wind, you do not have to re-wash," he further explained.

"So even farting is a sin!" I made light of it and laughed.

"No. I see you are still playing and pretending. Farting, as you say, is not a sin. It is an indication that you must wash before making your next prayer. Everyone passes wind," he said and he was still calm. But in his eyes I could see that he wished I was a little smarter. I am smart. Just not really interested in getting all involved in doing this and that religious thing.

"So let me ask you. Why do you and I need to make a prayer right now?" he said.

"It was your idea! I guess because the great big book says so," I said without laughter this time. I was laughing inside, though.

"I see it is difficult for your surface mind to connect up with your inner self and there is some disconnect with your soul," he said.

"You sound like a doctor. You're sixteen. Talk about getting up a game of basketball or meeting a girl you like. But probably most girls won't like you. It's not your look. But take it from me, you're way too serious." I tried to put him up on game. He ignored my advice.

"I washed in order to make a prayer. I am making the prayer to give thanks to Allah for the mercy that Allah allowed me, to travel to you and to arrive at the Last Stop Before the Drop safely. I am giving thanks for the gift of mercy to heal you to be able to stand from the ground by the gutter where you were paralyzed and unable to walk and talk. I am thanking Allah for the mercy to travel with you, and for both of us having arrived here safely. And for Allah's mercy in opening your mind, heart, and soul just enough for you to say, 'Lah-il-la-ha-illa-huwa,' which I told you before, means, 'There is no God but Allah.' You said these words not once, but several times. And for a period of time it was all that you would say," he said. He was low-key reminding me of just how desperate I was before he showed up. Yeah, I said the words. But, it's not like I remembered what they meant. I just remembered that I needed to say them to get out of the Last Stop Before the Drop.

"And you answered 'yes' that you are ready to stop playing and stop pretending that you do not understand when you do. I'm grateful for all of these gifts from Allah. Are you?" He asked me this with a solidness that I have only seen in one man while being alive on Earth, Midnight. The man who I loved with my whole heart, who if he would have loved me too, my whole life would have been better than the most beautiful dream sprinkled with my most incredible fantasy that I have ever dreamed or imagined.

"Yes," was all I said after my somewhat long pause.

"Saying you are grateful is easy. Making the prayers and expressing your thankfulness in this humbled way is showing that you are grateful, through action, not only words," he explained.

"I like action," I said.

"Let's get started with our prayer. Stand behind me," he said.

"Why? If I am your mother like you said I am, I should stand in front of you and you should stand behind me."

"Prayers are performed how Allah requires us to do them, not how each of us prefers that they should or should not be done. And Allah is the Best Knower. You and I are not." He spoke sternly, so to dead all of the religious talk, I got behind him. He raised his hands in the air and held them close to his ears. I followed his action. But damn, I felt like I was about to get arrested. Isn't that what the police always say, "Put your hands in the air"? Either that or I was at some dope-ass party where the DJ would be like, "Now throw your hands in the air and wave them like you just don't care." I smiled at the thought of being at a party. *Good thing Young Drummer ain't no mind reader.* Plus, he couldn't see me smiling. I was standing behind him.

Young Drummer said, "God is the Greatest," three times. I did not say anything. He continued on, speaking now in a different language. One minute he was standing. Next minute he was bent forward. The next minute he was on his knees. Next moment he lowered his forehead to the ground. He repeated these kinds of actions. When he was finally back to standing and out of his trance, he said, "Now that our prayers are completed, shortly I will need to return to my position." Then he pointed one finger up.

"Your position?"

"Yes, after my mercy with you today, *Alhamdulillah,* I must return to my duty of guarding the boundary of Heaven along with many others on duty for the same reason. We protect Heaven's perimeter, bomb the devils who try to enter the Heavens and create and expand their mischief and wickedness, by luring the good souls who are striving to stay on the straight path. There is no evil in Heaven. Allah never allows evil to enter a Paradise that they have not earned and/or atoned for."

"War on Earth, war in the Last Stop Before the Drop, war in Heaven," I commented casually, singing my words like a song. Not like I was expecting a reply!

"There is no war in Heaven. Allah forbids and Allah is All-powerful. The ones whose souls dwell in Heaven are protected. The ones whose souls have not earned Heaven are not protected, which is why evil can access and mislead them," he said, thoroughly convinced of his own words. "Like how evil accessed and misled you, Ma," he added, and I thought he could have left that out.

"Let's take a walk." He led the way. As we rounded the massive fountain, I saw a lot of other young men and young women speaking to someone older who was listening attentively. I was not accustomed to some little kid or teenager or young adult trying to teach someone old enough to be their mother or father. When I was a young kid, a teenager, and a young adult, I didn't try to teach the older people shit. I just swerved around them, ignored or tricked them somehow. I was young and swift. Halfway around the huge fountain, we faced a forest.

"A forest?" I said, as I followed behind him. I had not ever in my lifetime walked into any forest. I never even seen one. Sometimes driving or riding shotgun in a whip on a highway I would see a lineup of trees. But that's not how this forest that Young Drummer and me and many others were walking towards was. I noticed everyone was walking in clusters of two or more people who were walking and talking together. There were no unaccompanied people. There were no solo joggers or hikers. There were no loners wearing earplugs and headphones or carrying iPods or iPhones or iPads or selfie sticks or anything that a person could enjoy alone. There were no homeless-type people sitting, standing, begging, or laying around

"This is Usra Shajara Muntaza or, as you would understand in English, it's called Family Tree Park. By the Mercy and Grace of Allah, all UBS escort their no-longer-living-on-Earth parent or parents who aborted them into this park. You are no longer in the Last Stop Before the Drop, but you are not even close to Heaven. This park is located in the City of Mercy. It is a welcome gift to the dark souls who willed to come here. It is a glimpse of Allah's unimaginable creations and magnificence and a place for the UBS to say their final farewells. Also located inside of this park is the place where all souls escorted here, after willingly seeking the only way out of the Last Stop Before the Drop, will learn to acknowledge, understand, and humble themselves. You and them will remain in this city until your humbling is sincere. Let's go in, Ma," he said. I walked in beside him. I saw trees of every kind. They were beautiful in such a way that I could not explain to myself what I was seeing or feeling. Then I realized, these trees were like jewels to me. My eyes needed only to take a close look. When I did, the authenticity, beauty, and design captured and held my stare.

"Purple trees. That's dope," I said aloud.

"Those are known as wisteria trees," Young Drummer said. And, as he said, I saw other UBS giving the tour and explaining to their, I guess, parents or parent. They were at a standstill admiring what I was admiring and what anyone who could recognize true art would admire. There were more purple wisterias than my eyes could properly count. The forest that he called a park was so vast that even though there were many families, it didn't look or feel crowded like how crowded a picnic is in Brooklyn's Prospect Park on a hot August summer day. Every little cluster had their own space. In fact, I was wrapped in the feeling like it was only me and him even though it was not. Zigzagging patterns of steps and cement benches were woven before, after, and in between the powerfully purple trees. Some parents broke off the straight path to sit with their UBS. Young Drummer and I continued walking till the tens of purple trees ended and the tens of blue trees began, a beautiful blend of colors.

"Those are known as jacaranda trees," Young Drummer said. "And all of the trees that you see here in the City of Mercy, you would not see gathered together in the same city, state, or country if you were on living Earth. On Earth the trees are placed in a specific region and need a certain climate and timing to blossom and grow. All of nature was created by Allah. As you can see, in the City of Mercy, Allah does as Allah pleases to do." We walked through the blue forest for some time, and I again heard the sound of water nearby.

"Another fountain?" I asked him.

"No, it's a brook. A freshwater stream that runs throughout the park," he said calmly. He seemed to know so much.

The scent in this forest was unlike the scent that introduced Young Drummer when he arrived in the Last Stop location to come get me. It was a different kind of perfume than his cologne. Maybe it was the blended scents of all of the different trees. I thought if I could get leaves from each kind of tree here, I probably could make the dopest, most expensive perfume line ever to be offered in high-end perfumeries and department stores. After the blue, we walked through a valley of unbelievable maple trees lined up and interlocked except for the path we walked on, which was now filled with red leaves, as though only the maple section was experiencing autumn, while the other trees were in the summer season. Then the maple tunnel turned into a forest of bright-red trees that were rooted in the soil and striking a conceited pose like, *Yeah, you seen the rest, now take a look at the best!*

"Those are known as flamboyant trees," Young Drummer said. I knew that was the feeling those trees gave off. The flamboyant trees gave way to eucalyptus trees that smelled so refreshing it made me want to stand still and just inhale, exhale. But he needed to keep moving. So we did. Eucalyptus trees gave way to rainbow eucalyptus trees and then to amazing cherry trees. Now I felt I had seen trees of every shade of every color. He stopped. So I stopped.

"Ma, do you see that door up ahead in between the angel oaks?"

"Yes," was all I said. Only a blind fool could not see the incredibly crafted and sculpted door made from ivory. Whose idea was it to use elephant tusks in such a manner?

"That is the entrance. I cannot go through those doors with you."

"Why not?" I asked, and actually felt a little afraid to be without him.

"Each soul must enter through those doors alone and of its own will," he said solemnly.

"Yeah, but what's in there?" I asked, feeling suddenly suspicious.

"I cannot tell you, first because I have never been inside. It is not my place. It is a place for you and those souls in your category." It sounded like some polite way to insult me and associate me with some group I probably would never associate myself with.

"What, is Allah supposed to be in there?" I asked. It looked like he became quietly angry. I had never seen him angry. He always kept a cool composure. But I could see his jaw flexing. I learned way back that it is a telltale sign that a man is angry but holding back his anger.

"The ivory building is called Aldhdhat Aineikas, meaning 'self-reflection.' It is a place where the souls who enter will face themselves. Ma, this is not a movie. Don't expect Allah to be a man hidden behind a curtain yelling out commands to you. Don't expect Allah to be a con artist. Don't expect Allah to sit side by side with you in conversation, like a beggar begging you to want to be good. Don't expect Allah to be a pimp or a wimp. Allah cannot be seduced, nor would you ever have the opportunity to seduce Allah. That's silly. All of these are thoughts left over from your ignorance. Allah is beyond your or my comprehension. Even a man or woman who has studied and accumulated degrees and awards and finance and fame cannot imagine or know the mind or image of Allah." He folded his arms in front of himself.

"Ma, what I can say is this. The same way that Heaven is not promised to any soul, a soul must earn Heaven, or somehow be granted Allah's mercy. Allah does as Allah pleases. The City of Mercy is not promised to you or available for you to become a resident. It is a temporary realm where you must give your greatest effort to acknowledge and then strip off all of your evil and replace it with a genuine humility. Do you know what humility is?"

"Not exactly." I didn't want to say any more answers and have him correct me.

"To be humble. To humble yourself. Each of us must seek to humble ourselves then actually do it. A person or soul who is humble acknowledges and accepts the order of the living. Meaning, a person who doesn't confuse himself with God, or think of himself as high and important, royal or in control. A person who does not worship himself or think that he created himself or anyone else. A person who does not pretend and take credit for things that he or she deserves no credit for, Ma, say like your beautiful face and appearance . . ." He switched gears and I liked it.

"A person who is humble would be grateful to Allah for designing and causing and allowing him or her to have a beautiful outer appearance. A person who is not humble and does not want to be humble will use the beauty that Allah created, designed, and allowed as though it is a beauty they gave to themselves. Or that it is a beauty that originates with their parents. But no, your outer and inner self originates with Allah. Be humble. Don't use your beauty as a weapon, a license, or a tool. Thank Allah for it and for all else that Allah has provided you. That's being humble, having humility." I was thinking, *This young nigga is trying to take the hustle out of a hustler.* My whole generation, culture, and music is the opposite of what he is talking about. Niggas love to show off. That's the motherfucking point. Getting the things that you can flash and create envy and cause other niggas to bow down to is the drive, the action of life. Niggas live and breathe that! And the mothers and fathers of niggas live and breathe that too. Hell! Everybody does. No matter the race or whatever, everybody is making moves to get them from a certain level to the next level, to the top. The top is where you are envied, admired, served, and known. Icon status!

"There are seven magnificent structures lined up in a row, starting with the Self-Reflection Center. Connected are Fahum, Haya, Hidara, Hikma, Mutawadie, and Masjid. In your English language, the names of each of the structures after the Center of Self-Reflection are the House of Understanding, the House of Truth, the House of Culture, the House of Wisdom, the House of Humility, and the Grand Mosque, of course," he said.

"I thought you said you never been in there. So how would you know all of that?" I asked suspiciously. He smiled. "Is there any trust in you about anything or anyone good? Or about Allah, the Greatest? I did not lie to you. I have never been past those ivory doors. Once you go in, you will never come out. You will never be able to tell anyone what is in there. I happen to know an old wise soul. He worked in there. He told me nothing of the details but assured me of the layout. That's why I know a limited amount about the facility." But I was thinking, *What if it is like the nightclub? A place that appears to be so awesome, but is actually deadly?*

He saw me thinking. He may have even felt my worry.

"Ma, do not play or pretend that you do not understand

anymore. From now on and while you are here, do not lie when asked any question. Do not lie period for any reason, not even because you feel embarrassed or ashamed or because you think that a lie will protect your survival or advantage over something or someone. Do not assume that those inside appointed to assist you are naïve and stupid and can be tricked or manipulated. They are not. They are the sharpest and best equipped for the job of helping you to cleanse your own soul. Otherwise they would have never been appointed to do so. Ma, do not start a gang or a movement or throw parties or anything close to that. Do not listen to any other rebellious or evil soul who tries to influence you from doing any other thing other than cleansing your soul in accordance with what the program offers to you. If you do, you will not be asked why you did it. You will not be able to offer even one excuse for even one of your lies. Your first lie in there will be your last. There will be no lawyer to represent you, and no witness who can defend you. There will be no alibi you can invent. There will be no one who can do anything on your behalf. The ground beneath you will simply open up. Your sour soul will fall down into it and will burn. It will be a thousand times or more worse than anything that happened or that you felt or saw in the Last Stop Before the Drop. Your soul will remain on fire and it cannot be accessed, interrupted or stopped by anyone other than Allah. Your mind will remain. So you will be aware in a conscious state and continuous burning," he warned.

"Young Drummer, listen up. The one who you and your sister Bomber Girl call Shayton was accused of burning people in his bogus nightclub that was really a massive oven. So now that you threaten me with being burnt up, you are proving that Allah and Shayton both want the same things and take the same action. So what makes one better than the other?" I challenged him. I think he needed to be challenged. I don't think anyone should be so sure about any one person or thing. There gotta be like at least 3 percent of doubt. Otherwise if you go so hard and the person you loved or made a deal with, or the friend you found, or thing you believed in or was loyal to turns out to be incorrect, won't that cause you to lose your mind?

At least that's how I felt when Succubus and her father, who apparently was Shayton, were arguing. She revealed so many things about him and the sideways filthy shit that he do and the fucked up way that he went about it, I felt completely deceived. I was completely down for him only to discover that what he and I had was not special. Every night he brought a new bitch into the Light House, pumped her in the ass, turned her into some type of creature, and threw her in a wall or cage or tank. Every night he threw a crowd of hundreds, maybe thousands, into his nightclub fire pit. He was handsome, charming, and deceptive. He made each of us make the choice to destroy ourselves as though he was not controlling the action and the actual reason it was all happening. That's why if I had not had that 3 percent doubt and suspicion that all hustlers, gamblers, and go-getters gotta keep for everybody and every situation, I might have crumbled. When I found out he was lying and fucking everybody, even men . . . I mean I don't give a fuck what two men decide to do with each other. But if you are supposed to be my man or any woman's man, and you are also out there fucking men without saying that's what you're doing, that's wrong. That's bringing me into some bullshit I never signed up for and never agreed with. That will cause a good bitch or an evil bitch to go crazy and hunt for your head.

That's one thing I could give Young Drummer. He needed to reserve at least 3 percent doubt in case the whole Allah thing was not real, or true, or in effect. That's the only way he would be able to bounce back onto his feet if he found out he got betrayed or defrauded by his faith.

"Are you hearing me, Ma? Follow instructions of the ones put in place here to help you. This city as you can see has sunlight, nature with healing capabilities; clean, clear water; pure foods; and peace. It is one tiny glimpse of the Grace of Allah. Lastly, remember that I have told you that Allah is All-Knowing, All-Seeing, All-Hearing, and Forever Present. There is no secret that you can have or hide or withhold, that Allah is unaware of." Then he hugged me.

I felt hot tears spilling from my eyes. I was like *WTF? Winter Santiaga, what's going on? What's going wrong with you?* He stepped aside and flagged me forward. I walked slowly in a line of every kind of person of every color, race, and culture, men and women both. They may have each felt the same way that I did. They were shedding quiet tears and also moving slowly in single file.

29.

A dot, a tiny dot with a tiny pin that must be placed behind the ear of each person walking through the even-more-amazing-when-seen-up-close ivory doors. The dot was like one stud earring that once inserted could not be seen by anyone unless they pulled your ear back, or you pulled it back to reveal it. Once I put mine in my right ear as instructed, I was guided to the entry line for women. Of course the men had an entry line exclusively for them as well, although we were all entering the same building.

I was glad that there were men here, unlike at the convent. A bitch has got to have something to look at and someone to admire, talk to, and potentially hook up with. I know Young Drummer said not to, but isn't it natural for it to happen? That's not a lie. I remember that he warned me not to lie. I was concentrating extra hard on that one. I don't like the consequences that he described. I don' ever want to be a burnt bitch.

Women wearing fine fabrics, immaculately pressed so much so that everything they wore seemed brand-new, guided the women's lineup. Each of them had fine footwear and each pair of shoes and heels were different. I liked that because it was not all uniformed cheapness like the horrible convent sandals. I also liked it because even though they were clothed similarly, they were obviously able to express their fashion personality on their feet. The line was silent. There really was no need for guides. The sensual scents lured each of us in. The first stop was set up like a spa. It was crystal clean. We were each instructed to remove our clothes, shower in the marbled-out shower stalls, and take from the pile of bright white fluffy towels. One for the body, one for the hair, and one washcloth. Our clothes were all sorted in bins, I assumed for laundering. Once we arrived on the other side of the showering area, we were each given a tapered, long-sleeved, mint-green, shoulder-to-ankle dress and a hooded black robe to wear over the dress. The shoes being issued were black leather slides. I could do that. They are seven steps up from dollar-store flip-flops and the manmade plastic convent sandals.

We exited the spa area into some kind of main hall. It smelled incredible and looked even more incredible. This afterlife, City of Mercy, reminded me of the exquisiteness of Midnight's properties and palaces, although not exactly. The Self-Reflection Center did not have diamond, platinum, pearl, or pure gold doors. I was recalling the unique and unmatched architecture of Midnight's place. It outshined every place anywhere in the universe, to me. If Midnight's property had those purple wisteria trees, or was located inside of that forest that the City of Mercy has, it would be unfair. No, a crime against every person dead or alive for him to have it all. I smiled at the thought.

Someone kicked my chair. I turned around. It was Pretty. She was wearing the same thing I was wearing and the same that the seven hundred or so women gathered in the main hall were wearing. She was smiling brightly.

"Hey!" was all I said. I was so excited to see her. It allowed me to feel more comfortable and familiar. Not on some type of lesbian vibe. I am still strictly dickly. What she and I did, we both did for his pleasure. And even though we both felt pleasure, I am sure she knows it was a mistake for us to go that far just to entertain that man who I had lost my lust, love, and respect for.

"As-Salaam-Alaikum," a voice from the front of the hall said over a microphone. I turned back from Pretty to face front. "In

the name of Allah, the Beneficent, the Merciful . . . " the voice
said. I was like, *Oh here we go, using words that regular people don't
ever use. What is 'beneficent'?* Then it was as though she heard my
thoughts. She said, "Welcome to the Center of Self-Reflection.
We mean to make everything simple and clear every step of the
way, as you journey towards reflecting, cleansing, learning, understanding and putting into practice what you have learned,
understood, and felt. There will be many words that I will say
that you may not have heard before. I greeted you in the words of
peace and welcomed you in the name of Allah as everything begins with Allah.

"That is how we set the right tone. In your previous life, you
were not knowing, or not acknowledging the ONE who created
your soul and every living thing and the sun and the moon and all
stars and of course the wondrous sky. There is no woman or man or
Prophet who would or who could rightfully say they created any of
that. Nor could they say that they lent a hand in the creation of any
of it. Nor can they duplicate the creation of any of it. So praise be
to Allah, Lord of the Worlds. Allah the beneficent, meaning kind
in action, giving good, and causing everything good that happens.
Merciful, meaning knowing your heart, your intentions, and your
circumstances and, despite the fact that you have not earned it or
may not even deserve it, giving you a new opportunity to do better,
live better, be better than you chose to do on your own. Allah is . . .
the Most Beneficent, the Most Merciful, and the Most Compas-
sionate. It is Allah who each soul must seek and ask and pray for
help. Allah is ONE."

After her welcome talk, we were directed to a hall of computers
in groups of one hundred at a time. There were a hundred computers atop of individual stands with touch screens. One woman
standing at each screen. I was dazzled. On lockup, I couldn't wait
to get free to have my hands on all of the new technology. While
behind bars, the world had moved from hard lines and pagers to
cell phones with no texting, to cell phones with texting, to cell

phones with Wi-Fi, music, movies, and television, and to a social
media explosion. Of course I was aware of it. Technology is a part
of fashion. Bitches were styling and profiling by having their tech
be the highest available on the market. Even some were making
designer cell phone cases and diamond jewels and accessories for
their phones and pads and tablets. Now here I was, a dead bitch in
a high-tech hall filled with light and marble floors and walls and
high ceilings. I didn't have to pay for my stay. I didn't have to sell
anything, gang up or knock no one out, steal, strip, suck, or fuck
for my access. In everyday people's language, that is the real definition of merciful.

I was offered a menu of languages. I of course chose my language, English. The English page popped up. "Type in your name."
I began typing in *Brooklyn,* I pressed the *b,* then the *r,* then the
o, and remembered. *Do not tell a lie.* I paused for a minute and
asked myself, *Does that also mean not to type a lie?* I wasn't sure. But
whatever, I deleted. Then I typed in my real name, Winter Santiaga. The next prompt was for me to press print. I did. A ticket
printed out and I took it. It had my name printed on it. Below
my name was an appointment notification for me with a self-
reflection counselor named Dr. Amal Janebi for tomorrow at 7
a.m. It listed my dormitory assignment, the Princess Residence,
room 7. On the backside there was a small map of the route from
the hall to the dorm. I pressed "continue" on the touch screen. The
following screen gave me an assignment. "Write specifically and
clearly what you believe are the reasons that your soul was sent
to the Last Stop Before the Drop." I read the question over and
over again. Then there was a second assignment. "Write an essay
describing any and all of the things that you were and are grateful
for, prior to, and after, life." The third task was listed as a group assignment to be completed along with residence roommates. I was
instructed to bring the essays and a copy of the completed group
assignment to the self-reflection counselor, Dr. Amal. I pressed
"continue." Behind a green backdrop was printed in huge letters

the words THANK YOU. The screen switched to a flashing exit sign. I stepped back. I looked around the hall trying to see where Pretty was. I did not see her. I looked down at the map. A guide stationed by my computer was watching me. I decided to follow the map rather than to ask her for help. It seemed that was her plan too. She did not step up to point the route out to me. But in her eyes was the words, *Keep it moving.* I guess so, they had to do this same routine six more times to accommodate the six hundred or so women remaining in the previous hall.

"I prayed that we would be in the same room," Pretty said as I entered room seven. Instead of the roach-motel feeling I got from the convent, this room was made of pink marble and was wide and long enough to comfortably accommodate seven. At least I counted seven single beds each placed against one of the walls. There was a stand with a book holder atop. And on it was that great big book, oh no. The same unreasonably long book that Bomber Girl had given me. Beside that stand was another stand with a great big dictionary. There was one two-seater desk and two tablets laid at the center of it, as well as a stack of paper, pencils, and pens. There were five girls in the room. I was quickly deciding whether I needed to approach this situation like jail or not. The bed next to Pretty where I wanted to set up was occupied. Should I ask her to get up? Or should I just take it? Or should I just walk to one of the only two beds available? So I yanked the girl from the bed opposite Pretty's. Her ass hit the floor. She jumped up. I expected her to back down. Instead she cocked her hand back and slapped me across my face with full force. "Who do you think you are?" she said with an unintimidated fierceness. "Your bed is there. Go to it, quietly." She ordered me like I was her underling. I could feel the sting from the slap. If I had a mirror and a reflection, I would probably see a bright red handprint on my beautiful skin.

"You didn't have to go that far," Pretty scolded the slapper.

"You want to be next?" the slapper asked Pretty boldly. I rushed forward and pushed her with full force. She fell back. Two of the girls that were seated on their beds watching us rushed over and helped the slapper up. I sized up the situation. Okay, two against three, and one neutral bitch, seated at the desk writing and ignoring. The slapper was back on her feet and refocused. She charged at me. Pretty tripped her but she broke the fall and grabbed me around the waist and ran me towards a vacant bed. I fell back on the mattress. She landed on top of me. We was thumping. Pretty was trying to pull us apart. The two other bitches were trying to rescue the slapper. But we were entangled and jabbing each other wherever our fists landed. Pretty took off one slide and commenced to beating the slapper with it. The slapper got enraged. She mustered up some type of superpower and threw me off of her. She got close up in Pretty's face saying, "You dare to touch me with something from off of your foot." She grabbed Pretty's slide from her hand and slapped Pretty's face with the bottom of the shoe. I threw off the hooded garment I was wearing, twisted it how we twisted towels on lock to whip bitches who needed whipping. But I used it as a rope instead. It landed over the slapper and I used it to drag her back from Pretty's face. Now the slapper was like a rebellious dog on my leash. The slapper went crazy. She was kicking her feet and flailing her arms trying to land hits and get loose at the same time. Pretty dived down and hugged the slapper's calves to keep her still. One of the two bitches who had just been watching ran over and stuck me in the ass with a sharp thing. It felt like it pierced my ass, causing me to involuntarily let go of the twisted whipping roping garment. The other of the two walked in between the brawl separating me and Pretty on one side and the slapper and the one girl helping her on the other said, "Listen, I don't want any trouble here. Yesterday I would've pounded in your face for starting this bullshit. But I'm trying. We were all getting along before you just got here. Please take one of the two open beds available." She was talking down to me. I smiled at her to throw her off guard. I walked towards her like I was about to apologize. Soon as she returned the smile I snuffed her. When I did our residence door opened. All of us scattered to any open bed and sat. Guess we all thought it was the authorities. It wasn't. It was Bridgette.

She looked around at our tight, warlike faces. "What the fuck!" she said. "We are all women. We are not the villains. We are the victims who fight the goddamn villains!" she said in her passionate style, then rushed in and leaped on to Pretty's bed and hugged her. "Come on everybody, group hug." Pretty and Bridgette ended up walking over to where I was seated on the bed and hugging me. After the hug, we all three sat on the same bed with our backs up against the wall. The slapper and her two assistants moved back to their original beds where they were seated when I had first arrived. The bitch at the desk never even looked up from what she was doing. The way I factored it, now it's three against three. The study bitch don't count. No matter what Bridgette said, she was gonna be on me and Pretty's side. I didn't give a fuck that I rolled the slapper first and bed-jacked her. The way she slapped me was the same as if she said, "You no-class, low-class slave . . ." Or some shit like that. I could feel that she thought she was superior and I was way beneath her. I'll never let nobody get away with ever thinking some shit like that even quietly in their own mind. She and me are gonna face off again sooner than later.

Pretty, seeing the anger still moving in me, tried to dramatically switch the topics and thought process.

"So there is this assignment that everybody in the room has to work on together," Pretty announced. Now she sounded like a college bitch to me. I remember that she said she went to some university.

"I hate group assignments. I hate group dorms. I hate when anyone forces me to be a part of any group anything," the study bitch said, finally looking up from her work. "It's always a bunch of sorry somethings. I already did the definitions. Take your copies. Go ahead, take credit for what I did," she said and she was a bitter bitch.

"We still have to do the sentences. We can complete that part.

Then everyone will have contributed to the group assignment," Pretty said, emphasizing the word *group* just to get on study bitch's nerves.

"Cool. So we will go around the room. I'll write the sentences. What's the first word?" Bridgette asked.

"Worship," study bitch said. "To show extreme devotion to. To hold up higher than anything else. To love and trust without question or criticism." She defined *worship*.

"My entire nation worshipped my father," the slapper said, taking her turn first.

"Your sentence doesn't show that you know the meaning of the word worship," study bitch said, challenging the slapper.

"It does! People in my country lived and died for my father. People in my country murdered for my father. My father only needed to say that he didn't like someone, or no longer needed someone, and by the next morning that person or those people would be found dead. Not just dead nicely. Dead in pieces. An arm here, the feet in a river. The head in a freezer," the slapper, said sending a chill through the warm pink Princess Residence. I'm like now I know why the bitch is so bold.

"Your father is just another dictator!" Bridgette screamed out too loud. We were all seated in the same space.

"This is why I hate group assignments. Focus! Form one sentence which proves that you know and understand the meaning of the word," you know who said. Everybody sat thinking.

"People did not worship your father. They feared him. He must have been ruthless and reckless. The people feared for their own lives. That's the reason they would carry out your father's orders and wishes. Not because they worshipped him," I said to the slapper, not really giving a fuck about the sentence assignment.

"Silence! You don't know what the fuck you are talking about. Your father would have worshipped my father on his knees, making him only one of my father's millions of servants," the slapper bitch said. And before Bridgette could complete her outburst, "Why are we discussing our goddamn fathers? My father was a thug! He ruled over the trucking industry. So what! That's him not me! . . . " I was dragging the slapper by her wrists. Her two helpers were each holding one of her feet. We were all pulling in opposite directions. Instead of saving the slapper from me, her dumb helpers were helping to painfully stretch the slapper out. Bridgette ran over and sat on the slapper's back causing both sides to let go, and the slapper's body to hit the floor.

"My father, Ricky Santiaga, was top hustler. He ran a hundred-million-dollar empire. I worship him and so did everybody else. Study bitch said that to worship means to love and trust without question. To hold up higher than all else. To have an extreme devotion to. That's my father. Your father, from what you said, no one loved or trusted him, not even you. That's why you could talk about him the way you do. You're not devoted to your father. I am devoted to mine!" I was screaming. Not my usual style. I was teaching the slapper bitch a lesson. Oddly, I taught a lesson to myself. But like Brooklyn Momma said, "Your private business and your business-business, ain't nobody's business." So I didn't say nothing to no one about the lesson I just taught myself. "Without a doubt or a question, I worship my father," I said to study bitch. "Write that down."

The whole day in the Princess Residence went the same way. Every single word in the twenty-one-word word list set it off. When we first started the assignment the alliances were clearly drawn. Me, Bridgette, and Pretty versus everyone else. But as the talk and anger, debate and fighting escalated, it highlighted how different we all were, even though Bridgette claimed we were all the same. Overall, the self-reflection word game did what I imagine they wanted it to do. It caused us to think about ourselves more intensely than we had ever had. It caused me to go a few layers deeper than my look, which is still extremely fucking important. It caused me to look much more closely at what Young Drummer, Bomber Girl, and these people here are trying to do. They want me to love my family and friends and things that I do really love. But, they want me to worship only Allah. I understand. The problem is this. I now realized that worship contains love, trust, and devotion without question. The truth is, because I am concentrating extremely hard not to lie . . . The truth is I do not love or trust Allah. I do not even know Allah. How could I love and trust one who I don't know? Therefore, I cannot worship only Allah. Worship contains love.

30.

Lights-out. The seven of us were more comfortable with one another in the dark. In the light we had each shown our real faces and fists and ways and means. Tomorrow we would face ourselves one on one.

"Bridgette, how did you end up here at the City of Mercy?" Pretty asked.

"My aborted son had told me a long time ago that it's the only way out. After bouncing around the entire Last Stop Before the Drop, I realized he was right. Hell, I went to the Last Stop synagogue first. They wouldn't even let me in! Talking about I'm not one of them. I was like, 'Well, open the goddamn door. Maybe I can become one of ya.' Nope, never happened." She laughed. "Then I went to the convent. They let everybody in. I used that place like a hotel and a headquarters. But the convent still wasn't a way out. Then my son, he's one of the UBS you saw on the stage. He was the first speaker, bright blue eyes like his father. Anyway, on his third mercy, he was like, 'Time's up, take it or leave it.' I said yes, and then the magic words, *Lah-il-la-ha-illah-huwa*, and he brought me here to the City of Mercy. Interesting place. Good looking. But way too many goddamn rules. I mean it's a high standard, and a lot of requirements."

"You sure never answer a question without doing a whole soliloquy," study bitch said to Bridgette. "And those weren't magic words you said to get here. They were sacred words from the Quran that we all need to study."

"Soliloquy!" Bridgette spit back.

"It just means like a long solo speech. Just you doing all of the talking," Pretty explained.

"Study bitch is another college bitch," I said, 'cause I could recognize the type and her style.

"Ivy League, Dartmouth," study bitch said proudly. Whatever that meant.

"Oh you went to Dartmouth! I went to University of Pennsylvania!" Pretty said, excited. "Well, my daughter brought me here. She's one of the UBS. I can't help but love her. She's very precious to me," Pretty added.

"Stop lying," slapper bitch said to Pretty. "If she was precious you would never have killed her. All UBS are aborted souls. Your daughter included."

"Just stop!" Bridgette's voice boomed. "I told you we are all victims. We are all the same. That includes you," Bridgette said to slapper bitch. Slapper bitch laughed hard. I mean she cracked up.

"Hell no, we are not! I'm not the same as any bitch, living or dead. And, I had to kill my son. How else could I have explained that I am his mother, and his real grandfather is his father also? I did him a favor," slapper bitch said, then stopped laughing. Then the shit slapper had just said made everybody think twice and feel sorry for her. Everyone stopped speaking for some time.

"What's your M.O.D.?" Pretty asked aloud into the darkness, softly and suddenly, but without saying who she was speaking to.

"M.O.D.?" Bridgette asked.

"Method of death," Pretty explained, like it was a casual question.

"I killed myself," Pretty then added softly, confessing into the dark air.

"I killed myself too," study bitch admitted. "I jumped right into the gorge and got impaled on a sharp rock," she said without any emotion of any kind.

"I murdered myself," slapper bitch, daughter of the dictator, confessed, which is the same as suicide, but I guess she needed to state the same thing in some unique way for some dumb reason.

"I was raped and murdered," one of the slapper's helpers said.

"My mother killed me," the other slapper's helper said.

"My goddamn husband murdered me," Bridgette said in her wide-awake voice.

"I was shot dead. That's four murders and three suicides," I said.

"And don't forget to add on that we each killed at least one of our children, so that's at least seven dead kids between all of us," one of slapper bitch's helpers said.

Then came my second realization on the night of the same day. I could never have committed suicide. *I love myself to an extreme. I trust myself. I am devoted to myself. I worship myself.* I was not thinking a lie. I was thinking only the truth. Young Drummer said that he loves me, but that he does not worship me. He worships and fears only Allah. There is a separation between love and worship then. Even though love contains love. Worship contains love. But love of anything or anyone else should not contain worship, even love of self. For me and for all of these souls to get out of the City of Mercy, which is an incredible "temporary" place to be, we have to make a sincere prayer to Allah, the One who created all souls. *Sincere* means "genuine, real, not mixed and not deceitful, pure." I was blown away by that definition. Especially when I put two and two together and understood I had to make a sincere prayer. No one knows better than me what genuine, pure, not mixed means. This is the law of high fashion. If I want a mink coat, it should be 100 percent the fur of the mink. Not half or a quarter of or three-quarters of or a pinch of rat or dog hair or faux fibers or fillers. Genuine means genuine. The same goes for pure gold versus 14-karat gold or 18-karat gold, or etcetera. That's not pure. Pure means pure, period.

So to make one sincere prayer could take me forever. But I don't have forever. The City of Mercy, Young Drummer said, is temporary in preparation of a sincere prayer, made by a soul who is not pretending and not playing. Bomber Girl said that the Last Stop Before the Drop had a population of five million souls. I had laughed at that. I never believed that. But now that I saw that the only way out was to make one sincere prayer, I saw why five hundred million souls are stuck there in the Last Stop Before the Drop. The only way up is sincerity. The alternative is down, which is the Eternal Fire. I don't ever want to be a burnt bitch. I'm clear.

The Eternal Fire was created by Allah. It is the place where souls who refuse to learn, grow, and change for the better are dropped and forever tormented. The Eternal Fire was created by Allah for those souls who refuse to worship Allah. "That's me!" I shouted like a person rudely awoken from a nightmare terror. I sat up in my bed. It was not a nightmare because I was never asleep. *Do not tell a lie,* I reminded myself. It was not a nightmare. I haven't gone to sleep yet, I confirmed. So the third realization was that worship contains love, yes. But worship also must contain fear. I reflected on what Young Drummer had said, *I love you, Ma. I do not worship you. I love and fear only Allah.* Bingo, that was it. In order to worship Allah, a person must have a genuine love for Allah and a genuine fear of Allah. Only with the genuine fear and genuine love can it be sincere worship.

Thinking further, with my hustler's mind, which is the mind I must use in order to figure out any complicated thing, Allah created evil. Allah created Shayton and all of Shayton's army, which Shayton pretends to have created himself. Allah created the Eternal Fire. The same Allah who created the beautiful purple wisteria trees, the powerful sun, glowing moon, and shining stars also created the devil, the devil's army, and the Eternal Fire. Pure genius! Because a bitch like me would never ever love Allah without fear. A bitch like me would never ever love Allah without knowing Allah personally. A bitch like me would never ever love Allah without first fucking with evil, actually fucking the devil and his son. A bitch like me would never even recognize evil if I saw it face-to-face, and I did, unless evil slapped me violently, then raped me with full aggression and hate and disregard the way Iblis did. I wouldn't recognize it. And I didn't. A bitch like me would have never had even a slight chance at Heaven, without an extended stay in the Last Stop Before the Drop.

Bridget is wrong. We are the villains. We have been pretending while dead and alive to be the victims, each of us. Allah, who we don't know and who none of us love or fear, is Mercy.

"Brooklyn, are you asleep?" Pretty asked me.

"My name is not Brooklyn. It's Winter," I replied without even thinking. She giggled.

"My name is not Pretty. It's Sarah."

"What's up, Sarah," I asked, half in my thoughts, and half talking and half listening to her in the dark room.

"Do you think Allah will forgive someone like me, who did the things that I did?" I don't know why she was asking me a question like that. I had no idea about Allah. But I could hear Pretty's weepy voice. I had heard females on lock in the dark trying to disguise their tears.

"If Allah is the Most Merciful, based on the meaning of that, it's possible," I told her.

"I really want to see my daughter in Heaven," Pretty said. "I never wanted to abort her. I always wanted her. But everyone made it so awful. They treated me like pregnancy was the greatest evil. The same family that threw me a huge party for getting in to three top universities igged me like I was trash. It was like, 'If you don't abort the baby, we don't love you. If you do abort the baby and continue on to college, we will love you and continue on as though this little "mistake" never happened.' They made it like keeping my daughter was something only the lowest and dumbest of girls would do. My father threatened me. He drove me to the abortion clinic in another state in a rental car so no one would recognize his vehicle. When we got there he shoved the cash into my hand. He didn't even go in with me. He was always worried about his reputation. Said he had parishioners everywhere. But the reason I hate myself is I could have ran away. Once I got out of the rental, I was alone. I didn't have to walk into that clinic. Even once I was inside, I could have screamed for help. I didn't. I followed my father's words. He always said he spoke the words of God. When it was all over, I hated myself. I hated him and I hated God. From then on I was determined to destroy all three."

"What a bastard," Bridgette joined in. "His mother should have aborted *him!*" she said, going overboard as usual.

"Say a prayer," study bitch said. "Everything I've read says that Allah is our only help. Everyone else who we seek for help and answers is useless. It's on the first page of the Quran, the Book of Guidance. 'In the name of Allah.' Did you even bother to read it? It will come in handy for our interviews with the self-reflection counselor." Sounded like she was treating this situation like it was her top college.

Pretty answered, "I will." She got up and walked to the big book and flipped on the little light above it.

"Turn off the light! It's night time!" slapper bitch yelled.

"Bitch, you have on a sleeping mask. Close your eyes and go to sleep then," I told her.

"Even with the mask on, I need complete darkness to sleep," she said. We all igged her.

31.

Dr. Amal Janebi didn't look or behave like my prison psych. She was the opposite. Instantly I felt a strong like for her. It was not anything she said. She was in the corner office. Her desk was a semicircle made of 90 percent glass and 10 percent steel. It was placed in the middle of her large suite with a floor-to-ceiling glass wall behind her. The sunlight poured in, causing her face to have an extra glow. Through the glass desk I saw her crocodile stilettos. They was so fire. I wanted to pull up close on them, which I would never do. The illest thing, however, was that her couch, her divan, and her revolving doctor's chair were all made from genuine crocodile. Made me want to stand up and applaud her for whatever it took for her to chill so fucking hard that she got the corner office, the luxury furnishings, and the window with the sunlight. She was not young. She was not nearly old. She may have been around thirty it seems, like around my age or so. She had long, jet black hair that cascaded down with curls. Beautiful eyes and smooth skin. She was slim but shapely. Her Cartier reading glasses were laid on her desktop. She wore three pure gold bangles. Her ears dangled diamonds. Her marriage finger was laced with a "can't say no" rock so large it needed round-the-clock security. She wore the long, tapered, mint-green shoulder-to-shoe dress that we all wore. But of course her setting, accessories, and jewels made it crystal clear that she was not the same as the rest of us. All of it was more convincing than the degrees she held. They were posted on a side wall as though even she knew they weren't the biggest thing she had going on. I decided before the session even began, I would give it to her hands down. Why not? She took it. She had achieved what I had been saying about all of these counselors, therapists, psychologists, psychiatrists that I have encountered in my short lifetime. If you want someone to cooperate with you, to listen, to hear, consider what you are saying and suggesting, you have to be someone that your patient or client would like to become. Even a prisoner does not want to become like the cheap, style-less, unattractive, frustrated prison personnel. So we bullshit them the way they bullshit us. Not today. She won.

"We are both women," she began. "You may remove your abaya. Let your hair down. Feel comfortable. Would you like a glass of water?"

"No, thank you, Dr. Amal. I don't want water. If you are testing to see if I am an evil spirit or not, I am not."

She laughed. "You may have noticed that here in the City of Mercy we are not security heavy. The reason is because this area is under the mercy of Allah. There is nothing evil any soul can do here. There is no way back for any soul either. It's either up or down, by Allah's permission and none other. So please relax. I am a doctor, a psychiatrist, a guide, but as I am sure you have realized by now, there is only ONE JUDGE. When Allah grants mercy or gives out punishment, there is none who can lessen it or increase it or interfere." I took off my abaya and made myself comfortable on the crocodile. "Ask me anything," the doctor said. "Once you have exhausted all of your questions, I will lead the conversation."

"Are you Spanish, black, or white?" I asked her because I wasn't sure. To me she had the complexion of olive oil.

"Americans always want an answer to this race question. It is a strange preoccupation, but I will allow it. I am an Emirati," she said, and smiled nicely.

"Emirati," I repeated. Even that name is hot to death.

"Yes if there was a category, I would be placed in the Arab category. I don't flaunt that. I know Americans don't tend to meet, trust, or like Arabs. Also, many Americans have never heard of, or are completely unfamiliar with, the gulf countries." She is right. I don't really know anything about them or their countries or gulf, which is just the name of a gas station to me. And, I never even heard of an Emirati. Dope name though.

"I have had many American souls, who were a huge portion of the population of the Last Stop Before the Drop. They processed through here. Sad that the majority of them only encounter Arabs and the Arabic language and Arabic countries and lands after death. Not to say that all Arabs are good people. There is also a population of Arabs in the Last Stop Before the Drop. It is significant, however, that Allah chose the language of Arabic as the language that the Holy Quran was revealed and written in. This is what makes it special. Arabs, the people of course, are simply flawed like all humans," she said softly.

"So you have the advantage," I said.

"Pardon?" she said.

"You are closer to it because it comes from you. It looks and sounds familiar to you. It's in your language. The rest of us don't feel the familiarity, affection or love for your thing that you feel," I said to her. Then I started thinking and checking. *I am not telling a lie. I am not telling a lie*, I assured myself.

"Yes, but the Faith is for all. The message of the Holy Quran is for all," she said confidently.

"So let me ask you something. If the only way up is to make a sincere prayer, but a soul doesn't feel familiar and does not have an affection, devotion, or love for Allah, is it possible to go up based strictly only on the fact that I fear Allah? I fear the Hell Fire? Can worship be accepted without a real love, but with a real fear instead?" I reworded myself. It was as though I was asking her and asking myself at the same time.

"Powerful question. I think it is an excellent start that you have given the matter of your soul deep thought," she said. Inside I was celebrating. *That's right! Acknowledge, I am not a dumb bitch like Succubus said I was. As long as I decide to put my mind to something, that's what matters to me. I don't want anyone other than me to try to force my mind on to a matter.*

"There are seven academies here at the City of Mercy. You are at academy one, Self-Reflection. *InshAllah,* by the time you advance through each academy you will be very familiar with Allah. As you read Quran, your soul and heart will open up and you yourself will be moved to love Allah, *InshAllah.* You will grow to love Allah and worship with love and fear." I gave her a piercing look. She needed to know that, like study bitch, I wanted the answer to my question and that's it. She read my stare. She said, "Allah is the Judge. Allah is All-Knowing. Allah will judge if your fearful prayer is sincere. I cannot. No one else but Allah can."

"Okay, cool. So my next question is, can I skip the other six academies and make my fearful prayer, as you call it, and receive a decision? Is there an express line in the City of Mercy?" She laughed naturally. Then she tried to pull back her laughter professionally.

"You are staying in the Princess Residence, here in the Self-Reflection Center."

"Yes," was all I answered. I knew that it was not a question and that she already knew where I was staying. Everything here is digital and advanced.

"Of course. Every soul assigned to that particular residence has a special set of matters of the mind and soul to overcome. There is this condition known as the Princess complex. A woman does not actually have to be a princess to have this condition and this complex. It is a state of mind, brought on to women who have either been spoiled rotten, misled from a young age, or worshipped instead of loved, or overprotected instead of living, or violated in some awful manner by the people closest to them, family," she explained. "Or it could be rooted in something simple. You could be a woman who was read to, or who has read a lot of ridiculous stories that are read and told all around the world to children and young adults. Stories where you are a princess who is exalted, deserves to be served and worshipped, protected and cherished, and beautiful and rich, of course. Many women have these stories engraved into their souls, where they should not be, because they are not truthful stories nor are they realistic or good."

"I don't see nothing wrong with being a princess, or feeling like one even if you are not. Look at you, Dr. Amal, you are chilling very hard. Somewhere your father or mother or lover or whatever must have treated you like a princess. My father did. I wouldn't trade it for the world."

"Therein lies the problem," she said, standing up from her chair and walking around to where I sat on my own crocodile. She sat across from me on her divan. My eyes fixed on those mean-ass croc stilettos. And her flawless pedicure.

"A child captured by these stories grows up to be an adult who believes that she is always right. That her choices are correct. That her actions cannot be challenged. That everyone else is beneath her, or him in the case of a prince or king complex," she explained. I was glad she threw in that a man can have this complex too. Even though I didn't give a fuck, really.

"The problem is that these stories do not convey the proper order to life. Allah is ONE. That's first. If children are taught by their parents to know and understand this, and to read Quran as the main book that is repeatedly read, and to make their prayers properly, then their minds would not be in a state of disorder and chaos and confusion. Once you know that Allah is ONE. Once you read even the first chapter of the Holy Quran, you, no matter who you are, will learn your position in all things. Allah is ONE, Allah is the only ONE to be worshipped. If you knew this, you would never worship anything else or anyone else, not even your mother who birthed you or your father who raised you. And, most importantly, you would not waste your entire life wanting, expecting, and organizing others to bow down and worship you." She said it sweetly, but I could feel the kick in it. I was 'bout to swerve around all of this religious talk.

"Is there an express line?" I asked again calmly and sweetly. I even threw a smile on it.

"There is!" She caught it. She leaned forward and said. "But allow me to caution you. I, Dr. Amal Janebi, am nothing but a warner. The express line as you call it, is usually used by souls who already know that there is no God but Allah. Souls who already have read Quran, who were born into the Faith, practiced the Faith, and somehow chose an evil detour and ended up at the Last Stop Before the Drop. Since they knew the truth all along, and knew they were wrong for each and every misstep, their return to the truth makes it possible for them to advance swiftly." She stood up. Walking gracefully around her office as she spoke more to me.

"The question for you, Ms. Santiaga, is do you believe and think that you can properly self-reflect, which is mandatory, before advancing directly to submitting your prayers of sincerity?" she challenged. And she had used the word I hate, *mandatory*. Of course I know what that means. I did fifteen mandatory years on lock. Self-reflection is mandatory to pray my way out. I want to self-reflect, make one sincere prayer and be gone, either way. I had decided that last night after all the bitches stopped talking in the dark so I could think.

"So are you saying that if I complete today's session with you and give you my essay assignments and the group vocabulary sentences, that completes my self-reflection?" I asked.

"No. I will of course collect those from you right now. In order to bypass completion of the self-reflection period, or full term, you may request to advance directly to the Truth Booth, which is the final test of the Self-Reflection Center. Inside of that booth alone, you will face yourself. You will face all of your good, bad, and evil. You will be questioned. If you pass, you will advance beyond the six academies. If you fail, you will not. Additionally, there is a possibility—if you are unable to confront yourself properly and honestly, and if you deny, hide, cover up, mislead, deceive, or lie—that you may receive an immediate permanent judgment from the Most High. No one else controls what will happen in that booth. It is you facing you, and Allah who is All-Hearing, All-Seeing, All-Powerful, doing as Allah judges and pleases. Allah is swift in all accounts. You will never ever be cheated of anything good of you or evil of you," she warned.

"I'm ready," I said, placing my essays and sentences on her tabletop. I stood up.

"I recommend that you take some time to think about your decision. If you attend the academies, you will learn so many amazing truths. You will see yourself clearly. You will understand the Faith clearly. You will be able to sort your rights from wrongs because you will have mastered understanding of the rules and limits set for humanity by the Most High. Your soul will be more at ease in admitting to your errors. Each and every soul can only enter the Truth Booth once. There are no do-overs or makeups. The outcome is final unless it pleases Allah. Otherwise, Allah does as Allah pleases."

"I am ready," I confirmed again. It was not a lie. I am ready to get this over with. I am not a study bitch. I am not interested in working my way through, reading my way through, writing my way through or even praying my way through. There is no God but Allah. Worship only Allah. Love my father but do not worship my father or any other man including Jesus or any other woman including Brooklyn Momma. Also, do not worship any other thing including fashion, jewels, money, whips, sex, fame, or material items. The thin line that separates love from worship, I can see it now. I still do not love Allah. I do fear Allah. Because of my fear, I will worship only Allah. I was not lying about it. If I pray and don't lie, that's my sincerity. If sincerity was the core requirement, I was betting it all on my sincerity and letting it ride.

"I am ready for the Truth Booth," I stated clearly and confidently.

32.

Circular, sturdy, made of sparkling white, mountain rocks, single-occupancy booths. They were located in between the Manzil Mutawadie and the masjid—meaning, between the House of Humility and the mosque. There were eleven rows of eleven of these beautiful enclosures that were framed by a garden. I had not known what to expect. However, everything in the City of Mercy was way more than I expected and much more than I could have ever imagined.

As I walked the outdoor path that extended up until and after each of the seven buildings, I paused at the House of Wisdom. There was a fountain there, where some women, also fully covered, were seated. Across what they call the pavilion was another fountain and the walking path for men. There was a small gathering of about seven males, all immaculately dressed in brilliant white long garments and kufis.

A few thoughts occurred to me. I thought it was dope that they allowed all of us souls to move around outdoors without armed or unarmed security guards on post. Moreover, there were no escorts, hand- or ankle cuffs, chains, whips, or monitors. It felt like the City of Mercy was the truest location. None of us had to be tased, tranquilized, shot, roped, chained, beaten, or threatened into submission. We each knew that we were experiencing Allah's mercy, and that we had to be responsible for ourselves, straighten up and act right based on our own will, and our love and/or our fear of Allah.

Whether or not all of us love Allah—because I still do not—I don't know. However, I do know that we had each done more than enough, had more than enough done to us, and all felt and feared the range of Allah's power. So nobody made any reckless moves. It was all peace.

As some women ran their fingers through the water, and I stood facing the sun and hoping for a favorable outcome to my Truth Booth experience, I sensed something. My eyes searched. I saw a physique I could never forget. The shoulders, the back, and the ass—or should I say the print or outline of the shoulders, the back, the ass—was all that could be seen beneath the flawless white garment that he wore. But only he had this uniquely perfect physique. And only he wore Timbs on his feet. I waited for him to turn around just to confirm. When he did, my eyes ran across the pavilion where Dat Nigga was standing. It was some seconds before he saw me seeing him. When he saw, he looked only long enough to recognize me. Then he switched his gaze swiftly. He faced front and walked forward towards the men's path that led to the Truth Booths.

I felt like I had a rock in my throat. I was not angry that he didn't run or drive over to get me. I wasn't tight that he wasn't blown away by my look. I did not chase him. I waited for him to enter his circular booth before I started walking towards mine. Soon as he did and the awesome, cylinder doors closed behind him, I began my walk again. Part of me wanted to run back to the Self-Reflection Center, find Dr. Amal, and ask her if an evil spirit, which is what the nuns said Dat Nigga was, could become good. Could a person who sold their soul to the devil get it, buy it, win it, snatch it back, or acquire it mercifully? Could a spirit that was created to do evil get a raise, a promotion, a pass, an opportunity from Allah? I felt my heart race at the notion. *Is mercy deep enough, true enough, warm enough to welcome Winter Santiaga and Dat Nigga?* I didn't run back to ask. It's funny how if you start to listen to a certain group of people's reasoning behind a thing . . . you can eventually use that reasoning on your own to arrive at the same conclusion that the person who taught you something would accept or say.

I was glad that Dat Nigga was here. He must have betrayed his father. He must have shouted "Lah-il-la-ha-illah-huwa!" out of pure agony, like I did. He must have abandoned his whips, chips, house, monkey bars, alcohol, men, women, and weed. He had to have separated himself from the whole evil team. It must have been hard for him. Once he got to the City of Mercy—and I'd love to hear the story of how that occurred—he must have chosen to express straight to the Truth Booth. Dat Nigga and I were both impatient people addicted to action. There was no way either of us could sit still for too long, doing nothing but reading, writing, studying, praying, and talking about Faith.

Although I didn't know if I could ever forgive Dat Nigga, like how Allah might forgive him, I'd rather him go to Heaven than burn in hell. I don't know if I could fuck with any guy who has a history of doing some of the nasty shit that him and his brother and father did. Although I realize that each of the three of them did different evil, different ways. As for Dat Nigga, first I'd have to forget his whispering in my ear, "I'm an ass man." I'd have to forget that he fucked Succubus, his own sister of the same father. But I'd damn sure remember everything else. I still could feel the good feeling and impact of his *everything else.*

Standing outside of my designated Truth Booth cylinder, row one, number eleven, I shook off my memory of Dat Nigga. I am abandoning my cravings. I am emptying my mind so I can think straight and not lie once I step inside. I know a lie would be the end of me. The end, not in a good way. In a tragic way, with my mind fully awake, aware, and conscious to experience the torment.

I pressed the silver button. The cylinder door slid open. I stepped inside. It was completely dark. A pleasant female voice said, "Welcome." Crazy, the voice sounded like my voice. But, there was no one inside except for me, Dr. Amal had assured me.

"Inside of the Truth Booth, there is only your soul and your self-reflection experience. No one is recording, filming or watching or monitoring from afar. There is always the Forever-Present Allah, the All-Knowing, All-Hearing, All-Seeing, Who will know what happens within your experience, and only Allah is the Judge."

I lifted my arms and moved them around the darkness, making sure I was alone. Yeah, I know what she assured me. But I keep 3 percent doubt for the sake of my own survival. Soon as I began moving my arms, a light switched on. It was like a motion-detector-type thing. Now it is confirmed. I am the only one in here. There is no one else but me. Replaying Dr. Amal's instructions in my mind, I took out from my inside abaya pocket the tiniest paper envelope I had ever seen. Dr. Amal said to get started I needed to place the soul dot into the thin slot on the right of where I was standing. I found the slot easily. Back in Brooklyn hustle days, hustlers always had clever slots and compartments. Ways to hide things that had to be hidden or to see things without others seeing that you're seeing. I'm not saying that this thin slot was the same kind of thing. I'm not comparing the crack rock, which is small, to the soul dot, which is even tinier than a tiny pebble. I slipped it in, then faced forward.

Only after the dot was deposited did I realize that I am facing a mirror. I am a dead bitch. In the Truth Booth, some way, somehow, I can now recognize a mirror, and I now have a reflection. I can see myself. Overwhelmed, tears burst out from my eyes and my breath escaped from my mouth without me ordering it to do so. I stood crying uncontrollably in the mirror, spellbound by my own beautiful reflection. I put my hands to my face. So did my reflection. I felt my skin. So did my reflection. My eyes searched for my scar. So did my reflection. It was not there. *Al-hum-doo-lah-lah*, I thought without even thinking. I stared into my own eyes. My reflection stared back at me. A sudden urge rushed over me. I removed the hood of my abaya. Then I removed the abaya completely. I removed the tapered mint-shoulder-to-ankle dress. I slid out of their leather slides. I was more comfortable naked. Now that I could see my own reflection, I wanted to see it all. I was alone. So nudity was just fine,

isn't it? I asked myself. *Hell yeah, it's just fine.* If I was alone and no
one was filming or recording me or watching me, like she said they
wouldn't and weren't, it had to be fine. It was nobody else's fucking
business what I did with myself. And in the instructions, no one
said I shouldn't.

Starting at my neck, I began caressing myself. My hands criss-
crossed. My right hand caressed my left shoulder. My left hand
caressed my right. I moved them down my arms, feeling even my
elbows, forearms, and then held my hands up, admiring my fingers. When my reflection did the same as I did, I dropped my
hands down. My eyes searched my reflection for the position of my
breasts. They were not sixteen-years-young upright. But they were
not low, drooping, or dropped. They were plump and gorgeous. I
caressed them. I pinched my own nipples, not for pleasure but to
feel real. Then moved my fingers over my tight belly and around
back to hips, thighs, and ass. I was searching for blemishes. There
were none. Now I squatted, admiring the reflection of my toes and
feet and even ankles. *Check, check, check . . . all good.* I stood up.

Returning to the instructions, I pressed the inside silver button that was positioned over the tiny slot where I had deposited the
dot. When I did, the lights went out. The floor moved me 180 degrees without my expecting it, or doing any movement myself.

"Winter," a voice spoke into the atmosphere. I was 100 percent
that the voice was my voice. However, my lips were not moving.
My brain did not tell my lips to move or to talk to me. So what's
up? "Yes?" I answered myself.

"Do you worship only Allah?" my voice asked me.

"Yes, now I do," I said, my mind quick thinking that short answers are better and safer. Plus I do fear Allah and that's my reason
to worship. With that thought, images bled through the darkness.
No, the images were on the wall of the cylinder, same as a movie
screen. Not a regular movie. It was like an IMAX theater. The images and the sounds surrounded me in the cylinder booth, amazingly. It's me, being projected onto the wall as if I am starring in a

movie. But it's teenage me in the film scene. I was in some apartment. I was on a bed facedown, ass up, giving head. I couldn't see to
who though. The images moved. I was in a cheap car with a cheap
interior, my face buried in a lap giving head. Must've been Sterling,
a sucker nigga and the only nigga I ever let drive me in an inferior
whip during a personal emergency. The images moved. I was in a
different apartment—no, it's a basement. I was on my knees, facedown, ass up, giving head. I couldn't see to who though. But the
basement was fucked up. There was a cheap curtain hanging, keeping me from seeing whoever else was there. I could hear the sounds
of fucking and sucking. But I could only see myself giving head.
Oh yeah. I recognize it. It's Boom's basement. The movie continued. The images moved. I was on the floor. It was a dope floor, like
in a five-star hotel. I was facedown, ass up, giving head. I couldn't
see to who. But, I could hear the lusty breathing and pulling, mine
and his breath. The images moved and the scene changed, but the
action didn't. I was in an apartment on the floor, facedown, ass
up, giving head. I couldn't see him. I knew though the apartment
was mine and Bullet's. So I had to be giving Bullet my specialty
blow job. I laughed. Then I pulled my laughter back swiftly. The
scene changed. I was hanging upside down giving head. The scene
changed. I was on the floor, ass up, facedown, giving head. Oh yeah,
it's in the Light House. The images froze, my lips on a dick. I recognize my lips and the dick of course. Now I'm standing here in
the booth like, *What the fuck? So what's the point?* "Yeah, a bitch
likes fucking, likes pleasing her man. Is something wrong with
that?" I asked aloud. And suddenly, I actually got a reply. Not a
man's voice with a thundering tone like how they deepen and double up a man's voice on a horror film or even when it's suppose to
be like the fake voice of God. It was a woman's voice. It's mine. It's
me talking on the film soundtrack. I was speaking in my *fuck you
bitch tone of voice.* But I was talking to myself even though in actu-
ality, I was standing right there in the booth with my mouth closed
and not speaking at all.

"You bowed down from age twelve and throughout your entire young life to suck dick, you stupid bitch," my own voice said to me. Now I'm thinking, how is myself gonna have an attitude with myself? Or how is she . . . I mean, how am I gonna accuse myself as though I wasn't there doing the same thing as myself?

"But you never bowed down to the ONE who made your soul. Even in your afterlife, you were *still bowing down to suck dick. You even sucked the dick of the devil*, the voice that was mine said to me in a low volume but with accusatory anger. The images on the wall screen switched. The setting was the fountain located before the forest that led to the City of Mercy. The sound of the fountain gushing water was engulfing me. It was powerful like in a dope-ass movie with a top sound system and soundtrack. But on the screen, it was me when I had been standing behind Young Drummer as he prayed. I was standing behind him pretending, and not praying, and deceiving him. Of course, I remember. I remember everything. She, who is me, started talking down to me again.

"Up until this very second you *still* have never gotten on your knees to bow down in prayer to the ONE who gave you life, Allah, the ONE, the Most Merciful, the Most Gracious, the All-Powerful," my own voice said to me like she was really into it.

"I thought I was supposed to do the sincere prayer after the Truth Booth," I reminded my voice that was speaking while my lips were not speaking. "I thought those were the instructions," I further explained.

"Are you setting up to hustle Allah?" my voice asked me as though she is slicker than me and 'bout to catch me, who is her, in a lie.

"No!" I replied truthfully. Then there was silence. The frozen images went black. I became consumed by fear. Am I about to drop? I dropped down to my knees. It didn't matter what I do in here in the booth. No one could see Winter Santiaga on her knees except for me. "Okay, I get it," I said. "Worship only Allah. Worship contains not only fear, it contains prayer. It may have looked like I was worshipping these dudes I was giving head to. I mean, in order to pray it involves bending forward, getting on my knees, bowing down. True, I never did that. I never prayed. But yes, I sucked a lot of dick. I don't think it's really similar. I mean, but the stances are similar. But it's not the same thing." I paused. "Please forgive me," I said, lowering my head to the floor.

"Bitch, stand up. Stop pretending," my voice said to me in surround sound.

"Bitch, shut up!" I said to my voice. I didn't stand up. "I am not pretending. I'm doing it now. I'm praying now."

"Is that how your unborn son taught you to pray?" my voice asked me.

"No!" I leaped up. I bent back down and grabbed my clothing and put it back on. "I'll get dressed and pray. But you are making a big deal out of this. It's no big deal! I was going to pray. I just didn't think this was the right timing. You're acting all high and mighty. It's not like I'm a murderer," I yelled at myself, or at the sound and talk of my own voice that I was not controlling.

The wall screen switched back on. The images began to move. The setting was a packed outdoor parking lot. It was nighttime and zoomed in on some nervous old lady in the scene. She looked lost. Then there I was, suddenly in the scene with her. She was fumbling with her keys. The camera shifted from her and zoomed in close on me. I didn't look nervous. I looked young, determined, and fashionable as usual. But then . . . I cocked my right hand all the way back behind me. I was holding something. Then, fast as lightning, I used the something that I was holding to smash the nervous old lady in the head. She withered. I robbed her. Got her for her Gucci driving shoes, credit cards, and a little cash. The focus of the images on the wall screen moved from me and onto her. The frame froze on her shocked expression. A little blood trickled down from her scalp.

I screamed, "Blood!" I don't remember that. I didn't see no blood on her that night. Yeah, I remember her. I hit her with a sock filled with rocks. True dat. I did. "I'm not lying. It should not count as a lie. You're lying!" I said, screaming at the wall screen. "I knocked her out. I didn't murder her, though," I yelled at the accusation that the film scene starring the real me in my real life, which I clearly remember, was making. The images moved. The scene and setting switched. The camera zoomed in on the same nervous old lady. When I first chose her for a vic, she seemed like she had that old people's shaking disease. In the image on the wall screen now, she is not shaking. She is completely still. She's naked on a steel table. Her body is fucked-up shape wise. I didn't do that. I just hit her once. She probably died of diabetes or some other old people's disease. Then I heard the sound. It was a hospital sound. It was the sound of flatlining. The sound that machine makes when someone's heart is no longer beating. I know that much. I am not a dumb bitch.

"You murdered her," my voice said to me. But it wasn't me talking. My lips were not moving. My brain was not telling my voice to say these things to me.

"Okay, when I was seventeen, I murdered a senior citizen. When I said a few minutes ago that I am not a murderer, I did not lie. I just didn't know and had no way of knowing that she died. Since I did not know, that should not count as a lie that I told while here in the Truth Booth. I never ever been no murderer. So I did not lie. I just didn't know. I am not lying in the Truth Booth," I said, realizing I was repeating myself. I was pleading with my own voice, which I didn't control.

The images moved. The scene and the setting changed. I was in a doctor's office. I could see all of the medical equipment and supplies. There was a nurse or a doctor there, but I could only see her body in her doctor's clothes. Her head was not in the shot for some strange reason. The sound switched on. The eighteen-years-young Winter Santiaga was on the wall screen. Young Winter said, "Just take it out now." Of course I recognized it all. It's the real-life me! It was when I was in the abortion clinic demanding an abortion and angry that I had to make an appointment to come back and get it done. I wanted the thing out right then and there.

"You murdered your twins," my voice said to me with a calm force, and without my real-life lips moving. There was a disgust in her voice that a bitch who is me should not have in her voice against her own damn self. Trying to restrain my anger, I explained.

"Abortion is not the same as murder. Abortion does not count. If abortion was murder, it wouldn't be legal, right? On that day, I was doing something perfectly legal. I mean, it wasn't really me who killed the twins anyway. It was that damned doctor whose face I couldn't even see on the screen. It's not like I took a knife and stabbed myself in the belly. So how was it murder? Why are you saying that I murdered them? I didn't kill them. The doctor did. Either it's that or it's that *abortion is not murder*, like I said in the first place!" I defended myself from myself. These were my lips moving and saying. I was telling my voice the truth, not a lie. The wall screen shut off. The booth went black. There was silence. Pissed, I folded my arms in front of me. I felt set up. I stood there so long my arms felt like a twisted pretzel. My body muscles were so tight. It was a standoff between me and my voice, concerning our disagreement about the meaning of thesereal-life situations.

After a while, it seemed like if I didn't say or do something, the session would not ever end. I screamed, "Okay, I murdered three people: a senior citizen, Young Drummer, and Bomber Girl. I did not tell a lie. I didn't think that abortion was or is murder. My session should not stop just because of this small misunderstanding. You are treating me like a prisoner. I already did that. I already did fifteen years on lockdown for nothing. I'm not a criminal. But I paid that debt. Winter Santiaga is innocent! But I served the time. I did not snitch. I paid the debt. It was somebody else's debt. I paid it!" I yelled. The wall screen lit up. The images began moving. It was a bathroom. It was not a bathroom in my Brooklyn apartment or in our Long Island mansion, or even in the apartment that Bullet and I shared. I was in the big fancy bathroom in the mirror. I had a bag of coke in my hand. I cut it open and tasted it. The scene froze.

"That's not the same thing," I hollered. "That's not what I got arrested for. I tasted the cocaine just to make sure that them two bitches, who y'all took out of that scene, wasn't trying to trick me. I didn't want to show up with coke and be a fool in front of my man Bullet. What if I didn't taste it? What if the package turned out to be flour or baking soda or some shit like that?" I said, exasperated. "C'mon, I didn't lie. I really did not get locked up for what happened in that bathroom that night. I got locked up for some drugs and guns that were in a rental car that wasn't even mine. So that's what I meant when I said I am not a criminal." The screen shut off. The cylinder was back to black. I didn't want to stand there for a whole hour. I was figuring out the routine. I had to confess to my own voice whatever the truth was. I spent my whole lifetime not snitching on nobody no matter what. Now, in the end, I was being forced to snitch on my damn self. I started laughing. But believe me, it was not with joy.

"Okay, I am not innocent. I was not innocent. I was never innocent. I was not a drug dealer. But I did hold my nigga's guns and drugs and move them from here to there. If that makes me a criminal, then yes, the truth is, I am a criminal. I am not innocent. How you like that? I did not lie," I said. However, my voice did not say anything back to me.

The screen switched on. It froze on some type of weird word list. "Say aloud which of these sins you have committed in your Earth lifetime and/or afterlife." Those were the instructions listed above the word list. I just stared at the list. I thought it was some last trick that would be their final attempt to break me. They wanted to turn me into a liar. But, I came to the Truth Booth with my mind determined to win. So I started at the top, scanning the words and calling out aloud the wrongs that I had committed in my life and afterlife.

"Fornication," I said aloud. I remember Pretty taught me the meaning of that word. "Yeah, I fucked a bunch of niggas who I wasn't married to and who weren't married to me. But I did not fuck married niggas. That has to count for something," I said aloud to the voice that was my own. Then a thought occurred to me and I swiftly explained myself. "Yeah, I wanted to fuck Midnight even though I know and knew that he was married. But the truth is that I never fucked him and I never fucked no married man."

"Continue," my voice said to me. My eyes refocused on the list and scrolled down. I saw the word *sodomy*. I knew that was ass-fucking. But I didn't think that I could be guilty of sodomy. I don't have a dick. If I did, I wouldn't put it in an ass. So since I did not put a dick in anyone's ass, I skipped that one.

I felt like I was aging while reading the haram list. Haram being the word used in the City of Mercy for forbidden things. The nuns called them sins. It was all the same shit I guess. And between the harams and the sins, there were more than sixty words on the screen. I have felt teenage young my whole life. I even felt like a teenager before I actually became a teenager. I even felt like a teenager when I was no longer a teenager. I felt like a teenager even the day I got released after serving fifteen years. No one could convince me then that I was a day older than nineteen. But in this booth reading this list, I felt squeezed. Kind of how I felt when I was lying in my casket, with my eyes and lips stitched shut and my bones breaking and my body deteriorating.

Okay, I need to focus. So far I had called out that I committed three murders and fornication. I hesitated. My eyes hovered over the word *theft*. I am not a thief. *Simone's the thief!* I thought to myself. "Wait a minute," I asked out loud. "Should I confess to being a thief just because of the one incident with the old lady, the Gucci shoes, cash and credit cards? I already confessed to the murder!" I hollered in frustration. My own voice, which I heard clearly in surround sound; my own voice, which I did not control; my own voice, which had been making all of these accusations against me, did not reply. The screen with the word list switched off. The film of incidents of my real life began once again. But where was this place I was seeing on the wall screen? Obviously, it's some church. So now I was like, *What the fuck does that have to do with me? I never attended nobody's church. That isn't the sanctuary in the convent.* That was the only church-like place I been to. Who are these people packed in the pews? Way more people than the convent had at the Last Stop Before the Drop. The images moved. I was in a bathroom again. But this time, I was inside the toilet stall with the door locked shut. I wasn't shitting, though. I had the toilet seat down and I was using the top of it to sort money. The bills were disorganized. So I was separating the ones, fives, tens, and twenties like Poppa Santiaga taught me to do. He liked clean, neat bills. All bill faces facing the same direction. The wall screen froze on my pretty fingers with the bills in my hand. The image faded. The booth went dark. Instead of waiting, I just got it over with. I couldn't win this game with a lie. So why delay? "Theft!" I screamed out that one word. I was keeping it short. I did not need to add on the circumstance or explain how I stole the money from the church event that was put together to raise funds for HIV-positive children and their families. I know I did. I know the reason why I did. But this bitch who was me, or this voice that was my own, or this film of my life that I didn't agree to or benefit from didn't know my reasoning. My reasoning couldn't be captured on film. Not even a film that seemed to be coming from the soul dot. My reasoning for all the shit I did was in my head and no one else's. So yeah, fuck it. I called out, "Theft!" Now I would be thrown in the low category with a real thief bitch like Simone.

The list returned to the screen. I just started reading off damn near every *haramful* sinful word. I needed to get this over with. I needed to tell the truth, progress to the masjid, and make my sincere prayer, which I could do because I was not telling any lies. And I did fear Allah. Or better yet, I should say I feared the range of power that Allah is and that Allah seems to have over my life, death, and afterlife.

"Fornication, sodomy, murder, theft, liar, cheater, arrogance, niggardly, ingrate, selfish, hostile, vanity, lust, wrath, envy, greed . . . " I shouted them all. I left some out that I was sure didn't apply to me. "Done!" I shouted and dropped to the floor, worn out from this bullshit. "What's next? What's next?" I shouted from the floor in the semidark booth. Only the light from the word list glowed.

"Are you forgetting anything?" my own voice, which I do not control, asked me.

"Why don't you tell me, bitch! You seem to know every goddamn thing about me!" I said salty.

"It's you who must confess it and correct," my own voice said to me. "Review the list one more time to be sure. When you are sure, press the red button on the left," my voice instructed me. My immediate thought was, *Maybe I should just confess to everything on the list.* That way my voice couldn't possibly catch me in a lie. But then I thought, *If I confess to something that I am not guilty of, that would definitely be a lie!* Gluttony was on the list. I didn't confess to that. I never been a big food eater. True, I am not a glutton. That had to do with pigging out, I reminded myself. I have the definitions of these words that study bitch looked up and we discussed and fought over in my mind permanently. I already confessed to greed. That was greed over money, whips, houses, fashions, jewels, and beautiful shit like that. I stood up, reviewed the list again. I stopped at the word *sloth*. I was like, *Nah.* I never been a lazy bitch. Even organizing a crew or a gang is hard work. Yeah, when you're on top of any gang, crew or business, you let the low ones do some of the dirty work for you. But that's the commonsense way for them to earn their way up out of their low position. I looked it over. I was done. I pressed the red button. The light came on. The floor of the booth turned me a 180 back to the mirror. I saw my reflection and smiled. My beauty awed even me. *My look, I've got my look,* I assured myself, but only inside of my own mind. I was not talking aloud or screaming or explaining to my own voice, the one that was outside of my own body and outside of my own control.

I touched my hair. Stroking it was calming to me. It had grown back nicely. When I lifted my hand to stroke other strands, the hair I had been stroking fell out. Some was in my hand. Some was slowly cascading to the floor of the booth. I was looking down at my feet where the hair fell. As I looked down, more strands are appearing on my feet in clumps. I looked up and my hair was shedding. I touched it. My touch seemed to cause the shedding to increase. I placed both hands on my head and tried to press down and hold on to the hair that remained. I stood there for what seemed like hours, holding the remaining patches of hair. When I let go out of pure exhaustion, all of my remaining hair fell to the floor. "What the fuck!" I screamed at my reflection. I was bald. I was bald like how Brooklyn Momma turned bald as she changed into Crackhead Momma. "Momma shaved her hair off herself!" I hollered at the bald reflection that was also hollering. I yelled at my own voice that had not spoken in a long while. "Momma made the choice to shave her head. She wanted to look like Grace Jones! So what the fuck is this? I did not will for this. I did not ask to be bald. Why the fuck would I do that? Even Momma looked terrible after she made that move," I shouted. But there was no reply. Me and my reflection still looked exactly the same, bald. The lights stayed on, even though I realized I had been cursing. But I was not cursing and mixing curses with sacred words like Bomber Girl warned me not to do. Besides, I was talking to myself. So who cared if I was cursing my damn self out?

Suddenly, my face darkened. I pushed myself closer to the mirror. Had someone dimmed the lights in here? I looked around. No, the lights were still the same. I returned my gaze to the mirror. My face had darkened another few shades. It wasn't pretty dark, like the color of the beautiful black skin of Midnight. It was like ashy dark. I started to try and rub it off. Thought maybe there were some invisible bugs like the ones from the Last Stop Before the Drop attacking my look. But my blackening face didn't rub off like ash or soil would. It didn't feel like a rash, either. When I pulled my darkened face back, I saw that where I had been rubbing and touching my face now had marks even blacker than my darkened skin. "What the fuck is this?" I shouted. Then the black marks cracked and opened somehow. Inside there was red. "Oh my fucking God. Why are you doing this. This is bullshit," I screamed impulsively. My mouth began hurting. I covered it with my palm. It did not help ease the pain. When I removed my hand, a few of my teeth were inside of my palm and the others began falling out and hitting the floor of the booth like spilled raw rice or beans. I started crying furiously. Not a whimper. It was the cry of the whipped mixed with intense anger, no agony. My gums were pulsating. "Fuck it! I don't need teeth. I don't eat nothing down here anyway!" I shouted. I began feeling cold. I touched my shoulders and hugged myself. When I did, I felt that the skin on my shoulders and my arms as I moved my hands downward was filled with those open wounds. They felt like the wounds on my face. I realized that wherever I placed my own touch, some horrible ugliness would happen in that same body part. I was like, *What kind of shit is this?* "I can't even touch myself now?" I screamed. "Is touching myself a sin? You are too much. You want too much. Farting is a sin. Touching myself is a sin. This is not Mercy. This is bullshit. You are the goddamn liar. You are way worser than Shayton. At least he was fun while it lasted. At least he turns people into animals. I'd rather be a serpent, a dog, or even a rat!" I said screaming and crying. But my tears made the wounds on my face burn. *I hate burning,* I reminded myself. *Calm down,* I reminded myself. When I went to wipe my own tears, I felt fur against my face. When I looked at my reflection, my hand was black. My nails were long and black. I shouted. It was not words. It was a scream coming from deep in my gut, a roar.

"It's all fucked up now! You fucked up my look! You fucked up my currency! It doesn't even matter anymore. Nothing matters anymore." I tried to keep talking and screaming at the horrible reflection that is me. I couldn't. My tongue was in the process of growing longer and longer. It blocked me from speaking. Sounded like I talk with a lisp. It soon grew long enough to sit on my left titty. It turned colors, from pink to purple to black. Now I was officially scared of my own self. The floor beneath spun me in a 180 away from my own reflection. I was *Yeah, I don't need no goddamn mirror. I don't need any damned thing. I don't worship Allah. I definitely don't love Allah. I never did!* The lights in the booth turned off. The wall screen flashed on. When it did, I told myself in my own mind without a voice of my own, "I'm not going to watch anymore." I tried to move my eyes away, but they were locked in the direction of the screen. I tried to move my head. Both my head and neck were locked, like a paralyzed person. On the screen close-up was me, riding in Dat Nigga's whip. I opened my window and threw the Holy Quran out into the darkness.

"*Yeah that was me! I threw out that ridiculous big-ass book. So what. I don't give a flying fuck!*" The floor beneath me opened up. I was sucked through the floor by a powerful heated vacuum. It was not the thrill of the roller coaster. It was not the high or soaring feeling I had while my hand was being held by Young Drummer. It wasn't like the people who I had seen enjoying hang gliding on the TV. It was a dangerous, endless heated falling—maybe like being trapped alive in an exploded airplane and on fire the whole way down. A shocking, terrifying drop with no warning and no bungee cord to rebound. No parachute to open up. No net to catch me. No, I was not simply falling. I was being thrown and slammed and forced down. I could feel that it was intentional, awfully mean, and a forceful, painful, punishing fall.

33.

"Have you seen the script?" the showrunner asked me.

"I received it. I didn't read it, though," I said at the same time as I glanced towards the trash bin where I had thrown the script. She followed my eyes. Her facial reaction revealed that she saw it there.

"This is supposed to be a reality show. So, I'm gonna keep it natural," I said calmly.

"Natural will only work for you, Winter, for several reasons. First of all, because you're the star. Second of all, because your beauty, coupled with your mysterious life, will captivate the viewers and keep them from reaching for the remote. Lastly, because this is your first appearance during season one, and it's the season finale at the same time," she explained in a desperate tone.

"Exactly." My one-word response.

"However, everybody else on the show needs to play off of you. So we need you to at least remain in the framework of the script," she pleaded. I just looked at her. She knew that meant to get out. She was standing in my private V.I.P. greenroom, which was filled with welcome-back bouquets of red roses, congratulatory vases of white calla lilies, and clay-potted blue morning glories. No matter how stunning my surroundings are, inside of me my memory is demanding my attention and always reminding me. Right now, my memory was showing me images of the wisteria trees, the willow trees, the blue jacarandas. I had never heard of any of those trees before my death. Even if I had, it wouldn't have mattered to me.

"Are you hearing me?" The showrunner politely interrupted my thoughts. She had pulled the script pages from the trash and placed them on the countertop in front of me. I didn't acknowledge. She left.

I know that I have the top reality show being viewed by millions across the globe. I know that I broke all records by being the star of the top reality show and the star of the top show period. We had even outdistanced scripted shows and sitcoms in terms of the numbers of people viewing my show in America and all around the world. Moreover, we had done something unplanned, unexpected, completely original and unique. We claimed the top slot without the star, that's me, ever saying even one word or making any live appearances on her own show. Elisha said even a genius could never have conceived such an idea. At that time, I wasn't sure if he was bigging himself up, since he was the one who decided to move forward with the show even after my being shot dead. But later he clarified his statement saying that the whole show was a "Godsend." That led me to asking him, "Since the show is already in the top slot, and there's only the finale remaining, why should I appear? It might be more powerful to end the season without me. Let me debut on the first show of season two."

"Trust me. This finale needs you. You have worked so hard to get back everything you almost completely lost. Winter, you will give the whole world hope. You look so unbelievably beautiful and healthy, no one would believe that you had ever experienced the tragedy that you experienced," he said passionately. I was swooning over him saying out loud how beautiful I look. Then on the inside my memory reminded me not to swoon. Not to need and desire constant signs, words, and acknowledgment of my amazing outward appearance.

"Well, Elisha, since they saw my tragedy on camera, they will definitely believe it," I said. I was low-grade stabbing him for showing such a gruesome event. He knew that back then for me it was all about my look. Of course he did. He was the one who had my wardrobe secured and delivered to me exactly as I had ordered for him to do. He was the one who threw in the diamond necklace and other powerful perks. Therefore he must have known that I would never agree to being filmed getting shot dead. But a dead person has no defense. I'm not mad at him, though. He has made me into what I always wanted to be, a rich bitch.

Someone knocked. "I'm Mika from wardrobe," she said. She was a petite girl pushing a wheeled cart that held the bagged clothes I had ordered custom-designed two months ago, to be worn for my finale appearance. She left the cart and exited after saying only "Thank you" to me, as though I had delivered the clothes to myself. That's the level I'm at now. People thank me out loud for even being able to work for me, with me, or to serve me. She closed the door.

I stood up, walked over, and locked it. Since my return, I spend a lot of time alone behind closed and locked doors. However, it is not like before. Nothing is the same as it was before. The closed and locked doors that I am behind are exquisite rooms, suites, apartments, houses, and spaces. I have locked the doors myself. I am not locked in or imprisoned. I can unlock anytime. I can walk out anytime. And I do, when I feel like it.

While I am dressing myself finely, I am thinking about my game face. It takes more effort for me to maintain it now. When I make my debut on the finale of my show, I need my game face, to face Simone, Natalie, and all of my girls for the first time since getting shot, flatlining and pronounced dead, revived and hooked up to life support, comatose for weeks and then returning to real life, breathing on my own, seeing and being seen. They would never know that I know who each of them really is and what they had actually done to me. How could they know? It was only me, out of my crew, who got murdered and traveled to the unknown. I now know that the unknown is called the unknown for a reason. The living have no knowledge of it. My girls will never know or possibly imagine that I saw them have that secret hood after-party conversation about me on the night of my death. Simone would never know that I heard her bold drunken confession. None of my girls would know that I know, that they had all agreed to remain silent about my murder. They sold me out, chasing the money bag. I ain't mad at them, though. I'm no snitch. In the aftermath of the same circumstance, I might have done the same thing, easily. But even though I am not mad, I still don't want to let on that I know what they did. I want to see how well they play it. I want to see how mean their game faces are now. I want to experience their reactions. Simone, after believing that she had successfully murdered me, had said, "Winter does the least and gets the most." She must have been right. They got their little appearance fee crumbs for being the help, I mean for being the support cast on my show. While I laid in a coma, I collected more than a million dollars, after the original contracted sum of eight hundred thousand dollars. Plus, there were bonuses and perks direct deposited into my account. They're probably still mad at that, if they had somehow gotten anyone to break the confidentiality agreement and run their mouths about my deal. What the fuck did they expect? I'm Winter Santiaga, *bitches, bow down,* I thought. Then my memory reminded me not to say or dare even think, or need or desire others to bow down to me and for me. It wasn't an easy thing to erase from my core. Besides, the name of my reality show is *Bow Down, Starring Winter Santiaga.* I had asked Elisha to name it that before I was ever released or shot dead. I can change the show name now that I know better. Show execs would fight me the whole way though. Why would they want to change the biggest reality-show title moneymaker?

There was a knock at the door.

"Winter, it's Porsche. It's showtime," she said softly. The whole show crew and staff knew that Porsche was the only one who could get me out of any room that I was in, behind closed doors, that I locked. I let her in. She immediately hugged me tightly as though she had not just seen me at home a few hours ago. Porsche is like that, to the extreme.

"You look so perfect," she said, unlocking me from her hug. "What made you select the alligator couture?" she asked, smiling. Then she began circling around me, checking out my authentic green alligator stilettos, my alligator trench dress, and even my alligator handbag. "Your ponytails make you look as young as me," she said. Since Porsche is only twenty-five years young (and at the top of her game), it was a real compliment she was giving me. And because she was the one saying it, I know that it's true. She's not Hollywood fake. She's all the way at the opposite of that. "Your hair is so long and lovely. Look how it shines," she said, stroking it. Then got excited when she saw my limited-edition alligator hair ties. "Oh, that's dope!" She laughed approvingly.

Porsche was the one who had maintained my hair throughout my death. Others don't call it my death. They call it a coma. But only I really know. It was my death and I experienced my afterlife. It was a whole life after death that I went through. I don't tell nobody. Regular people would just write it off as a dream. That's bullshit corny to me. That's false. It was not a dream. Doctors even said that during a coma there is no brain activity, no dreaming. But fuck them on that point too. They don't know. Only I know what happened. Only my soul knows. I refuse to explain or argue with any regular bitch or motherfucker about what happened to me. I refuse to argue with doctors. I don't say shit back to them or ask them any questions about me.

Porsche hates doctors, hospitals, and medicine. I didn't know that about her before. I found out after I came through. When I regained consciousness, she was the one who was beside me. Matter of fact, she was standing over me, her head pushed down too close in my face, her pretty eyes so widened at the shock of my eyes opening after having been so closed that they could've been mistaken as stitched shut. Before I could think anything, because my thoughts were moving very, very slow, she spilled tears onto my face. Then she withdrew her face and used her bare fingers to wipe away her tears from my skin. The nurses told me that it was Porsche who had washed my body daily. Porsche who insisted on keeping my hair washed and combed and clipped. She even did my finger- and toenails. Porsche massaged my legs regularly and turned my body position so that I wouldn't get bedsores. She helped my blood to circulate. Porsche read me stories while I laid there comatose. One nurse told me that most of the time Porsche was actually talking to me as though I were alive, conscious, and could hear her. She seemed to even respond to me as though I had replied to her talk, which sounds a little crazy. More than reading and talking, Porsche was singing and humming and of course crying all in between. Porsche doesn't like being in the limelight. She doesn't want to be on camera. However, one thing anybody who knows Porsche knows is that she will do anything to please her husband, Elisha. The two of them have a love so deep and so active that anyone and everyone who sees them together can feel it. Some admire their love. Some find it annoying. Some hate how it highlights that they don't have the same love in their own lives. I probably am in all three categories. I would only think that to myself, of course.

Elisha got Porsche to agree to allow him to install cameras for the show in the room where I was laid out. She agreed because it was Elisha asking. She had one condition, though. It was that she controlled the camera angle. She could only be filmed from behind, sitting in front of me, who was lying in the hospital bed. She was blocking anyone from seeing me close up or in any detail. They would see only the pretty sheets that she required me to have. What's so crazy is that Porsche, who didn't want to be a star, became the star. Not for her beautiful look, although she is flawless. She didn't flaunt it. She didn't allow them to put her face on camera. She became the star because no one had ever seen on a reality show a person or sister who had had so deep of a real love for her own sister, that's me. On and off camera, Porsche had sacrificed her own time, focus, and attention to my recovery. She and I had never even watched one episode of my reality show up until this second. Porsche's reason is that that's not what she cared about. As for me, I was busy relearning how to talk right, stand up right, walk right, and think straight after the coma. Porsche would be right there looking over the shoulder of her handpicked personal healer as she performed acupuncture on me. I never heard of it till that lil' lady started sticking me with these pins in weird places like the top middle of my scalp, the insides of my ankles, and even between my thumb and index finger. Porsche would oversee my various physical therapists, watching me crawl on the floor, stand upright shaking on my feet, take a few steps, collapse, get up and finally walk, then run on the treadmill. The illest thing was, Porsche would be doing whatever I was doing as if she needed to do it. She didn't. She would be right across from me crawling, standing, walking, running while cheesing, smiling, beaming and cheering me on.

Even though the show viewers could not see Porsche faced forward, the audience of millions fell in love with her effort and her singing and humming to me as I lay there. Elisha, who never missed a valuable opportunity, recorded his wife's impromptu performances over my dead-like body. Out of those recordings, he created a show soundtrack titled *Bow Down* that big banked. His wife refused to perform any of her original tracks or cover songs or hummings. The music still sold and hit like crazy. Meanwhile, my reality show, applauded for its unique cinematography—thanks to Elisha's director's eye—had become a combination of the investigation of my execution, the medical story of my flat lining and coming back, the cast of my bitches and their crazy-ass nigga boyfriends, kids, and lives. Since the start of reality shows, all reality shows have stupid bitches doing dumb shit and the weak niggas they know, and the crazy bastards they gave birth to. It was, however, when the cameras redirected to Porsche and what she was doing, and how passionately and honestly that she was doing it, that grabbed the viewers by the heart. That's how Elisha described it. He said his wife "resonates." I don't know that word. I'm not a college bitch. All I know is with Porsche and her emotions everything is extreme. She was extreme in her care for me, in her love of me and of her love of everyone and everything that she loved. It was only a handful of people and handful of things. Once she claimed it and loved it though, she was loyal to the fullest extent. Wait a minute. My memory was reminding me. Porsche loves like Brooklyn Momma used to love.

"Time to go. I'll walk you out, just you and me. The on-set cameras will be rolling so expect it. Winter, are you nervous?" Porsche asked me.

"I'm good," was all I said. That's how it was between me and my middle sister. I would always have something urgent that I wanted to say to her. But for some reason, I wouldn't. I knew the words to say. I knew clearly what I wanted her to know. Sometimes I wanted to tell her what I had learned from living life, also from getting shot dead, my afterlife, and my return to life. But then, my tongue would feel heavy. The words that needed to be spoken, I never spoke. Even before I was murdered, it was like that between me and my sister Porsche. My mind was reminding me of how I wanted to say certain things to her at my mother's funeral long ago. I had one opportunity and maybe even, only one minute to say some urgent things. I didn't. Even now I know I should thank her, tremendously. I know what she gave up to get us to this point. I know that she didn't have to do shit for me. She was already rich, married, chilling, a mother of three. She didn't have to bother at all.

On my inside, I worried about Porsche's deep love problem. I wanted to tell her what I had learned about the difference between loving, which is a good and powerful thing, and worshipping. I wanted to warn her to continue to love but not to worship her husband, Elisha, or even her children. Worship is reserved for only ONE.

"Action!" Elisha's voice called out. I couldn't see him, though. Porsche nudged me forward and dropped back from the camera's view. The finale had a live audience. It was packed. There were so many blinding lights hanging from above. The cameras were very close to where I stood. I walked up, following the marked stage floor. I knew to hit my mark and then to let all else flow. When the audience saw me they jumped out of their seats and cheered. I wondered if I was supposed to interact with them. I should have checked the script. This didn't seem like any of the reality shows I had seen before I got shot up and declared dead then brought back to life. Where is Simone and Natalie, Asia and Toshi, Reese and . . . Hold up. *I hear music.* Because of Brooklyn Momma, I can name that tune in three seconds. It's the tinkle of the xylophone. For some reason, I am catching feelings. It's an old joint, from when my parents were teens. The rough and soothing voice of Bill With-ers. The song title is "Just the Two of Us"! *Momma used to sing it,* my mind reminded me. I began looking up and around the studio. Up high there was a green light glowing. It gave me the feeling of when I was trapped in the darkness of the Last Stop Before the Drop and suddenly a green glow emerged followed by a lavender sky and a diamond rain. *But I am not dead or comatose anymore.* My mind reminded me. *I am alive. I am in the studio, on set, surrounded by a whole lot of people, more than a hundred.*

I collapsed onto the floor. As Bill Withers sang, "We can make it if we try . . ." it was Santiaga. He walked on stage opposite me. He glided in smoothly on the words of the song. Just seeing him free. Just seeing him walking. Just seeing him so cool and so hand-some. Just seeing him . . . He came to me. Face-to-face, he ex-tended his hand. I placed my hand in his hand. He pulled me close. He hugged me and lifted me up. It was a spinning hug, my alligator stilettos swinging in the air. I am crying now uncontrollably. I am on camera crying uncontrollably but I don't give a fuck. Millions of people around the world are seeing me weeping on camera.

"Baby girl," was all he said. He was still calling me Baby Girl because I was his first born. His first baby, his first daughter. Even though he had three more after me, *I am "Baby Girl."*

"Cut," I heard Elisha say. But my father kept hugging and spin-ning me. The song switched to "Ribbons in the Sky" by Stevie

Wonder. He put me down gently and held me until a little wave of dizziness drifted away. As I steadied, the set changed as the audience chattered loudly. My poppa and me was still just admiring one another. It was so hard for me not to be caught up into him. He was standing right there in front of me. He's family. He's familiar. He is the one I know. He must have just got out. No, he's too well-suited. His scent is wonderful. His look is rough, sexy, and calm. They must have hid Poppa from me. He was the first person I asked for when I came through and out of my coma. He was still on lock, they told me. If I worked hard and recovered, I would be able to go visit him. Oh, Elisha . . . What a surprise, no prison wear, chains, cuffs, or dirty plastic dividers on a bullshit visitation separating us. No monitored over the old-school, old wall phone conversation. No corrections officers, police, guards, or escorts. Elisha, my brother-in-law, had kept his word. Poppa is here, free and fit, and beautiful.

A red light flashed. The audience grew quiet and took their seats. My father and I were left center stage. I was trying not to worship him. I was trying to keep it all in the love category. I was fighting myself on the inside. Love and worship war in my soul. I was trying but I could see my father. I could not see God. I know my father the most. I love him the most. He taught me most, almost everything I know.

My memory reminded me. It is a Mercy that I am alive. It is a Mercy that Poppa is free. It is a Mercy more than anything else. No matter how hard anyone fought to make this moment happen, without the Mercy it could never have happened. I know. It is a Mercy that I am receiving. No, it is a Mercy that the whole Santiaga family is receiving.

"Alhamdulillah" was the first word I spoke on camera. Probably no one understood what or why. But, I do.

34.

We dominated. The news the next day was all about us. All about *Bow Down, Starring Winter Santiaga.* The morning shows was abuzz because of the ratings that broke all records ever known. Viewers from around the world tuned in to see me at my finest. Even in countries where our show didn't air, legit and illegit satellites were making it possible for all to see. One morning-show host showed clips of teens gathered in one hood hut in Rio de Janeiro, Brazil, to check my show. Kids in the barrio in Cuba and Puerto Rico were glued to the tube. Places I never heard of heard of me—more than heard of me: knew me, sweated me. Ghana and Nigeria, Senegal and South Africa, Zimbabwe and Kenya, yup, I only know of them because they knew of me first. They're my fans, my viewers. Jamaica, Bahamas, Barbados, Aruba, Turks & Caicos, yeah I knew all of them of course. They were the hustler's playground.

Funny thing is, when you're dominating, which is way higher than simply trending . . . every kind of media, social or otherwise, every magazine, newspaper, online service, gossip mag and rag, blogger, podcast, YouTuber, and radio or whatever, are each coming from a different angle. The fashion media was on Santiaga's dick. He was wearing Stefano Ricci and killing it. There were images of only my alligator stilettos, starring my pretty feet and perfect pedi. Each of my body parts were captured in close-ups, posted and praised. Comments were streaming in from everywhere. Where did you buy those shoes? How can I get an alligator trench? Who did your diamonds? Grown-ass women and female celebs were rocking ponytails within twenty-four hours of viewing my show.

The political shows didn't give a fuck about the Santiaga's fashion. They just wanted to know who let us out of prison. It was as though they wanted us to be locked up forever. Investigative reporters were already digging. They wanted to know the details of my father's release. No comment from Elisha and my team. By morning time the next day, I knew the deal. It was the governor of New York that set Santiaga free by pardon. It was an entanglement of circumstances. All of the veins leading to Elisha. It was amazing to me the doors that would open for him. I know I would never know if money changed hands. I don't need to know either. All I know is that my father is free and poised to be king. Okay, not king. Let me calm down. All I know is shit changes. The high and lows happen. The tables turn. That having been said, my father is back to where he belongs. And . . . even the governor of New York and president of the United States of America are black men!

Entertainment outlets all focused on Elisha and tried to get photo exclusives of Porsche. Porsche turned down *The Tonight Show,* Jimmy Kimmel, *Good Morning America,* Jimmy Fallon, Katie Couric, and even Ellen, Oprah, and Gayle King. Once it was absolutely clear that she was not available, producers and publicists started coming for me. I agreed, of course, to all the elaborate photo shoots for the top magazines. That was fun and easy for me. Like being a supermodel or some shit. But as far as in-depth interviews where I had to talk, I hesitated before agreeing. I want to be interviewed only in a place where I can say whatever I want. Nobody beeping out, cutting, editing, and limiting what I say. I didn't want to be packaged like some fake-ass bitch. They'd have to invite me and take what they get. Go on live and cross their fingers that I don't say or do nothing too wild or too forbidden. But I'm a cool bitch. I already know what it means to be dead. I already know what it means to come back to life. So of course I wasn't planning on playing myself, like others do easily.

Party and publicity invites piled up to a paper mountain. My digital likes and followers and fans bursted into seven figures. Elisha was tight that all of this extra popularity on top of the already super popularity happened after the finale. The new season would not start for a few months. That meant other shows would be eating up the excitement that he created on *Bow Down*. I gotta give it up, though, my brother-in-law is extra clever. He surprised everyone, his staff and crew. He went off-script, the same one I had tossed in the trash. He made the finale with only me and my father. He restricted the cast that had carried the show for the whole season. My reunion with them was to be the show opener in the autumn season. Elisha knew how to keep his audiences in film and television, as well as cable, hanging off a cliff. Then he would milk their anticipation and open up with the viewership numbers higher than other shows' finale numbers.

I decided to accept an invitation based on the fact that it was what was familiar and comfortable to me. It came from Angie Martinez. She was the voice on Hot 97 that ruled in the '90s. Now she switched over to Power 105. I didn't like the switch. But she's a cool bitch. She knows everybody and everybody knows her. She's New York style. Our style is definite and different. In our state, the Blacks and Latinos are the same. We living the same. We struggling the same. We earning the same. We hang out together. We all speak English. And, unless it's over some hot boy or top hustler, we don't fight on no Black vs. Latino–type vibe. When a fight is over a top nigga all bets are off. A black chick will fight another black chick just as furiously as she would fight a Latina. Even when I found out on lock that in other states in America, it's the Blacks vs. the Latinos, I thought that was dumb and corny and basically backwards. So Angie Martinez was my pick. Besides, if I let her interview me, I know all of my niggas will be listening. That's what I really cared about. It was okay to be known all around the world. But at the end of the day, I'm thinking about Brooklyn niggas and New York State. I'm wanting my chicks on lock who are still there to taste my victory. I wanted hustlers in their whips that came up after my pops to know and then to show him some motherfucking respect. I wanted to certify that the Santiagas are back on our feet, strong, rich, legit, and doing it.

Here's how my first post-finale interview went.

Her: I know you probably get asked the same questions over and over again.

Me: Definitely.

Her: So let me take it from another angle. What do you think is the reason your show has become the phenomenon that it is?

Me: 'Cause niggas love victory. Niggas love drugs, hustling, and stories about drugs and hustling. Niggas love money. Niggas love fashion. Niggas love passion. We got all of that going on at the same time.

Her: But there has to be more to it. There are so many shows, films, stories about hustlers, hustling, drugs, etc. Your show has surpassed them all.

Me: True, there are other shows, and movies with actors and actresses and shit like that. But our story is original. The Santiaga's ain't acting. We come from that golden age of stand-up hustlers and hustling and the women who rode with the niggas the whole ride through. No flipping or snitching. So many have tried to cash in on what was our lifestyle, our thing, our hoods. We genuine. This story is authentic for us. If there is money to be made off of our lifestyle, business and true stories, our fashions and look and even lows, who should make that money besides us?

Her: Whoa! the streets are cosigning. Look how the board lit up with callers from every borough of New York.

Me: The whole world loves a happy ending. We made a strong comeback. We got back up without diming out, betraying or embarrassing the hood, our culture, our people. That's why they showing love.

Her: Let me ask you about your father.

Me: Be careful.

Her: I've interviewed hundreds if not thousands of people: stars, rappers, CEOs, producers, directors, community leaders, students, activists, moguls, icons. For every person I've interviewed, I've heard almost as many true, hateful, hard-luck sad stories about absent fathers, abusive fathers, mentally and physically ill fathers, disappointing fathers, hated fathers, shrewd, manipulative, cunning, and thieving fathers. But you, Winter, stand out and probably will forever be remembered as the most loving, loyal daughter that a father ever had. Now you spoke about being popular because of your hood background, drugs, hustling, prison, and an undeniably amazing comeback. But I watch your show because of your family relationships. Rich or poor, for better or worse, that's the one thing almost no one seems to be able to get right. It's incredible to me to see how your sister Porsche adores you. How you adore your father. I know the only person in the world who probably loves your father more than you is your moms. I heard your parents never divorced. That's big.

I sat back. I had tears in my eyes. But I refused to allow them to spill. She brought up Momma. Didn't her producers tell her that Momma was dead? Why was she forcing me into a memory that I did not want to remember?

Me: Momma . . . Lana, . . . yes. Lana Santiaga loves
        her husband more than anyone ever loved any man,
        true.

Her: See, I thought so, that's beautiful. To have love,
        honesty, and warmth in a family, that's something
        money can't buy. That's what we all wanted . . . but
        so few of us received.

She promised the many callers to hold on and that she would definitely allow them to ask questions and for me to answer their questions. Then, she teased them by placing them all on hold, saying that she wanted to ask her audience a question first. So she asked the listeners:

Her: If your father walked into your living room today,
        the way Winter Santiaga's father walked in on the
        reality-show-set living room, millions of us all saw
        for sure, do you think that simply seeing him would
        cause you to collapse and spill tears the way Winter
        Santiaga did on her show finale? Winter, you're
        real. You've said that you are no actress. Those
        were real tears I saw and we all experienced, weren't
        they? You were actually shocked to see your father
        on your own show, weren't you?

Me: I don't know how many bitches you had sit in this
        interview chair. But I for one don't have even one
        percent of anything fake. These are my eyes, my
        eyelashes. This is my hair. This is my ass, my body.
        My feet. Nothing borrowed, rented, plastered,

plastic or lasered on, touched up, shifted, stolen, filled, or purchased. This is the same me who came out of my momma's coochie. Y'all got to see my tears once. I hope you taped it, downloaded it or plan to buy the DVD. Otherwise, you gon' have to wait till reruns. From finale forward, no more tears. We going all the way up.

Her: I like that! I love that! I feel your confidence.

Then she went to the callers.

Caller: Marry me.

Two words was all the caller said. He had a nice voice though.

Me: Nigga, I don't know you!

I responded the only way I know how. But just as I did, I thought the voice sounded familiar. It did. I would, however, need him to say more than two words to confirm.

Her: Caller, hold on. Don't hide behind the radio show. Sounds like you popping the question that most girls can't get their man to pop, because you are not here in my studio, standing in front of Winter Santiaga, and holding the rock you would need to have on you to marry this superstar!

Caller: I'm down in the lobby. I got the diamond fresh in the box from the jeweler.

Her: I take it back. You can't come at her like that. I love the callers but that feels like some stalker-type shit. Winter, does this caller make you feel like you need security?

Me: I know who you are, nigga. Fall back.

Then I saw her press a button and terminate his call. A new caller popped on. But I wasn't listening no more. That nigga Bullet got me vexed. What the fuck is he talking about, "Marry me!" He left me sitting in the rented car. The car he had me rent in my name to run his drug and gun hustle. That wasn't the problem, though. He let me take the fall for him. He never came for me. He never got a lawyer for me. He never put money on my books. He never visited. He never wrote. Point-blank. He never loved me. And I served fifteen mandatory years without betraying his fucked-up ass.

Me: I want to say something to all the niggas listening. A bitch wants a nigga who is loyal to her the same level that she is loyal to him. A bitch wants a nigga who loves her all the way up to worshipping her but who never crosses that line. A bitch wants a man who she don't have to teach how to be a man. He should already know and already been living it. A bitch wants a man who doesn't abuse his kids or anybody else's kids for that matter. And if you the nigga out there who fits this description, but you ain't rich, a bitch like me will forgive you and share her bounty without bragging about it or mushing it in your face. But if you're listening and you are rich that's okay too, of course. But let me make it clear: Winter Santiaga ain't no nigga's fuck piece, no matter who he is or how rich he is. I'm holding out for a man worthy of being my husband. A man almost as good as my father, which I already know is next to impossible. A solid, unapologetic man who doesn't suck or fuck men. Who never allows men to suck or fuck him.

Her: We'll be back after a commercial break.

*   *   *

Later that night, I locked my bedroom door even though my apartment door was already securely locked. I'm not scared of no niggas running up in my place. I am still living alone in a wing of the Porsche/Elisha Brooklyn mansion. I don't plan to stay long. I plan to build my fashion empire. At the same time, I plan to marry the man who meets my loyalty and love level. Now that I'm known around the world, I know I have my choice of all the top picks. No matter who I choose, he will still have to get the nod of approval from Santiaga, my father and my first love.

I'm washing my naked body. I'm preparing to make a prayer. That's why my door is locked. I don't want anyone, not even family, to see me pray or to even know that I pray. At the same time, I know from being shot dead and from the death after life, and the life after death, that there is a God. God is One, All-Powerful, and All-Knowing. That One God is the only One to be feared and worshipped. I know there are consequences to each of my choices and actions. I know how hellish those consequences are because I already experienced them. I know what mercy means. I'm grateful for many things, but especially I am grateful to be alive.

At the same time, I'm no fanatic. I got pride. Don't know if I will ever be able to let pride go even though I know it's wrong. I don't know if I even want to. I don't cover my hair or wear religious-type clothing. For me that ain't it. But I do worship One God and make my prayers in the early morning and late night, when no one can see me. Once I find and marry a real man who makes my heart and my pussy thump, who loves me right up to the line of worship, I'll let him be the only one that sees me bow down beside him, bowing down beside me, to the One who created us both and us all.